Sports fans and science fiction fans alike have something to cheer about—thirteen stories by twelve outstanding science fiction writers who speculate on sports in the probable, the possible and the impossible future. For whatever the future may hold, sports will play an important part. In these stories, the Last Superbowl is played out before empty stands in Hoboken, New Jersey; the Martians can't hit a curve ball to the satisfaction of a Dodgers fan; in combat football, scoring is based on the number of casualties and fatalities. Man is measured anew against himself, against other men, against machine, against beast. The editors of this first anthology of its kind have compiled intriguing glimpses of sports through the future and the future through sports.

run to starlight

run to starlight

sports through science fiction

Edited and with introductions by
Martin Harry Greenberg
Joseph D. Olander
Patricia Warrick

delacorte press/new york

Library of Congress Cataloging in Publication Data

Main entry under title:
Run to starlight.

CONTENTS: Martin, G. R. R. The last super bowl game.
—Spinrad, N. The national pastime.—Martin, G. R. R. Run
to starlight. [etc.]
    1. Sports stories. 2. Science fiction. [1. Sports stories.
    2. Science fiction. 3. Short stories]
I. Greenberg, Martin Harry. II. Olander, Joseph D.
III. Warrick, Patricia S. IV. Title.
PZ5.R84   [Fic]   75-8005
ISBN 0-440-07401-0

1887604

acknowledgments

"The Last Super Bowl Game" by George R. R. Martin: Copyright © 1975 by George R. R. Martin. Portions of this story appeared earlier in *Gallery*, February 1975, under the title "The Last Super Bowl." Copyright © 1975 by Brookbridge Publishing Corp. Reprinted by permission of the author.

"The National Pastime" by Norman Spinrad: Reprinted by permission of the author's agent, Lurton Blassingame. Copyright © 1973 by Harry Harrison.

"Run to Starlight" by George R. R. Martin. Copyright © 1974 by Ultimate Publishing Co., Inc. Reprinted from *Amazing Science Fiction* by permission of the author.

"Dodger Fan" by Will Stanton: © 1957 by Mercury Press, Inc. Reprinted from *The Magazine of Fantasy and Science Fiction*. Used by permission of the author.

"The Celebrated No-Hit Inning" by Frederik Pohl: Copyright © 1956 by King-Size Publications, Inc. Reprinted by permission of the author.

"Naked to the Invisible Eye" by George Alec Effinger: © 1973 by George Alec Effinger. Used by permission of the author.

"Goal Tending" by E. Michael Blake: Copyright © 1975 by E. Michael Blake. All rights reserved. Used by permission of the author.

"To Hell with the Odds" by Robert L. Fish: Every effort has been made to contact the author. If the author will write to them, the publishers will be happy to arrange formal acknowledgment and customary payment. Copyright © 1967 by Mercury Press, Inc. Reprinted from *The Magazine of Fantasy and Science Fiction*.

"Title Fight" by William Campbell Gault: Copyright © 1956 by William Campbell Gault. Used by permission of the author.

"Steel" by Richard Matheson: Copyright © 1956 by Richard Matheson. Reprinted by permission of Harold Matson Company, Inc.

"The Immortal Game" by Poul Anderson: Reprinted by permission of the author and his agents, Scott Meredith Literary Agency, Inc., 580 Fifth Avenue, New York, New York 10036.

"The Immortal Game" chess match is reprinted from THE ENCYCLOPAEDIA OF CHESS by Anne Sunnucks by permission of St. Martin's Press, Inc.

"The Doors of His Face, the Lamps of His Mouth" by Roger Zelazny: Copyright © 1965 by Mercury Press, Inc., for publication in *The Magazine of Fantasy and Science Fiction*, reprinted by permission of the author and Henry Morrison, Inc., his agents.

"Poor Little Warrior!" by Brian W. Aldiss: Reprinted by permission of the author and his agent, A. P. Watt & Son.

To Sally, Cookie, and
Jim—three good sports

contents

introduction

football

baseball

basketball

golf

introduction

The word *science* in science fiction seems out of place in a book of sports stories. On reflection, however, the world of sports relies heavily on science and technology. From the television sets which bring sports into our homes to the automobiles which take us to the sports, science and technology are important elements in sports as we know them. They also affect the sports themselves, from lightweight shoulder pads in football to the "live ball" in baseball.

A "sport" can be just about anything which either involves overt physical activity or requires physical fitness. Organization can change an activity into a sport. For example, walking is an activity which can provide pleasure and exercise for most of us. When walking is organized into clubs, meets, and races, however, it is transformed into a sport. Most sports involve some form of *competition*. In addition, most sports involve winning and losing, and athletes seek to defeat or outscore other athletes. "The thrill of victory" and "the agony of defeat" are sensations familiar to all who have participated in sports. Many commentators have argued that this is the greatest weakness of sports—the emphasis on winning has gone too far—and "winning isn't the most important thing, it is the only thing." Others point out that the drive to win is not a function of sports per se but simply a reflection of values inherent in our society. Sports, after all, are a reflection of the society in which they take place. The ugly side of sports depicted in some of the stories in this collection exists because of the ugly side of our society and of the imperfect nature of human beings.

On the other hand, sports also foster *cooperation*, especially team sports. They teach such positive values as working together or sacrificing one's self for the good of the group. This *competition-cooperation* is the great dichotomy of sports. Sports, moreover, are also goal-oriented, stressing commitment, self-discipline, and concentration—all of which are necessary for goal achievement. For the true sportsman, giving one's best is more important than winning. The old cliché, "It is not winning or losing but how you play the game that counts," still has validity today.

However, sports are also big business. Some estimates of their income run as high as four billion dollars a year in terms of equipment, tickets, and television rights. Professional sports franchises go for millions of dollars, and top sports stars earn hundreds of thousands of dollars a year. The stakes are rising each year. College athletics no longer simply produce well-rounded and fit young men and women; they also provide badly needed revenue for their schools. In professional sports, the unionization of players has added a political dimension to sports.

Sports are played at all educational levels in the

United States. They really become organized in junior high school with intramural competition. At the high school level, sports form a substantial part of the culture of the school. At the college level, sports continue to feature organized competition, but selectivity increases and recruitment of athletes becomes a business in itself. School sports tend to foster an "us and them" mentality which some commentators feel is unhealthy. In the light of this phenomenon, it is not especially surprising that sports have been compared to other conflict situations such as *war*. Indeed, sports may very well have developed as training for warfare. From a military point of view, sports can teach strategy, aggressiveness, and teamwork. It has been said often that the British prepared for war "on the playing fields of Eton," an upper-class school which trained the British elite. More recently, sports have been considered as surrogates for war and aggressive behavior, providing society with the means for sublimating violence. Finally, at the international level, matches between national teams can be viewed as an extension of foreign policy, reaching their greatest level every four years in the Olympic Games. To some, these games have become a reflection of national power, which is unfortunate since sports should not be used as propaganda.

The Olympic Games originated in Greece as festivals. After this period, sports grew very slowly. In fact, it was not until the modern era and its accompanying increase in leisure time that sports really developed. Most modern sports are simply modifications of earlier forms; for example, cricket into baseball, rugby into football, and field hockey into ice hockey. Basketball is a major exception to this general rule. Sports which were not native to a particular culture have spread around the world because of advances in transportation and communications technology. Today, one can find Chinese playing volleyball, Spaniards playing basketball, Japanese playing baseball, and Russians playing ice hockey. This is a trend which we can expect to continue and accelerate.

Science fiction projects current social trends into the future. It is a literature which has examined the possibilities of future society in all its varied forms, real and imagined. Although science fiction has not produced a large number of sports stories—which is one reason that this is the first anthology of its kind—it nevertheless has given us a number of truly memorable ones, especially in recent years. Whatever the future may hold for us, we can be sure that sports will be an important part of it.

football

America is football crazy. In fact, the game has surpassed baseball in the opinion polls as America's favorite spectator sport. A number of reasons have been put forth to explain football's popularity, some of which are explored in the stories in this section.

Football is a fast, violent game which began in England. It was imported into the United States during the nineteenth century through the development of two English games—soccer and rugby. Soccer is a fast kicking game which is played on a field resembling today's football gridiron. Since tackling was permitted, rugby added the dimension of body contact to soccer. In its early American form, football involved as many as thirty players on each side of a team, with kicking still the basic component of the sport.

The first "real" football game was played on November 6, 1869, in New Brunswick, New Jersey, between Rutgers College and the College of New Jersey. The first football game to employ tackling, however, occurred in Canada, where McGill University of Montreal adopted this style. The Canadian version of the sport rapidly caught on in the United States, although no formal rules existed. Usually, the two teams simply agreed on the rules for a particular game, a procedure which frequently led to violent arguments and ultimately to the adoption of fairly uniform codes for the sport.

As time went on, towns and cities in the United States began to field their own teams, a process which anticipated the organizational structure of today's professional football. Because football is a contact sport, fierce brawls often broke out during games, both among players and among their supporters. The violent aspect of football generated much debate and controversy, an argument which has continued to the present day. In fact, as rough an individual as President Theodore Roosevelt once wanted to ban the sport because of its violence.

A revolutionary development in the sport occurred in 1906, when the first forward pass was thrown, although this aspect of the game did not become popular until a number of years later. The passing game then became an integral part of football, contributing much to its increasing popularity. A large number of colleges and universities started to field teams, and today more than six hundred institutions of higher learning and thousands of high schools play the game. With the introduction of post-season bowl games, college football reached its present peak. These events have grown into spectacular "happenings" with elaborate parades, half-time shows, and other activities surrounding the main event.

Professional football dates from the late 1800s when some of the existing local town teams began to pay their star players. The first documented professional game took place in Pennsylvania between teams from Latrobe and Jeannette. The pro version of the sport grew slowly, always overshadowed by the college game, until the 1920s. At that time, college stars like Red Grange joined professional teams, which increased attendance and fan interest. However, professional football's present success and popularity are largely creations of technology, since television has contributed a great deal to football's national appeal. Since the advent of the televised pro game, football has been booming. As a matter of fact, its popularity has become so great that a new league—the World Football League—was launched in 1974 in order to compete with the established National and American conferences in the United States.

The culmination of the football season is the Super Bowl, played between the champions of the National and American conferences. "Super Sunday" has thus become an important day in the lives of the American people, with more than fifty million fans glued to their television sets watching twenty-two men colliding with each other!

The Last
Super Bowl
Game

george r. r. martin

It happens every January, after the excitement of the
college bowl games has died down and the snow is fresh
on the ground over much of America. The tension builds
as the middle of the month approaches, reaching fever
pitch the day of the great event. As the game begins, a
great silence comes over the land; for this is one of the
most important moments for millions of people—Super
Sunday—the day of the Super Bowl Game.

The pre-game hysteria before Super Sunday is so tremendous that the game itself seems almost anticlimactic.
There have been close games, uneven games, even boring
games—boring, that is, to sportswriters and commentators, rarely to fans, to whom the event itself could never
be boring. Early in its history, the Super Bowl was not
only a test of skill and commitment for two football
teams but also a rite of passage for a new league. The upstart American Football League burst upon the scene
like a rocket, with players like Joe Namath making what
seemed to be wild claims about the excellence of their
teams. Many fans of the old and established National
Football League viewed the newcomer with a combination of distaste and disgust, believing that no team could

defeat their champion. It was the victory of the New York Jets which proved the legitimacy and talent of the American Football League and brought it equal status with the National Football League. Perhaps one day we will witness this same occurrence with a team from the new World Football League.

In this fine story by one of the brightest young talents in science fiction, we witness a future in which football as we know it has come to the end of the line—the last "real" game is being played on a field in Hoboken, New Jersey. Football has become a victim of technology and can no longer compete with the creations of a massive computer. It is the culmination of a trend—a paradox. Technology, in the form of television, has made professional football what it is today. However, some argue that television will eventually kill football through overexposure. It is still too early to tell, but the handwriting may very well be on the wall.

The Last
Super Bowl
Game

The last Super Bowl was played in January, 2016, on a muddy field in Hoboken, New Jersey.

It was attended by 832 aging fans, 12 sportswriters, a Boy Scout troop, and the commissioner of the National Football League. The commissioner brought the Boy Scouts. He was also a scoutmaster.

The Packers were the favorites, and that was as it should be. It was somehow right, and appropriate, and just that the Packers should be in the final game.

They were still the Green Bay Packers, after all, the same now, at the end, as in the dim beginnings so many years ago. The teams of the great cities had come and gone, but the Packers stayed on, eternal and unchanging.

They had a perfect record going into the championship, and a defense the likes of which football had never seen. Or at least so the sportswriters wrote. But claims like that had to be taken with several grains of salt. Sportswriters were a dying breed, and they exaggerated a lot to stave off extinction.

The underdogs in the last, lonely showdown were the Hoboken Jets. Formerly the Jersey City Jets. Formerly the Newark Jets. Formerly the New York Jets. The sportswriters, in their fading wisdom, had decreed that the Jets would lose by two touchdowns.

Not that Hoboken had a bad team. They were pretty good, actually. They'd won their conference going away. But then, it was a weak conference, and the Jet defense was a little sloppy. They didn't have a great offense either.

What they did have was Keith Lancer. Lancer, so said the sportswriters, was the greatest quarterback ever to throw a football. Better than Namath, Unitas, Graham, Baugh, any of them. A golden arm; great range, fantastic accuracy. He was a scrambler too. And a brilliant field general.

But he was only one man, and he had never faced a team like the Packers. The Packer front four were creatures out of nightmare. Their rush had been known to drive brilliant quarterbacks into blithering, terrified idiocy.

The sportswriters claimed the Packer defense would grind Lancer into little bits and scatter him all over the field. But that was just what the sportswriters claimed. And nobody listened to sportswriters anymore.

It was a classic confrontation. Offense against defense. One brilliant man against a smoothly oiled machine. A lone hero against a horde of monsters.

The last page of football history. But a great page, a great moment, a great game.

And it was played before 832 fans, 12 sportswriters, a

Boy Scout troop, and the commissioner of the National Football League.

It had begun, long ago, when someone decided to settle an old argument.

Arguments are the stuff of which sports are made. They go on and on, forever, and no one has ever stopped to figure out how many bars they keep in business. The arguments were all different, but all the same. Who's the greatest heavyweight champion of all time? Who should play center field on the all-time All Star team? Name the best football team ever.

Ask a man those questions and listen to his answers. Then you'll know when he was growing up, and where he once lived, and what kind of a man he was.

Eternal questions, never-ending arguments, the raucous music of the locker room and the tavern. Not questions that could be answered. Nor questions that should be answered. There are some things man was not meant to know.

But one day someone tried to answer them. He used a computer.

Computers were still in diapers back then. But still they were treated with deference. They didn't make mistakes. When a computer said something, the man in the street generally listened. And believed.

So they decided to ask a computer to pick the greatest heavyweight champion of all time.

But they didn't merely ask a question. They had more imagination than that. They arranged a tournament, a great tournament between all the heavyweight champions of history, each fighting in his prime. They fed each man's style into the machine, and told it about his strengths and weaknesses and habits and quirks.

And the machine digested all the glass chins and snappy left jabs and dazzling footwork, and set to work producing simulated fights. One by one the heavyweight champions eliminated each other in computerized bouts that were jazzed up and dramatized and broadcast over the radio.

Rocky Marciano won the thing.

It began to rain shortly after the two teams had come onto the field. Not a heavy rain, at first. Just a thin, cold, soggy-wet drizzle that came down and down and wouldn't stop.

Green Bay won the toss and elected to receive. Hoboken decided to defend the south goal.

The kickoff was shallow and wobbly, probably because of the rain and the muddy condition of the field. Mike Strawn, the Packers' speed merchant, fielded the kick and ran it back fifteen yards before being pulled down at the thirty.

The Packer offense took the field. They were a coldly determined bunch that afternoon. They had something to prove. They were tired of hearing, over and over again, about how defense made the Packers great. And Dave Sandretti, the Packers' scrappy young quarterback, was especially tired of hearing about Keith Lancer.

Sandretti went to the air immediately, hitting on a short, flat pass to the sideline for a quick first down. On the next play he handed off, and Mule Mitchell smashed through the center of the Jet line for a four-yard gain.

Then Strawn went around end for another first down. The Packers drove.

Their offense was nothing fancy. The Packer coach believed in basic football. But it was effective. Alternating skillfully between his short passes and his potent running game, Sandretti moved the Packers across the fifty and into enemy territory before the drive finally bogged down near the thirty-five.

The field-goal attempt was wide. The Jets took over on their own twenty.

Inevitably, other tournaments followed in the wake of the first one. They settled the argument about the greatest middleweight champion of all time, and the best college football team, and the finest baseball squad ever assembled.

And each simulated fight and computerized game seemed to draw larger radio audiences than the one before it. People liked the idea. They didn't always agree with the computer's verdict, but that was okay. It gave them something new to argue about.

It wasn't long before the sponsors of the computerized tournaments realized they had a gold mine on their hands. And, once they did realize it, it took them no time at all to abandon their original purposes. Settling the old arguments, after all, was dangerous. It might lead to loss of interest in forthcoming computerized bouts.

So they announced that the computer's verdicts were far from final. Different tournament pairings might give different results, they claimed. And so it was when they ran the heavyweight elimination over again.

The lords of sport looked on tolerantly. Computerized

sports were an interesting sideshow, they thought, but hardly anything to worry about. After all, a phony football game broadcast over the radio could never match the violent color and excitement of the real thing on television.

They even went so far as to feature computer simulations in their pre-game shows, to add a little spice to the presentation. The computer predictions were almost always wrong, and the computer games were drab compared to the spectacle that invariably followed.

The lords of sport were absolutely certain that computer simulations would never be anything more than minor sideshows. Absolutely certain.

At first, Lancer set out to establish his running game.

He abandoned that idea two plays later, after the Packer defense had twice snagged Jet runners short of the line of scrimmage. On third and fifteen, Lancer took to the air for the first time. The pass was complete for a first down.

On first and ten, he went for a long bomb. It fell incomplete when his receiver slipped on the muddy field. But the Jets got a first down anyway. The Packer rush put a bit too much pressure on Lancer, and got assessed fifteen yards for roughing the passer. Lancer had been hit solidly by two defensemen after getting the pass away.

He got up covered with mud, a little shaken, and very mad. When Lancer was mad, the Jets were mad. The team began to move.

If the Packer offense was the soul of simplicity, the Jet offense was a study in devious complexity. Lancer used a whole array of different formations, kept his backfield in constant motion with shift after shift, and had a mind-boggling number of plays to choose from. The Packers knew all that, of course. They had studied game films. But watching films was not quite the same thing as facing an angry Keith Lancer.

Lancer let the Packers have both barrels now. He started to razzle-dazzle with a vengeance. The Packer rush dumped him a few more times. But in between, the Jets were registering long gains.

It took Lancer nine plays to put Hoboken into the end zone. The Jets went ahead, 7-0.

The sportswriters started muttering.

The problem with the early computer simulations was their lack of depth. Computer games were presented either as flat, colorless predictions, or as overdramatized radio shows. Which was all right. But not to be compared to actually watching a real game.

Then someone got a bright idea. They made a movie.

Rocky Marciano had been retired for years, but he was still around. Muhammad Ali was still one of the premier heavyweights of the era. So they paired them in a computer fight, got Marciano back into reasonable shape, and had the two men act out the computer's prediction of what would have happened if they had met when each was in his prime. Marciano won by a knockout.

The film got wide publicity, and was shown in theaters from coast to coast. It outdrew the crowds that real bouts got in the same theaters when they appeared via closed-circuit television.

The newspapers seemed confused over how to cover it. Some sent movie critics. But many sent sportswriters. And while most of those sportswriters treated it as a joke, a minor and inconsequential diversion, others wrote up the fight quite seriously.

The handwriting was on the wall. But the lords of sport didn't read it. After all, the circumstances that allowed a film like this to be made were pretty unique, they reasoned. The computer people could hardly dig up John L. Sullivan or the Four Horsemen or Babe Ruth for future films. And the public would never accept actors.

So there was nothing to worry about. Nothing at all.

Through the mud and the steadily building rain, the Packers came driving back. They relied mostly on their running game, on Mule Mitchell's tanklike rushes and Mike Strawn's darting zigzags and quick end runs. But Sandretti's passing played a role, too. He didn't have Lancer's arm, by any means. But he was good, and he was accurate, and when the chips were down he seldom missed.

Back upfield they moved, back into Jet territory. The first quarter ended with them on the Jet thirty.

The drive continued in the second period, but once again the Packers seemed to run out of gas when they got within the shadow of the goalposts. They had to settle for a field goal.

More movies followed the success of the first. But the lords of sport had been correct. The idea had built-in limitations. A lavish production that used actors to pit

Jack Dempsey against Joe Louis underlined that point. It was a total bust. The fans wanted the real thing. Or close to it, anyway.

But some films could be made, and they were made, and they made money. It became a respectable movie subgenre. One studio, Versus Productions, specialized in film versions of computer sports, and made modest profits.

But real sports continued to do better than ever. The public had more and more leisure, and a voracious hunger for vicarious violence. The lords of sport feasted on huge television contracts, and grew fat and rich. And blind.

They hardly even noticed when some of the old computer films began to turn up on late shows here and there.

They should have.

Lancer got the Jets driving again. But this time their momentum ebbed quickly. The Packer defense wasn't about to get pushed around all day. They were quick to adapt, and now they were beginning to get used to Lancer's bag of tricks.

The Hoboken drive sputtered to a halt on the Green Bay forty, when Lancer was dumped twice in a row by the Packer rush. The field-goal attempt was a valiant but misguided effort to buck the wind and the rain. It fell absurdly short.

The Packers took over. At once they began to move. Sandretti clicked on a series of passes, and Mitchell punched through the Hoboken line again and again.

When the Packers crossed the fifty, the Jets decided to

surprise Sandretti with a blitz. They did surprise him. Once.

The next time they tried it, Sandretti flipped a screen pass to Strawn in the flat. He shook off one tackler, sidestepped two more, and outran everybody else on the field.

That made it 10–7 Packers. The sportswriters began to breathe a little easier.

It was such a simple idea.

The name of the man who first thought of it is lost. But there is a legend. The legend says it was an electronics engineer employed by one of the networks, and that the idea came to him when he was watching a television rerun of a computer fight movie.

It wasn't a very good movie, and his attention began to wander, says the legend. He began to think about why filmed computer simulations had never really made it big. The problem, he decided, was actors.

Computer simulations had more veracity and realism than fictional fight movies. But they lost it when they used actors. The public wouldn't buy actors. But, without actors, the possible number of productions was severely limited.

What was needed was another way to make the simulations.

He looked at the television wall, the legend says. And the idea came.

He wasn't watching a picture. Not really. He knew that. He was watching a pattern of multicolored dots. A complex pattern that deluded the human eye into thinking it was a picture. But it wasn't. There was nothing there but a bunch of electronic impulses.

If you got those impulses to join together and form an image of some actor playing Joe Louis, then there was no damn reason in the world that you couldn't get them to join together to form an image of Joe Louis himself.

It was easier if there was a pattern to be broken down and reassembled, of course. But that didn't mean it was impossible to build patterns out of whole cloth. And it wouldn't matter if those patterns had ever really existed anywhere but on the television screen. The images could be made just as real.

Yes. It could work. If you had an instrument fast enough to assemble such complex patterns and change them smoothly enough to simulate motion and action. If you had a computer, a big one. Yes.

The next day, the legend says, the nameless electronics engineer went to speak to the president of his network.

On the second play after the kickoff, the Packers blitzed. Their normal rush was fierce enough. Their blitz was devastating. The Hoboken line shattered under the impact, and the Packers stormed through, hungry for quarterback blood.

Lancer, back to pass, searched desperately for a receiver. He found none. He danced out of the way of the first Packer to reach him, tucked the ball under his arm, and tried to scramble. He got about five yards back toward the line of scrimmage before the Green Bay meat grinder closed in around him.

Afterward, he couldn't get up. They carried him off the field, limping.

There was a stunned silence, then a slowly building cheer as Lancer was carried to the sidelines.

Or as much of a cheer as could be produced by 832 fans, 12 sportswriters, a Boy Scout troop, and the commissioner of the National Football League.

Sports were very big business, and all three networks fought tooth and nail in the bloody bidding wars for the right to telecast the major events. And of all the wars, the football wars were the most gory.

One network won the NFL that year. Another won the NCAA. The third, according to tradition, was in for a bad time. It was going to get badly bludgeoned in the ratings until those contracts ran out.

But that year, the third network refused to lie down meekly and accept its fate. It broke with tradition. It scheduled something new. A show called "Unplayed Football Classics."

The show featured televised computer simulations of great games between the top football teams, both pro and college, in the history of the game. It did not use actors. A gigantic network computer, specially designed and built for the purpose, produced the simulations from scratch.

The show was a bombshell. A glorious, shouting, screaming, disgustingly successful smash hit.

With Lancer out, the Jets went nowhere. They bogged down in the mud and were forced to punt.

Sandretti, sensing that the Hoboken team was badly

shaken by the loss of its star quarterback, pressed his advantage ruthlessly. He went for the bomb on the first play from scrimmage.

Strawn, sent out wide on the play, snagged the long throw neatly and took it all the way in for another Packer touchdown. The extra point made it 17–7.

All of a sudden, it seemed to be raining a little harder on the Hoboken side of the field. A few of the 832 fans, those of the least faith, began to drift from the stadium.

"Unplayed Football Classics" was followed by "Matchup," a boxing show that telecast the imaginary bouts most requested by the viewers. Other spin-offs followed in good time when "Matchup," too, made it big.

After the third year of smash ratings, "Unplayed Football Classics" was sent into the front lines. Its time slot was moved so it conflicted, directly, with the NFL Game-of-the-Week.

The resulting holocaust was a ratings draw. But even that was enough to wake the lords of sport from their slumber and set them to yelping. For the very first time, computer simulations had demonstrated that they could compete successfully with the real product.

The lords of sport fought back, at first, with an advertising campaign. They set out to convince the public that the computer games were cheap imitations that no *real* sports fan would accept for a moment as a substitute for the real thing.

They failed. The fans were too far removed from the stadium to grasp the point. They were a generation of sports fans that had never seen a football game, except over television. And, over television, the computer games were just as dramatic and unpredictable and exciting as anything the NFL could offer.

So, the games weren't real. So what. They *looked* real. It wasn't like they used actors, or anything.

The lords of sport reeled from their failure, grasped for another weapon. The lawsuits began.

You can't call your simulated team the Green Bay Packers, the lawyers for the lords told the computer people. That name is our property. You can't use it. Or the names of all those players. You'll have to make up your own.

They went to court to prove their point.

They lost.

After all, the judges ruled, they weren't using real games. Besides, they asked the lords of sport, why didn't you object to all those people who did the same thing on radio? No, it's too late. You've set your precedents already.

Meanwhile, the third network was building a bigger computer. It was called Sportsmaster.

Hoboken held onto the ball for the rest of the second quarter, but only to run out the clock. There wasn't enough time left to do anything before the half, anyway.

The halftime show was a dreary affair. The NFL had long passed the point when it could stage big productions. But, given its budget, it still tried. There were a few high school bands on hand, and a holoshow that was an utter disaster thanks to the rain.

It didn't matter. Nobody was watching, anyway. The fans had all gone for hot dogs, and the sportswriters were down in the locker room trying to find out how Keith Lancer was.

The Boy Scouts, meanwhile, went to the Packer locker room, to get autographs—on orders from the scoutmaster, who was also commissioner of the National Football League.

Sportsmaster was the largest civilian computer ever built, and there were some that said it was even bigger than the Pentagon computer that controlled the nation's defenses. Its master memory banks contained all the data on sports and sports figures that anyone anywhere had ever bothered to put down on paper or film or tape. It was designed to prepare detailed, full-color, whole-cloth simulations, for both standard television wall-screens and the new holovision sets.

Its method of operation was an innovation, too. Instead of isolated games, Sportsmaster featured league competition, complete with seasons and schedules. But in the Sportsmaster Baseball League, every team was a pennant winner. In the Sportsmaster Boxing Tournament, every fighter was a champion. In the Sportsmaster Football League, every competitor had at least a divisional crown to its credit.

Sportsmaster games would not be presented as mere television shows. They would be presented as events, as news, it was decreed. The network sponsoring Sportsmaster immediately began to give the same buildup to future computer simulations as to real sports events. The newspapers, at first, refused to go along. Most insisted on covering Sportsmaster broadcasts in the entertainment section instead of the sports pages.

For a while they insisted, that is. Then, one by one, they began to come around. The fans, it seemed, wanted sports coverage of Sportsmaster presentations.

And the lords of sport suddenly faced war.

Hoboken took the kickoff at the opening of the second half. But Keith Lancer still sat on the sidelines, and without him the Jets seemed vaguely unsure of what they were supposed to do with the ball. They made one first down, then stalled and were forced to punt.

The Packer offense came back onto the field, and they radiated a cold confidence. With methodical precision, Sandretti led his team down the field. He was taking no chances now, so he kept the ball out of the air and relied on his running backs. Again and again Mitchell slammed into the line, and Strawn danced through it, to pick up a yard or two or four. Slowly but inexorably the Packer steamroller ground ahead.

The drive was set back by a few penalties, and slowed here and there when the Jet defense toughened momentarily. But it was never stopped. It was late in the third quarter before Mitchell finally plunged over tackle into the end zone for another Packer touchdown.

Then came the extra point, and it was 24–7 Packers, and a lot of the fans seemed to be leaving.

For a decade the war raged, fierce and bloody. At first, Sportsmaster was the underdog, fighting for acceptance, fighting to be taken seriously. The NFL and the NHL and the NBA won all the early battles.

And then the gap began to close. The viewers and the

fans got used to Sportsmaster, and the distinction began to blur. After all, the games all looked the same over television. Except that the Sportsmaster leagues seemed to have better teams, and their games seemed to be a little more exciting.

That was deliberate. The Sportsmaster people had programmed in a drama factor. They were careful about it, however. They knew that nothing can kill a sport faster than obvious staging of games for effect. The predictable, standard scripts of wrestling and roller derby were strictly avoided. Sportsmaster games remained always as unpredictable as the real thing.

Only, they were slightly more exciting, on the average. There were dull games in the Sportsmaster leagues, of course. But never quite as many as in the real leagues.

The turning point in the war was the Battle of the Super Bowl in January, 1994.

In the NFL Super Bowl, the New York Giants were facing the Denver Broncos. The Broncos were one of the most exciting teams in decades; blinding speed, a colorful quarterback, and the highest-scoring offense in football history. The Giants were the mediocre champions of a weak division, who had gotten lucky in the play-offs.

In the Sportsmaster Super Bowl, the 1993 Denver Broncos were facing the Green Bay Packers of the Vince Lombardi era.

In the NFL Super Bowl, the Broncos beat the Giants 34–9 in an utterly undistinguished game. The outcome of the contest was never in doubt for a second.

In the Sportsmaster Super Bowl, the Broncos beat the Packers 21–17, on a long bomb thrown with seconds remaining on the clock.

The two Super Bowls got almost identical ratings. But those who watched the NFL game found that they had missed a classic to watch a dud. It was the last time that would happen, they vowed.

Sportsmaster began to pull ahead.

It was the moment of truth for Hoboken.

The Jets took the Packer kickoff, and started upfield with determination. Yard by yard they fought their way through the mud and the rain, back into the game. And the Packer defense made them pay for every inch with blood.

The Jets drove to the fifty, then past it. They moved into Packer territory. When the quarter ended, they were on the Packer thirty-three-yard line.

Two plays into the fourth quarter, the second-string quarterback fumbled on a handoff. The Packers recovered.

Sandretti took over, and the Packers moved the ball back toward midfield. They picked up one first down. But then, suddenly, the Jet defense got tough.

They stopped the Packers on the forty-five. Green Bay was forced to punt. The punt, against the wind, was a bad one. The Jets called for a fair catch and took the ball on their own thirty.

First and ten. The Jets tried an end sweep. No gain.

Second and ten. A reverse. A three-yard loss.

Third and thirteen. The Jets called time out.

And Keith Lancer came back in.

He wasn't limping now. But he still looked unsteady, wobbly on his feet. This was it for the Jets, the fans told themselves. This was the do-or-die play. A pass, of course. It had to be a pass.

The Packers were thinking the same thing. When the ball was snapped and Lancer faded back, their front four came roaring in like demons out of hell.

Lancer lateraled to one of his halfbacks on the sideline. The rushers changed direction in midstride, and streaked past him.

Lancer, suddenly ignored, ran slowly upfield and caught the pass for a first down. He was tackled with a vengeance. But all that got the Packers was a fifteen-yard penalty.

Lancer stayed in, and started passing. In seven plays, he put Hoboken on the scoreboard again to cut the Packer margin to 24–14.

The long twilight of spectator sports had begun.

Sportsmaster II was unveiled in 1995, a computer bigger and more sophisticated than the original. Sportsmaster, Inc., was sliced from the network that had founded it by government decree, since the combined empire was growing too large.

By the late 1990s, television confrontations between Sportsmaster shows and real sports events were confrontations in name only. Sportsmaster ran away with the ratings with monotonous regularity.

In 1996, the network that had been broadcasting NFL games refused to pick up the contract unless the price was slashed almost in half. The league was forced to agree.

In 1998, the NBA television contract was worth only a fourth of what it had gone for five years earlier.

In 1999, no one bid for the right to telecast NHL hockey.

Still, the sports promoters hung on. They still had some television audiences. And the games themselves were still packed.

But the Sportsmaster men were ruthless. They analyzed the reasons why real sports still attracted people. And came up with some innovations.

People who still went to games did so because they preferred to view sports outdoors, or as part of a crowd, they decided. Fine. So they built Sportsmaster Theaters, where fans could eat hot dogs and watch the games as part of a crowd. And they erected a giant Sportsmaster Stadium, where the simulations were staged outdoors as full-color, three-dimensional holoshows.

In 2003, the Super Bowl was not a sellout. The World Series had already failed to sell out for several years running. The live crowds started to shrink.

And didn't stop.

Despite the Jet touchdown, the Packers were still comfortably out in front. The game was theirs, if they could only run out the clock.

Sandretti kept his team on the ground, handing off to Mitchell and Strawn, chalking up one first down after another the hard way by churning through the mud. The Jets began to use their time-outs. The minutes flew by.

The Packers finally were held just past the midfield stripe. But Sandretti had wreaked his damage. There was time left for maybe one Jet drive, but hardly for two.

But Hoboken did not give up. Their time-outs were gone, and the clock was against them. But Lancer was in the game again. And that made anything possible.

The Packers went into a prevent defense to guard against the bomb. They were willing to give up the short gain, the first down. That was all right. Lancer. could drive for a touchdown if he wanted to, so long as it wasn't a quick score.

The Jet quarterback tried one bomb, but it fizzled, incomplete, in the rain. Packer defenders were all over the Hoboken deep men. The Jets had no recourse but to drive for the score, eat up the clock, and pray for a break.

They drove. Lancer, no longer wobbly, hit on one short pass after another. Hoboken moved upfield. Hoboken scored. The extra point was dead on target. The score stood at 24–21.

But there was less than a minute left to play.

In 2005, they introduced Sportsmaster III, and the Home Matchmaker. It was a fatal blow.

Sportsmaster III was ten times the size of Sportsmaster II, and had more than a hundred times the capacity. It was built underground in Kansas, and was larger than most cities. Regional extensions were scattered over the nation.

The Home Matchmakers were expensive devices that linked up directly with the Sportsmaster extensions, and through them, with Sportsmaster III. They were programming devices. They allowed each Sportsmaster subscriber to select his own games for home viewing.

Sportsmaster III could accommodate any request, could set up any match, could arrange any conditions. If a subscriber wanted to see the 1962 Los Angeles Rams play the 1980 Notre Dame junior varsity in the Astrodome, Sportsmaster III would digest that request, search its awesome memory banks, and beam up simulation to the subscriber's holovision.

The variations were infinite. The subscriber could punch in weather, injuries, and location. The subscriber could select his own team of All Stars, and pit them against someone else's team, or against a real team of any era. With Sportsmaster III and the Home Matchmaker, the sports fan could sit at home and watch any sort of contest he could dream up.

At first, the Home Matchmakers were very costly. Only the very rich could afford them. Others were forced to pool their resources, form Sportsmaster clubs, and vote on the games they wanted to see.

But soon the price began to come down.

And when it got low enough, spectator sports died.

Boxing went first. It had always been the weak sister. The champions continued to defend their crowns, but there were fewer and fewer challengers, since the game was far from lucrative. The intervals between fights grew steadily longer. And after a while, there were no more fights.

The other sports followed. People continued to play tennis and golf, but they were no longer willing to pay to watch others play. Not when they could watch much better matches, of their own selection, on Sportsmaster hookups. Tournament after tournament was canceled. Until there were no more left to cancel.

The NHL and the NBA both disbanded in 2010. They had been suffering billion-dollar losses for several years before they closed up shop.

Baseball, hoary with age, held on four years longer. It moved its teams to progressively smaller cities, where the novelty always brought out crowds for a while. It slashed costs desperately. It sold stadiums, cut salaries to the bone, skimped on field and equipment maintenance. It went before Congress, and argued that the national pastime should be preserved with a subsidy.

And, in 2014, it folded.

Football was the last to go. Since the 1970s, it had been the biggest, and the richest, and the most arrogant sport of all. It had fought the most bitterly in the days of ads and lawsuits, and it had carried the brunt of the battle throughout the long television war.

And now it refused to die. It used every trick the baseball leagues had tried, and then some. It cut teams, added teams, moved teams, changed the rules, began sideshows. But nothing worked. No one came. No one was interested.

And so it was that the last Super Bowl was played in January, 2016, on a muddy field in Hoboken, New Jersey.

It was going to be an on-sides kick. The Jets knew that. The Packers knew that. Every fan in the stadium knew that. They were all waiting.

But even as they lined up for the kickoff, the rains came.

They came in earnest, a torrent, a sudden downpour. The sky darkened, and the wind howled, and the water came rushing down and down and down. It was a blinding rain, lashing at the mud, sending the remaining fans scrambling for shelter.

In that rain came the kickoff.

It was an on-sides kick, of course. Neither team could see the ball very well. Both converged on it. A Packer reached it first. He threw himself on top of it.

And the mud-covered ball squirted out from under him. Squirted toward Hoboken.

The Jets had the break they needed. It was first and ten near the fifty, and it was their ball. But the clock was ticking, and the rain was a shrieking wall of water that refused to let up.

Lancer and the Jet offense came running back onto the field, and lined up quickly. They didn't bother with a huddle. They had their plays down already.

The Packer defensemen walked out slowly, dragging their heels through the mud, dawdling, eating up the clock. Finally they got lined up, and the ball was snapped.

It was impossible to pass in that rain. Impossible. You couldn't throw through that much water. You couldn't run through mud like that, and puddles that looked like oceans. You couldn't even see the ball in that kind of rain.

It was impossible to pass in that rain. But the Jets had to pass. Their time was running out.

So Lancer passed. Somehow, somehow, he passed.

His first throw was a bullet to the sidelines, good for twenty yards. The receiver didn't see the ball coming. But he caught it anyway, because Lancer laid it right into his hands. Then he stepped out of bounds, and stopped the clock.   1887604

There were eighteen seconds left to play.

Lancer passed again. Somehow, through that blinding rain, in that sea of mud, somehow, he passed again. It was complete.

It was complete to the other sideline, to the five. The receiver clutched at the ball, and bobbled it for a second, then grasped it tightly, and took a step toward the goal line.

And the Packer defender roared into him like a Mack truck and knocked him out of bounds. The clock stopped again. With about six seconds left.

It was the last touchdown drive. The very, very last. And now was its climax.

They lined up at the three, with seconds left. Both teams looked the same by now; spattered, soaking, hulking figures in uniforms that had all turned an identical mud-brown.

It was the last confrontation. The Packer defense, in its ultimate test: a wall, an iron-hard, determined, teeth-clenched, mud-brown human wall. Lancer, the last great quarterback: wet and muddy and injured and angry and brilliant.

And the rain, the pounding rain around them both. The ball was snapped.

Lancer took it. The Jet line surged forward, smashing at the Packers, fighting to clear a hole, clearing one. Lancer moved to it, through it, toward the goal line, the goal line only feet away.

And something rose up from the ground and hit him. Hard and low.

It was the last touchdown drive, the last ever. And it was brilliant and it was poetic and they should have scored. They should have scored.

But they didn't.

And the gun sounded, and the game was over, and the Packers had won. The players began to drift away to the locker room.

And Keith Lancer, who drove for the final touchdown, and didn't make it, picked himself up from the mud, and sighed, and helped up the man who had tackled him.

They shook hands in the rain, and Lancer smiled to hide the tears. And so, strangely, did the Packer. They walked together from the field.

Neither one bothered to look up at the stands.

The empty stands.

The
National
Pastime

norman spinrad

The "national pastime" is a phrase associated with baseball. Yet it is becoming increasingly clear that football,
especially in its professional form, has replaced that
sport as the favorite of the American people. A number
of views have been advanced to explain this shift, mostly
centering around the controlled violence found in football. Some critics have argued that since America is a
"violent society," it is only natural that Americans
would love violent sports. Others have pointed out what
they believe to be the "warlike" aspects of football—
terms like "the bomb," "the blitz," and "offense" and
"defense." Some persons have even maintained that these
characteristics of football are healthy—that all societies
need some form of outlet for their aggressions and
frustrations and that these are better taken out vicari-
ously through watching pro football than by directly
punching one's neighbor in the mouth.

Certainly all these arguments have some element of
truth in them, but they all bear close examination. All
societies seem to have an element of violence in their
national sports, whether it is the cockfight and bullfight
of Latin America or the rise of boxing in countries such

as Japan. Similarly, many other games can be considered surrogates for war, including chess, which has never been as popular in this country as it has in Europe.

This well-written story examines some of these themes through its portrayal of a new form of football called "Combat Football." It attempts to project developments in the near future in which athletic teams represent social groups instead of geographic regions, and fan involvement becomes active rather than passive. This does not imply that fans are always passive. Anyone who has been caught in the middle of a soccer riot in Europe or in Latin America can attest to the nonpassive attitudes of some fans! But, typically, fans' participation in spectator sports is psychological and spiritual rather than actual. In "The National Pastime," however, the fans not only riot, they also become part of the score and the game. A clear case of "group therapy" with a vengeance!

The
National
Pastime

The Founding Father

I know you've got to start at the bottom in the television business, but producing sports shows is my idea of cruel and unusual punishment. Sometime in the dim past, I had the idea that I wanted to make films, and the way to get to make films seemed to be to run up enough producing and directing credits on television, and the way to do *that* was to take whatever came along, and what came along was an offer to do a series of sports specials on things like kendo, sumo wrestling, jousting, Thai boxing, in short, ritual violence. This was at the height (or the depth) of the antiviolence hysteria, when you couldn't so much as show the bad guy getting an on-camera rap in the mouth from the good guy on a moron western. The only way you could give the folks what they really wanted was in the All-American wholesome package of a sporting event. Knowing this up front —unlike the jerks who warm chairs as network executives—I had no trouble producing the kind of sports specials the network executives knew people wanted to see without quite knowing why, and thus I achieved the status of boy genius. Which, alas, ended up in my being offered a long-term contract as a producer in the sports department that was simply too rich for me to pass up, I mean I make no bones about being a crass materialist.

So try to imagine my feelings when Herb Dieter, the network sports programming director, calls me in to his inner sanctum and gives me The Word. "Ed," he tells me, "as you know, there's now only one major football league, and the opposition has us frozen out of the picture with long-term contracts with the NFL. As you also know, the major league football games are clobbering us in the Sunday afternoon ratings, which is prime time as far as sports programming is concerned. And as you know, a sports programming director who can't hold a decent piece of the Sunday afternoon audience is not long for this fancy office. And as you know, there is no sport on God's green earth that can compete with major league football. Therefore, it would appear that I have been presented with an insoluble problem.

"Therefore, since you are the official boy genius of the sports department, Ed, I've decided that you must be the solution to my problem. If I don't come up with something that will hold its own against pro football by the beginning of next season, my head will roll. Therefore, I've decided to give you the ball and let you run with it. Within ninety days, you will have come up with a solution or the fine-print boys will be instructed to find a way for me to break your contract."

I found it very hard to care one way or the other. On the one hand, I liked the bread I was knocking down, but on the other, the job was a real drag and it would probably do me good to get my ass fired. Of course the whole thing was unfair from my point of view, but who could fault Dieter's logic, he personally had nothing to lose by ordering his best creative talent to produce a miracle or be fired. Unless I came through, *he* would be fired, and then what would he care about gutting the sports department, it wouldn't be his baby anymore. It wasn't very nice, but it was the name of the game we were playing.

"You mean all I'm supposed to do is invent a better sport than football in ninety days, Herb, or do you mean something more impossible?" I couldn't decide whether I was trying to be funny or not.

But Dieter suddenly had a 20-watt bulb come on behind his eyes (about as bright as he could get). "I do believe you've hit on it already, Ed," he said. "We can't get any pro football, so you're right, you've got to *invent* a sport that will outdraw pro football. Ninety days, Ed. And don't take it too hard; if you bomb out, we'll see each other at the unemployment office."

So there I was, wherever *that* was. I could easily get Dieter to do for me what I didn't have the willpower to do for myself and get me out of the stinking sports department—all I had to do was *not* invent a game that would outdraw pro football. On the other hand, I liked living the way I did, and I didn't like the idea of losing *anything* because of failure.

So the next Sunday afternoon, I eased out the night before's chick, turned on the football game, smoked two joints of Acapulco Gold, and consulted my muse. It was the ideal set of conditions for a creative mood: I was being challenged, but if I failed, I gained too, so I had no inhibitions on my creativity. I was stoned to the point where the whole situation was a game without serious consequences; I was hanging loose.

Watching two football teams pushing each other back
and forth across my color television screen, it once again
occurred to me how much football was a ritual sublima-
tion of war. This seemed perfectly healthy. Lots of cultures are addicted to sports that are sublimations of the
natural human urge to clobber people. Better the sub-
limation than the clobbering. People dig violence,
whether anyone likes the truth or not, so it's a public
service to keep it on the level of a spectator sport.

Hmmm . . . that was probably why pro football had
replaced baseball as the National Pastime in a time
when people, having had their noses well rubbed in the
stupidity of war, needed a war substitute. How could
you beat something that got the American armpit as
close to the gut as that?

And then from the blue grass mountaintops of Mexico,
the flash hit me: the only way to beat football was at its
own game! Start with football itself, and convert it into
something that was an even *closer* metaphor for war,
something that could be called—

!!COMBAT FOOTBALL!!

Yeah, yeah, Combat football, or better, COMBAT
football. Two standard football teams, standard football
field, standard football rules, except:

Take off all their pads and helmets and jerseys and
make it a warm-weather game that they play in shorts
and sneakers like boxing. More meaningful, more inti-
mate violence. Violence is what sells football, so give 'em
a bit more violence than football, and you'll draw a bit
more than football. The more violent you can make it
and get away with it, the better you'll draw.

Yeah . . . and you could get away with punching, after all boxers belt each other around and they still allow boxing on television; sports have too much All-American Clean for the antiviolence freaks to attack, in fact, where their heads are at, they'd *dig* Combat football. Okay. So in ordinary football, the defensive team tackles the ball carrier to bring him to his knees and stop the play. So in Combat, the defenders can slug the ball carrier, kick him, tackle him, why not, anything to bring him to his knees and stop the play. And to make things fair, the ball carrier can slug the defenders to get them out of his way. If the defense slugs an offensive player who doesn't have possession, it's ten yards and an automatic first down. If anyone but the ball carrier slugs a defender, it's ten yards and a loss of down.

Presto: Combat football!

And the final touch was that it was a game that any beer-sodden moron who watched football could learn to understand in sixty seconds, and any lout who dug football would have to like Combat better.

The boy genius had done it again! It even made sense after I came down.

Farewell to the Giants

Jeez, I saw a thing on television last Sunday you wouldn't believe. You really oughta watch it next week, I don't care who the Jets or the Giants are playing. I turned on the TV to watch the Giants game and went to get a beer, and when I came back from the kitchen I had some guy yelling something about today's professional Combat football game, and it's not the NFL announcer, and it's a team called the New York Sharks playing a team called the Chicago Thunderbolts, and they're playing in L.A. or Miami, I didn't catch which, but someplace with palm trees anyway, and all the players are bare-ass! Well, not really bare-ass, but all they've got on is sneakers and boxing shorts with numbers across the behind—blue for New York, green for Chicago. No helmets, no pads, no protectors, no jerseys, no nothing!

I check the set and sure enough I've got the wrong channel. But I figured I could turn on the Giants game anytime, what the hell, you can see the Giants all the time, but what in hell is *this*?

New York kicks off to Chicago. The Chicago kick-returner gets the ball on about the 10—bad kick—and starts upfield. The first New York tackler reaches him and goes for him and the Chicago player just belts him in the mouth and runs by him! I mean, with the ref standing there watching it, and no flag thrown! Two more tacklers come at him on the 20. One dives at his legs, the other socks him in the gut. He trips and staggers out of the tackle, shoves another tackler away with a punch in the chest, but he's slowed up enough so that three or four New York players get to him at once. A couple of them grab his legs to stop his motion, and the others knock him down, at about the 25. Man, what's going on here?

I check my watch. By this time the Giants game has probably started, but New York and Chicago are lined up for the snap on the 25, so I figure what the hell, I gotta see some more of this thing, so at least I'll watch one series of downs.

On first down, the Chicago quarterback drops back

and throws a long one way downfield to his flanker on maybe the New York 45; it looks good, there's only one player on the Chicago flanker, he beats this one man and catches it, and it's a touchdown, and the pass looks right on the button. Up goes the Chicago flanker, the ball touches his hands—and pow, right in the kisser! The New York defender belts him in the mouth and he drops the pass. Jeez, what a game!

Second and ten. The Chicago quarterback fades back, but it's a fake, he hands off to his fullback, a gorilla who looks like he weighs about two-fifty, and the Chicago line opens up a little hole at left tackle and the fullback hits it holding the ball with one hand and punching with the other. He belts out a tackler, takes a couple of shots in the gut, slugs a second tackler, and then someone has him around the ankles; he drags himself forward another half yard or so, and then he runs into a good solid punch and he's down on the 28 for a three-yard gain.

Man, I mean *action!* What a game! Makes the NFL football look like something for faggots! Third and seven, you gotta figure Chicago for the pass, right? Well on the snap, the Chicago quarterback just backs up a few steps and pitches a short one to his flanker at about the line of scrimmage. The blitz is on and everyone comes rushing in on the quarterback and before New York knows what's happening, the Chicago flanker is five yards downfield along the left sideline and picking up speed. Two New York tacklers angle out to stop him at maybe the Chicago 40, but he's got up momentum and one of the New York defenders runs right into his fist—I could hear the thud even on television—and falls back right into the other New York player, and the Chicago flanker is by them, the 40, the 45, he angles back toward the center of the field at midfield, dancing away from one more tackle, then on maybe the New York 45 a real fast New York defensive back catches up to him from behind, tackles him waist-high, and the Chicago flanker's motion is stopped as two more tacklers come at him. But he squirms around inside the tackle and belts the tackler in the mouth with his free hand, knocks the New York back silly, breaks the tackle, and he's off again downfield with two guys chasing him— 40, 35, 30, 25, he's running away from them. Then from way over the right side of the field, I see the New York safety man running flat out across the field at the ball carrier, angling toward him so it looks like they'll crash like a couple of locomotives on about the 15, because the Chicago runner just doesn't see this guy. Ka-boom! The ball carrier running flat out runs right into the fist of the flat-out safety at the 15 and he's knocked about ten feet one way and the football flies ten feet the other way, and the New York safety scoops it up on the 13 and starts upfield, 20, 25, 30, 35, and then slam, bang, whang, half the Chicago team is all over him, a couple of tackles, a few in the gut, a shot in the head, and he's down. First and ten for New York on their own 37. And that's just the first series of downs!

Well let me tell you, after that you know where they can stick the Giants game, right? This Combat football, that's the real way to play the game, I mean it's football and boxing all together, with a little wrestling thrown in, it's a game with *balls*. I mean, the *whole game* was like that first series. You oughta take a look at it next week.

Damn, if they played the thing in New York we could even go out to the game together. I'd sure be willing to spend a couple of bucks to see something like that.

Commissioner Gene Kuhn Addresses the
First Annual Owners' Meeting of the
National Combat Football
League

Gentlemen, I've been thinking about the future of our great sport. We're facing a double challenge to the future of Combat football, boys. First of all, the NFL is going over to Combat rules next season, and since you can't copyright a sport (and if you could the NFL would have us by the short hairs anyway) there's not a legal thing we can do about it. The only edge we'll have left is that they'll have to at least wear heavy uniforms because they play in regular cities up north. But they'll have the stars, and the stadiums, and the regular hometown fans and fatter television deals.

Which brings me to our second problem, gentlemen, namely that the television network which created our great game is getting to be a pain in our sport's neck, meaning that they're shafting us in the crummy percentage of the television revenue they see fit to grant us.

So the great task facing our great National Pastime, boys, is to ace out the network by putting ourselves in a better bargaining position on the television rights while saving our million-dollar asses from the NFL competition, which we just cannot afford.

Fortunately, it just so happens your commissioner has been on the ball, and I've come up with a couple of new gimmicks that I am confident will insure the posterity and financial success of our great game while stiff-arming the NFL and the TV network nicely in the process.

Number one, we've got to improve our standing as a live spectator sport. We've got to start drawing big crowds on our own if we want some clout in negotiating with the network. Number two, we've got to give the customers something the NFL can't just copy from us next year and clobber us with.

There's no point in changing the rules again because the NFL can always keep up with us there. But one thing the NFL is locked into for keeps is the whole concept of having teams represent cities; they're committed to that for the next twenty years. We've only been in business four years and our teams never play in the damned cities they're named after because it's too cold to play bare-ass Combat in those cities during the football season, so it doesn't have to mean anything to us.

So we make two big moves. First, we change our season to spring and summer so we can play up north where the money is. Second, we throw out the whole dumb idea of teams representing cities; that's old-fashioned stuff. That's crap for the coyotes. Why not six teams with *national* followings? Imagine the clout that'll give us when we renegotiate the TV contract. We can have a flexible schedule so that we can put any game we want into any city in the country any time we think that city's hot and draw a capacity crowd in the biggest stadium in town.

How are we gonna do all this? Well look, boys, we've

got a six-team league, so instead of six cities, why not match up our teams with six national groups?

I've taken the time to draw up a hypothetical league lineup just to give you an example of the kind of thing I mean. Six teams: the Black Panthers, the Golden Supermen, the Psychedelic Stompers, the Caballeros, the Gay Bladers and the Hog Choppers. We do it all up the way they used to do with wrestling, you know, the Black Panthers are all spades with naturals, the Golden Supermen are blond astronaut types in red-white-and-blue bunting, the Psychedelic Stompers have long hair and groupies in miniskirts up to their navels and take rock bands to their games, the Caballeros dress like gauchos or something, whatever makes Latin types feel feisty, the Gay Bladers and Hog Choppers are mostly all-purpose villains—the Bladers are black-leather and chain-mail faggots and the Hog Choppers we recruit from outlaw motorcycle gangs.

Now is that a *league*, gentlemen? Identification is the thing, boys. You gotta identify your teams with a large enough group of people to draw crowds, but why tie yourself to something local like a city? This way, we got a team for the spades, a team for the frustrated Middle Americans, a team for the hippies and kids, a team for the spics, a team for the faggots, and a team for the motorcycle nuts and violence freaks. And any American who can't identify with any of those teams is an odds-on bet to hate one or more of them enough to come out to the game to see them stomped. I mean, who wouldn't want to see the Hog Choppers and the Panthers go at each other under Combat rules?

Gentlemen, I tell you it's creative thinking like this that made our country great, and it's creative thinking like this that will make Combat football the greatest gold mine in professional sports.

Stay Tuned, Sports Fans . . .

Good afternoon, Combat fans, and welcome to today's major league Combat football game between the Caballeros and the Psychedelic Stompers brought to you by the World Safety Razorblade Company, with the sharpest, strongest blade for your razor in the world.

It's 95 degrees on this clear New York day in July, and a beautiful day for a Combat football game, and the game here today promises to be a real smasher, as the Caballeros, only a game behind the league-leading Black Panthers, take on the fast-rising, hard-punching Psychedelic Stompers and perhaps the best running back in the game today, Wolfman Ted. We've got a packed house here today, and the Stompers, who won the toss, are about to receive the kickoff from the Caballeros. . . .

And there it is, a low bullet into the end zone, taken there by Wolfman Ted. The Wolfman crosses the goal line, he's up to the 5, the 10, the 14, he brings down number 71 Pete Lopez with a right to the windpipe, crosses the 15, takes a glancing blow to the head from number 56 Diaz, is tackled on the 18 by Porfirio Rubio, number 94, knocks Rubio away with two quick rights to the head, crosses the 20, and takes two rapid blows to the midsection in succession from Beltran and number 30 Orduna, staggers, and is tackled low from behind by the quick-recovering Rubio and slammed to the ground under a pile of Caballeros on the 24.

First and ten for the Stompers on their own 24. Stompers quarterback Ronny Seede brings his team to the line of scrimmage in a double flanker formation with Wolfman Ted wide to the right. A long count—

The snap, Seede fades back to—

A quick handoff to the Wolfman charging diagonally across the action toward left tackle, and the Wolfman hits the line on a dead run, windmilling his right fist, belting his way through one, two, three Caballeros, getting two, three yards, then taking three quick ones to the rib cage from Rubio, and staggering right into number 41 Manuel Cardozo, who brings him down on about the 27 with a hard right cross.

Hold it! A flag on the play! Orduna number 30 of the Caballeros and Dickson number 83 of the Stompers are whaling away at each other on the 26! Dickson takes two hard ones and goes down, but as Orduna kicks him in the ribs, number 72, Merling of the Stompers, grabs him from behind and now there are six or seven assistant referees breaking it up. . . .

Something going on in the stands at about the 50 too— a section of Stompers rooters mixing it up with the Caballero fans—

But now they've got things sorted out on the field, and it's 10 yards against the Caballeros for striking an ineligible player, nullified by a 10-yarder against the Stompers for illegal offensive striking. So now it's second and seven for the Stompers on their own 27—

It's quieted down a bit there above the 50-yard line,

but there's another little fracas going in the far end zone and a few groups of people milling around in the aisles of the upper grandstand—

There's the snap, and Seede fades back quickly, dances around, looks downfield, and throws one intended for number 54, Al Viper, the left end, at about the 40. Viper goes up for it, he's got it—

And takes a tremendous shot along the base of his neck from number 94 Porfirio Rubio! The ball is jarred loose. Rubio dives for it, he's got it, but he takes a hard right in the head from Viper, then a left. Porfirio drops the ball and goes at Viper with both fists! Viper knocks him sprawling and dives on top of the ball, burying it and bringing a whistle from the head referee as Rubio rains blows on his prone body. And here come the assistant referees to pull Porfirio off as half the Stompers come charging downfield toward the action—

They're at it again near the 50-yard line! About forty rows of fans going at each other. There goes a smoke bomb!

They've got Rubio away from Viper now, but three or four Stompers are trying to hold Wolfman Ted back and Ted has blood in his eye as he yells at number 41, Cardozo. Two burly assistant referees are holding Cardozo back. . . .

There go about a hundred and fifty special police up into the midfield stands. They've got their Mace and prods out. . . .

The head referee is calling an official's time-out to get things organized, and we'll be back to live National Combat Football League action after this message. . . .

The Circus Is in Town

"We've got a serious police problem with Combat football," Commissioner Minelli told me after the game between the Golden Supermen and the Psychedelic Stompers last Sunday in which the Supermen slaughtered the Stompers 42–14 and during which there were ten fatalities and 189 hospitalizations among the rabble in the stands.

"Every time there's a game, we have a riot, your honor," Minelli (who had risen through the ranks) said earnestly. "I recommend that you should think seriously about banning Combat football. I really think you should."

This city is hard enough to run without free advice from politically ambitious cops. "Minelli," I told him, "you are dead wrong on both counts. First of all, not only has there *never* been a riot in New York during a Combat football game, but the best studies show that the incidence of violent crimes and social violence diminishes from a period of three days before a Combat game clear through to a period five days afterward, not only here, but in every major city in which a game is played."

"But only this Sunday ten people were killed and nearly two hundred injured, including a dozen of my cops—"

"In the *stands*, you nitwit, not in the streets!" Really, the man was too much!

"I don't see the difference—"

"Ye gods, Minelli, can't you see that Combat football keeps a hell of a lot of violence off the streets? It keeps it in the stadium, where it belongs. The Romans understood that two thousand years ago! We can hardly stage gladiator sports in this day and age, so we have to settle for a civilized substitute."

"But what goes on in there is murder. My cops are taking a beating. And we've got to assign two thousand cops to every game. It's costing the taxpayers a fortune, and you can bet . . . *someone* will be making an issue out of it in the next election."

I do believe that the lout was actually trying to pressure me. Still, in his oafish way, he had put his finger on the one political disadvantage of Combat football: the cost of policing the games and keeping the fan clubs in the stands from tearing each other to pieces.

And then I had one of those little moments of blind inspiration when the pieces of a problem simply fall into shape as an obvious pattern of solution.

Why bother keeping them from tearing each other to pieces?

"I think I have the solution, Minelli," I said. "Would it satisfy your sudden sense of fiscal responsibility if you could take all but a couple dozen cops off the Combat football games?"

Minelli looked at me blankly. "Anything less than two thousand cops in there would be mincemeat by half-time," he said.

"So why send them in there?"

"Huh?"

"All we really need is enough cops to guard the gates, frisk the fans for weapons, seal up the stadium with the help of riot doors, and make sure no one gets out till things have simmered down inside."

"But they'd tear each other to ribbons in there with no cops!"

"So let them. I intend to modify the conditions under which the city licenses Combat football so that anyone who buys a ticket legally waives his right to police protection. Let them fight all they want. Let them really work out their hatreds on each other until they're good and exhausted. Human beings have an incurable urge to commit violence on each other. We try to sublimate that urge out of existence, and we end up with irrational violence on the streets. The Romans had a better idea—give the rabble a socially harmless outlet for violence. We spend billions on welfare to keep things pacified with bread, and where has it gotten us? Isn't it about time we tried circuses?"

As American as Apple Pie

Let me tell it to you, brother, we've sure been waiting for the Golden Supermen to play the Panthers in *this* town again, after the way those blond mothers cheated us 17–10 the last time and wasted three hundred of the brothers! Yeah man, they had those stands packed with honkies trucked in from as far away as Buffalo—we just weren't ready, is why we took the loss.

But this time we planned ahead and got ourselves up for the game even before it was announced. Yeah, instead of waiting for them to announce the date of the next Panther–Supermen game in Chicago and then scrambling with the honkies for tickets, the Panther Fan Club made under-the-table deals with ticket brokers for blocs of tickets for whenever the next game would be, so that by the time today's game was announced, we controlled two-thirds of the seats in Daley Stadium and the honkies had to scrape and scrounge for what was left.

Yeah man, today we pay them back for that last game! We got two-thirds of the seats in the stadium and Eli Wood is back in action and we gonna just go out and *stomp* those mothers today!

Really, I'm personally quite cynical about Combat; most of us who go out to the Gay Bladers games are. After all, if you look at it straight on, Combat football is rather a grotty business. I mean, look at the sort of people who turn out at Supermen or Panthers or for God's sake *Caballero* games: the worst sort of proletarian apes. Aside from us, only the Hogs have any semblance of class, and the Hogs have beauty only because they're so incredibly up-front gross, I mean all that shiny metal and black leather!

And of course that's the only real reason to go to the Blader games: for the spectacle. To see it and to be part of it! To see seminaked groups of men engaging in violence and to be violent yourself—and especially with those black-leather and chain-mail Hog Lovers!

Of course I'm aware of the cynical use the loathsome government makes of Combat. If there's nastiness between the blacks and P.R.s in New York, they have the league schedule a Panther–Caballero game and let them get it out on each other safely in the stadium. If there's college campus trouble in the Bay Area, it's a Stompers–Supermen game in Oakland. And us and the Hogs when just *anyone* anywhere needs to release general hostility. I'm not stupid, I know that Combat football is a tool of the Establishment. . . .

But Lord, it's just so much bloody *fun*!

We gonna have some fun today! The Hogs is playing the Stompers and that's the wildest kind of Combat game there is! Those crazy freaks come to the game stoned out of their minds, and you know that at least Wolfman Ted is playing on something stronger than pot. There are twice as many chicks at Stomper games than with any other team the Hogs play because the Stomper chicks are the only chicks beside ours who aren't scared out of their boxes at the thought of being locked up in a stadium with twenty thousand hot-shot Hogger rape artists like us!

Yeah, we get good and stoned, and the Stomper fans get good and stoned, and the Hogs get stoned, and the Stompers get stoned, and then we all groove on beating the piss out of each other, *whoo*-whee! And when we win in the stands, we drag off the pussy and gang-bang it.

Oh yeah, Combat is just good clean dirty fun!

It makes you feel good to go out to a Supermen game, makes you feel like a real American is supposed to, like a man. All week you've got to take crap from the niggers and the spics and your goddamn crazy doped-up kids and hoods and bums and faggots in the streets, and you're not even supposed to think of them as niggers and spics and crazy doped-up kids and bums and hoods and faggots. But Sunday you can go out to the stadium and watch the Supermen give it to the Panthers, the

Caballeros, the Stompers, the Hogs, or the Bladers and maybe kick the crap out of a few people whose faces you don't like yourself.

It's a good healthy way to spend a Sunday afternoon, out in the open air at a good game when the Supermen are hot and we've got the opposition in the stands outnumbered. Combat's a great thing to take your kid to, too!

I don't know, all my friends go to the Caballero games, we go together and take a couple of six packs of beer apiece, and get *muy boracho* and just have some crazy fun, you know? Sometimes I come home a little cut up and my wife is all upset and tries to get me to promise not to go to the Combat games anymore. Sometimes I promise, just to keep her quiet, she can get on my nerves, but I never really mean it.

Hombre, you know how it is, women don't understand these things like men do. A man has got to go out with his friends and feel like a man sometimes. It's not too easy to find ways to feel *muy macho* in this country, *amigo*. The way it is for us here, you know. It's not as if we're hurting anyone we shouldn't hurt. Who goes out to the Caballero games but a lot of dirty gringos who want to pick on us? So it's a question of honor, in a way, for us to get as many *amigos* as we can out to the Caballero games and show those *cabrones* that we can beat them anytime, no matter how drunk we are. In fact, the drunker we are, the better it is, "*¿tu sabes?*"

Baby, I don't know what it is, maybe it's just a chance to get it all out. It's a unique trip, that's all, there's no other

way to get that particular high, that's why I go to Stompers games. Man, the games don't mean anything to me
as games; games are like *games*, dig. But the whole Combat scene is its own reality.

You take some stuff—acid is a groovy high but you're
liable to get wasted, lots of speed and some grass or hash
is more recommended—when you go in, so that by the
time the game starts you're really loaded. And then man,
you just groove behind the violence. There aren't any
cops to bring you down. What chicks are there are there
because they dig it. The people you're enjoying beating
up on are getting the same kicks beating up on you, so
there's no guilt hang-up to get between you and the
total experience of violence.

Like I say, it's a unique trip. A pure violence high
without any hang-ups. It makes me feel good and
purged and kind of together just to walk out of that
stadium after a Combat football trip and know I sur-
vived; the danger is groovy too. Baby, if you can dig it,
Combat can be a genuine mystical experience.

Hogs Win It All, 21–17, 1,578(23)–989(14)!

Anaheim, October 8. It was a slam-bang finish to the
National Combat Football League Pennant Race, the
kind of game Combat fans dream about. The Golden
Supermen and the Hog Choppers in a dead-even tie for
first place, playing each other in the last game of the
season, winner take all, before nearly 60,000 fans. It
was a beautiful sunny 90-degree Southern California day
as the Hogs kicked off to the Supermen before a crowd
that seemed evenly divided between Hog Lovers who

had motorcycled in all week from all over California and Supermen Fans whose biggest bastion is here in Orange County.

The Supermen scored first blood midway through the first period when quarterback Bill Johnson tossed a little screen pass to his right end, Seth West, on the Hog 23, and West slugged his way through five Hog tacklers, one of whom sustained a mild concussion, to go in for the touchdown. Rudolf's conversion made it 7–0, and the Supermen Fans in the stands responded to the action on the field by making a major sortie into the Hog Lover section at midfield, taking out about 20 Hog Lovers, including a fatality.

The Hog fans responded almost immediately by launching an offensive of their own in the bleacher seats, but didn't do much better than hold their own. The Hogs and the Supermen pushed each other up and down the field for the rest of the period without a score, while the Supermen Fans seemed to be getting the better of the Hog Lovers, especially in the midfield sections of the grandstand, where at least 120 Hog Lovers were put out of action.

The Supermen scored a field goal early in the second period to make the score 10–0, but more significantly, the Hog Lovers seemed to be dogging it, contenting themselves with driving back continual Supermen Fan sorties, while launching almost no attacks of their own.

The Hogs finally pushed in over the goal line in the final minutes of the first half on a long pass from quarterback Spike Horrible to his flanker Greasy Ed Lee to make the score 10–7 as the half ended. But things were not nearly as close as the field score looked, as the Hog

Lovers in the stands were really taking their lumps from the Supermen Fans, who had bruised them to the extent of nearly 500 takeouts, including 5 fatalities, as against only about 300 casualties and 3 fatalities chalked up by the Hog fans.

During the halftime intermission, the Hog Lovers could be seen marshaling themselves nervously, passing around beer, pot, and pills, while the Supermen Fans confidently passed the time entertaining themselves with patriotic songs.

The Supermen scored again halfway through the third period, on a handoff from Johnson to his big fullback Tex McGhee on the Hog 41. McGhee slugged his way through the left side of the line with his patented windmill attack, and burst out into the Hog secondary swinging and kicking. There was no stopping the Texas Tornado, though half the Hog defense tried, and McGhee went 41 yards for the touchdown, leaving three Hogs unconscious and three more with minor injuries in his wake. The kick was good, and the Supermen seemed on their way to walking away with the championship, with the score 17–7, and the momentum, in the stands and on the field, going all their way.

But in the closing moments of the third period, Johnson threw a long one downfield intended for his left end, Dick Whitfield. Whitfield got his fingers on the football at the Hog 30, but Hardly Davidson, the Hog cornerback, was right on him, belted him in the head from behind as he touched the ball, and then managed to catch the football himself before either it or Whitfield had hit the ground. Davidson got back to midfield before three Supermen tacklers took him out of the rest of the game with a closed eye and a concussion. All at once, as time ran out in the third period, the 10-point Supermen lead didn't seem so big at all as the Hogs advanced to a first down on the Supermen 35 and the Hog Lovers in the stands beat back Supermen Fan attacks on several fronts, inflicting very heavy losses.

Spike Horrible threw a 5-yarder to Greasy Ed Lee on the first play of the final period, then a long one into the end zone intended for his left end, Kid Filth, which the Kid dropped as Gordon Jones and John Lawrence slugged him from both sides as soon as he became fair game.

It looked like a sure pass play on third and five, but Horrible surprised everyone by fading back into a draw and handing the ball off to Loser Ludowicki, his fullback, who plowed around right end like a heavy tank, simply crushing and smashing through tacklers with his body and fists, picked up two key blocks on the 20 and 17, knocked Don Barnfield onto the casualty list with a tremendous haymaker on the 7, and went in for the score.

The Hog Lovers in the stands went Hog-wild. Even before the successful conversion by Knuckleface Bonner made it 17–14, they began blitzing the Supermen Fans on all fronts, letting out everything they had seemed to be holding back during the first three quarters. At least 100 Supermen Fans were taken out in the next three minutes, including two quick fatalities, while the Hog Lovers lost no more than a score of their number.

As the Hog Lovers continued to punish the Supermen Fans, the Hogs kicked off to the Supermen, and stopped them after two first downs, getting the ball back on their own 24. After marching to the Supermen 31 on a sustained and bloody ground drive, the Hogs lost the ball again when Greasy Ed Lee was rabbit-punched into a fumble.

But the Hog fans still sensed the inevitable and pressed their attack during the next two Supermen series of downs, and began to push the Supermen Fans toward the bottom of the grandstand.

Buoyed by the success of their fans, the Hogs on the field recovered the ball on their own 29 with less than two minutes to play when Chain Mail Dixon belted Tex McGhee into a fumble and out of the game.

The Hogs crunched their way upfield yard by yard, punch by punch, against a suddenly shaky Supermen opposition, and all at once, the whole season came down to one play:

With the score 17–14 and 20 seconds left on the clock, time enough for one or possibly two more plays, the Hogs had the ball third and four on the 18-yard line of the Golden Supermen.

Spike Horrible took the snap as the Hog Lovers in the stands launched a final all-out offensive against the Supermen Fans, who by now had been pushed to a last stand against the grandstand railings at fieldside. Horrible took about ten quick steps back as if to pass, and then suddenly ran head down fist flailing at the center of the Supermen line with the football tucked under his arm.

Suddenly Greasy Ed Lee and Loser Ludowicki raced ahead of their quarterback, hitting the line and staggering the tacklers a split second before Horrible arrived, throwing them just off balance enough for Horrible to punch his way through with three quick rights, two of them k.o. punches. Virtually the entire Hog team roared through the hole after him, body-blocking, and elbowing, and crushing tacklers to the ground. Horrible punched out three more tacklers as the Hog Lovers pushed the first contingent of fleeing Supermen Fans out onto the field, and went in for the game and championship-winning touchdown with two seconds left on the clock.

When the dust had cleared, not only had the Hog Choppers beaten the Golden Supermen 21–17, but the Hog Lovers had driven the Golden Supermen Fans from their favorite stadium, and had racked up a commanding advantage in the casualty statistics, 1,578 casualties and 23 fatalities inflicted, as against only 989 and 14.

It was a great day for the Hog Lovers and a great day in the history of our National Pastime.

The Voice of Sweet Reason

Go to a Combat football game? Really, do you think I want to risk being injured or possibly killed? Of course I realize that Combat is a practical social mechanism for preserving law and order, and to be frank, I find the spectacle rather stimulating. I watch Combat often, almost every Sunday.

On television, of course. After all, everyone who is anyone in this country knows very well that there are basically two kinds of people in the United States: people who go out to Combat games and people for whom Combat is strictly a television spectator sport.

Run to Starlight

george r. r. martin

Sports are many things to many different kinds of people: a way to keep fit, a way to make money, or a way for one nation or group to "prove" its superiority over another. This latter attitude creates a truly unfortunate state of affairs, because sports need no social justification. They can simply be enjoyed for themselves. However, man is a social animal and tends to categorize people into groups, often reducing social situations to competition between "us" and "them."

It has long been claimed that sports can help to reduce the negative images that groups possess of each other. Those who hold this view believe that by bringing together members of different groups in friendly competition, each will better understand the other and come to appreciate everyone's basic humanity. Unfortunately, some attitudes have proved hard to crack; for example, the idea that a black man cannot be an effective quarterback in the National Football League, or that blacks lack the mental capacity to manage in professional sports. (This last attitude is particularly foolish, since Ray Scott of the Detroit Pistons won the Coach of

the Year award in 1973–74.) Prejudice is still with us—
and sports are no exception.

This story concerns prejudice in sports and in life—a
form of prejudice made more severe because it involves
humans and aliens. It recalls memories that many Americans would rather forget: memories of Jackie Robinson
being called names and having pitches thrown at his
head. Yet it recalls some memories which Americans can
be proud of: Branch Rickey having the courage to bring
blacks into baseball, Robinson and other blacks proving
their ability and their guts, and Americans cheering
Hank Aaron on by the millions. It also shows that in
sports competition there need not be only winners and
losers. There can be situations in which all sides truly
"win."

Run to Starlight

Hill stared dourly at the latest free-fall football results from the Belt as they danced across the face of his desk console, but his mind was elsewhere. For the seventeenth time that week, he was silently cursing the stupidity and shortsightedness of the members of the Starport City Council.

The damn councilmen persisted in cutting the allocation for an artificial gravity grid out of the departmental budget every time Hill put it in. They had the nerve to tell him to stick to "traditional" sports in planning his recreational program for the year.

The old fools had no idea of the way free-fall football was catching on throughout the system, although he'd tried to explain it to them God knows how many times. The Belt sport should be an integral part of any self-respecting recreational program. And on Earth, that meant you had to have a gravity grid. He'd planned on installing it beneath the stadium, but now—

The door to his office slid open with a soft hum. Hill looked up and frowned, snapping off the console. An agitated Jack De Angelis stepped through.

"What is it now?" Hill snapped.

"Uh, Rog, there's a guy here I think you better talk to," De Angelis replied. "He wants to enter a team in the City Football League."

"Registration closed on Tuesday," Hill said. "We've already got twelve teams. No room for any more. And why the hell can't you handle this? You're in charge of the football program."

"This is a special case," De Angelis said.

"Then make an exception and let the team in if you want to," Hill interrupted. "Or don't let them in. It's your program. It's your decision. Must I be bothered with every bit of trivia in this whole damned department?"

"Hey, take it easy, Rog," De Angelis protested. "I don't know what you're so steamed up about. Look, I . . . hell, I'll show you the problem." He turned and went to the door. "Sir, would you step in here a minute?" he said to someone outside.

Hill started to rise from his seat, but sank slowly back into the chair when the visitor appeared in the doorway.

De Angelis was smiling. "This is Roger Hill, the director of the Starport Department of Recreation," he said smoothly. "Rog, let me introduce Remjhard-nei, the head of the Brish'diri trade mission to Earth."

Hill rose again, and offered his hand numbly to the visitor. The Brish'dir was squat and grotesquely broad. He was a good foot shorter than Hill, who stood six feet four, but still gave the impression of dwarfing the director somehow. A hairless, bullet-shaped head was set squarely atop the alien's massive shoulders. His eyes were glittering green marbles sunk in the slick, leathery gray skin.

There were no external ears, only small holes on either side of the skull. The mouth was a lipless slash.

Diplomatically ignoring Hill's openmouthed stare, Remjhard bared his teeth in a quick smile and crushed the director's hand in his own. "I am most pleased to meet you, sir," he said in fluent English, his voice a deep bass growl. "I have come to enter a football team in the fine league your city so graciously runs."

Hill gestured for the alien to take a seat, and sat down himself. De Angelis, still smiling at his boss's stricken look, pulled another chair up to the desk for himself.

"Well, I . . ." Hill began uncertainly. "This team, is it a . . . a Brish'diri team?"

Remjhard smiled again. "Yes," he answered. "Your football, it is a fine game. We of the mission have many times watched it being played on the 3V wallscreens your people were so kind as to install. It has fascinated us. And now some of the half-men of our mission desire to try to play it." He reached slowly into the pocket of the black-and-silver uniform he wore, and pulled out a folded sheet of paper.

"This is a roster of our players," he said, handing it to Hill. "I believe the newsfax said such a list is required to enter your league."

Hill took the paper and glanced down at it uncertainly. It was a list of some fifteen Brish'diri names, neatly typed out. Everything seemed to be in order, but still—

"You'll forgive me, I hope," Hill said, "but I'm somewhat unfamiliar with the expressions of your people. You said . . . half-men? Do you mean children?"

Remjhard nodded, a quick inclination of his bullet-like head. "Yes. Male children, the sons of mission personnel. All are aged either eight or nine Earth seasons."

Hill silently sighed with relief. "I'm afraid it's out of the question, then," he said. "Mr. De Angelis said you were interested in the City League, but that league is for boys aged eighteen and up. Occasionally we'll admit a younger boy with exceptional talent and experience, but never anyone this young." He paused briefly. "We do have several leagues for younger boys, but they've already begun play. It's much too late to add another team at this point."

"Pardon, Director Hill, but I think you misunderstand," Remjhard said. "A Brish'dir male is fully mature at fourteen Earth years. In our culture, such a person is regarded as a full adult. A nine-year-old Brish'dir is roughly equivalent to an eighteen-year-old Terran male in terms of physical and intellectual development. That is why our half-men wish to register for this league and not one of the others, you see."

"He's correct, Rog," De Angelis said. "I've read a little about the Brish'diri, and I'm sure of it. In terms of maturity, these youngsters are eligible for the City League."

Hill threw De Angelis a withering glance. If there was one thing he didn't need at the moment, it was a Brish'diri football team in one of his leagues, and Remjhard was arguing convincingly enough without Jack's help.

"Well, all right," Hill said. "Your team may well be of age, but there are still problems. The Rec Department sports program is for local residents only. We simply don't have room to accommodate everyone who wants to participate. And your home planet is, as I understand, several hundred light-years beyond the Starport city limits." He smiled.

"True," Remjhard said. "But our trade mission has been in Starport for six years. An ideal location due to your city's proximity to Grissom Interstellar Spaceport, from which most of the Brish'diri traders operate while on Earth. All of the current members of the mission have been here for two Earth years, at least. We are Starport residents, Director Hill. I fail to understand how the location of Brishun enters into the matter at hand."

Hill squirmed uncomfortably in his seat, and glared at De Angelis, who was grinning. "Yes, you're probably right again," he said. "But I'm still afraid we won't be able to help you. Our junior leagues are touch football, but the City League, as you might know, is tackle. It can get quite rough at times. State safety regulations require the use of special equipment. To make sure no one is injured seriously. I'm sure you understand. And the Brish'diri . . ."

He groped for words, anxious not to offend. "The— uh—physical construction of the Brish'diri is so different from the Terran that our equipment couldn't possibly fit. Chances of injury would be too great, and the department would be liable. No. I'm sure it couldn't be allowed. Too much risk."

"We would provide special protective equipment," Remjhard said quietly. "We would never risk our own offspring if we did not feel it safe."

Hill started to say something, stopped, and looked to

De Angelis for help. He had run out of good reasons why the Brish'diri couldn't enter the league.

Jack smiled. "One problem remains, however," he said, coming to the director's rescue. "A bureaucratic snag, but a difficult one. Registration for the league closed on Tuesday. We've already had to turn away several teams, and if we make an exception in your case, well . . ." De Angelis shrugged. "Trouble. Complaints. I'm sorry, but we must apply the same rule to all."

Remjhard rose slowly from his seat, and picked up the roster from where it lay on the desk. "Of course," he said gravely. "All must follow the regulations. Perhaps next year we will be on time." He made a formal half-bow to Hill, turned, and walked from the office.

When he was sure the Brish'dir was out of earshot, Hill gave a heartfelt sigh and swiveled to face De Angelis. "That was close," he said. "Christ, a Baldy football team. Half the people in this town lost sons in the Brish'diri War, and they still hate them. I can imagine the complaints."

Hill frowned. "And you! Why couldn't you just get rid of him right away instead of putting me through that?"

De Angelis grinned. "Too much fun to pass up," he said. "I wondered if you'd figure out the right way to discourage him. The Brish'diri have an almost religious respect for laws, rules, and regulations. They wouldn't think of doing anything that would force someone to break a rule. In their culture, that's just as bad as breaking a rule yourself."

Hill nodded. "I would have remembered that myself if I wasn't so paralyzed at the thought of a Brish'diri football team in one of our leagues," he said limply. "And now that that's over with, I want to talk to you about that gravity grid. Do you think there's any way we could rent one instead of buying it outright? The council might go for that. And I was thinking. . . ."

A little over three hours later, Hill was signing some equipment requisitions when the office door slid open to admit a brawny, dark-haired man in a nondescript gray suit.

"Yes?" the director said, a trifle impatiently. "Can I help you?"

The dark-haired man flashed a government ID as he took a seat. "Maybe you can. But you certainly haven't so far, I'll tell you that much. My name's Tomkins. Mac Tomkins. I'm from the Federal E.T. Relations Board."

Hill groaned. "I suppose it's about that Brish'diri mess this morning," he said, shaking his head in resignation.

"Yes," Tomkins cut in at once. "We understand that the Brish'diri wanted to register some of their youngsters for a local football league. You forbade it on a technicality. We want to know why."

"Why?" said Hill incredulously, staring at the government man. "WHY? For god's sake, the Brish'diri War was only over seven years ago. Half of those boys on our football teams had brothers killed by the Bulletbrains. Now you want me to tell them to play football with the subhuman monsters of seven years back? They'd run me out of town."

Tomkins grimaced, and looked around the room. "Can that door be locked?" he asked, pointing to the door he had come in by.

"Of course," Hill replied, puzzled.

"Lock it, then," Tomkins said. Hill adjusted the appropriate control on his desk.

"What I'm going to tell you should not go beyond this room," Tomkins began.

Hill cut him off with a snort. "Oh, come now, Mr. Tomkins. I may be only a small-time sports official, but I'm not stupid. You're hardly about to impart some galaxy-shattering top secret to a man you met a few seconds ago."

Tomkins smiled. "True. The information's not secret, but it is a little ticklish. We would prefer that every Joe in the street doesn't know about it."

"All right, I'll buy that for now. Now, what's this all about? I'm sorry if I've got no patience with subtlety, but the most difficult problem I've handled in the last year was the protest in the championship game in the Class B Soccer League. Diplomacy just isn't my forte."

"I'll be brief," Tomkins said. "We—E.T. Relations, that is—we want you to admit the Brish'diri team into your football league."

"You realize the furor it would cause?" Hill asked.

"We have some idea. In spite of that, we want them admitted."

"Why, may I ask?"

"Because of the furor if they aren't admitted." Tomkins paused to stare at Hill for a second, then apparently reached a decision of some sort and continued. "The Earth–Brishun War was a ghastly, bloody deadlock, although our propaganda men insist on pretending it was a great victory. No sane man on either side wants it resumed. But not everyone is sane."

The agent frowned in distaste. "There are elements among us who regard the Brish'diri—or the Bulletbrains, or Baldies, or whatever you want to call them—as monsters, even now, seven years after the killing has ended."

"And you think a Brish'diri football team would help to overcome the leftover hates?" Hill interrupted.

"Partially. But that's not the important part. You see, there is also an element among the Brish'diri that regards humans as subhuman—vermin to be wiped from the galaxy. They are a very virile, competitive race. Their whole culture stresses combat. The dissident element I mentioned will seize on your refusal to admit a Brish'diri team as a sign of fear, an admission of human inferiority. They'll use it to agitate for a resumption of the war. We don't want to risk giving them a propaganda victory like that. Relations are too strained as it is."

"But the Brish'dir I spoke to . . ." Hill objected. "I explained it all to him. A rule. Surely their respect for law . . ."

"Remjhard-nei is a leader of the Brish'diri peace faction. He personally will defend your position. But he and his son were disappointed by the refusal. They will talk. They already have been talking. And that means that eventually the war faction will get hold of the story and turn it against us."

"I see. But what can I do at this point? I've already told Remjhard that registration closed Tuesday. If I understand correctly, his own morality would never permit him to take advantage of an exception now."

Tomkins nodded. "True. You can't make an exception. Just change the rule. Let in all the teams you refused. Expand the league."

Hill shook his head, wincing. "But our budget . . . it couldn't take it. We'd have more games. We'd need more time, more referees, more equipment."

Tomkins dismissed the problem with a wave of his hand. "The government is already buying the Brish'diri special football uniforms. We'd be happy to cover all your extra costs. You'd get a better recreational program for all concerned."

Hill still looked doubtful. "Well—"

"Moreover," Tomkins said, "we might be able to arrange a government grant or two to bolster other improvements in your program. Now, how about it?"

Hill's eyes sparkled with sudden interest. "A grant? How big a grant? Could you swing a gravity grid?"

"No problem," said Tomkins. A slow grin spread across his face.

Hill returned the grin. "Then, mister, Starport's got itself a Brish'diri football team. But, oh, are they going to scream!" He flicked on the desk intercom. "Get Jack De Angelis in here," he ordered. "I've got a little surprise for him."

The sky above Starport Municipal Stadium was bleak and dreary on a windy Saturday morning a week later, but Hill didn't mind it at all. The stadium force bubble kept out the thin, wet drizzle that had soaked him to the bone on the way to the game, and the weather fitted his mood beautifully.

Normally, Hill was far too busy to attend any of his department's sporting events. Normally *everyone* was too busy to attend the department's sporting events. The Rec Department leagues got fairly good coverage in the local newspaper, but they seldom drew many spectators. The record was something like four hundred people for a championship game a few years ago.

Or rather, that *was* the record, Hill reminded himself. No more. The stadium was packed today, in spite of the hour, the rain, and everything else. Muncipal Stadium was *never* packed except for the traditional Thanksgiving Day football game between Starport High and its archrival Grissom City Prep. But today it was packed.

Hill knew why. It had been drilled into him the hard way after he had made the damn fool decision to let the Brish'diri into the league. The whole city was up in arms. Six local teams had withdrawn from the City League rather than play with the "inhuman monsters." The office switchboard had been flooded with calls daily, the vast majority of them angry denunciations of Hill. A city council member had called for his resignation.

And that, Hill reflected glumly, was probably what it would come to in the end. The local newspaper, which had always been hard-line conservative on foreign affairs, was backing the drive to force Hill out of office. One of its editorials had reminded him gleefully that Starport Municipal Stadium was dedicated to those who had given their lives in the Brish'diri War, and had screamed about "desecration." Meanwhile, on its sports pages, the paper had taken to calling the Brish'diri team "the Baldy Eagles."

Hill squirmed uncomfortably in his seat on the fifty-yard line, and prayed silently that the game would begin. He could feel the angry stares on the back of his neck, and he had the uneasy impression that he was going to be hit with a rock any second now.

Across the field, he could see the camera installation of one of the big 3V networks. All five of them were here, of course; the game had gotten planetwide publicity. The newsfax wires had also sent reporters, although they had seemed a little confused about what kind of a story this was. One had sent a political reporter, the other a sportswriter.

Out on the stadium's artificial grass, the human team was running through a few plays and warming up. Their bright-red uniforms were emblazoned with "Ken's Computer Repair" in white lettering, and they wore matching white helmets. They looked pretty good, Hill decided from watching them practice. Although they were far from championship caliber. Still, against a team that had never played football before, they should mop up.

De Angelis, wearing a pained expression and a ref's striped shirt, was out on the field talking to his officials. Hill was taking no chances with bad calls in this game. He made sure the department's best men were on hand to officiate.

Tomkins was also there, sitting in the stands a few sections away from Hill. But the Brish'diri were not. Remjhard wanted to attend, but E.T. Relations, on Hill's advice, had told him to stay at the mission. Instead, the game was being piped to him over closed-circuit 3V.

Hill suddenly straightened in his seat. The Brish'diri team, which called itself the Kosg-Anjehn after a flying carnivore native to Brishun, had arrived, and the players were walking slowly out onto the field.

There was a brief instant of silence, and then someone in the crowd started booing. Others picked it up. Then others. The stadium was filled with the boos. Although, Hill noted with relief, not everyone was joining in. Maybe there were some people who saw things his way. The Brish'diri ignored the catcalls. Or seemed to, at any rate. Hill had never seen an angry Brish'dir, and was unsure how one would go about showing his anger.

The Kosg-Anjehn wore tight-fitting black uniforms, with odd-looking elongated silver helmets to cover their bullet-shaped heads. They looked like no football team Hill had ever seen. Only a handful of them stood over five feet, but they were all as squat and broad as a tackle for the Packers. Their arms and legs were thick and stumpy, but rippled with muscles that bulged in the wrong places. The helmeted heads, however, gave an impression of frailty, like eggshells ready to shatter at the slightest impact.

Two of the Brish'diri detached themselves from the group and walked over to De Angelis. Evidently they felt they didn't need a warm-up, and wanted to start immediately. De Angelis talked to them for an instant, then turned and beckoned to the captain of the human team.

"How do you think it'll go?"

Hill turned. It was Tomkins. The E.T. agent had stopped him and struggled through the crowd to his side.

"Hard to say," the director replied. "The Brish'diri have never really played football before, so the odds are they'll lose. Being from a heavy-gravity planet, they'll be stronger than the humans, so that might give them an edge. But they're also a lot slower from what I hear."

"I'll have to root them home," Tomkins said with a smile. "Bolster the cause of interstellar relations and all that."

Hill scowled. "*You* root them home if you like. I'm pulling for the humans. Thanks to you, I'm in enough trouble already. If they catch me rooting for the Brish'-diri, they'll tear me to shreds."

He turned his attention back to the field. The Computermen had won the toss, and elected to receive. One of the taller Brish'diri was going back to kick off.

"Tuhgayh-dei," Tomkins provided helpfully. "The son of the mission's chief linguist." Hill nodded.

Tuhgayh-dei ran forward with a ponderous, lumbering gallop, nearly stopped when he finally reached the football, and slammed his foot into it awkwardly but hard. The ball landed in the upper tier of the stands, and a murmur went through the crowd.

"Pretty good," Tomkins said. "Don't you think?"

"Too good," replied Hill. He did not elaborate.

The humans took the ball on their twenty. The Computermen went into a huddle, broke it with a loud clap, and ran to their positions. A ragged cheer went up from the stands.

The humans went down into the three-point stance. Their Brish'diri opponents did not. The alien linemen just stood there, hands dangling at their sides, crouching a little.

"They don't know much about football," Hill said. "But after that kickoff, I wonder if they have to."

The ball was snapped, and the quarterback for Ken's Computer Repair, a rangy ex–high school star named Sullivan, faded back to pass. The Brish'diri rushed forward in a crude blitz, and crashed into the human line-men.

An instant later, Sullivan was lying facedown in the grass, buried under three Brish'diri. The aliens had blown through the offensive line as if it didn't exist.

That made it second and fifteen. The humans huddled again, came out to another cheer, not quite so loud as the first one. The ball was snapped. Sullivan handed off to a beefy fullback, who crashed straight ahead.

One of the Brish'diri brought him down before he went half a yard. It was a clumsy tackle, around the shoulders. But the force of the contact knocked the fullback several yards in the wrong direction.

When the humans broke from their huddle for the third time, the cheer could scarcely be heard. Again Sullivan tried to pass. Again the Brish'diri blasted through the line en masse. Again Sullivan went down for a loss.

Hill groaned. "This looks worse every minute," he said.

Tomkins didn't agree. "I don't think so. They're doing fine. What difference does it make who wins?"

Hill didn't bother to answer that.

There was no cheering when the humans came out in punt formation. Once more the Brish'diri put on a strong rush, but the punter got the ball away before they reached him.

It was a good, deep kick. The Kosg-Anjehn took over on their own twenty-five-yard line. Marhdaln-nei, Remjhard's son, was the Brish'diri quarterback. On the first play from scrimmage, he handed off to a halfback, a runt built like a tank.

The Brish'diri blockers flattened their human opponents almost effortlessly, and the runt plowed through the gaping hole, ran over two would-be tacklers, and burst into the clear. He was horribly slow, however, and the defenders finally brought him down from behind after a modest thirty-yard gain. But it took three people to stop him.

On the next play, Marhdaln tried to pass. He got excellent protection, but his receivers, trudging along at top speed, had defensemen all over them. And the ball, when thrown, went sizzling over the heads of Brish'diri and humans alike.

Marhdaln returned to the ground again after that, and handed off to the runt halfback once more. This time he tried to sweep around end, but was hauled to the ground after a gain of only five yards by a quartet of human tacklers.

That made it third and five. Marhdaln kept to the ground. He gave the ball to his other halfback, and the brawny Brish'dir smashed up the middle. He was a little faster than the runt. When he got in the clear, only one man managed to catch him from behind. And one wasn't enough. The alien shrugged off the tackle and lumbered on across the goal line.

The extra point try went under the crossbar instead of over it. But it still nearly killed the poor guy in the stands who tried to catch the ball.

Tomkins was grinning. Hill shook his head in disgust. "This isn't the way it's supposed to go," he said. "They'll kill us if the Brish'diri win."

The kickoff went out of the stadium entirely this time. On the first play from the twenty, a Brish'diri lineman roared through the line and hit Sullivan just as he was handing off. Sullivan fumbled.

Another Brish'dir picked up the loose ball and carried it into the end zone while most of the humans were still lying on the ground.

"My God," said Hill, feeling a bit numb. "They're too strong. They're too damn strong. The humans can't cope with their strength. Can't stop them."

"Cheer up," said Tomkins. "It can't get much worse for your side."

But it did. It got a lot worse.

On offense, the Brish'diri were well-nigh unstoppable. Their runners were all short on speed, but made up for it with muscle. On play after play, they smashed straight up the middle behind a wall of blockers, flicking tacklers aside like bothersome insects.

And then Marhdaln began to hit on his passes. Short passes, of course. The Brish'diri lacked the speed to cover much ground. But they could outjump any human, and they snared pass after pass in the air. There was no need to worry about interceptions. The humans simply couldn't hang on to Marhdaln's smoking pitches.

On defense, things were every bit as bad. The Computermen couldn't run against the Brish'diri line. And Sullivan seldom had time to complete a pass, for the alien rushers were unstoppable. The few passes he did hit on went for touchdowns; no Brish'dir could catch a human from behind. But those were few and far between.

When Hill fled the stadium in despair at the half, the score was Kosg-Anjehn 37, Ken's Computer Repair 7.

The final score was 57–14. The Brish'diri had emptied their bench in the second half.

Hill didn't have the courage to attend the next Brish'diri game later in the week. But nearly everyone else in the city showed up to see if the Kosg-Anjehn could do it again.

They did. In fact, they did even better. They beat Anderson's Drugs by a lopsided 61–9 score.

After the Brish'diri won their third contest, 43–17, the huge crowds began tapering off. The Starport Municipal Stadium was only three-quarters full when the Kosg-Anjehn rolled over the Stardusters, 38–0, and a mere handful showed up on a rainy Thursday afternoon to see the aliens punish the United Veterans Association, 51–6. And no one came after that.

For Hill, the Brish'diri win over the U.V.A.-sponsored team was the final straw. The local paper made a heyday out of that, going on and on about the "ironic injustice" of having the U.V.A. slaughtered by the Brish'diri in a stadium dedicated to the dead veterans of the Brish'diri War. And Hill, of course, was the main villain in the piece.

The phone calls had finally let up by that point. But the mail had been flowing into his office steadily, and most of it was not very comforting. The harassed rec director got a few letters of commendation and support, but the bulk of the flood speculated crudely about his ancestry or threatened his life and property.

Two more city councilmen had come out publicly in favor of Hill's dismissal after the Brish'diri defeated the U.V.A. Several others on the council were wavering, while Hill's supporters, who backed him strongly in private, were afraid to say anything for the record. The municipal elections were simply too close, and none of them was willing to risk his political skin.

And of course the assistant director of recreation, next in line for Hill's job, had wasted no time in saying *he* would certainly never have done such an unpatriotic thing.

With disaster piling upon disaster, it was only natural that Hill reacted with something less than enthusiasm when he walked into his office a few days after the fifth Kosg-Anjehn victory and found Tomkins sitting at his desk waiting for him.

"And what in the hell do you want now?" Hill roared at the E.T. Relations man.

Tomkins looked slightly abashed, and got up from the director's chair. He had been watching the latest free-fall football results on the desk console while waiting for Hill to arrive.

"I've got to talk to you," Tomkins said. "We've got a problem."

"We've got lots of problems," Hill replied. He strode angrily to his desk, sat down, flicked off the console, and pulled a sheaf of papers from a drawer.

"This is the latest of them," he continued, waving the papers at Tomkins. "One of the kids broke his leg in the Starduster game. It happens all the time. Football's a rough game. You can't do anything to prevent it. In a normal case, the department would send a letter of apology to the parents, our insurance would pay for it, and everything would be forgotten.

"But not in this case. Oh, no. This injury was inflicted

while the kid was playing against the Brish'diri. So his parents are charging negligence on our part and suing the city. So our insurance company refuses to pay up. It claims the policy doesn't cover damage by inhuman, superstrong, alien monsters. Bah! How's that for a problem, Mr. Tomkins? Plenty more where that came from."

Tomkins frowned. "Very unfortunate. But my problem is a lot more serious than that." Hill started to interrupt, but the E.T. Relations man waved him down. "No, please, hear me out. This is very important."

He looked around for a seat, grabbed the nearest chair, and pulled it up to the desk. "Our plans have backfired badly," he began. "There has been a serious miscalculation—our fault entirely, I'm afraid. E.T. Relations failed to consider *all* the ramifications of this Brish'diri football team."

Hill fixed him with an iron stare. "What's wrong now?"

"Well," Tomkins said awkwardly, "we knew that refusal to admit the Kosg-Anjehn into your league would be a sign of human weakness and fear to the Brish'diri war faction. But once you admitted them, we thought the problem was solved.

"It wasn't. We went wrong when we assumed that winning or losing would make no difference to the Brish'diri. To us, it was just a game. Didn't matter who won. After all, Brish'diri and Terrans would be getting to know each other, competing harmlessly on even terms. Nothing but good could come from it, we felt."

"So?" Hill interrupted. "Get to the point."

Tomkins shook his head sadly. "The point is, we didn't know the Brish'diri would win so *big*. And so *regularly.*" He paused. "We—uh—we got a transmission late last night from one of our men on Brishun. It seems the Brish'diri war faction is using the one-sided football scores as propaganda to prove the racial inferiority of humans. They seem to be getting a lot of mileage out of it."

Hill winced. "So it was all for nothing. So I've subjected myself to all this abuse and endangered my career for absolutely nothing. Great! That was all I needed, I tell you."

"We still might be able to salvage something," Tomkins said. "That's why I came to see you. If you can arrange it for the Brish'diri to *lose*, it would knock holes in that superiority yarn and make the war faction look like fools. It would discredit them for quite a while."

"And just how am I supposed to *arrange* for them to lose, as you so nicely put it? What do you think I'm running here, anyway, professional wrestling?"

Tomkins just shrugged lamely. "I was hoping you'd have some ideas," he said.

Hill leaned forward, and flicked on his intercom. "Is Jack out there?" he asked. "Good. Send him in."

The lanky sports official appeared less than a minute later. "You're on top of this city football mess," Hill said. "What's the chances the Kosg-Anjehn will lose?"

De Angelis looked puzzled. "Not all that good, offhand," he replied. "They've got a damn fine team."

He reached into his back pocket and pulled out a notebook. "Let me check their schedule," he continued, thumbing through the pages. He stopped when he found the place.

"Well, the league's got a round-robin schedule, as you

know. Every team plays every other team once, best record is champion. Now the Brish'diri are currently 5–0, and they've beaten a few of the better teams. We've got ten teams left in the league, so they've got four games left to play. Only, two of those are with the weakest teams in the league, and the third opponent is only mediocre."

"And the fourth?" Hill said hopefully.

"That's your only chance. An outfit sponsored by a local tavern, the Blastoff Inn. Good team. Fast, strong. Plenty of talent. They're also 5–0, and should give the Brish'diri some trouble." De Angelis frowned. "But, to be frank, I've seen both teams, and I'd still pick the Brish'diri. That ground game of theirs is just too much." He snapped the notebook shut and pocketed it again.

"Would a close game be enough?" Hill said, turning to Tomkins again.

The E.T. Relations man shook his head. "No. They have to be beaten. If they lose, the whole season's meaningless. Proves nothing but that the two races can compete on roughly equal terms. But if they win, it looks like they're invincible, and our stature in Brish'diri eyes takes a nosedive."

"Then they'll have to lose, I guess," Hill said. His gaze shifted back to De Angelis. "Jack, you and me are going to have to do some hard thinking about how the Kosg-Anjehn can be beaten. And then we're going to call up the manager of the Blastoff Inn team and give him a few tips. You have any ideas?"

De Angelis scratched his head thoughtfully. "Well . . ." he began. "Maybe we . . ."

During the two weeks that followed, De Angelis met
with the Blastoff Inn coach regularly to discuss plans
and strategy, and supervised a few practice sessions. Hill,
meanwhile, was fighting desperately to keep his job, and
jotting down ideas on how to beat the Brish'diri during
every spare moment.

Untouched by the furor, the Kosg-Anjehn won its
sixth game handily, 40–7, and then rolled to devastating
victories over the circuit's two cellar-dwellers. The mar-
gins were 73–0 and 62–7. That gave them an unblem-
ished 8–0 ledger with one game left to play.

But the Blastoff Inn team was also winning regularly,
although never as decisively. It too would enter the last
game of the season undefeated.

The local paper heralded the showdown with a sports
page streamer on the day before the game. The lead
opened, "The stakes will be high for the entire human
race tomorrow at Municipal Stadium, when Blastoff Inn
meets the Brish'diri Baldy Eagles for the championship
of the Department of Recreation City Football League."

The reporter who wrote the story never dreamed how
close to the truth he actually was.

The crowds returned to the stadium for the championship game, although they fell far short of a packed
house. The local paper was there too. But the 3V networks and the newsfax wires were long gone. The
novelty of the story had worn off quickly.

Hill arrived late, just before game time, and joined
Tomkins on the fifty-yard line. The E.T. agent seemed
to have cheered up somewhat. "Our guys looked pretty

good during the warm-up," he told the director. "I think we've got a chance."

His enthusiasm was not catching, however. "Blastoff Inn might have a chance, but I sure don't," Hill said glumly. "The city council is meeting tonight to consider a motion calling for my dismissal. I have a strong suspicion that it's going to pass, no matter who wins this afternoon."

"Hmmmm," said Tomkins, for want of anything better to say. "Just ignore the old fools. Look, the game's starting."

Hill muttered something under his breath and turned his attention back to the field. The Brish'diri had lost the toss once more, and the kickoff had once again soared out of the stadium. It was first and ten for Blastoff Inn on its own twenty.

And at that point the script suddenly changed.

The humans lined up for their first play of the game, but with a difference. Instead of playing immediately in back of the center, the Blastoff quarterback was several yards deep, in a shotgun formation.

The idea, Hill recalled, was to take maximum advantage of human speed, and mount a strong passing offense. Running against the Brish'diri was all but impossible, he and De Angelis had concluded after careful consideration. That meant an aerial attack, and the only way to provide that was to give the Blastoff quarterback time to pass. Ergo, the shotgun formation.

The hike from center was dead on target, and the Blastoff receivers shot off downfield, easily outpacing the ponderous Brish'diri defensemen. As usual, the Kosg-Anjehn crashed through the line en masse, but they had covered only half the distance to the quarterback before he got off the pass.

It was a long bomb, a psychological gambit to shake up the Brish'diri by scoring on the first play of the game. Unfortunately, the pass was slightly overthrown.

Hill swore.

It was now second and ten. Again the humans lined up in a shotgun offense, and again the Blastoff quarterback got off the pass in time. It was a short, quick pitch to the sideline, complete for a nine-yard gain. The crowd cheered lustily.

Hill wasn't sure what the Brish'diri would expect on third and one. But whatever it was, they didn't get it. With the aliens still slightly off balance, Blastoff went for the bomb again.

This time it was complete. All alone in the open, the fleet human receiver snagged the pass neatly and went all the way in for the score. The Brish'diri never laid a hand on him.

The crowd sat in stunned silence for a moment when the pass was caught. Then, when it became clear that there was no way to prevent the score, the cheering began, and peaked slowly to an earsplitting roar. The stadium rose to its feet as one, screaming wildly.

For the first time all season, the Kosg-Anjehn trailed. A picture-perfect placekick made the score 7–0 in favor of Blastoff Inn.

Tomkins was on his feet, cheering loudly. Hill, who had remained seated, regarded him dourly. "Sit down," he said. "The game's not over yet."

The Brish'diri soon underlined that point. No sooner did they take over the ball than they came pounding back upfield, smashing into the line again and again. The humans alternated between a dozen different defensive formations. None of them seemed to do any good. The Brish'diri steamroller ground ahead inexorably.

The touchdown was an anticlimax. Luckily, however, the extra point try failed. Tuhgayh-dei lost a lot of footballs, but he had still not developed a knack for putting his kicks between the crossbars.

The Blastoff offense took the field again. They looked determined. The first play from scrimmage was a short pass over the middle, complete for fifteen yards. Next came a tricky double pass. Complete for twelve yards.

On the following play, the Blastoff fullback tried to go up the middle. He got creamed for a five-yard loss.

"If they stop our passing, we're dead," Hill said to Tomkins, without taking his eyes off the field.

Luckily, the Blastoff quarterback quickly gave up on the idea of establishing a running game. A prompt return to the air gave the humans another first down. Three plays later, they scored. Again the crowd roared.

Trailing now, 14–6, the Brish'diri once more began to pound their way upfield. But the humans, elated by their lead, were a little tougher now. Reading the Brish'diri offense with confident precision, the defensemen began gang-tackling the alien runners.

The Kosg-Anjehn drive slowed down, then stalled. They were forced to surrender the ball near the fifty-yard line.

Tomkins started pounding Hill on the back. "You did it," he said. "We stopped them on offense too. We're going to win."

"Take it easy," Hill replied. "That was a fluke. Several

of our men just happened to be in the right place at the right time. It's happened before. No one ever said the Brish'diri scored every time they got the ball. Only most of the time."

Back on the field, the Blastoff passing attack was still humming smoothly. A few accurate throws put the humans on the Kosg-Anjehn's thirty.

And then the aliens changed formations. They took several men off the rush, and put them on pass defense. They started double-teaming the Blastoff receivers. Except it wasn't normal double-teaming. The second defender was playing far back of the line of scrimmage. By the time the human had outrun the first Brish'dir, the second would be right on top of him.

"I was afraid of something like this," Hill said. "We're not the only ones who can react to circumstances."

The Blastoff quarterback ignored the shift in the alien defense, and stuck to his aerial game plan. But his first pass from the thirty, dead on target, was batted away by a Brish'diri defender who happened to be right on top of the play.

The same thing happened on second down. That made it third and ten. The humans called time out. There was a hurried conference on the sidelines.

When action resumed, the Blastoff offense abandoned the shotgun formation. Without the awesome Brish'diri blitz to worry about, the quarterback was relatively safe in his usual position.

There was a quick snap, and the quarterback got rid of the ball equally quickly, an instant before a charging Brish'dir bore him to the ground. The halfback who got the handoff streaked to the left in an end run.

The other Brish'diri defenders lumbered toward him en masse to seal shut the sideline. But just as he reached the sideline, still behind the line of scrimmage, the Blastoff halfback handed off to a teammate streaking right.

A wide grin spread across Hill's face. A reverse!

The Brish'diri were painfully slow to change directions. The human swept around right end with ridiculous ease and shot upfield, surrounded by blockers. The remaining Brish'diri closed in. One or two were taken out by team blocks. The rest found it impossible to lay their hands on the swift, darting runner. Dodging this way and that, he wove a path neatly between them and loped into the end zone.

Once more the stadium rose to its feet. This time Hill stood up too.

Tomkins was beaming again. "Ha!" he said. "I thought you were the one who said we couldn't run against them."

"Normally we can't," the director replied. "There's no way to run over or through them, so runs up the middle are out. End runs are better, but if they're in their normal formation, that too is a dreary prospect. There is no way a human runner can get past a wall of charging Brish'diri.

"However, when they spread out like they just did, they give us an open field to work with. We can't go over or through them, no, but we sure as hell can go *between* them when they're scattered all over the field. And Blastoff Inn has several excellent open-field runners."

The crowd interrupted him with another roar to herald a successful extra-point conversion. It was now 21–6.

The game was far from over, however. The human defense was not nearly as successful on the next series of downs. Instead of relying exclusively on the running game, Marhdaln-nei kept his opponents guessing, with some of his patented short, hard pop passes.

To put on a more effective rush, the Blastoff defense spread out at wide intervals. The offensive line thus opened up, and several humans managed to fake out slower Brish'diri blockers and get past them to the quarterback. Marhdaln was even thrown for a loss once.

But the Blastoff success was short-lived. Marhdaln adjusted quickly. The widely spread human defense, highly effective against the pass, was a total failure against the run. The humans were too far apart to gang-tackle. And there was no way short of mass assault to stop a Brish'dir in full stride.

After that, there was no stopping the Kosg-Anjehn, as Marhdaln alternated between the pass and the run according to the human defensive formation. The aliens marched upfield quickly for their second touchdown.

This time, even the extra point was on target.

The Brish'diri score had taken some of the steam out of the crowd, but the Blastoff Inn offense showed no signs of being disheartened when they took the field again. With the aliens back in their original blitz defense, the human quarterback fell back on the shotgun once more.

His first pass was overthrown, but the next three in a

row were dead on target and moved Blastoff to the Kosg-Anjehn forty. A running play, inserted to break the monotony, ended in a six-yard loss. Then came another incomplete pass. The toss was perfect, but the receiver dropped the ball.

That made it third and ten, and a tremor of apprehension went through the crowd. Nearly everyone in the stadium realized that the humans had to keep scoring to stay in the game.

The snap from center was quick and clean. The Blastoff quarterback snagged the ball, took a few unhurried steps backward to keep at a safe distance from the oncoming Brish'diri rushers, and tried to pick out a receiver. He scanned the field carefully. Then he reared back and unleashed a bomb.

It looked like another touchdown. The human had his alien defender beaten by a good five yards and was still gaining ground. The pass was a beauty.

But then, as the ball began to spiral downward, the Brish'diri defender stopped suddenly in midstride. Giving up his hopeless chase, he craned his head around to look for the ball, spotted it, braced himself—

—and jumped.

Brish'diri leg muscles, evolved for the heavy gravity of Brishun, were far more powerful than their human counterparts. Despite their heavier bodies, the Brish'diri could easily outjump any human. But so far they had only taken advantage of that fact to snare Marhdaln's pop passes.

But now, as Hill blinked in disbelief, the Kosg-Anjehn defenseman leaped at least five feet into the air to meet the descending ball in midair and knock it aside with a vicious backhand slap.

The stadium moaned.

Forced into a punting situation, Blastoff Inn suddenly seemed to go limp. The punter fumbled the snap from center, and kicked the ball away when he tried to pick it up. The Brish'dir who picked it up got twenty yards before he was brought down.

The human defense this time put up only token resistance as Marhdaln led his team downfield on a series of short passes and devastating runs.

It took the Brish'diri exactly six plays to narrow the gap to 21–19. Luckily, Tuhgayh-nei missed another extra point.

There was a loud cheer when the Blastoff offense took the field again. But right from the first play after the kickoff, it was obvious that something had gone out of them.

The human quarterback, who had been giving a brilliant performance, suddenly became erratic. To add to his problems, the Brish'diri were suddenly jumping all over the field.

The alien kangaroo pass defense had several severe limitations. It demanded precise timing and excellent reflexes on the part of the jumpers, neither of which was a Brish'diri forte. But it was a disconcerting tactic that the Blastoff quarterback had never come up against before. He didn't know quite how to cope with it.

The humans drove to their own forty, bogged down, and were forced to punt. The Kosg-Anjehn promptly marched the ball back the other way and scored. For the first time in the game, they led.

The next Blastoff drive was a bit more successful, and reached the Brish'diri twenty before it ground to a halt. The humans salvaged the situation with a field goal.

The Kosg-Anjehn rolled up another score, driving over the goal line just seconds before the half ended.

The score stood at 31–24 in favor of the Brish'diri.

And there was no secret about the way the tide was turning.

It had grown very quiet in the stands.

Tomkins, wearing a worried expression, turned to Hill with a sigh. "Well, maybe we'll make a comeback in the second half. We're only down seven. That's not so bad."

"Maybe," Hill said doubtfully. "But I don't think so. They've got all the momentum. I hate to say so, but I think we're going to get run out of the stadium in the second half."

Tomkins frowned. "I certainly hope not. I'd hate to see what the Brish'diri war faction would do with a really lopsided score. Why, they'd—" He stopped, suddenly aware that Hill wasn't paying the slightest bit of attention. The director's eyes had wandered back to the field.

"Look," Hill said, pointing. "By the gate. Do you see what I see?"

"It looks like a car from the trade mission," the E.T. agent said, squinting to make it out.

"And who's that getting out?"

Tomkins hesitated. "Remjhard-nei," he said at last.

The Brish'dir climbed smoothly from the low-slung black vehicle, walked a short distance across the stadium grass, and vanished through the door leading to one of the dressing rooms.

"What's he doing here?" Hill asked. "Wasn't he supposed to stay away from the games?"

Tomkins scratched his head uneasily. "Well, that's what we advised. Especially at first, when hostility was at its highest. But he's not a *prisoner*, you know. There's no way we could force him to stay away from the games if he wants to attend."

Hill was frowning. "Why should he take your advice all season and suddenly disregard it now?"

Tomkins shrugged. "Maybe he wanted to see his son win a championship."

"Maybe. But I don't think so. There's something funny going on here."

By the time the second half was ready to begin, Hill was feeling even more apprehensive. The Kosg-Anjehn had taken the field a few minutes earlier, but Remjhard had not reappeared. He was still down in the alien locker room.

Moreover, there was something subtly different about the Brish'diri as they lined up to receive the kickoff. Nothing drastic. Nothing obvious. But somehow the atmosphere was changed. The aliens appeared more carefree, more relaxed. Almost as if they had stopped taking their opponents seriously.

Hill could sense the difference. He'd seen other teams with the same sort of attitude before, in dozens of other contests. It was the attitude of a team that already knows how the game is going to come out. The attitude of a team that knows it is sure to win—or doomed to lose.

The kickoff was poor and wobbly. A squat Brish'dir took it near the thirty and headed upfield. Two Blastoff tacklers met him at the thirty-five.

He fumbled.

The crowd roared. For a second the ball rolled loose on the stadium grass. A dozen hands reached for it, knocking it this way and that. Finally, a brawny Blastoff lineman landed squarely on top of it and trapped it beneath him.

And suddenly the game turned around again.

"I don't believe it," Hill said. "That was it. The break we needed. After that touchdown pass was knocked aside, our team just lost heart. But now, after this, look at them. We're back in this game."

The Blastoff offense raced onto the field, broke their huddle with an enthusiastic shout, and lined up. It was first and ten from the Brish'diri twenty-eight.

The first pass was deflected off a bounding Brish'dir. The second, however, went for a touchdown.

The score was tied.

The Kosg-Anjehn held onto the kickoff this time. They put the ball in play near the twenty-five.

Marhdaln opened the series of downs with a pass. No one, human or Brish'dir, was within ten yards of where it came down. The next play was a run. But the Kosg-Anjehn halfback hesitated oddly after he took the handoff. Given time to react, four humans smashed into him at the line of scrimmage. Marhdaln went back to the air. The pass was incomplete again.

The Brish'diri were forced to punt.

Up in the stands, Tomkins was laughing wildly. He began slapping Hill on the back again. "Look at that!

Not even a first down. We held them. And you said they were going to run us out of the stadium."

A strange half-smile danced across the director's face. "Ummm," he said. "So I did." The smile faded.

It was a good, solid punt, but Blastoff's deep man fielded it superbly and ran it back to the fifty. From there, it took only seven plays for the human quarterback, suddenly looking cool and confident again, to put the ball in the end zone.

Bouncing Brish'diri had evidently ceased to disturb him. He simply threw the ball through spots where they did not happen to be bouncing.

This time the humans missed the extra point. But no one cared. The score was 37–31. Blastoff Inn was ahead again.

And they were ahead to stay. No sooner had the Kosg-Anjehn taken over again than Marhdaln threw an interception. It was the first interception he had thrown all season.

Naturally, it was run back for a touchdown.

After that, the Brish'diri seemed to revive a little. They drove three-quarters of the way down the field, but then they bogged down as soon as they got within the shadow of the goalposts. On fourth and one from the twelve-yard line, the top Brish'diri runner slipped and fell behind the line of scrimmage.

Blastoff took over. And scored.

From then on, it was more of the same.

The final score was 56–31. The wrong team had been run out of the stadium.

Tomkins, of course, was in ecstasy. "We did it. I knew

we could do it. This is perfect, just perfect. We humiliated them. The war faction will be totally discredited now. They'll never be able to stand up under the ridicule." He grinned and slapped Hill soundly on the back once again.

Hill winced under the blow, and eyed the E.T. man dourly. "There's something funny going on here. If the Brish'diri had played all season the way they played in the second half, they never would have gotten this far. Something happened in that locker room during the halftime."

Nothing could dent Tomkins's grin, however. "No, no," he said. "It was the fumble. That was what did it. It demoralized them, and they fell apart. They just clutched, that's all. It happens all the time."

"Not to teams this good, it doesn't," Hill replied. But Tomkins wasn't around to hear. The E.T. agent had turned abruptly and was weaving his way through the crowd, shouting something about being right back.

Hill frowned and turned back to the field. The stadium was emptying quickly. The rec director stood there for a second, still looking puzzled. Then suddenly he vaulted the low fence around the field, and set off across the grass.

He walked briskly across the stadium and down into the visitors' locker room. The Brish'diri were changing clothes in sullen silence, and filing out of the room slowly to the airbus that would carry them back to the trade mission.

Remjhard-nei was sitting in a corner of the room.

The Brish'dir greeted him with a slight nod. "Director Hill. Did you enjoy the game? It was a pity our half-men failed in their final test. But they still performed creditably, do you not think?"

Hill ignored the question. "Don't give me the bit about failing, Remjhard. I'm not as stupid as I look. Maybe no one else in the stadium realized what was going on out there this afternoon, but I did. You didn't lose that game. You threw it. Deliberately. And I want to know why!"

Remjhard stared at Hill for a long minute. Then, very slowly, he rose from the bench on which he was seated. His face was blank and expressionless, but his eyes glittered in the dim light.

Hill suddenly realized that they were alone in the locker room. Then he remembered the awesome Brish'diri strength, and took a hasty step backward, away from the alien.

"You realize," Remjhard said gravely, "that it is a grave insult to accuse a Brish'dir of dishonorable conduct?"

The emissary took another careful look around the locker room to make sure the two of them were alone. Then he took another step toward Hill.

And broke into a wide smile when the director, edging backward, almost tripped over a locker.

"But, of course, there is no question of dishonor here," the alien continued. "Honor is too big for a half-man's play. And, to be sure, in the rules that you furnished us, there was no provision requiring participants to . . ." He paused. ". . . to play at their best, shall we say?"

Hill, untangling himself from the locker, sputtered. "But there are unwritten rules, traditions. This sort of thing simply is not sporting."

Remjhard was still smiling. "To a Brish'dir, there is nothing as meaningless as an unwritten rule. It is a contradiction in terms, as you say."

"But *why?*" said Hill. "That's what I can't understand. Everyone keeps telling me that your culture is virile, competitive, proud. Why should you throw the game? Why should you make yourself look bad? WHY?"

Remjhard made an odd, gurgling noise. Had he been a human, Hill would have thought he was choking. Instead, he assumed he was laughing.

"Humans amuse me," the Brish'dir said at last. "You attach a few catch phrases to a culture, and you think you understand it. And if something disagrees with your picture, you are shocked.

"I am sorry, Director Hill. Cultures are not that simple. They are very complex mechanisms. A word like *pride* does not describe everything about the Brish'diri.

"Oh, we are proud. Yes. And competitive. Yes. But we are also intelligent. And our values are flexible enough to adjust to the situation at hand."

Remjhard paused again, and looked Hill over carefully. Then he decided to continue. "This football of yours is a fine game, Director Hill. I told you that once before. I mean it. It is very enjoyable, a good exercise of mind and body.

"But it is only a game. Competing in games is important, of course. But there are larger competitions. More important ones. And I am intelligent enough to know which one gets our first priority.

"I received word from Brishun this afternoon about the use to which the Kosg-Anjehn victories were being put. Your friend from Extra Terrestial Relations must have told you that I rank among the leaders of the Brish'diri Peace Party. I would not be here on Earth otherwise. None of our opponents is willing to work with humans, whom they consider animals.

"Naturally I came at once to the stadium and informed our half-men that they must lose. And they, of course, complied. They too realize that some competitions are more important than others.

"For in losing, we have won. Our opponents on Brishun will not survive this humiliation. In the next Great Choosing, many will turn against them. And I, and others at the mission, will profit. And the Brish'diri will profit.

"Yes, Director Hill," Remjhard concluded, still smiling, "we are a competitive race. But competition for control of a world takes precedence over a football game."

Hill was smiling himself by now. Then he began to laugh. "Of course," he said. "And when I think of the ways we pounded our heads out to think of strategies to beat you. When all we had to do was tell you what was going on." He laughed again.

Remjhard was about to add something when suddenly the locker-room door swung open and Tomkins stalked in. The E.T. agent was still beaming.

"Thought I'd find you here, Hill," he began. "Still trying to investigate those conspiracy theories of yours, eh?" He chuckled and winked at Remjhard.

"Not really," Hill replied. "It was a harebrained theory. Obviously it was the fumble that did it."

"Of course," Tomkins said. "Glad to hear it. Anyway, I've got good news for you."

"Oh? What's that? That the world is saved? Fine. But I'm still out of a job come tonight."

"Not at all," Tomkins replied. "That's what my call was about. We've got a job for you. We want you to join E.T. Relations."

Hill looked dubious. "Come now," he said. "Me? An E.T. agent? I don't know the first thing about it. I'm a small-time local bureaucrat and sports official. How am I supposed to fit into E.T. Relations?"

"As a sports director," Tomkins replied. "Ever since this Brish'diri thing broke, we've been getting dozens of requests from other alien trade missions and diplomatic stations on Earth. They all want a crack at it too. So, to promote goodwill and all that, we're going to set up a program. And we want you to run it. At double your present salary, of course."

Hill thought about the difficulties of running a sports program for two dozen wildly different types of extraterrestials.

Then he thought about the money he'd get for doing it.

Then he thought about the Starport City Council.

"Sounds like a fine idea," he said. "But tell me. That gravity grid you were going to give to Starport—is that transferable too?"

"Of course," Tomkins said.

"Then I accept." He glanced over at Remjhard. "Although I may live to regret it when I see what the Brish'diri can do on a basketball court."

baseball

Babe Ruth, Roger Maris, Ty Cobb, Sandy Koufax, Willie Mays, Hank Aaron—these names are familiar to millions of Americans, practitioners of the art of baseball. For several generations baseball was *the* American game. Most Americans have forgotten that the genesis of the sport goes back to the British game of cricket. However, it was an American—Abner Doubleday—who first laid out a ball field, in Cooperstown, New York, in 1839, in something resembling contemporary diamonds. Cooperstown later became the site of baseball's Hall of Fame.

Baseball grew slowly. The first real game did not take place until 1846, when the New York Nine played the New York Knickerbockers. Baseball was organized professionally in 1871 with the formation of the National Association, later called the National League. In 1900, a rival league, the American League, was founded and raided the National League for players, much in the same way as the American and World Football Leagues would do more than a half-century later.

Baseball is a very personal sport. In some ways, it is not a team game at all. The batter, the pitcher, and the fielders are isolated during the game, and their actions can be closely followed. For this reason, fans quickly develop personal favorites, and the exploits of individual players are avidly followed. This "star" system helped make baseball popular.

But this popularity did not save the game from some rather embarrassing moments, most notably the Black Sox scandal surrounding the 1919 World Series, when a number of Chicago White Sox players accepted payoffs in order to fix games. Nevertheless, both the fans and the game quickly recovered from this shock, and baseball surged back stronger than ever. Superstars like Babe Ruth—and innovations like the "live ball," which made home runs more likely—made the sport the national game of America. One other important technological development took place with the introduction of night baseball, which made the game accessible to millions of working men and women.

In the post–World War II era, other changes occurred in the game. One of the most important of these was the entry of black persons as players. Jackie Robinson and those who followed him brought new talent to baseball and made major contributions to race relations in the United States. Later, Latin ball players would play a similar role. Another physical change involved the shifting of teams from one city to another, including the move of the Brooklyn Dodgers to Los Angeles and of the New York Giants to San Francisco.

Although overshadowed by football among younger fans, baseball has grown in popularity around the world. It is played widely in Latin America as well as in Japan, whose professional leagues have attracted American talent. It is also clear that the slow death predicted for baseball by some a few years ago was premature. Baseball and its stars will continue to capture the attention and the imagination of millions of people. Who knows, someday the game may find its way to the stars. . . .

Dodger Fan

will stanton

The sports fan is a very special creature. He will frequently travel hundreds of miles through rain, snow, and sleet to watch "his" team lose the big one. During the sports seasons, the fan's work suffers, his marriage may go on the rocks, and he becomes a stranger to his children. In cities like Green Bay, Wisconsin, wills and divorces are contested over who gets season tickets!

Psychologists tend to disagree over the exact causes of this devotion, but the majority say that man has a basic desire to *belong*—to identify with a particular group. In an age of increasing dehumanization and loss of identity, we can expect the fanatic fan to continue to share his team's losses and victories.

Among the most famous sports fans in history were those of the old Brooklyn Dodgers, who visited Ebbetts Field and yelled, "Kill the umpire." These men and women rejoiced at the great Dodger teams of the 1950s and then felt betrayed when the team was moved to Los Angeles. Some of them—including one of your editors, who once saw fifty-seven Dodger home games in one season—have never forgiven owner Walter O'Malley for taking the club out of Brooklyn.

The Dodgers were one of those teams which featured great players who will live in the hearts of their fans forever. Names like Carl Furillo, Roy Campanella, Duke Snider, Pee Wee Reese, Jackie Robinson, and Gil Hodges have become part of the history and folklore of baseball as we know it today. These are the men whose impact on Brooklyn was vividly portrayed in Roger Kahn's *The Boys of Summer*.

Journey back with us, then, to an earlier era and meet one of the fans who helped produce the legend of the Brooklyn Dodgers.

Dodger Fan

"Some vacation." Jerome snapped off the TV. "All year I look forward to a little rest and relaxation. And what happens? The first game we lose on an error and a wild pitch—twelve innings. Game two is rained out. Today we get our hits—grand total."

Cleo, his wife, unwrapped a fresh stick of gum. "Five hits," she said. "Campy two, Duke one—"

"Who cares?" He walked to the window and looked out disgustedly. "You call that baseball?" He picked up his hat and headed for the door. "Some vacation."

"Erskine pitches tomorrow," Cleo said.

"Tomorrow the President could pitch," Jerome said, "I wouldn't be watching." He left the apartment and headed down the street. After a couple of blocks he hesitated and then stepped back and looked up at the gold sign. He couldn't remember seeing it before.

WANT TO VISIT MARS? STEP INSIDE

Jerome stepped inside. He hadn't been going anyplace in particular. The man behind the counter was very friendly.

"Glad to have you aboard," he said. "You're the first to come in all day, and I was beginning to wonder. You see, I took a special course in Earth Psychology, so this is of great interest to me. What prompted you to visit Mars?"

"I just wanted to get out of town," Jerome said, "Detroit, Baltimore, Mars—it don't make any special difference."

"I graduated with honors, you know, from the Academy of Earthly Advertising and Customer Response. I was groomed for this job. So naturally your reaction—"

"If you got a trip to Philly, I'll take that," Jerome said. "Anything so I don't have to hear about that crummy outfit they call a ball club. Mars is OK."

"I see. You understand the trip would be brief. We must depend on the space-warp continuum, which will be effective for only six more days. We would have to leave at once."

"It's my vacation," Jerome said. "I can do what I want."

When he stepped down on Mars, all of the big wheels were waiting. The chairman of Lions Interplanetary, the Editor of *Martian Digest*, the head of the Future Voters' League, and others. The welcoming address was delivered by the President of the Solar Council.

"In conclusion," he said, "at this first meeting of the dominant cultures of the planetary system, may I extend to you, Jerome of Earth, the keys to our cities and the hearts of our people, in the fervent hope—"

Jerome had taken a pair of clippers from his pocket and was trimming his nails. "Likewise," he said.

"—in the fervent hope," said the President, "that the

civilizations we represent may gain by this association some insight—"

"Looks like a mighty nice little planet you've got here," Jerome said.

After the ceremonies there was a small banquet at the Palace with some informal entertainment, and somewhat later Jerome was installed in the visitors' suite. He slept well.

The next morning he was treated to a gala patio breakfast, with the Royal Martian Ballet performing on the terrace below. "You are surprised to feel so much at home," said the President, smiling. "You see, we have been listening to your radio for many years, and so have learned your language, your customs, your likes and dislikes—"

"I like my eggs over easy," Jerome said. "But these are OK." He poked at them politely with his fork. "Anyhow, it's a change."

"We have planned so long for this occasion," said the President, "to show you our way of life, only to find our time so short—"

"Why don't we just drive around for a while," said Jerome. "If you got a car?"

They visited the Bureau of Statistical Research and Loving Kindness, and the Criminal Building, and Jerome left his footprints in concrete at the Sanctorium of the Daughters of the Martian Revolution.

"Actually," said the President, "the Revolution never amounted to much, but these ladies are the daughters of it and they're quite well-to-do. Now this afternoon—"

"As long as it's my vacation," said Jerome, "let's take in a ball game."

"First of all there is the Memorial Service of the Young Republicans' Club and then—" He paused. "A ball game, you say. Yes." He seemed to be thinking. "Very well, then, suppose we begin by having a bite of lunch."

There were fourteen courses, with appropriate wines and Solar Cola, so the luncheon was rather long. Long enough for the Martian Engineers and the Royal Construction Corps to erect a triple-decked stadium, and for two baseball teams to learn the game by means of microwave hypnosis. And for 120,000 volunteer fans to receive a short treatment of mass suggestion. Jerome and the President arrived at the park and took their seats. The umpire dusted off home plate, the first baseman took a chew of tobacco, the batter knocked the dirt out of his spikes, and the game began.

In the first inning there was a triple play and a triple steal. One of the managers was thrown out and the umpire was hit by a pop bottle. Jerome frowned. "I only wish Cleo was here," he said.

"You miss her a great deal," said the President.

"She never did see an ump get flattened," he said. "Not from this close anyhow."

In the second inning there was an inside-the-park grand slam home run, the third baseman made a triple error, and Jerome caught a pop foul. "Pretty fair seats," he said.

Returning to the Palace, the President outlined the rest of the day's schedule. "We're having a cocktail party in your honor," he said, "followed by a state dinner and the première of a new opera. Then a reception and a masked ball—"

"I thought I'd turn in early tonight," Jerome said. "Have a sandwich and a beer in my room and read the baseball almanac awhile."

"A sandwich and a beer in your room," said the President, "I see. Well, there should be beer in the icebox. If there's any special kind of sandwich you'd like we can stop at a delicatessen—"

"No special kind," Jerome said. The car turned in at the Palace.

The second morning was as busy as the first. The Tri-Centennial Military Review and Air Command Proceedings took up most of it so there was barely time to visit the Museum of Metaphysics and Household Design before lunch.

"This afternoon," said the President over the soup, "we have a program of unusual interest—"

"Who's pitching?" Jerome asked.

The Royal Construction Corps was forced to call on its civilian reserve to help rebuild the stadium it had torn down the night before. No one on Mars had considered the possibility that anybody would want to see more than one baseball game.

Driving home after the game, the President smiled. "Nothing wrong with a little relaxation, is there? Especially since tomorrow is going to be our big day. Something like your Independence Day: the Annual Opening of the Canals, address by the Philosopher-in-Chief, Dedication of the Five Hundredth Congress of Scientific—"

"Sounds great," said Jerome. "Be playing a double-header, I presume?"

"—of Scientific and Cultural Evalua—" The President

paused. "A double-header, you say. Well, yes—naturally. If you'll excuse me a moment I have to make a phone call." He was in time. They had only ripped out the first three rows of seats.

Returning to the Palace the third day, Jerome seemed restless. "Nice of you to ask me up," he said, "and all, but I'd better be getting home."

"There are still two days," the President said. "It will be years before conditions will enable us to communicate with Earth again. There is much we have to give you: a cure for the common cold—the formula for universal peace—plans for a thirty-five-inch color TV set the average boy can build for ten dollars—"

"I wouldn't mind staying on," Jerome said, "I'd like to see that little southpaw pitch tomorrow, but I got to get home. I promised Cleo I'd pick up the laundry, for one thing—"

"We had envisioned an exchange program," said the President, "of specialized personnel. Some of us going to Earth—some of you coming here."

"We could use a left-handed pitcher," Jerome said. "Probably we could give you a pretty good third baseman."

The President nodded. "At a moment like this there isn't very much I can say."

The trip to Earth was uneventful. Jerome was glad to be home. He hurried up to the apartment. Cleo was sitting in the same chair, watching the game.

"What inning?" he asked.

"Last of the third, no score," she said. "Been away?"

"Yeah." He settled down on the couch. "Newcombe pitching, huh?"

She nodded. "Got his fast ball working pretty good. Where'd you go—Canarsie?"

"Mars," he said. He started to unlace his shoes. "Campy's thumb bother him any?"

"Still got it taped, but he's swinging OK." She unwrapped a stick of gum. "What's it like up there—nice?"

"Yeah," he said, "seemed like a pretty good crowd, what I saw of them. What did Reese do last time up?"

"Grounded to short," she said. "Why don't you come to the meeting Thursday—the Current Events Club? Give a little talk about them? Might be interesting."

Jerome went up to the set and adjusted the dial. "Talk about who?"

"Now you got it too dark," she said. "Talk about these friends you went to see. Up to Mars. They worthwhile getting to know?"

Jerome shook his head slowly. "Can't hit the curve ball," he said.

The Celebrated No-Hit Inning

frederik pohl

Athletes are human beings. This truism accounts for the fact that a certain percentage of them are "problem" athletes. Many so-called problem athletes simply want to be treated as human beings or to be paid what they think they are worth. However, there are also a few who are real individualists, unable to adjust to the needs of team play or to accommodate the demands of the news media. Some, like Duane Thomas, have never reached their real potential because of disagreements with the "front office" or with coaches. Others, like baseball player Richie Allen, have overcome these difficulties through a change of teams and personal maturity.

In Fred Pohl's fine story, we meet a very temperamental baseball star who has the opportunity to play against the greatest player of all time. However, he discovers that the definition of what constitutes a superstar is relative to the time in which it occurs.

The
Celebrated No-Hit
Inning

This is a true story, you have to remember. You have to keep that firmly in mind because, frankly, in some places it may not *sound* like a true story. Besides, it's a true story about baseball players, and maybe the only one there is. So you have to treat it with respect.

You know Boley, no doubt. It's pretty hard not to know Boley, if you know anything at all about the National Game. He's the one, for instance, who raised such a scream when the sportswriters voted him Rookie of the Year. "I never *was* a rookie," he bellowed into three million television screens at the dinner. He's the one who ripped up his contract when his manager called him, "The hittin'est pitcher I ever see." Boley wouldn't stand for that. "Four-eighteen against the best pitchers in the league," he yelled, as the pieces of the contract went out the window. "Fogarty, I am the hittin'est *hitter* you ever see!"

He's the one they all said reminded them so much of Dizzy Dean at first. But did Diz win thirty-one games in his first year? Boley did; he'll tell you so himself. But politely, and without bellowing . . .

Somebody explained to Boley that even a truly great

Hall-of-Fame pitcher really ought to show up for spring training. So, in his second year, he did. But he wasn't convinced that he *needed* the training, so he didn't bother much about appearing on the field.

Manager Fogarty did some extensive swearing about that, but he did all of his swearing to his pitching coaches and not to Mr. Boleslaw. There had been six ripped-up contracts already that year, when Boley's feelings got hurt about something, and the front office were very insistent that there shouldn't be any more.

There wasn't much the poor pitching coaches could do, of course. They tried pleading with Boley. All he did was grin and ruffle their hair and say, "Don't get all in an uproar." He could ruffle their hair pretty easily, since he stood six inches taller than the tallest of them.

"Boley," said Pitching Coach Magill to him desperately, "you are going to get me into trouble with the manager. I need this job. We just had another little boy at our house, and they cost money to feed. Won't you please do me a favor and come down to the field, just for a little while?"

Boley had a kind of a soft heart. "Why, if that will make so much difference to you, Coach, I'll do it. But I don't feel much like pitching. We have got twelve exhibition games lined up with the Orioles on the way north, and if I pitch six of those that ought to be all the warm-up I need."

"Three innings?" Magill haggled. "You know I wouldn't ask you if it wasn't important. The thing is, the owner's uncle is watching today."

Boley pursed his lips. He shrugged. "One inning."

"Bless you, Boley!" cried the coach. "One inning it is!"

Andy Andalusia was catching for the regulars when Boley turned up on the field. He turned white as a sheet. "Not the fast ball, Boley! Please, Boley," he begged. "I only been catching a week and I have not hardened up yet."

Boleslaw turned the rosin bag around in his hands and looked around the field. There was action going on at all six diamonds, but the spectators, including the owner's uncle, were watching the regulars.

"I tell you what I'll do," said Boley thoughtfully. "Let's see. For the first man, I pitch only curves. For the second man, the screwball. And for the third man—let's see. Yes. For the third man, I pitch the sinker."

"Fine!" cried the catcher gratefully, and trotted back to home plate.

"He's a very spirited player," the owner's uncle commented to Manager Fogarty.

"That he is," said Fogarty, remembering how the pieces of the fifth contract had felt as they hit him on the side of the head.

"He must be a morale problem for you, though. Doesn't he upset the discipline of the rest of the team?"

Fogarty looked at him, but he only said, "He win thirty-one games for us last year. If he had *lost* thirty-one he would have upset us a lot more."

The owner's uncle nodded, but there was a look in his eye all the same. He watched without saying anything more, while Boley struck out the first man with three sizzling curves, right on schedule, and then turned around and yelled something at the outfield.

"That crazy— By heaven," shouted the manager, "he's chasing them back into the dugout. I *told* that—"

The owner's uncle clutched at Manager Fogarty as he was getting up to head for the field. "Wait a minute. What's Boleslaw doing?"

"Don't you see? He's chasing the outfield off the field. He wants to face the next two men without any outfield! That's Satchell Paige's old trick, only he never did it except in exhibitions where who cares? But that Boley—"

"This is only an exhibition, isn't it?" remarked the owner's uncle mildly.

Fogarty looked longingly at the field, looked back at the owner's uncle, and shrugged.

"All right." He sat down, remembering that it was the owner's uncle whose sprawling factories had made the family money that bought the owner his team. "Go ahead!" he bawled at the right fielder, who was hesitating halfway to the dugout.

Boley nodded from the mound. When the outfielders were all out of the way he set himself and went into his windup. Boleslaw's windup was a beautiful thing to all who chanced to behold it—unless they happened to root for another team. The pitch was more beautiful still.

"I got it, I got it!" Andalusia cried from behind the plate, waving the ball in his mitt. He returned it to the pitcher triumphantly, as though he could hardly believe he had caught the Boleslaw screwball—after only the first week of spring training.

He caught the second pitch, too. But the third was unpredictably low and outside. Andalusia dived for it in vain.

"Ball one!" cried the umpire. The catcher scrambled up, ready to argue.

"He is right," Boley called graciously from the mound. "I am sorry, but my foot slipped. It was a ball."

"Thank you," said the umpire. The next screwball was a strike, though, and so were the three sinkers to the third man—though one of those caught a little piece of the bat and turned into an into-the-dirt foul.

Boley came off the field to a spattering of applause. He stopped under the stands, on the lip of the dugout. "I guess I am a little rusty at that, Fogarty," he called. "Don't let me forget to pitch another inning or two before we play Baltimore next month."

"I won't!" snapped Fogarty. He would have said more, but the owner's uncle was talking.

"I don't know much about baseball, but that strikes me as an impressive performance. My congratulations."

"You are right," Boley admitted. "Excuse me while I shower, and then we can resume this discussion some more. I think you are a better judge of baseball than you say."

The owner's uncle chuckled, watching him go into the dugout. "You can laugh," said Fogarty bitterly. "You don't have to put up with that for a hundred fifty-four games, and spring training, *and* the Series."

"You're pretty confident about making the Series?"

Fogarty said simply, "Last year Boley win thirty-one games."

The owner's uncle nodded, and shifted position uncomfortably. He was sitting with one leg stretched over a large black metal suitcase, fastened with a complicated lock. Fogarty asked, "Should I have one of the boys put that in the locker room for you?"

"Certainly not!" said the owner's uncle. "I want it

right here where I can touch it." He looked around him. "The fact of that matter is," he went on in a lower tone, "this goes up to Washington with me tomorrow. I can't discuss what's in it. But as we're among friends, I can mention that where it's going is the Pentagon."

"Oh," said Fogarty respectfully. "Something new from the factories."

"Something very new," the owner's uncle agreed, and he winked. "And I'd better get back to the hotel with it. But there's one thing, Mr. Fogarty. I don't have much time for baseball, but it's a family affair, after all, and whenever I can help— I mean, it just occurs to me that possibly, with the help of what's in this suitcase— That is, would you like me to see if I could help out?"

"Help out how?" asked Fogarty suspiciously.

"Well— I really mustn't discuss what's in the suitcase. But would it hurt Boleslaw, for example, to be a little more, well, modest?"

The manager exploded, "No."

The owner's uncle nodded. "That's what I've thought. Well, I must go. Will you ask Mr. Boleslaw to give me a ring at the hotel so we can have dinner together, if it's convenient?"

It was convenient, all right. Boley had always wanted to see how the other half lived; and they had a fine dinner, served right in the suite, with five waiters in attendance and four kinds of wine. Boley kept pushing the little glasses of wine away, but after all the owner's uncle was the owner's uncle, and if *he* thought it was all right— It must have been pretty strong wine, because Boley began to have trouble following the conversation.

It was all right as long as it stuck to earned-run

averages and batting percentages, but then it got hard to follow, like a long, twisting grounder on a dry September field. Boley wasn't going to admit that, though. "Sure," he said, trying to follow; and, "You say the *fourth* dimension?" he said; and, "You mean a time machine, like?" he said; but he was pretty confused.

The owner's uncle smiled and filled the wineglasses again.

Somehow the black suitcase had been unlocked, in a slow, difficult way. Things made out of crystal and steel were sticking out of it. "Forget about the time machine," said the owner's uncle patiently. "It's a military secret, anyhow. I'll thank you to forget the very words, because heaven knows what the General would think if he found out— Anyway, forget it. What about you, Boley? Do you still say you can hit any pitcher who ever lived and strike out any batter?"

"Anywhere," agreed Boley, leaning back in the deep cushions and watching the room go around and around. "Any time. I'll bat their ears off."

"Have another glass of wine, Boley," said the owner's uncle, and he began to take things out of the black suitcase.

Boley woke up with a pounding in his head like Snider, Mays, and Mantle hammering Three-Eye League pitching. He moaned and opened one eye.

Somebody blurry was holding a glass out to him. "Hurry up. Drink this."

Boley shrank back. "I will not. That's what got me into this trouble in the first place."

"Trouble? You're in no trouble. But the game's about to start and you've got a hangover."

Ring a fire bell beside a sleeping Dalmatian; sound the Charge in the ear of a retired cavalry major. Neither will respond more quickly than Boley to the words, "The game's about to start."

He managed to drink some of the fizzy stuff in the glass and it was a miracle; like a triple play erasing a ninth-inning threat, the headache was gone. He sat up, and the world did not come to an end. In fact, he felt pretty good.

He was being rushed somewhere by the blurry man. They were going very rapidly, and there were tall, bright buildings outside. They stopped.

"We're at the studio," said the man, helping Boley out of a remarkable sort of car.

"The stadium," Boley corrected automatically. He looked around for the lines at the box office but there didn't seem to be any.

"The *studio*. Don't argue all day, will you?" The man was no longer so blurry. Boley looked at him and blushed. He was only a little man, with a worried look to him, and what he was wearing was a pair of vivid orange Bermuda shorts that showed his knees. He didn't give Boley much of a chance for talking or thinking. They rushed into a building, all green and white opaque glass, and they were met at a flimsy-looking elevator by another little man. This one's shorts were aqua, and he had a bright-red cummerbund tied around his waist.

"This is him," said Boley's escort.

The little man in aqua looked Boley up and down.

"He's a big one. I hope to goodness we got a uniform to fit him for the Series."

Boley cleared his throat. "Series?"

"And you're in it!" shrilled the little man in orange. "This way to the dressing room."

Well, a dressing room was a dressing room, even if this one did have color television screens all around it and machines that went *wheepety-boom* softly to themselves. Boley began to feel at home.

He blinked when they handed his uniform to him, but he put it on. Back in the Steel & Coal League, he had sometimes worn uniforms that still bore the faded legend 100 *Lbs. Best Fortified Gro-Chick*, and whatever an owner gave you to put on was all right with Boley. Still, he thought to himself, *kilts!*

It was the first time in Boley's life that he had ever worn a skirt. But when he was dressed it didn't look too bad, he thought—especially because all the other players (it looked like fifty of them, anyway) were wearing the same thing. There is nothing like seeing the same costume on everybody in view to make it seem reasonable and right. Haven't the Paris designers been proving that for years?

He saw a familiar figure come into the dressing room, wearing a uniform like his own. "Why, Coach Magill," said Boley, turning with his hand outstretched. "I did not expect to meet you here."

The newcomer frowned, until somebody whispered in his ear. "Oh," he said, "you're Boleslaw."

"Naturally I'm Boleslaw, and naturally you're my pitching coach, Magill, and why do you look at me that way when I've seen you every day for three weeks?"

The man shook his head. "You're thinking of Grand-daddy Jim," he said, and moved on.

Boley stared after him. Granddaddy Jim? But Coach Magill was no granddaddy, that was for sure. Why, his eldest was no more than six years old. Boley put his hand against the wall to steady himself. It touched something metal and cold. He glanced at it.

It was a bronze plaque, floor to ceiling high, and it was embossed at the top with the words *World Series Honor Roll*. And it listed every team that had ever won the World Series, from the day Chicago won the first Series of all in 1906 until—until—

Boley said something out loud, and quickly looked around to see if anybody had heard him. It wasn't something he wanted people to hear. But it was the right time for a man to say something like that, because what that crazy lump of bronze said, down toward the bottom, with only empty spaces below, was that the most recent team to win the World Series was the Yokohama Dodgers, and the year they won it in was—1998.

1998.

A time machine, thought Boley wonderingly, I guess what he meant was a machine that traveled in *time*.

Now, if you had been picked up in a time machine that leaped through the years like a jet plane leaps through space, you might be quite astonished, perhaps, and for a while you might not be good for much of anything, until things calmed down.

But Boley was born calm. He lived by his arm and his eye, and there was nothing to worry about there. Pay him his Class C league contract bonus, and he turns up

in Western Pennsylvania, all ready to set a league record
for no-hitters his first year. Call him up from the minors
and he bats .418 against the best pitchers in baseball. Set
him down in the year 1999 and tell him he's going to
play in the Series, and he hefts the ball once or twice
and says, "I better take a couple of warm-up pitches. Is
the spitter allowed?"

They led him to the bullpen. And then there was the
playing of the National Anthem and the teams took the
field. And Boley got the biggest shock so far.

"Magill," he bellowed in a terrible voice, "what is that
other pitcher doing out on the mound?"

The manager looked startled. "That's our starter,
Padgett. He always starts with the number-two defensive
lineup against right-hand batters when the outfield shift
goes—"

"Magill! I am not any *relief* pitcher. If you pitch
Boleslaw, you *start* with Boleslaw."

Magill said soothingly, "It's perfectly all right. There
have been some changes, that's all. You can't expect the
rules to stay the same for forty or fifty years, can you?"

"I am not a *relief* pitcher. I—"

"Please, please. Won't you sit down?"

Boley sat down, but he was seething. "We'll see about
that," he said to the world. "We'll just see."

Things had changed, all right. To begin with, the studio
really was a studio and not a stadium. And although it
was a very large room, it was not the equal of Ebbetts
Field, much less the Yankee Stadium. There seemed to
be an awful lot of bunting, and the ground rules confused Boley very much.

Then the dugout happened to be just under what seemed to be a complicated sort of television booth, and Boley could hear the announcer screaming himself hoarse just overhead. That had a familiar sound, but—

"And here," roared the announcer, "comes the all-important nothing-and-one pitch! Fans, what a pitchers' duel *this* is! Delasantos is going into his motion! He's coming down! He's delivered it! And it's *in there* for a count of nothing and two! Fans, what a pitcher that Tiburcio Delasantos *is!* And here comes the all-important nothing-and-two pitch, and—and—yes, and he struck him out! *He struck him out!* He struck him *out!* It's a *no-hitter*, fans! In the all-important second inning, it's a no-hitter for Tiburcio Delasantos!"

Boley swallowed and stared hard at the scoreboard, which seemed to show a score of 14–9, their favor. His teammates were going wild with excitement, and so was the crowd of players, umpires, cameramen, and announcers watching the game. He tapped the shoulder of the man next to him.

"Excuse me. What's the score?"

"Dig that Tiburcio!" cried the man. "What a first-string defensive pitcher against left-handers he *is!*"

"The score. Could you tell me what it is?"

"Fourteen to nine. Did you *see* that—"

Boley begged, "Please, didn't somebody just say it was a no-hitter?"

"Why, sure." The man explained: "The inning. It's a no-hit *inning*." And he looked queerly at Boley.

It was all like that, except that some of it was worse. After three innings Boley was staring glassy-eyed into space. He dimly noticed that both teams were trotting off the field and what looked like a whole new corps of players were warming up when Manager Magill stopped in front of him. "You'll be playing in a minute," Magill said kindly.

"Isn't the game over?" Boley gestured toward the field.

"Over? Of course not. It's the third-inning stretch," Magill told him. "Ten minutes for the lawyers to file their motions and make their appeals. You know." He laughed condescendingly. "They tried to get an injunction against the bases-loaded pitchout. Imagine!"

"Hah-hah," Boley echoed. "Mister Magill, can I go home?"

"Nonsense, boy! Didn't you hear me? You're on as soon as the lawyers come off the field!"

Well, that began to make sense to Boley and he actually perked up a little. When the minutes had passed and Magill took him by the hand, he began to feel almost cheerful again. He picked up the rosin bag and flexed his fingers and said simply, "Boley's ready."

Because nothing confused Boley when he had a ball or a bat in his hand. Set him down any time, anywhere, and he'd hit any pitcher or strike out any batter. He knew exactly what it was going to be like, once he got on the playing field.

Only it wasn't like that at all.

Boley's team was at bat, and the first man up got on with a bunt single. Anyway, they *said* it was a bunt single. To Boley it had seemed as though the enemy pitcher had charged beautifully off the mound, fielded the ball with machinelike precision, and flipped it to the first-base player with inches and inches to spare for the out. But the umpires declared interference by a vote of eighteen to seven, the two left-field umpires and the one with the field glasses over the batter's head abstaining; it seemed that the first baseman had neglected to say "Excuse me" to the runner. Well, the rules were the rules. Boley tightened his grip on his bat and tried to get a lead on the pitcher's style.

That was hard, because the pitcher was fast. Boley admitted it to himself uneasily; he was *very* fast. He was a big monster of a player, nearly seven feet tall and with something queer and sparkly about his eyes; and when he came down with a pitch there was a sort of a hiss and a *splat*, and the ball was in the catcher's hands. It might, Boley confessed, be a little hard to hit that particular pitcher, because he hadn't yet seen the ball in transit.

Manager Magill came up behind him in the on-deck spot and fastened something to his collar. "Your intercom," he explained. "So we can tell you what to do when you're up."

"Sure, sure." Boley was only watching the pitcher. He looked sickly out there; his skin was a grayish sort of color, and those eyes didn't look right. But there wasn't anything sickly about the way he delivered the next pitch, a sweeping curve that sizzled in and spun away.

The batter didn't look so good either—same sickly gray skin, same giant frame. But he reached out across the plate and caught that curve and dropped it between third base and short; and both men were safe.

"You're on," said a tinny little voice in Boley's ear; it was the little intercom, and the manager was talking to him over the radio. Boley walked numbly to the plate. Sixty feet away, the pitcher looked taller than ever.

Boley took a deep breath and looked about him. The crowd was roaring ferociously, which was normal enough —except there wasn't any crowd. Counting everybody, players and officials and all, there weren't more than three or four hundred people in sight in the whole studio. But he could *hear* the screams and yells of easily fifty or sixty thousand— There was a man, he saw, behind a plate-glass window who was doing things with what might have been records, and the yells of the crowd all seemed to come from loudspeakers under his window. Boley winced and concentrated on the pitcher.

"I will pin his ears back," he said feebly, more to reassure himself than because he believed it.

The little intercom on his shoulder cried in a tiny voice: "You will not, Boleslaw! Your orders are to take the first pitch!"

"But, listen—"

"Take it! You hear me, Boleslaw?"

There was a time when Boley would have swung just to prove who was boss; but the time was not then. He stood there whi.e the big gray pitcher looked him over with those sparkling eyes. He stood there through the windup. And then the arm came down, and he didn't stand there. That ball wasn't invisible, not coming right at him; it looked as big and as fast as the Wabash Cannonball and Boley couldn't help it, for the first time in his life he jumped a yard away, screeching.

"Hit batter! Hit batter!" cried the intercom. "Take your base, Boleslaw."

Boley blinked. Six of the umpires were beckoning him on, so the intercom was right. But still and all—

Boley had his pride. He said to the little button on his collar, "I am sorry, but I wasn't hit. He missed me a mile, easy. I got scared is all."

"Take your base, you silly fool!" roared the intercom. "He *scared* you, didn't he? That's just as bad as hitting you, according to the rules. Why, there is no telling what incalculable damage has been done to your nervous system by this fright. So kindly get the bejeepers over to first base, Boleslaw, as provided in the rules of the game!"

He got, but he didn't stay there long, because there was a pinch runner waiting for him. He barely noticed that it was another of the gray-skinned giants before he headed for the locker room and the showers. He didn't even remember getting out of his uniform; he only remembered that he, Boley, had just been through the worst experience of his life.

He was sitting on a bench, with his head in his hands, when the owner's uncle came in, looking queerly out of place in his neat pin-striped suit. The owner's uncle had to speak to him twice before his eyes focused.

"They didn't let me pitch," Boley said wonderingly. "They didn't want Boley to pitch."

The owner's uncle patted his shoulder. "You were a guest star, Boley. One of the all-time greats of the game. Next game they're going to have Christy Mathewson. Doesn't that make you feel proud?"

"They didn't let me pitch," said Boley.

The owner's uncle sat down beside him. "Don't you see? You'd be out of place in this kind of a game. You got on base for them, didn't you? I heard the announcer say it myself; he said you filled the bases in the all-important fourth inning. Two hundred million people were watching this game on television! And they saw you get on base!"

"They didn't let me hit either," Boley said.

There was a commotion at the door and the team came trotting in, screaming victory. "We win it, we win it!" cried Manager Magill. "Eighty-seven to eighty-three! What a squeaker!"

Boley lifted his head to croak, "That's fine." But nobody was listening. The manager jumped on a table and yelled, over the noise in the locker room:

"Boys, we pulled a close one out, and you know what that means. We're leading in the Series, eleven games to nine! Now let's just wrap those other two up, and—"

He was interrupted by a bloodcurdling scream from Boley. Boley was standing up, pointing with an expression of horror. The athletes had scattered and the trainers were working them over; only some of the trainers were using pliers and screwdrivers instead of towels and liniment. Next to Boley, the big gray-skinned pinch runner was flat on his back, and the trainer was lifting one leg away from the body—

"Murder!" bellowed Boley. "That fellow is murdering that fellow!"

The manager jumped down next to him. "Murder? There isn't any murder, Boleslaw! What are you talking about?"

Boley pointed mutely. The trainer stood gaping at him, with the leg hanging limp in his grip. It was completely removed from the torso it belonged to, but the torso seemed to be making no objections; the curious eyes were open but no longer sparkling; the gray skin, at closer hand, seemed metallic and cold.

The manager said fretfully, "I swear, Boleslaw, you're a nuisance. They're just getting cleaned and oiled, batteries recharged, that sort of thing. So they'll be in shape tomorrow, you understand."

"Cleaned," whispered Boley. *"Oiled."* He stared around the room. All of the gray-skinned ones were being somehow disassembled; bits of metal and glass were sticking out of them. "Are you trying to tell me," he croaked, "that those fellows aren't fellows?"

"They're ball players," said Manager Magill impatiently. "Robots. Haven't you ever seen a robot before? We're allowed to field six robots on a nine-man team, it's perfectly legal. Why, next year I'm hoping the Commissioner'll let us play a whole robot team. *Then* you'll see some baseball!"

With bulging eyes Boley saw it was true. Except for a handful of flesh-and-blood players like himself the team was made up of man-shaped machines, steel for bones, electricity for blood, steel and plastic and copper cogs for muscle. "Machines," said Boley, and turned up his eyes.

The owner's uncle tapped him on the shoulder worriedly. "It's time to go back," he said.

So Boley went back.

He didn't remember much about it, except that the owner's uncle had made him promise never, never to tell anyone about it, because it was orders from the Defense Department, you never could tell how useful a time machine might be in a war. But he did get back, and he woke up the next morning with all the signs of a hang-over and the sheets kicked to shreds around his feet.

He was still bleary when he staggered down to the coffee shop for breakfast. Magill the pitching coach, who had no idea that he was going to be granddaddy to Magill the Series-winning manager, came solicitously over to him. "Bad night, Boley? You look like you have had a bad night."

"Bad?" repeated Boley. "Bad? Magill, you have got no idea. The owner's uncle said he would show me some-thing that would learn me a little humility and, Magill, he came through. Yes, he did. Why, I saw a big bronze tablet with the names of the Series winners on it, and I saw—"

And he closed his mouth right there, because he remembered right there what the owner's uncle had said about closing his mouth. He shook his head and shuddered. "Bad," he said, "you bet it was bad."

Magill coughed. "Gosh, that's too bad, Boley. I guess— I mean, then maybe you wouldn't feel like pitching another couple of innings—well, anyway, one inning— today, because—"

Boley held up his hand. "Say no more, please. You want me to pitch today, Magill?"

"That's about the size of it," the coach confessed.

"I will pitch today," said Boley. "If that is what you want me to do, I will do it. I am now a reformed char-acter. I will pitch tomorrow, too, if you want me to pitch tomorrow, and any other day you want me to pitch. And if you do not want me to pitch, I will sit on the sidelines. Whatever you want is perfectly all right with me, Magill, because, Magill, I—hey! Hey, Magill, what are you doing down there on the floor?"

So that is why Boley doesn't give anybody any trouble anymore, and if you tell him now that he reminds you of Dizzy Dean, why, he'll probably shake your hand and thank you for the compliment—even if you're a sportswriter, even. Oh, there still are a few special little things about him, of course—not even counting the things like how many shutouts he pitched last year (eleven) or how many home runs he hit (fourteen). But everybody finds him easy to get along with. They used to talk about the change that had come over him a lot and wonder what caused it. Some people said he got religion and others said he had an incurable disease and was trying to do good in his last few weeks on earth; but Boley never said, he only smiled; and the owner's uncle was too busy in Washington to be with the team much after that. So now they talk about other things when Boley's name comes up. For instance, there's his little business about the pitching machine—when he shows up for batting practice (which is every morning, these days), he insists on hitting against real live pitchers instead of the machine. It's even in his contract. And then, every March he bets nickels against anybody around the training camp that'll bet with him that he can pick that year's Series winner. He doesn't bet more than that, because the Commissioner naturally doesn't like big bets from ball players.

But, even for nickels, don't bet against him, because he isn't ever going to lose, not before 1999.

Naked to the Invisible Eye

george alec effinger

Baseball has declined in relation to sports like football and basketball in recent years, but the major leagues are still.healthy. Like the future envisioned for football by George R. R. Martin, however, this story shows the further decline of spectator sports in general. But the decline is not technologically based, as it is in Martin's story. Here it declines because of the presence of a true superstar.

It is interesting to speculate whether the truly *perfect* ball player could ever kill interest in a sport. It seems very likely, however, since perfection is boring. This is the reason that utopian stories rarely appear in contemporary science fiction, while the dystopian story with its element of conflict and the need for change is very popular.

The protagonist in this story is a Latin pitcher with a unique means of "psyching out" opposing batters. Psychology is a very important aspect of sports, one which is receiving increasing attention from coaches, players, and fans. Were it not for the factor of psychology, the "better" team would win every time, there would be no upsets, and sports would be a lot duller. Psychology thus provides a rationale behind the claim that "on any given day, the worst team in the league can beat the best." It is difficult enough for one individual to become highly motivated for a sports event. Think how difficult it must be for a coach to motivate an entire team, day after day, week after week. For pitcher Rudy Ramirez, however, it is not difficult at all. If you can't "get yourself up," then the trick is to get the other guy down!

Naked to the
Invisible Eye

There were less than a thousand spectators in the little ball park, their chatter nearly inaudible compared to the heartening roar of the major league crowds. The fans sat uneasily, as if they had wandered into the wake of a legendary hero. No longer was baseball the national pastime. Even the big league teams, roving from franchise to franchise in search of yesterday's loyal bleacher fanatics, resorted to promotional gimmicks to stave off bankruptcy. Here, the Bears were in third place, with an unlikely shot at second. The Tigers had clinched the pennant early, now leading the second-place Kings by nine gam·s and the Bears by an even more discouraging number. There was no real tension in this game—oh, with a bad slump the Bears might fall down among the cellar teams, but so what? For all intents and purposes, the season had ended a month ago.

There was no tension, no pennant race any longer, just an inexpensive evening out for the South Carolina fans. The sweat on the batter's hands was the fault of his own nervous reaction; the knots in his stomach were shared by no one. He went to the on-deck circle for the pine-tar rag while he waited for the new pitcher to toss his warm-ups.

The Bear shortstop was batting eighth, reflecting his anemic .219 average. Like a great smoothed rock this fact sat in the torrent of his thinking, submerged at times but often breaking through the racing surface. With his unsteady fielding it looked as if he would be out of a job the next spring. To the players and to the spectators the game was insignificant; to him it was the first of his last few chances. With two runs in already in the eighth, one out and a man on first, he went to the plate.

He looked out toward the kid on the mound before settling himself in the batter's box. The pitcher's name was Rudy Ramirez, he was only nineteen and from somewhere in Venezuela. That was all anybody knew about him; this was his first appearance in a professional ball game. The Bear shortstop took a deep breath and stepped in.

That kid Ramirez looked pretty fast during his warm-ups, he thought. The shortstop damned the fate that made him the focus of attention against a complete unknown. The waters surged; his thoughts shuffled and died.

The Venezuelan kid looked in for his sign. The shortstop looked down to the third-base coach, who flashed the *take* signal; that was all right with him. *I'm only batting .219, I want to see this kid throw one before. . . .*

Ramirez went into his stretch, glanced at the runner on first. . . .

With that kid Barger coming off the disabled list I might not be able to. . . .

Ramirez' right leg kicked, his left arm flung back. . . .
The shortstop's shrieking flood of thought stilled, his
mind was as quiet as the surface of a pond stagnating.
The umpire called the pitch a ball.

Along the coaching lines at third Sorenson was relaying
the *hit-and-run* sign from the dugout. *All right,* thought
the shortstop, *just make contact, get a good ground ball,
maybe a hit, move the man into scoring position.* . . .

Ramirez nodded to his catcher, stretched, checked the
runner. . . .

*My luck, I'll get an easy double-play ball to the right
side.* . . .

Ramirez kicked, snapped, and pitched. . . .

The shortstop's mind was silent, ice-cold, dead, watching the runner vainly flying toward second, the catcher's
throw beating him there by fifteen feet. Two out. One
ball and one strike.

Sorenson called time. He met the shortstop halfway
down the line.

"You damn brainless idiot!" said the coach. "You saw
the sign, you *acknowledged* the sign, you stood there
with your thumb in your ear looking at a perfect strike!
You got an awful short memory?"

"Look, I don't know—"

"I'll tell you what I *do* know," said Sorenson. "I know
that'll cost you twenty dollars. Maybe your spot in the
lineup."

The shortstop walked to the on-deck circle, wiped his
bat again with the pine tar. His head was filled with
anger and frustration. Back in the batter's box he stared
toward the pitcher in desperation.

On the rubber Ramirez worked out of a full windup

with the bases empty. His high kick hid his delivery until the last moment. The ball floated toward the plate, a fat balloon belt-high, a curve that didn't break. . . .

The hitter's mind was like a desert, his mind was like an empty glass, a blank sheet of paper, his mind was totally at rest. . . .

The ball nicked the outside corner for a called strike two. The Tiger catcher chuckled. "Them people in the seats have to pay to get in," he said. "They're doin' more'n you!"

"Shut up." The Bear shortstop choked up another couple of inches on the handle. *He'll feed me another curve, and then the fast ball.* . . .

Ramirez took the sign and went into his motion.

Lousy kid. I'm gonna rap it one down his lousy throat. . . .

The wrist flicked, the ball spun, broke. . . .

The shortstop watched, unawed, very still, like a hollow thing, as the curve broke sharply, down the heart of the plate, strike three, side retired.

The Tigers managed to score an insurance run in the top half of the ninth, and Rudy Ramirez went back to the mound with a five-to-three lead to protect. The first batter that he was scheduled to face was the Bear pitcher, who was replaced in the order by pinch hitter Frank Asterino.

A sense of determination, confidence made Asterino's mind orderly. It was a brightly lit mind, with none of the shifting doubts of the other. Rudy felt the will, he weighed the desire, he discovered the man's dedication and respected it. He stood off the rubber, rubbing the shine from the new ball. He reached for the rosin bag, then dropped it. He peered in at Johnston, his catcher. The sign: the fast ball.

Asterino guarded the plate closely. Johnston's mitt was targeted on the inside—start off with the high hard one, loosen the batter up. Rudy rocked back, kicked that leg high, and threw. The ball did not go for the catcher's mark, sailing out just a little. A not-overpowering pitch right down the pipe—a true gopher ball.

Rudy thought as the ball left his hand. He found that will of Asterino's, and he held it gently back. *Be still. Do not move; yes, be still.* And Asterino watched the strike intently as it passed.

Asterino watched two more, both curves that hung tantalizing but untouched. Ramirez grasped the batter's desire with his own, and blotted up all the fierce resolution there was in him. Asterino returned to the bench amid the boos of the fans, disappointed but unbewildered. He had struck out but, after all, that was not so unusual.

The top of the batting order was up, and Rudy touched their disparate minds. He hid their judgment behind the glare of his own will, and they struck out; the first batter needed five pitches and the second four. They observed balls with as much passive interest as strikes, and their bats never left their shoulders. No runs, no hits, no errors, nothing across for the Bears in the ninth. The ball game was over; Rudy earned a save for striking out the four batters he faced in his first pro assignment.

Afterward, local reporters were met by the angry manager of the Bears. When asked for his impression of the young Tiger pitcher he said, "I didn't think he looked *that* sharp. How you supposed to win managing a damn bunch of zombies?" In the visitors' clubhouse Tiger manager Fred Marenholtz was in a more expansive mood.

"Where did Ramirez come from?" asked one reporter.

"I don't really know," he said. "Charlie Cardona checks out Detroit's prospects down there. All I know is the telegram said that he was signed, and then here he is. Charlie's dug up some good kids for us."

"Did he impress you tonight?"

Marenholtz settled his wire-rim glasses on his long nose and nodded. "He looked real cool for his first game. I'm going to start him in the series with the Reds this weekend. We'll have a better idea then, of course, but I have a feeling he won't be playing Class B ball long."

After the game with the Bears, the Tigers showered quickly and boarded their bus. They had a game the next night against the Selene Comets. It was a home game for the Tigers, and they were all glad to be returning to Cordele, but the bus ride from the Bears' stadium would be four or five hours. They would get in just before dawn, sleep until noon, have time for a couple of unpleasant hamburgers, and get to the park in time for practice.

The Tigers won that game, and the game the next night, also. The Comets left town and were replaced by the Rockhill Reds, in for a Saturday afternoon game and a Sunday double-header. This late in the summer the pitching staffs were nearly exhausted. Manager Marenholtz of the Tigers kept his promise to the newspaper-

men; after the Saturday loss to the Reds he went to
Chico Guerra, his first-string catcher, and told him to get
Rudy Ramirez ready for the second game the next day.
Ramirez was eager, of course, and confident. Marenholtz was sitting in his office when Rudy came into the
locker room before the Sunday double-header, a full
half hour before practice began. Marenholtz smiled,
remembering his own first game. He had been an outfielder; in the seventh inning he had run into the left-
field wall chasing a long fly. He dropped the ball,
cracked his head, and spent the next three weeks on the
disabled list. Marenholtz wished Ramirez better luck.

The Tigers' second-string catcher, Maurie Johnston,
played the first game, and Guerra sat next to Ramirez
in the dugout, pointing out the strengths and weaknesses
of the opposing batters. Ramirez said little, just nodding
and smiling. Marenholtz walked by them near the end
of the first game. "Chico," he said, "ask him if he's
nervous."

The catcher translated the question into Spanish.
Ramirez grinned and answered. "He say no," said
Guerra. "He jus' wan' show you what he can do."

The manager grunted a reply and went back to his
seat, thinking about cocky rookies. The Tigers lost the
first game, making two in a row dropped to the last-
place Reds. The fans didn't seem to mind; there were
only twenty games left until the end of the season, and
there was no way possible for the Tigers to fall from first
place short of losing all of them. It was obvious that
Marenholtz was trying out new kids, resting his regulars
for the Hanson Cup play-offs. The fans would let him
get away with a lot, as long as he won the cup.

Between games there was a high school band marching in the outfield, and the local Kiwanis Club presented a plaque to the Tigers' center fielder, who was leading the league with forty-two home runs. Ramirez loosened up his arm during all this; he stood along the right-field foul line and tossed some easy pitches to Guerra. After a while the managers brought out their lineup cards to the umpires and the grounds crew finished grooming the infield. Ramirez and Guerra took their positions on the field, and the rest of the team joined them, to the cheers of the Tigers' fans.

Skip Stackpole, the Reds' shortstop and leadoff batter, was settling himself in the batter's box. Rudy bent over and stared toward Guerra for the sign. An inside curve. Rudy nodded.

As he started into his windup he explored Stackpole's mind. It was a relaxed mind, concentrating only because Stackpole enjoyed playing baseball; for him, and for the last-place Reds, the game was meaningless. Rudy would have little difficulty.

Wait, thought Rudy wordlessly, forcing his will directly into Stackpole's intellect. *Not this one. Wait.* And Stackpole waited. The ball broke sharply, over the heart of the plate, for the first strike. There was a ripple of applause from the Tiger fans.

Guerra wanted a fast ball. Rudy nodded, kicked high, and threw. *Quiet*, he thought, *do not move*. Right down the pipe, strike two.

This much ahead of the hitter, Guerra should have called for a couple of pitches on the outside, to tease the batter into swinging at a bad pitch. But the catcher thought that Stackpole was off balance. The Reds had never seen Ramirez pitch before. Guerra called for another fast ball. Rudy nodded and went into his windup. He kept Stackpole from swinging. The Reds' first hitter was called out on strikes; the Tiger fans cheered loudly as Guerra stood and threw the ball down to third base. Ramirez could hear his infielders chattering and encouraging him in a language that he didn't understand. He got the ball back and looked at the Reds' second man.

The new batter would be more of a challenge. He was hitting .312, battling with two others for the last place in the league's top ten. He was more determined than anyone Ramirez had yet faced. When Rudy pitched the ball, he needed more mental effort to keep the man from swinging at it. The pitch was too high. Ramirez leaned forward; Guerra wanted a low curve. The pitch broke just above the batter's knees, over the outside corner of the plate. One ball, one strike. The next pitch was a fast ball, high and inside. Ball two. Another fast ball, over the plate. *Wait*, thought Rudy, *wait*. The batter waited, and the count was two and two. Rudy tried another curve, and forced the batter to watch it helplessly. Strike three, two out.

Ramirez felt good, now. The stadium full of noisy people didn't make him nervous. The experienced athletes on the other team posed no threat at all. Rudy knew that he could win today; he knew that there wasn't a batter in the world that could beat him. The third hitter was no problem for Rudy's unusual talent. He struck out on four pitches. Rudy received a loud cheer from the fans as he walked back to the dugout. He smiled and waved, and took a seat next to the water cooler with Guerra.

The Tigers scored no runs in their part of the first inning, and Rudy went back to the mound and threw his allotment of warm-ups. He stood rubbing up the ball while the Reds' cleanup hitter settled himself at the plate. Rudy disposed of the Reds' best power hitter with three pitches, insolently tossing three fast balls straight down the heart of the plate. Rudy got the other two outs just as quickly. The fans gave him another cheer as he walked from the mound.

The Tigers got a hit but no runs in the second, and Ramirez struck out the side again in the top of the third. In the bottom of the third Doug Davies, the Tiger second baseman, led off with a sharp single down the left-field line. Rudy was scheduled to bat next; he took off his jacket and chose a light bat. He had never faced an opposing pitcher before. He had never even taken batting practice in the time he had been with the Tigers. He walked to the plate and took his place awkwardly.

He swung at two and watched two before he connected. He hit the ball weakly, on the handle of the bat, and it dribbled slowly down the first-base line. He passed it on his way to first base, and he saw the Reds' pitcher running over to field it. Rudy knew that he'd be an easy out. *Wait*, he thought at the pitcher, *stop. Don't throw it.* The pitcher held the ball, staring ahead dazedly. It looked to the fans as if the pitcher couldn't decide whether to throw to first, or try for the lead runner going into second. Both runners were safe before Rudy released him.

Rudy took a short lead toward second base. He watched the coaches for signs. On the next pitch Davis broke for third. Rudy ran for second base. The Reds' catcher got the ball and jumped up. *Quiet*, thought Rudy. *Be still.* The catcher watched both Davies and Rudy slide in safely.

Eventually, the Tigers' leadoff man struck out. The next batter popped up in the infield. The third batter in the lineup, Chico Guerra, hit a long fly to right field, an easy enough chance for the fielder. But Rudy found the man's judgment and blocked it with his will. *Not yet*, he thought, *wait*. The outfielder hesitated, seeming as if he had lost the ball in the setting sun. By the time he ran after it, it was too late. The ball fell in and rolled to the wall. Two runs scored and Guerra lumbered into third base.

"Now we win!" yelled Rudy in Spanish. Guerra grinned and yelled back.

The inning ended with the Tigers ahead, three to nothing. Rudy was joking with Guerra as he walked back on the field. His manner was easy and supremely confident. He directed loud comments to the umpire and the opposing batters, but his Spanish went uninterpreted by his catcher. The top of the Reds' batting order was up again in the fourth inning, and Rudy treated them with total disregard, shaking off all of Guerra's signs except for the fast ball, straight down the middle. Stackpole, the leadoff batter, struck out again on four pitches. The second batter needed only three, and the third hitter used four. No one yet had swung at a pitch. Perhaps the fans were beginning to notice, because the cheer was more subdued as the Tigers came back to the bench. The Reds' manager was standing up in the dugout, angrily condemning his players, who went out to their positions with perplexed expressions.

The game proceeded, with the fans growing quieter and quieter in the stands, the Reds' manager getting louder in his damnations, the Tiger players becoming increasingly uneasy about the Reds' lack of interest. Rudy didn't care; he kept pitching them in to Guerra, and the Rockhill batters kept walking back to their dugout, shrugging their shoulders and saying nothing. Not a single Rockhill Red had reached first base. The ninth inning began in total silence. Rudy faced three pinch hitters and, of course, struck them out in order. He had not only pitched a no-hit game, not only pitched a *perfect* game, but he had struck out twenty-seven consecutive batters. Not once during the entire game did a Rockhill player even swing at one of his pitches.

A perfect game is one of the rarest of baseball phenomena. Perhaps only the unassisted triple play occurs less frequently. There should have been a massive crowd pouring out to congratulate Rudy. Players and fans should have mobbed him, carried him off the field, into the clubhouse. Beer should have been spilled over his head. Pictures should have been taken with Fred Marenholtz' arm around Rudy's neck. Instead, the infielders ran off the field as quickly as they could. They patted Rudy's back as they passed him on the way to the dugout. The fans got up and went home, not even applauding the Tiger victory.

Marenholtz was waiting in the dugout. "Take a shower and see me in my office," he said, indicating both Guerra and Ramirez. Then the manager shook his head and went down the tunnel to the dressing room.

Marenholtz was a tall, thin man with sharp, birdlike features. He was sitting at his desk, smoking a cigar. He smoked cigars only when he was very angry, very worried, or very happy. Tonight, while he waited for Guerra and the new kid, he was very worried. Baseball, aged and crippled, didn't need this kind of notoriety.

There were half a dozen local newspapermen trying to force their way into the clubhouse. He had given orders that there would be no interviews until he had a chance to talk to Ramirez himself. He had phone calls from newscasters, scouts, fans, gamblers, politicians, and relatives. There was a stack of congratulatory telegrams. There was a very worried telegram from the team's general manager, and a very worried telegram from the front office of the Tigers' major league affiliate.

There was a soft knock on the door. "Guerra?" Marenholtz called out.

"Sí."

"Come on in, but don't let anybody else come in with you except Ramirez."

Guerra opened the door and the two men entered. Behind them was a noisy, confused crowd of Tiger players. Marenholtz sighed; he would have to find out what happened, and then deal with his team. Then he had to come up with an explanation for the public.

Ramirez was grinning, evidently not sharing Marenholtz' and Guerra's apprehension. He said something

to Guerra. The catcher frowned and translated for
Marenholtz. "He say, don' he do a good job?"

"That's what *I* want to know!" said Marenholtz.
"What *did* he do? You know it looks a little strange
that not one guy on that team took swing number one."

Guerra looked very uncomfortable. "*Sí*, maybe he just
good."

Marenholtz grunted. "Chico, did he look *that* good?"
Guerra shook his head. Ramirez was still smiling.
Marenholtz stood up and paced behind his desk. "I
don't *mind* him pitching a perfect game," he said. "It's a
memorable achievement. But I think his effort would be
better appreciated if one of those batters had tried
hitting. At least *one*. I want you to tell me why they
didn't. If you can't, I want you to ask *him*."

Guerra shrugged and turned to Ramirez. They con-
versed for a few seconds, and then the catcher spoke
to Marenholtz. "He say he don' want them to."

Marenholtz slammed his fist on his desk. "That's going
to make a great headline in the *Sporting News*. Look,
if somehow he paid off the Reds to throw the game, even
they wouldn't be so stupid as to do it that way." He
paused, catching his breath, trying to control his exas-
peration. "All right, I'll give him a chance. Maybe he *is*
the greatest pitcher the world has ever known. Though
I doubt it." He reached for his phone and dialed a
number. "Hello, Thompson? Look, I need a favor from
you. Have you turned off the field lights yet? OK, leave
'em on for a while, all right? I don't care. I'll talk to Mr.
Kaemmer in the morning. And hang around for another
half hour, OK? Well, screw the union. We're having a
little crisis here. Yeah, Ramirez. Understand? Thanks,

Thompson." Marenholtz hung up and nodded to Guerra. "You and your battery mate here are going to get some extra practice. Tell him I want to hit some off him, right now. Don't bother getting dressed again. Just put on your mask and get out on the field." Guerra nodded unhappily and led Rudy away.

The stadium was deserted. Marenholtz walked through the dugout and onto the field. He felt strangely alone, cold and worried; the lights made odd, vague shadows that had never bothered him before. He went to the batter's box. The white lines had been all but erased during the course of the game. He leaned on the bat that he had brought with him and waited for the two men.

Guerra came out first, wearing his chest protector and carrying his mask and mitt. Behind him walked Ramirez, silently, without his usual grin. He was dressed in street clothes, with his baseball spikes instead of dress shoes. Rudy took his place on the mound. He tossed a ball from his hand to his glove. Guerra positioned himself and Marenholtz waved to Rudy. No one had said a word.

Rudy wound up and pitched, a medium fast ball down the middle. Marenholtz swung and hit a low line drive down the right-field line that bounced once and went into the stands. Rudy threw another and Marenholtz hit it far into right center field. The next three pitches he sent to distant, shadowed parts of the ball park. Marenholtz stepped back for a moment. "He was throwing harder during the game, wasn't he?" he asked.

"I think so," said Guerra.

"Tell him to pitch me as hard as he did then. And throw some good curves, too." Guerra translated, and Ramirez nodded. He leaned back and pitched. Marenholtz swung, connected, and watched the ball sail in a huge arc, to land in the seats three hundred and fifty feet away in right field.

Rudy turned to watch the ball. He said nothing. Marenholtz tossed him another from a box on the ground. "I want a curve, now," he said.

The pitch came, breaking lazily on the outside part of the plate. Marenholtz timed it well and sent it on a clothesline into center field, not two feet over Ramirez' head. "All right," said the manager, "tell him to come here." Guerra waved, and Rudy trotted to join them. "One thing," said Marenholtz sourly. "I want him to explain why the Reds didn't hit him like that."

"I wanna know, too," said Guerra. He spoke with Ramirez, at last turning back to Marenholtz with a bewildered expression. "He say he don' wan' *them* to hit. He say you wan' hit, he *let* you hit."

"Oh, hell," said Marenholtz. "I'm not stupid."

Rudy looked confused. He said something to Guerra. "He say he don' know why you wan' hit *now*, but he do what you say."

The manager turned away in anger. He spit toward the dugout, thinking. He turned back to Guerra. "We got a couple of balls left," he said. "I want him to pitch me just like he did to the Reds, understand? I don't want him to *let* me hit. Have him try to weave his magic spell on me, too."

Rudy took a ball and went back to the mound. Marenholtz stood up to the plate, waving the bat over his shoulder in a slow circle. Ramirez wound up, kicked, and threw. His fastest pitch, cutting the heart of the plate.

Quiet, thought Rudy, working to restrain his manager's furious mind. *Easy, now. Don't swing. Quiet.*

Marenholtz' mind was suddenly peaceful, composed, thoughtless. The pitch cracked into Guerra's mitt. The manager hadn't swung at it.

Rudy threw ten more pitches, and Marenholtz didn't offer at any of them. Finally he raised his hand. Rudy left the mound again. Marenholtz stood waiting, shaking his head. "Why didn't I swing? Those pitches weren't any harder than the others," Marenholtz said.

"He just say he don' want you to swing. In his head he tell you. Then you don' swing. He say it's easy."

"I don't believe it," said the manager nervously. "Yeah, OK, he can do it. He *did* do it. I don't like it." Guerra shook his head. The three stood on the empty field for several seconds in uneasy silence. "Can he do that with anybody?" asked Marenholtz.

"He say, *sí.*"

"Can he do it any time? *Every* time?"

"He say, *sí.*"

"We're in trouble, Chico." Guerra looked into Marenholtz' frightened face and nodded slowly. "I don't mean just us. I mean *baseball*. This kid can throw a perfect game, every time. What do you think'll happen if he makes it to the majors? The game'll be dead. Poor kid. He scares me. Those people in the stands aren't going to like it any better."

"What you gonna do, Mr. Marenholtz?" asked Guerra.

"I don't know, Chico. It's going to be hard keeping a

bunch of perfect games secret. Especially when none of the hitters ever takes the bat off his shoulder."

The following Thursday the Tigers had a night game at home against the Kings. Rudy came prepared to be the starting pitcher, after three days' rest. But when Marenholtz announced the starting lineup, he had the Tigers' long relief man on the mound. Rudy was disappointed, and complained to Guerra. The catcher told him that Marenholtz was probably saving him for the next night, when the Kings' ace left-hander was scheduled to pitch.

On Friday Ramirez was passed over again. He sat in the dugout, sweating in his warm-up jacket, irritated at the manager. Guerra told him to have patience. Rudy couldn't understand why Marenholtz wouldn't pitch him, after the great game Ramirez had thrown in his first chance. Guerra just shrugged and told Rudy to study the hitters.

Rudy didn't play Saturday, or in either of the Sunday double-header's games. He didn't know that the newspapermen were as mystified as he. Marenholtz made up excuses, saying that Rudy had pulled a back muscle in practice. The manager refused to make any comments about Ramirez' strange perfect game, and as the days passed the clamor died down.

The next week Rudy spent on the bench, becoming angrier and more frustrated. He confronted Marenholtz several times, with Guerra as unwilling interpreter, and each time the manager just said that he didn't feel that Ramirez was "ready." The season was coming to its close, with only six games left, and Rudy was determined to play. As the games came and went, however, it became obvious that he wasn't going to get the chance.

On the day of the last game, Marenholtz announced that Irv Tappan, his number-one right-hander, would start. Rudy stormed out of the dugout in a rage. He went back to the locker room and started to change clothes. Marenholtz signaled to Guerra, and they followed Ramirez.

"All right, Ramirez, what're you doing?" asked the manager.

"He say he goin' home," said Guerra, translating Rudy's shouted reply.

"If he leaves before the game is over, he's liable to be fined. Does he know that?"

"He say he don' care."

"Tell him he's acting like a kid," said Marenholtz, feeling relieved.

"He say you can go to hell."

Marenholtz took a deep breath. "OK, Chico. Tell him we've enjoyed knowing him, and respect his talent, and would like to invite him to try out for the team again next spring."

"He say go to hell."

"He's going home?" asked Marenholtz.

"He say you 'mericanos jealous, and waste his time. He say he can do other things."

"Well, tell him we're sorry, and wish him luck."

"He say go to hell. He say you don' know your *ano* from a hole in the groun'."

Marenholtz smiled coldly. "Chico, I want you to do me a favor. Do yourself a favor, too; there's enough here for the two of us. You let him finish clearing out of here, and you go with him. I don't know where he's going this time of day. Probably back to the hotel where he stays. Keep with him. Talk to him. Don't let him get away, don't let him get drunk, don't let him talk to anybody else."

Guerra shrugged and nodded. Ramirez was turning to leave the clubhouse. Marenholtz grabbed Guerra's arm and pushed him toward the furious boy. "Go on," said the manager, "keep him in sight. I'll call the hotel in about three or four hours. We got a good thing here, Chico, my boy." The catcher frowned and hurried after Rudy.

Marenholtz sighed; he walked across the dressing room, stopping by his office. He opened the door and stared into the darkened room for a few seconds. He wanted desperately to sit at his desk and write the letters and make the phone calls, but he still had a game to play. The job seemed so empty to him now. He *knew* this would be the last regular game he'd see in the minor leagues. Next spring he and Ramirez would be shocking them all at the Florida training camps. Next summer he and Ramirez would own the world of major league baseball.

First, though, there was still the game with the Bears. Marenholtz closed the door to the office and locked it. Then he went up the tunnel to the field. All that he could think of was going back to the Big Time.

After the game, Fred Marenholtz hurried to his office. The other players grabbed at him, swatting at his back to congratulate him on the end of the season. The Tigers were celebrating in the clubhouse. Cans of beer were popping open, and sandwiches had been supplied by the front office. The manager ignored them all. He locked the door to the office behind him. He called Ramirez' hotel and asked for his room.

Guerra answered, and reported that Ramirez was there, taking a nap. The catcher was instructed to tell Rudy that together they were all going to win their way to the major leagues. Guerra was doubtful, but Marenholtz wouldn't listen to the catcher's puzzled questions. The manager hung up. He pulled out a battered address book from his desk drawer, and found the telephone number of an old friend, a contract lawyer in St. Louis. He called the number, tapping a pencil nervously on the desk top while the phone rang.

"Hello, Marty?" he said when the call was finally answered.

"Yes. Who's this calling, please?"

"Hi. You won't remember me, but this is Fred Marenholtz."

"Freddie! How are you? Lord, it's been fifteen years. Are you in town?"

Marenholtz smiled. Things were going to be all right. They chatted for a few minutes, and then Marenholtz told his old friend that he was calling on business.

"Sure, Freddie," said the lawyer. "For Frantic Fred Marenholtz, anything. Is it legal?" Marenholtz laughed.

The photographs on the office wall looked painfully old to Marenholtz. They were of an era too long dead, filled with people who themselves had long since passed away. Baseball itself had withered, had lost the lifeblood of interest that had infused the millions of fans each spring. It had been too many years since Fred Marenholtz had claimed his share of glory. He had never been treated to his part of the financial rewards of baseball, and after his brief major league career he felt it was time to make his bid.

Marenholtz instructed the lawyer in detail. Old contracts were to be broken, new ones drawn up. The lawyer wrote himself in for five percent as payment. The manager hung up the phone again. He slammed his desk drawer closed in sheer exuberance. Then he got up and left his office. He had to thank his players for their cooperation during the past season.

"Tell him he's not going to get anything but investigated if he doesn't go with us." It was late now, past midnight. Ramirez' tiny hotel room was stifling. Rudy rested on the bed. Guerra sat in a chair by the single window. Marenholtz paced around, his coat thrown on the bed, his shirt soaked with perspiration.

"He say he don' like the way you run the club. He don' think you run him better," said Guerra wearily.

"All right. Explain to him that we're not going to cost him anything. The only way *we* can make any money is by making sure *he* does OK. We'll take a percentage of what he makes. That's his insurance."

"He wan' know why you wan' him now, you wouldn' play him before."

"Because he's a damn fool, is why! Doesn't he know what would happen if he pitched his kind of game, week after week?"

"He think he make a lot of money."

Marenholtz stopped pacing and stared. "Stupid

Spanish idiot!" he said. Guerra, from a farming village in
Panama, glared resentfully. "I'm sorry, Chico. Explain it
to him." The catcher went to the edge of the bed and sat
down. He talked with Rudy for a long while, then
turned back to the manager.

"OK, Mr. Marenholtz. He didn' think anybody
noticed."

"Fine," said Marenholtz, taking Guerra's vacated chair.
"Now let's talk. Chico, what were you planning to do
this winter?"

Guerra looked puzzled again. "I don't know. Go
home."

Marenholtz smiled briefly and shook his head. "No.
You're coming with me. We're taking young Mr.
Ramirez here and turn him into a pitcher. If not that,
at least into an intelligent thrower. We got a job, my
friend."

They had six months, and they could have used more.
They worked hard, giving Rudy little time to relax. He
spent weeks just throwing baseballs through a circle of
wire on a stand. Guerra and Marenholtz helped him
learn the most efficient way to pitch, so that he wouldn't
tire after half a game; he studied films of his motions, to
see where they might be improved, to fool the hitters
and conserve his own energy. Guerra coached him on all
the fundamentals: fielding his position, developing a
deceptive throw to first base, making certain that his
windup was the same for every different pitch.

After a couple of months Ramirez' control was sharp
enough to put a ball into Guerra's mitt wherever the
catcher might ask. Marenholtz watched with growing
excitement—they were going to bring it off. Rudy was as

good as any mediocre pitcher in the majors. Marenholtz was teaching him to save his special talent for the tight situations, the emergencies where less attention would be focused on the pitcher. Rudy was made to realize that he had eight skilled teammates behind him; if he threw the ball where the catcher wanted it, the danger of long hits was minimized. A succession of pop-ups and weak grounders would look infinitely better than twenty-seven passive strikeouts.

Before the spring training session began, Rudy had developed a much better curve that he could throw with reasonable control, a passable change-up, a poor slider, and a slightly off-speed fast ball. He relied on Guerra and Marenholtz for instructions, and they schooled him in all the possible situations until he was fed up.

"Freddie Marenholtz! Damn, you look like you could still get out there and play nine hard ones yourself. Got that phenom of yours?"

"Yeah, you want him to get dressed?" Marenholtz stood by a batting cage in the training camp of the Nashville Cats, a team welcomed into the American League during the expansion draft three years previously. The Florida sun was already fierce enough in March to make Marenholtz uncomfortable, and he shielded his eyes with one hand as he talked to Jim Billy Westfahl, the Cats' manager.

"All right," said Westfahl. "You said you brought this kid Ramirez and a catcher, right? What's his name?"

"Guerra. Only guy Ramirez ever pitched to."

"Yeah, well, you know we got two good catchers in

Portobenez and Staefler. If Guerra's going to stick, he's going to have to beat them out."

Marenholtz frowned. Guerra was *not* going to beat them out of their jobs. But he had to keep the man around, both because he could soothe Ramirez' irrational temper and because Guerra presented a da⁻ıger to the plan. But the aging catcher might have to get used to watching the games from the boxes. He collected three and a half percent of Rudy's income, and Marenholtz couldn't see that Guerra had reason to complain.

Rudy came out of the locker room and walked to the batting cage. Guerra followed, looking uneasy among the major league talents. Ramirez turned to Westfahl and said something in Spanish. Guerra translated. "He say he wan' show you what he can do."

"OK, I'm game. *Somebody's* going to have to replace McAnion. It may as well be your kid. Let's see what he looks like."

Rudy pitched to Guerra, and Westfahl made a few noncommittal remarks. Later in the day Rudy faced some of the Cats' regulars, and the B squad of rookies. He held some of them back, pitched to some of them, and looked no less sharp than any of the other regular pitchers after a winter's inactivity. In the next few weeks Marenholtz and Guerra guided Rudy well, letting him use his invisible talent sparingly, without attracting undue notice, and Ramirez seemed sure to go north with the team when the season began. Guerra didn't have the same luck. A week before spring training came to an end he was optioned to the Cats' Double A farm club. Guerra pretended to be upset, and refused to report.

By this time Marenholtz had promoted a large amount of money. The newly appointed president of RR Star Enterprises had spent the spring signing contracts while his protégé worked to impress the public. Permissions and royalty fees were deposited from trading card companies, clothing manufacturers, grooming product endorsements (Rudy was hired to look into a camera and say, "I like it. It makes my hair neat without looking greasy." He was finally coached to say, "I like it," and the rest of the line was given to a sexy female model), fruit juice advertisements, and sporting goods dealers.

The regular season began at home for the Cats. Rudy Ramirez was scheduled to pitch the third game. Rudy felt little excitement before the game; what he did feel was in no way different in kind or quantity from his nervousness before his first appearance with the Cordele Tigers. The slightly hostile major league crowd didn't awe him: he was prepared to awe the four thousand spectators who had come to watch the unknown rookie.

Fred Marenholtz had briefed Rudy thoroughly; before the game they had decided that an impressive but nonetheless credible effort would be a four- or five-hit shutout. For an added touch of realism, Rudy might get tired in the eighth inning, and leave for a relief pitcher. Marenholtz and Guerra sat in field boxes along the first-base side, near the dugout. Ramirez could hear their shouts from the mound. He waved to them as he took his place before the National Anthem was sung.

Rudy's pitches were not particularly overpowering. His fast ball was eminently hittable; only the experience of the Cats' catcher prevented it from sailing time after time over the short-left-field fence. Ramirez' weeks of practice saved him: his pitches crossed the plate just above the batter's knees, or handcuffed him close around the fists, or nicked the outside edge of the plate. Rudy's curve was just good enough to keep the hitters guessing. The first batter hit a sharp ground ball to short, fielded easily for the first out. The second batter lofted a fly to right field for the second out. Rudy threw three pitches to the third batter, and then threw his first mistake, a fast ball belt-high, down the middle. Rudy knew what would happen—a healthy swing, and then a quick one-run lead for the White Sox. Urgently, desperately, he sought the batter's will and grasped it in time. The man stood stupidly, staring at the most perfect pitch he would see in a long while. It went by for a called strike three, and Rudy had his first official major league strikeout.

Marenholtz stood and applauded when Rudy trotted back to the dugout. Guerra shouted something in Spanish. Ramirez' teammates slapped his back, and he smiled and nodded and took his place on the bench. He allowed a double down the line in the second inning, set the White Sox down in order in the third and fourth, gave up a single and a walk in the fifth, a single in the sixth, no hits in the seventh, two singles in the eighth, and two to the first two batters in the ninth. Rudy had pitched wisely, combining his inferior skill with judicious use of his mental talent. Sometimes he held back a batter for just a fraction of a second, so that the hitter would swing late. Other times he would prevent a batter from running for a moment, to insure his being thrown out at first. He caused the opposition's defense to commit errors so that the Cats could score the runs to guarantee victory.

The manager of the Cats came out to the mound to talk with Ramirez in the ninth. Carmen Velillo, the Cats' third baseman, joined the conference to translate for Rudy. Ramirez insisted that he was strong enough to finish, but the manager brought in a relief pitcher. Rudy received a loud cheer from the fans as he went off the field. He didn't watch the rest of the game, but went straight to the showers. The Cats' new man put down the rally, and Ramirez had a shutout victory. After Rudy and Velillo had answered the excited questions of the newsmen, Marenholtz and Guerra met him for a celebration.

Marenholtz held interviews with reporters from national magazines or local weeklies. Coverage of Ramirez' remarkable success grew more detailed; as the season progressed, Rudy saw his picture on the front of such varied periodicals as *Sports Illustrated* and *Esquire*. By June Rudy had won eleven games and lost none. His picture appeared on the cover of *Time*. A small article in *Playboy* announced that he was the greatest natural talent since Grover Cleveland Alexander. He appeared briefly on late-night television programs. He was hired to attend supermarket openings in the Nashville area. He loved winning ball games, and Marenholtz, too, gloried in returning a success to the major leagues that had treated him so shabbily in his youth.

The evening before Ramirez was to start his twelfth ball game, he was having dinner with Marenholtz and Guerra. The older man was talking about his own short playing career, and how baseball had deteriorated since then. Guerra nodded and said little. Ramirez stared quietly at his plate, toying with his food and not eating. Suddenly he spoke up, interrupting Marenholtz' flow of memories. He spoke in rapid Spanish; Marenholtz gaped in surprise. "What's he saying?" he asked.

Guerra coughed nervously. "He wan' know why he need us," he said. "He say he do pretty good by himself."

Marenholtz put his cigar down and stared angrily at Ramirez. "I was wondering how long it would take him to think he could cut us out. You can tell him that if it hadn't been for us he'd either be in trouble or in Venezuela. You can tell him that if it hadn't been for us he wouldn't have that solid bank account and his poor gray mama wouldn't have the only color television south of the border. And if that doesn't work, tell him maybe he *doesn't* need us, but he signed the contracts."

Guerra said a few words, and Rudy answered. "What's he say now?" asked Marenholtz.

"Nothing," said Guerra, staring down at his own plate. "He jus' say he thank you, but he wan' do it by himself."

"Oh, hell. Tell him to forget that and pitch a good game tomorrow. *I'll* do the worrying. That's what I'm for."

"He say he do that. He say he pitch you a good game."

"Well, thank you, Tom, and good afternoon, baseball fans everywhere. In just a few moments we'll bring you live coverage of the third contest of this weekend series, a game between the Nashville Cats, leaders in the American League Midlands Division, and the Denver Athletics. It looks to be a pitchers' duel today, with young Rudy Ramirez, Nashville's astonishing rookie, going against the A's veteran right-hander, Morgan Stepitz."

"Right, Chuck, and I think a lot of the spectators in the park today have come to see whether Ramirez can keep his streak alive. He's won eleven, now, and he hasn't been beaten so far in his professional career. Each game must be more of an ordeal than the last for the youngster. The strain will be starting to take its toll."

"Nevertheless, Tom, I have to admit that it's been a very long time since I've seen anyone with the poise of that young man. He hasn't let his success make him overconfident, which for him is now the greatest danger. I'm sure that defeat, when it comes, will be a hard blow, but I'm just as certain that Rudy Ramirez will recover and go on to have a truly amazing season."

"A lot of fans have written in to ask what the record is for most consecutive games won. Well, Ramirez has quite a way to go. The major league record is nineteen, set in 1912 by Rube Marquard. But even if Ramirez doesn't go on to break that one, he's still got the start on a great season. He's leading both leagues with an Earned Run Average of 1.54, and has an excellent shot at thirty wins—"

"All right, let's go down to the field, where we'll have the singing of the National Anthem."

After the spectators cheered and settled back into their seats, after the Cats' catcher whipped the ball down to second base, and after the infielders tossed it around and, finally, back to the pitcher, Rudy looked around at the stadium. The Nashville park was new, built five years ago in hopes of attracting a major league franchise. It was huge, well-designed, and, generally, filled with noisy fans. The sudden success of the usually hapless Cats was easily traced: Rudy Ramirez. He was to pitch again today, and his enthusiastic rooters crowded the spacious park. Bed sheet banners hung over railings, wishing him luck and proclaiming Ramirez to be the best-loved individual on the continent. Rudy, still innocent of English, did not know what they said.

He could see Marenholtz and Guerra sitting behind the dugout. They saw him glance in their direction and stood, waving their arms. Rudy touched the visor of his cap in salute. Then he turned to face the first of the Athletics' hitters.

"OK, the first batter for the A's is the second baseman, number 12, Jerry Kleiner. Kleiner's batting .262 this season. He's a switch-hitter, and he's batting right-handed against the southpaw, Ramirez.

"Ramirez takes his sign from Staefler, winds up, and delivers. Kleiner takes the pitch for a called strike one. Ramirez has faced the A's only once before this season, shutting them out on four hits.

"Kleiner steps out to glance down at the third-base coach for the signal. He steps back in. Ramirez goes into his motion. Kleiner lets it go by again. No balls and two strikes."

"Ramirez is really piping them in today, Tom."

"That's right, Chuck. I noticed during his warm-ups that his fast ball seemed to be moving exceptionally well.

It will tend to tail in toward a right-handed batter. Here comes the pitch—strike three! Kleiner goes down looking."

"Before the game we talked with Cats' catcher Bo Staefler, who told us that Ramirez' slider is improving as the season gets older. That can only be bad news for the hitters in the American League. It may be a while before they can solve his style."

"Stepping in now is the A's right fielder, number 24, Ricky Gonzalvo. Gonzalvo's having trouble with his old knee injury this year, and his average is down to .244. He crowds the plate a little on Ramirez. The first pitch is inside, knocking Gonzalvo down. Ball one.

"Ramirez gets the ball back, leans forward for his sign. And the pitch . . . in there for a called strike. The count is even at one and one."

"He seems to have excellent control today, wouldn't you say, Tom?"

"Exactly. Manager Westfahl of the Cats suggested last week that the pinpoint accuracy of his control is sometimes enough to rattle a batter into becoming an easy out."

"There must be *some* explanation, even if it's magic."

"Ramirez deals another breaking pitch, in there for a called strike two. I wouldn't say it's all magic, Chuck. It looked to me as though Gonzalvo was crossed up on that one, obviously expecting the fast ball again."

"Staefler gives him the sign. Ramirez nods, and throws. Fast ball, caught Gonzalvo napping. Called strike three; two away now in the top of the first.

"Batting in the number three position is the big first baseman, Howie Bass. Bass' brother, Eddie, who plays for the Orioles, has the only home run hit off Ramirez this season. Here comes Ramirez' pitch . . . Bass takes it for strike one."

"It seems to me that the batters are starting out behind Ramirez, a little overcautious. That's the effect that a winning streak like his can have. Ramirez has the benefit of a psychological edge working for him, as well as his great pitching."

"Right, Tom. That pitch while you were talking was a called strike two, a good slider that seemed to have Bass completely baffled."

"Staefler gives the sign, but Ramirez shakes his head. Ramirez shakes off another sign. Now he nods, goes into his windup, and throws. A fast ball, straight down the middle, strike three. Bass turns to argue with the umpire, but that'll do him no good. Three up and three down for the A's, no runs, no hits, nothing across."

The Cats' fans jumped to their feet, but Fred Marenholtz listened angrily to their applause. He caught Rudy's eye just as the pitcher was about to enter the dugout. Before Marenholtz could say anything, Rudy grinned and disappeared inside. Marenholtz was worried that the sophisticated major league audience would be even less likely to accept the spectacle of batter after batter going down without swinging at Ramirez' pitches. The older man turned to Guerra. "What's he trying to do?" he asked.

Guerra shook his head. "I don' know. Maybe he wan' strike out some."

"Maybe," said Marenholtz dubiously, "but I didn't think he'd be that dumb."

The Cats got a runner to second base in their part of

the first inning, but he died there when the cleanup hitter sent a line drive over the head of the A's first baseman, who leaped high to save a run. Rudy walked out to the mound confidently, and threw his warm-ups.

"All right," said Marenholtz, "let's see him stop that nonsense now. This game's being televised all over the country." He watched Ramirez go into his motion. The first pitch was a curve that apparently didn't break; a slow pitch coming toward the plate as fat as a basketball. The A's batter watched it for a called strike. Marenholtz swore softly.

Rudy threw two more pitches, each of them over the plate for strikes. The hitter never moved his bat. Marenholtz' face was turning red with anger. Rudy struck out the next batter in three pitches. Guerra coughed nervously and said something in Spanish. Already the fans around them were remarking on how strange it was to see the A's being called out on strikes without making an effort to guard the plate. The A's sixth batter took his place in the batter's box, and three pitches later he, too, walked back to the bench, a bewildered expression on his face.

Marenholtz stood and hollered to Ramirez. "What the hell you doing?" he said, forgetting that the pitcher couldn't understand him. Rudy walked nonchalantly to the dugout, taking no notice of Marenholtz.

Guerra rose and edged past Marenholtz to the aisle. "You going for a couple of beers?" asked Marenholtz. "No," said Guerra. "I think I just *goin'*."

"Well, Tom, it's the top of the third, score tied at nothing to nothing. I want to say that we're getting that pitchers' battle we promised. We're witnessing one heck of a good ball game so far. The Cats have had only one hit, and rookie Rudy Ramirez hasn't let an Athletic reach first base."

"There's an old baseball superstition about jinxing a pitcher in a situation like this, but I might mention that Ramirez has struck out the first six men to face him. The record for consecutive strikeouts is eleven, held by Gaylord Perry of the old Cleveland Indians. If I remember correctly, that mark was set the last year the Indians played in Cleveland, before their move to New Orleans."

"This sort of game isn't a new thing for Ramirez, either, Tom. His blurb in the Cats' pressbook mentions that in his one start in the minor leagues, he threw a perfect game and set a Triangle League record for most strikeouts in a nine-inning game."

"OK, Chuck. Ramirez has finished his warm-ups here in the top of the third. He'll face the bottom of the A's order. Batting in the seventh position is the catcher, number 16, Tolly Knecht. Knecht's been in a long slump, but he's always been something of a spoiler. He'd love to break out of it with a hit against Ramirez here. Here's the pitch . . . Knecht was taking all the way, a called strike one."

"Maybe the folks at home would like to see Ramirez' form here on the slow-motion replay. You can see how the extra-high kick tends to hide the ball from the batter until the very last moment. He's getting the full force of his body behind the pitch, throwing from the shoulder with a last, powerful snap of the wrist. He ends up here perfectly balanced for a sudden defensive move. From the plate the white ball must be disguised by the uniform. A marvelous athlete and a terrific competitor."

"Right, Chuck. That last pitch was a good breaking ball; Knecht watched it for strike two. I think one of the reasons the hitters seem to be so confused is the excellent arsenal of pitches that Ramirez has. He throws his fast ball intelligently, saving it for the tight spots. He throws an overhand curve and a sidearm curve, each at two different speeds. His slider is showing up more and more as his confidence increases."

"Ramirez nods to Staefler, the catcher. He winds up, and throws. Strike three! That's seven, now. Knecht throws his bat away in frustration. The fans aren't too happy, either. Even the Cats' loyal crowd is beginning to boo. I don't think I've ever seen a team as completely stymied as the A's are today."

"I tell you, I almost wish I could go down there myself. Some of Ramirez' pitches look just too good. It makes me want to grab a bat and take a poke at one. His slow curves seem to hang there, inviting a good healthy cut. But, of course, from our vantage point we can't see what the batters are seeing. Ramirez must have tremendous stuff today. Not one Athletic hitter has taken a swing at his pitches."

When the eighth Athletic batter struck out, the fans stood and jeered. Marenholtz felt his stomach tightening. His mouth was dry and his ears buzzed. After the ninth batter fanned, staring uninterestedly at a mild, belt-high pitch, the stadium was filled with boos. Marenholtz couldn't be sure that they were all directed at the unlucky hitters.

Maybe I ought to hurry after Guerra, thought

Marenholtz. *Maybe it's time to talk about that bowling alley deal again. This game is rotten at its roots already. It's not like when I was out there. We cared. The fans cared. Now they got guys like Grobert playing, they're nearly gangsters. Sometimes the games look like they're produced from a script. And Ramirez is going to topple it all. The kid's special, but that won't save us. Good God, I feel sorry for him. He can't see it coming. He won't see it coming. He's out there having a ball. And he's going to make the loudest boom when it all falls down. Then what's he going to do? What's he going to do?*

Rudy walked jauntily off the field. The spectators around Marenholtz screamed at him. Rudy only smiled. He waved to Marenholtz, and pointed to Guerra's empty seat. Marenholtz shrugged. Ramirez ducked into the dugout, leaving Marenholtz to fret in the stands.

After the Cats were retired in the third, Rudy went out to pitch his half of the fourth. A policeman called his name, and Rudy turned. The officer stood in the boxes, at the edge of the dugout, stationed to prevent overeager fans from storming the playing field. He held his hand out to Rudy and spoke to him in English. Rudy shook his head, not understanding. He took the papers from the policeman and studied them for a moment. They were contracts that he had signed with Marenholtz. They were torn in half. Ramirez grinned; he looked up toward Marenholtz' seat behind the dugout. The man had followed Guerra, had left the stadium before he could be implicated in the tarnished proceedings.

For the first time since he had come to the United

States, Rudy Ramirez felt free. He handed the contracts back to the mystified police officer and walked to the mound. He took a few warm-ups and waited for Kleiner, the A's leadoff batter. Ramirez took his sign and pitched. Kleiner swung and hit a shot past the mound. Rudy entered Kleiner's mind and kept him motionless beside the plate for a part of a second. The Cats' shortstop went far to his left, grabbed the ball and threw on the dead run; the runner was out by a full step. There were mixed groans and cheers from the spectators, but Rudy didn't hear. He was watching Gonzalvo take his place in the batter's box. Maybe Rudy would let him get a hit.

basketball

Basketball certainly ranks as one of the fastest-growing sports in the world. It has spread from its birthplace in the United States and crossed the Atlantic to Western and Eastern Europe—and beyond. Millions of fans sat tensely on the edge of their seats as they watched the Soviet Union defeat the United States (in a still-controversial finale) in the last second of the final game of the 1972 Olympics.

Basketball is the only major sport which was created and developed in the United States. Its founder was a

physical education instructor in Springfield, Massachu-
setts, named James A. Naismith. Anyone who has spent
time in New England can tell you how severe the
winters there can be. The school and college systems had
long been concerned with the lack of team sports which
could be played indoors during the winter months. Pro-
fessor Naismith had this factor well in mind when he
conceived and developed the game of basketball. The
name of the game derives from the use of fruit baskets
which served as targets for the players to shoot at.

As was the case with the development of football,
basketball was played under different rules in different
places for many years. It was not until 1915 that a standard set of regulations came into common use. The game
was originally played by passing the ball from player to
player, since dribbling did not become popular until the
turn of the century. A major development in the style
of play occurred during the 1930s and 1940s, when
players like Hank Luisetti of Stanford introduced the
one-hand jump shot. Until that time, the stationary
two-hand set shot was dominant, and the new method
greatly speeded up the game and made it more popular.

Basketball was primarily a school and college sport
for most of its history, with several thousand colleges
and universities participating in conferences. Interest in
college basketball—as in college football—has been
heightened by the practice of ranking teams in the
opinion polls of coaches and reporters. The quest for
the "National Championship" and number-one status
has proved to be a strong motivation for players and for
coaches. The highlight of the college season is the
tournament, the major ones being the National Collegi-

ate Athletic Association (NCAA) and the National
Invitational (NIT).

Professional basketball has a much shorter history in
its organized form, although numerous individual teams
travel around the country playing local teams for money.
The pro game really came into its own after World
War II. The sport has been dominated since then by the
"big man," with players over seven feet no longer a
rarity. It has proved to be increasingly difficult to win
National or American Basketball Association titles without an outstanding big man like George Mikan, Bill
Russell, Wilt Chamberlain, or Kareem Abdul-Jabbar.

Professional and amateur leagues have developed in
other areas of the world, notably in Europe. International interest in basketball received a tremendous boost
from the appearances of the American-based Harlem
Globetrotters, an all-black team which combines excellent basketball ability with high comedy. They have
introduced this sport to millions of people the world over.

Goal Tending
e. michael blake

Basketball is a team sport. It requires hours of practice and drilling to acquire the timing necessary to produce the teamwork which is the hallmark of champions. It requires sacrifice of self for the good of the team—this means that individual players must pass off to teammates when they have the better shot, and place winning the game ahead of personal statistics and glory.

There have been teams throughout history which have had terrific personnel, but *great teams* are more than the sum of their individual parts. The great clubs, like the Boston Celtics and New York Knicks of the 1960s and 1970s, have meshed together as a unit, and while their members achieved outstanding individual statistics, they never did so at the expense of the total team effort. Other teams with excellent personnel have not attained the same success because their players tended to be individualists, concerned more with themselves than with the club.

A very few players have put themselves so far ahead of everything else that they have agreed to fix games so that their team would either lose or only win by a pre-arranged number of points. Game-fixing occurred during the early 1950s at the college level in the New York City area, and those found guilty were banned from basketball.

As this story indicates, although basketball may evolve into something quite different from today's game, the prerequisites for victory are unchanging: courage, determination, skill, and above all, *teamwork*.

Goal Tending

Number 25 leaned lightly against a sidewall, planting himself in five thousandths of a gravity. He held the ball one-handed, partway out from his body, but securely. Number 6 guarded him loosely, floating two meters away. This close to the wall, the defender had to tread air with his leg vanes to remain stationary. Twenty-five braced his right foot on the wall, faked the ball high-left, then straight out, then faked a whole move high-left—and, as 6 took the bait, zipped off a pass down-left diagonally. Six snapped back his arm vanes, reversing—too late. The ball crossed the ellipsoidal cavity, hit the wall with a crisp *bowk!* and barreled into 10's arms. Twenty-five righted himself from the reactions to his moves, flapping arms and pumping legs, air-swimming to the frontcourt action on the vanes of his uniform.

The uniform, seen by the observer beyond the clear wall of the playing volume, was red. The observer could be sure of this much, at least—red squad versus blue squad. Otherwise, he saw only a formless welter of anthropoid bodies—ethereally alien in the hologram monitor, savagely alien in the live action above him.

Knock it off, he told himself, *just pre-launch jitters.* His mood broken, he looked again at the scrimmage above, seeing it now as a sport.

Number 16 on the red squad—name? Gossage, was it? —flexed his arches, releasing grotesque flipperlike leg vanes. He clutched the ball close—as much to streamline himself as to assure possession—and drove under the focus ("under" from the observer's vantage). His teammates darted around him, moving well without the ball. Suddenly 16 saw a teammate sailing toward the back wall, ahead of her defender. Sixteen shot her a quick pass—she snared it, and slammed the ball into the very back of the ellipsoid. The ball bounced back through the focus, three and a half meters away. The scoreboard clanged.

I should know all their names, thought the observer; his own name was Ugo DiFazio, and he was General Manager of the team, the Vayu Centaurs.

"You're going to see an opening like that maybe once a night," the Coach barked into a microphone, "come on, get back to the mid-space patterns."

DiFazio watched the red and blue figures fan their arm and leg vanes and drift toward the center of the ellipsoid. He looked back to the Coach next to him at the table—and felt the jolt of a newly stiff neck. To make conversation, he asked, "Will the layover be any problem?"

"Not really," she returned, still looking at the hologram monitor, "at least, it'll affect everyone else the

same way. I'll hold a couple hours of conditioning and
agility workouts every day; even in full gravity, that'll
help."

DiFazio nodded. He'd lined up an axial-quarters common room for such workouts, as well as adjoining axial
accommodations, whirlpool baths, etc., etc. He was frequently surprised by the amount of weight he could
throw around, on the team's behalf. The same was
probably true of his counterparts on the seven other
teams—this sport had pull. The game of Foci would be
the foremost continuing public attraction/entertainment
for nearly half a million people cooped up in a colony
ship for two hundred years.

"Joy, tell me the truth," said DiFazio, "how would this
team stack up against a real powerhouse?"

Coach Joy Wegener chuckled. "No comparison. We'd
be laughed out of the Earth Orbital League. If you put
together an all-star team from this whole ship, you might
break even in one of the asteroid leagues, or make it out
of the Earth Orbital cellar."

"Are our fans likely to realize this?"

She shrugged—then barked again at the mike:
"Okkengoek, establish position! Stationary, *stationary!*"
In the monitor a tiny red figure vaned awkwardly, trying
to balance action and reaction. The Coach leaned back,
ran both hands through her long brown hair wearily.
"What'd you say? Oh. No, I don't think they'll know the
difference. These people are mostly grounders, aren't
they? New to space?"

"Yes, most of the homesites—"

"Homesites," she chuckled. The reaction to the laugh

lifted her gently from the chair. She let the minute gravity return her at its own slow pace; she seemed to savor the floating sensation. "Well, only a veteran spacer who knows his low gravity—and also happens to be an avid Foci fan—would see us for what we really are."

DiFazio bristled, but Wegener made no move to soften her words. She leaned forward to the monitor again, eyeing the tiny figures that flew through her patterns. And in the screen, she saw herself—in a conscious fantasy—blocking shots for Brazil, bulleting a perfect lead-pass for Israel, feeling the zero gravity make her big-boned body a thing of beauty and grace. Realization struck her: in four days, she would leave the solar system—the home roots, the major leagues, the countless fans—forever. *I should go out, take a last look—even go to a big-league game. I'll get tired enough of this place. I won't even live to see where we'll end up.*

But she knew, somehow, that she wouldn't take any last looks.

The ship had no name. It was the first of its kind, and cost overruns hinted that it might also be the last—so there was no need to call it anything but *the* ship. This got around the political problems involved in naming the first large-population ship ever to leave the solar system, a ship built and sponsored by many nations and interests—"*the* ship" could translate into any language, emphasis and all, even though English was the dominant language in space.

Construction had run twelve years, including internal preparation of the "homesites" built into the gargantuan vessel. Planning had started five years before that, and continued even now in offices, boardrooms, and courts of law. It was such an enormous venture that nobody was entirely sure where and when it had started. Perhaps it dated from the moment when the first interstellar mission had reached Alpha Centauri and sent back word that an earthlike planet awaited—one without a dominant species to conflict with human colonists.

Then it had begun to snowball. A feasibility study here, a new concept in design there. Suddenly the human beings who lived away from Earth—in orbital stations, on Luna, on and around Mars, in the asteroids —had a new neighbor: a structure that trailed Earth, in the same orbit around the sun, roughly one and a half million kilometers from the planet. At each close-approach of Luna, work teams ferried out new plans and materials. The bulk of metals and scale of engineering would have been unthinkable on Earth, or even on Luna —but in free fall, it was nothing more than staggeringly expensive. And the expense could be met, by various grants and by the sale of on-board "homesites" to would-be colonists. Resources were fed in from Mars and the asteroids. Shortcuts in free-fall construction were discovered on the job. These shortcuts would pay for themselves in the solar system only after *the* ship was long gone.

Finished, *the* ship was a cylinder eight kilometers long and four across. Eight fully-operating breeder reactors powered nothing but the drive engines; four more maintained the inside's needs. At takeoff, all of the people who had decided to live on this ship and send

their descendants to a new world—all 469,023 of them—
would huddle in small "axial" apartments toward the
middle of the ship. These apartments were built with
floors perpendicular to the axis of the ship-cylinder—so
that when *the* ship accelerated toward Alpha Centauri
at one gee, gravity would be normal in the apartments.
But the ship would only accelerate for one week—and
only reach two percent of the speed of light. Though
the original small-crew mission to Alpha Centauri had
been able to accelerate and decelerate most of the way—
pushing against relativistic contractions to a maximum
speed of nine-tenths light and reaching the new system
in less than seven years—*the* ship was too massive, too
nonrigid, to risk a sustained thrust.

At week's end, *the* ship would coast—leaving everyone
in free fall. Crewmen would then guide the residents to
their "homesites" on the inside rim of the cylinder—
built on nearly a hundred square kilometers of "land."
Here the curved wall of the cylinder would be reckoned
"down," when *the* ship fired new engines and began to
rotate along its axis. A full turn every ninety seconds
would ge: erate a centrifugal pull of one "gravity" at the
homesites.

But in the center of *the* ship—directly along the axis—
the rotational pull would be almost negligible. Here the
planners had housed important things—liquid Helium,
superheavy organic molecules, gyroscopic guidance
equipment.

And eight Foci-playing volumes.

Joy Wegener ambled down a residential street in the
ship-town of Vayu. Idly she watched her new neighbors

as they worried over their incoming truckloads of furniture and belongings. Here a woman badgered a crew member about the bolting-down procedure—she wanted to be *absolutely sure* about which way was down, and when there a man tried to count cartons while two small children shelled him with questions: "—can we hang-glide here, Papa? Are there real fish down at the beach? Will we ever get to space-walk?"

The Coach stopped to watch the kids. *Dutch or Belgian, from the sound of the accent. Both seem to like active games. Who knows, maybe they'll be in my starting lineup in twenty years or so.*

Twenty years, she thought again. *Two hundred years.*

She turned away, started down another street. Dredging her memory for specific regrets, something to attach to her prelaunch melancholy, she found nothing. There hadn't been much pain to endure, nor many promises unfulfilled. She'd never had children, but had never really wanted any; all of her relationships with men had been temporary, concluded in friendship and leaving just the right memories. No, her personal life didn't figure to be changed by her departure from most of the human race. *Still, it isn't something that allows you any second thoughts . . .*

The "town's" layout amused her. It looked like a bustling, thriving small city nestled in a fertile earthly valley, complete with hills on either side, hiding the upward curvature of the surface. A small river wound down from *the* ship's tail, through the center of town, and spilled at last into a beach-edged "sea." Manufactured clouds and optical tricks masked the actual boundaries—the fore and aft of *the* ship, the adjoining cities up the arc of the cylinder, the kilometer-high ceiling. All of the plants were real, green and healthy atop ten meters of topsoil—supported by a "bedrock" of ship-steel. Hidden drains would remove and store the water at launch time, when the present rotation was stopped.

It's all window-dressing, she thought, *an illusion to keep grounders from getting jittery. But—I like it, kind of. It's like what I remember of Saskatoon, when I was little . . .*

How will they keep everything from avalanching to the tail when we accelerate? she wondered. Then she remembered hearing about a sort of pseudo-stasis field that had just been developed—something to do with supercompressed air, ionic sprays, and standing waves broadcast in the air. *Whatever, it better not uproot my house.*

She had finished moving in two weeks earlier. The house was free, part of her contract with the team. The teams—already called the Centauran League—were in a unique position: employees of *the* ship's parent agency, but not crew members. *We're a public commodity,* she thought half ruefully, *but why should it be any different here?*

A neighborhood bulletin board caught her eye. Nearly all of the space was covered by a poster, which also overlapped at the bottom, leaving corners to flap in a programmed breeze. It read:

FOCI
Exhibition Game
Tonight

Vayu   Proxima
CENTAURS   *versus*   PANTHERS

*with an introduction
to the game and its rules*

1930 hours • Proxima Freefall Arena
Residents free • Visitors E 2.50

"An introduction to the game and its rules." Wegener suppressed a snob reaction. She had no call to act like an elitist; she hadn't made the decision to become a spacer. Her parents had taken her along into Canada's Earth orbital station when she was nine. And she'd originally studied to be a deep-vacuum stress engineer, until her passion for Foci outgrew the after-hours competition at the athletic club. Besides, she had been offered a good rookie contract when she was twenty. It would have taken her another two years of struggle and study to become an engineer—at lower pay.

Half a block ahead, a jogger loped down a cross street. "Hey, Phuon," called the Coach.

The jogger—black hair, brown skin, gray sweats—stopped, looked at her. "What's up, Coach?"

"What are you trying to do? We play *tonight*, you'll get a workout then." She approached him with a long, easy stride. "I don't want anyone too tensed up."

The jogger chuckled. The front of his jersey bore

black letters: INDONESIA. "Come on, Coach, I'm always tensed up." His English was heavily inflected, but understandable.

"I know. And if I gave you the chance, you'd foul out in the first half." *But I need a player like him,* she added mentally, *he's all hustle.*

Phuon Hamudi, backcourt scrambler, had spent two years in the Earth Orbital League—the Mecca of professional Foci. Indonesia, a recent expansion addition, had tried to buy respectability by importing journeyman players from other teams—other nations. This wasn't unusual; seldom were the parent nation's citizens a majority on any Earth Orbital Team. Wegener herself had never played for Canada. But Hamudi, fresh from a stiff qualifying exam in Djakarta, had turned down several offers to play pro soccer on Earth to take a job on his country's tight-budgeted new orbital station—and a tryout for its Foci team. He'd taken to the game surprisingly well, for someone new to free fall—improving in competition, making up for his lack of savvy with hustle and aggressiveness. He was improving enough, in fact, to become trade bait. When he'd learned that he was about to be dealt to EuroCom in a multiplayer swap, he'd quit—noisily. The team's small following earthside was outraged that Hamudi, a local hero, was being cast adrift. Indonesia had cancelled the trade, too late; Hamudi was already looking for a job out in the asteroid leagues. Then Joy Wegener, whom he remembered as a tough, canny, but aging starter for Israel, had contacted him about *the* ship.

He's still young, thought Wegener, walking alongside him, *he could've carved out quite a reputation for him-*

*self in the asteroids. Won't be long before the asteroids
achieve parity with Earth Orbital. Yet he'll spend his
prime here, and no matter how great he becomes, only a
few thousand people bound for a new sun will ever
know.*

The thought nagged her enough to make her ask:
"Not that I'm trying to hurt morale, but why *did* you
sign with us? I took the job because nobody else with
money would let me coach. A few, like Peugeot and
En-Yan, are past their primes and could have expected
salary cuts—and here, the competition will be less frantic
and they'll last longer. Kids like Okkengoek and
Carrasquez y Delon would have to spend a couple years
in the bushes, like Mars Orbital, before they could get a
chance at the big money. Then there's Jack Gossage,
who's been in so many fights with management that he
wound up blacklisted. But you?"

Hamudi, walking slowly back toward his house,
shrugged and half smiled. Always, something glowed in
his black eyes. "I guess this is part of it," he said, sweeping a hand out to the town of Vayu around him,
"creature comforts. The asteroids are still rather austere.
But here I get good pay, a house with a bit of room, and
a captive audience of fans. Which reminds me—is there
much interest in the game tonight?"

"Hard to say. They'll get a packed house, but the gate's
free."

"No, I mean from the news media. From Earth."

Wegener frowned. "Earth? Why?"

Hamudi grinned until he almost looked predatory. "I
heard something about this game being broadcast back to
Earth. Sort of as a novelty, something to tape with

special-interest sports, like water skiing and jai alai. It'd
be seen in Earth orbit, too. I could really show those
ingrates something!"

"You mean to tell me you're going to hot-dog it?"
Wegener snapped, "just as a last hurrah for your fans?
To make the Indonesian front office regret having
crossed you? Is this just a grudge match to you?"

"Hey, Coach, hold it," said Hamudi quickly, tonguing
lips nervously. "I wasn't going to get out of line—but it's
only an exhibition—"

This is what a coach has to do, thought Wegener
grimly, *even if she knows her team, and her league, play
low-grade ball. She still has to do what's best for the
team.* "I don't care what it is. You're not starting
tonight. And when I *do* put you in, you'd better stick to
the patterns and play teamwork—or I'll suspend you!"

Hamudi was speechless. His Coach turned and strode
away firmly.

"Charter citizens of Alpha Centauri—welcome to
Proxima Freefall Arena."

A partial cheer rose from the near-capacity crowd.
The "grounders" who had never been to a freefall arena
were having trouble adjusting. The seats were chair-
shaped, but tilted back so that the occupant was practi-
cally lying down. This was necessary, because the action
took place "above"—in the playing volume aligned to *the*
ship's axis. The occupants must also stay belted down—
too easy to jerk out of place, in one-hundredth gravity.
Ten meters above most seats was the clear wall of the
playing volume. At mid-court—the circle of seats around
the ellipse's minor axis—were the benches, scorer's con-

sole, and press box. Players and referees entered and left the volume along shinny-cables leading to hatches. Screened conduits at each end of the ellipse supplied ventilation. Except for these conduit-struts, nothing anchored the playing volume—so fans would have unobstructed views from nearly every seat in the 8700-capacity house.

"For the benefit of you new fans," the loudspeakers continued, "we'll now project a holographic introductory film in the playing volume." The volume glowed—animated bodies took form. They weaved through the motions described over the speakers. "Foci is a continuous-play goal-achievement game, like basketball, soccer, and the various forms of hockey. The variable factor among these games is goal tending—it is forbidden in basketball, the highest-scoring of all team games, but permitted in soccer and hockey, together the lowest-scoring. Goal tending is provisionally permitted in Foci, in the sense that a team may play zone defense and station a player near the goal. However, the convergence of electric eyes that pinpoint the goals—one at each focus of the ellipsoid—" (now each focus lit up brighter red than usual) "must not be touched by a defender, or a goal will be scored regardless of whether a shot is on the way. If, however, an opponent pushes a defender into the focus, a foul away from the ball is called against the opponents, and the ball turned over to the other team. This will be covered more fully later, when fouls are discussed."

Joy Wegener surged up a lower hatchway to her team's bench, where DiFazio waited. The Coach snapped, "All right, what is this? I've got a team down there in the locker room that I'm *trying* to get 'up' for an exhibition game in a throwaway league,. and you want me to come up here. Why?"

DiFazio was too surprised—and too tense—to get angry. He felt very much the way he looked, like a short, balding administrator who didn't really know very much about this game. "They want to interview you on the TV hookup to Earth. Your coaching debut, stuff like that."

Wegener stopped short. *Okay, Coach, what do you do?* Incongruously, she wondered if she looked all right. Seldom did she bother about personal vanity, usually content with her plain, semiattractive features.

In her silence, the speakers droned on: "—the most interesting aspect of this game is the very nature of the playing volume. In an ellipse, any straight line drawn through one focus and reflected ideally off the surface of the ellipse will pass through the other focus. So, if you put your home focus behind you and shoot straight at the wall, the rebound will take the ball through the other focus, and score a goal. This is the crux of the matter: goals can be scored *only* on rebounds, not on direct shots. And, since players are usually moving when they shoot, and the spin on the ball will alter the rebound, and there is a slight pseudogravity at the outside, this is hardly an 'ideal' ellipse. Mastering these intricacies is a task for only the most dedicated of athletes."

DiFazio spoke up again. "They've already interviewed Urdehelm. He was only too happy to get on the air."

Wegener grimaced. Trygve Urdehelm, Coach-General Manager of the rival Proxima Panthers, had built two championship teams in the asteroid leagues, but had never landed a job in Earth Orbital. Urdehelm was notoriously Machiavellian, and most owners feared he'd take over if let in.

"Okay, I'll give 'em a few minutes. Where are they?"

DiFazio pointed across the arena, cutting a chord under the playing volume, to a clutch of bodies and equipment in the press box. "Need time to cool off first?"

"No, I'm okay." She stepped off lightly through the slight gravity, still frowning. She had never gotten along well with the press, even under the best of conditions. During her playing days, sportscasters had always characterized her as a drudge worker—getting results with ferocity and stamina, wearing out opposition. She'd never had flashy moves, didn't score much, concentrated mostly on defense. But she had been a major factor in two Earth Orbital Championships for Brazil, while still in her early twenties; then, after contract renegotiations with Brazil had broken down, she had taken an attractive offer from Israel. In an expanded role as playmaker and unofficial assistant coach, she had nurtured the Eastern Division cellar-dweller and, in three years, made it a contender—both with her play and with her advice to the front office on which blue-chip players could be lured away from other teams.

". . . ball control," the speakers continued, "can be maintained by one player for only ten meters distance: this is largely a matter of referee's judgment. But once a player makes and maintains wall contact, he can't carry the ball any further and can advance it only by passing off . . ."

In 2025, Joy Wegener's Israel team had won the Earth Orbital Championship. Around then she was beginning to consider coaching, thinking herself heiress-apparent to the top job at Israel. She was 33, and the vigor she had maintained by playing in free fall was being spent in the ever-toughening competition. Unfortunately, the incumbent coach was showing no desire to step down; nor was the team's front office showing any interest in adding a nonplaying assistant coach to the payroll. Wegener had played three years more, waiting, slowly losing her edge. The tables were turning; now she was the one being worn out, by sharp young players on hungry teams. Israel never repeated as Champion.

". . . the goal region itself is a sphere 50 centimeters across; around it is a 'hands-off' sphere a full meter wide. This outer sphere, however, is widened to *two*-meter diameter during the last three minutes of each half. Thus, it becomes easier to score toward the end of the game—and it leaves less than two and a half meters between the back wall and the outer sphere . . ."

"Ah, Ms. Wegener," smiled Tasha Leminevski, a longtime Foci commentator working with the Earth crew. Leminevski had been a second-echelon announcer for two or three Earth Orbital teams, and may have jumped at the chance to cover a big sportscast, even if just a novelty. She was a trim, athletic woman, more graceful-looking than Wegener—but Leminevski's playing days had been few, two or three seasons spent mostly on the benches of the Russian teams in Earth Orbital, Novaya Russia and Marx-Gorodok. *Too indecisive,* Wegener recalled from her mental file of opponents, *all the agility in the world isn't worth a thing if*

*you can't make snap decisions in the heat of the action.
And she couldn't.*

Wegener smiled, almost at ease. "Welcome aboard. I
don't imagine you're coming along, though."

Leminevski laughed politely, flashing teeth ideal for
TV. "No, the lure of the stars hasn't taken me yet." It
was a strange, but diplomatic, answer; better than, "No,
I've got a steady job here." "I know you're busy, Coach.
We'll make this quick." Leminevski guided Wegener a
few steps sideways, then set herself alongside, while the
holocameras centered on them. Red lights sparked on the
cameras.

"I'm with Joy Wegener," Leminevski said, her trained
voice bell-clear even though English wasn't her native
tongue, "whom Foci fans will remember from her great
days with Brazil and Israel in the Earth Orbital League.
Joy is coaching now, overseeing the Vayu Centaurs.
Coach, first of all, let me say how impressed I am with
the Foci facilities on this magnificent ship. The arenas
on board are spacious, up to date, and this one is just full
of fans."

Wegener untensed slightly; evidently this crew wasn't
out to condescend. "It's very gratifying, Tasha. I
couldn't ask for better arenas, or better facilities in
general. And the fans—heh, well, Tash, that's always an
iffy thing, but we'll give 'em our best."

"I'm sure the fans would like to know why you
picked this particular coaching opportunity, which will,
after all, take you away from your home system for good.
There were other offers, weren't there? Colleges, instruc-
tional work, asteroid teams?"

"That's true, but none of them really offered anything

substantial. As you know, no team in Earth Orbital would even give me an assistant spot—mostly I was offered one-year playing contracts, with fuzzy half-promises about coaching, maybe. And the colleges, what few are established in free fall facilities, aren't well funded in Foci. The asteroids sent out a few feelers, but never talked about good money. The people here did, so here I am."

"Isn't this rather final?" Leminevski said, almost lamenting. "The Earth Orbital situation could change in a year or two."

Wegener didn't answer right away; she really didn't have a concrete answer. Then Leminevski pressed: "Is it because you want to make a contribution to the human race's growth to the stars?"

A sportscaster had no business asking a question like that. But it struck a chord. Wegener was uncomfortable again. "I—don't know if a half-ostracized Foci coach can make a 'contribution.' But these people are here, on this ship, and they'll need something like Foci to take their minds off the dull trip. And—maybe I can make that brand of Foci—something they'll want to watch." Blood flared in her ears. She was half embarrassed at the fool she must be making of herself, half disarmed to realize that she believed what she said.

Leminevski believed it too. She looked at the Coach, almost, in awe. "Thank you, Coach." The cameras' red lights died away.

Wegener stepped off, drifted back toward her locker room hatchway. *I was a hustling, aggressive player. I gave a hundred percent. And if that attitude isn't the same one that wants the human race to keep growing, questing, expanding, then at least they're closely related.*

And that's why Hamudi wants to play on this ship, instead of staying put in the solar system. Even if he doesn't know it himself.

Can I blame him for wanting to hot-dog it? He'd do more than just work off a grudge. He might just show the folks back home what kind of people the solar system is losing, and will keep losing.

Frowning in deep thought, the Coach dropped lightly into her locker room.

Proxima brought the ball upcourt hesitantly, looking for an opening in the Centaurs' coverage. Jack Gossage, at the center spot, was vaned out and ready. Proxima passed, passed again, wide of the well-guarded focus. At last, one pass went off target; in the scramble after the loose ball, Vayu's Jan Trbovich got possession—and, at a sign from his teammates, called a time-out.

Wegener took her eyes off the hologram monitor and stood up. She glanced at the benched Hamudi, and prepared herself.

All of her substitutes gathered around the Coach as she waited for the on-court players to make the easy drop-swing down from the ellipse. At last she brought them all together and spoke in the low, needlessly conspiratorial tone she used in time-outs. "Okay, early third quarter, we got 'em by five. I think they've tried about everything; if we start opening it up on offense, we've got 'em bagged. Am I right?"

Reaction was mixed. Carrasquez y Delon, a rookie, couldn't really evaluate the situation and didn't respond; Okkengoek, also a rookie, nodded her head emphatically but was probably just following the Coach's lead. Wegener looked mostly to her veterans—Gossage, Peugeot, Avery, Geld, En-Yan—for confirmation. And they agreed.

"Okay. Let's show Urdehelm that a pattern defense can click right into a pattern offense. Hamudi, go in for Avery."

Hamudi's eyebrows rose. He'd played sparingly in the first half, and hadn't expected to return until late in the game.

The Coach broke the huddle. At her table she punched out a message to the scorer's console: #3 HAMUDI, PHUON REPLACES #44 AVERY, SOLON/VAYU. She looked up, caught Hamudi's eye. He moved away from the shinny cable, approached her. She looked down until her own readout showed confirmation from the scorer, then looked back up at the small, wiry man. "Play the patterns. Give me precision and execution. We can handle everything they come up with; mostly we're in better shape. Just go out there and play a team game. Then—if we really put it out of reach —the last five minutes are all yours."

He looked at her for a moment, not knowing what to expect. She just looked back, with a gleam of her own. At last, Hamudi grinned, nodded quickly, and bounded to the shinny cable. As he hurried up, the traditional klaxon blatted out notice of a substitution. A phlegmatic voice on the loudspeakers followed. "Hamudi—in for—Avery."

The referees whistled time-in. Trbovich inbounded to Hamudi in backcourt, while the latter was on a slow forward vane. The newcomer eyed the goal situation

ahead—three teammates testing their coverage, a forecourt man directly ahead, a goalie hovering near the
focus. Hamudi passed off to Trbovich, then vaned
"down" toward a sidewall. He had seen how Ronit Geld
was testing her defender, and getting the better of the
matchup—she'd get the shot, if they got her the ball
before the defense could switch.

The forecourt defender took Trbovich, leaving
Hamudi uncovered. Hamudi vaned along the sidewall,
toward the focus; the goalie slipped between him and
the goal. Trbovich, in trouble, still got a pass off to Gossage. Suddenly Geld broke free, lurching back toward
midspace—but the pass went to Hamudi underneath.
The goalie tensed, ready to block a short cheap-shot—
but Hamudi whirled and fired a pass out to Geld, in
perfect position to bank one off the opposite ("above")
sidewall. With the goalie drawn to the other side of the
focus, there was no one to block the shot. It was long
and had to be accurate, but Geld made it look like a
cripple. Vayu led by seven.

When the referee handed the ball back to Proxima,
that team tried a fast break. Full of strong but raw talent
from the asteroid leagues, the Panthers were better
geared to a "running" game. But Geld, reacting off her
shot, was already most of the way back to take her goalie
assignment—and Hamudi hustled back to help. Proxima
pulled up in the forecourt, tried to set up a pattern. The
Centaurs, sparked out of third-quarter doldrums by
Hamudi's presence, stayed alert on defense and didn't
yield. Finally a Panther took a bad-angle low-percentage
shot, which Trbovich picked off wide of the focus.
Proxima was on the run.

The fans, both from Vayu and Proxima, were unmoved; a close game, either way, would have stirred more interest. Now Vayu was starting to pour it on, and it didn't look like the end would be exciting.

But the Centaurs didn't care. They gloried in the almost-smug awareness that they could win going away. At first Hamudi chafed at the confines of his playmaking, diversionary role—but soon he sharpened, working around Proxima's adjusted coverages, selecting the right option for each situation, even scoring a few points himself when he had the shots. He grew bolder on defense, deflecting passes, drawing offensive fouls. Wegener, staring into the monitor, smiled wolfishly. Hamudi could have starred in any league, given discipline.

However, the unsophisticated fans weren't aware that they were seeing play execution worthy of Earth Orbital. They saw only a slow, grueling contest which one side was coming to dominate. The cheers grew more and more ragged. DiFazio petitioned his Coach: "Can't they put in a little more razzle-dazzle? The crowd's getting bored."

"If they hang around," she returned, "they'll get all the razzle-dazzle they can fathom." She chuckled to herself. *"If they hang around?" They'll hang around for two hundred years.*

The third quarter ended with Vayu in front 62–48. Wegener rested Jack Gossage and Enriette Peugeot, inserted Horacio Carrasquez y Delon and Britte Okkengoek. She left in Hamudi. "This is it," she said.

"Say what, Coach?" asked Gossage, mopping sweat with a towel.

"Hamudi. With the kids in there, he has to take the lead and keep them from making mistakes."

Gossage stretched out. "Ol' Hamudi, he's like a time bomb out there. Just barely holding *himself* together."

The Coach smiled at the black American. Gossage had come to Foci after having infuriated just about every front office in earthside professional basketball—and had signed with an American team in Earth Orbital, North American Rockwell. He was supposed to have attracted earthside fans' interest; instead, he had brought his anti-management sentiments with him. In less than three years he had walked out on seven teams, including Nigeria.

Gossage had come up through playground ball, as so many ghetto youths had before him—and in the playgrounds, style counted for everything. He had had to learn defense and team play to get anywhere, but had maintained his good moves—in basketball, and later in Foci. Once, after watching Hamudi do solo moves in practice, Gossage had asked if there had been playground ball in Indonesia.

"He'll get his chance to unwind," Wegener told him now. "So will you, if you want one. How about it? Put on a show for the folks back home?"

Gossage shook his head. "They've had as much of me as I'm ever going to give 'em."

Here's another one bound for the stars, she thought, *struggling up through the playgrounds and planets, always outward . . . but I wonder how long it'll be before he picks on DiFazio, or me.*

It looks like we're taking bad traits along with the

good—we all tend to be self-centered, overly ambitious, combative.

Hamudi had trouble adjusting to Okkengoek and Carrasquez y Delon, who were relatively easy marks for their defenders. He steered the offense away from the focus, setting Trbovich and Geld as his primary targets. Soon this led to double-teaming on the veterans, as well as on Hamudi—and scoring got tougher. The rookies also endangered their own defense, either yielding too much or playing too tight and fouling. Hamudi planned on the fly, yelling the rookies through defensive switches to keep Proxima from gaining momentum. Trbovich picked off one pass and triggered a fast break, Hamudi taking the long lead pass, gliding behind the focus, and slamming the ball off the back wall for a cinch major-axis rebound through the goal. But Proxima continued to play around the rookies, and the Vayu lead hovered around twelve. This could vanish quickly toward the end, when the "hands-off" zone around each goal enlarged.

With 8:23 left in the game, Carrasquez y Delon committed his third foul. "Get back in, Jack," Wegener barked as Proxima set up for free throws. "I'm not going to wait around for him to get into foul trouble."

Gossage exhaled deeply, slapped on his vanes, and pushed himself up toward the shinny cable. Hamudi saw him coming—and from over twenty meters away, Wegener could see the Indonesian's smile of relief.

"Bum call, Coach," began Carrasquez y Delon, arriving at the bench. "I wasn't anywhere near—"

"Relax," said Wegener, almost serenely. Okkengoek stayed in the lineup, and would probably get to look good for a few minutes, as Hamudi worked Gossage into the attack. But the other rookie would get chances of his own, when the season started. *Who knows, they might turn into decent ballplayers.*

Solon Avery went in also, for Trbovich—no problem there. The fresh subs ignited the Centaurs again. The fans, thinking for a while that Proxima might catch up, started to lose interest again. A few made for the exits.

Vayu stretched the lead up to 17. With exactly five minutes left, Wegener made her last substitutions—Okkengoek and Geld out, Peugeot and En-Yan in. The newcomers made encouraging gestures to Hamudi. Wegener tilted her chair back—she wanted to see this live.

Proxima faded back on defense, expecting Hamudi to stick with the patterns. He passed off to Avery at midcourt, snapped out his vanes, and pumped in toward the focus. Four meters away, he veered to one side—drawing the goalie—then, instead of setting up on the wall, Hamudi bounced back the other way, snapped in his arm vanes to free his hands, whipped his head around in mid-flight, saw Avery's pass on the way, grabbed the ball, twisted, and shot off an unguarded wall—and scored. The Panthers, stunned, had no defense against the wide-open shot.

On defense, Gossage left his stationary pivot and managed to cover two Panthers—leaving Hamudi free to dart around brazenly, after the ball. The small man swooped and vaned around all five Panthers, who had grown used to a less fluid defense. At last Proxima got an opportunity—but Hamudi was there, executing a quick, spectacular barrel roll and blocking the shot cleanly from behind. Gossage hauled in the ball, looked downcourt—and Hamudi had everyone beat. The rattled Panthers were too busy bawling at the referees (surely Hamudi was doing *something* illegal). It was almost mechanical now—retract vanes, take the pass, dribble once off a near wall, swoop to rear, slam the ball. The frenzied Urdehelm called time.

Wegener had nothing much to say to her own troops, who spent most of the break pounding Hamudi on the back. She began to feel nostalgic. *If I worked at it for a few weeks, I could get myself in good enough shape to play. Watching Hamudi reminds me that I used to have* fun *playing this game.*

I could go in as a sub, pairing myself with each of the rookies in turn—get them educated that way. They've got a lot to learn.

And I've got a lot to teach. The people on this ship, even the grounders, all have a desire to achieve goals. Maybe I can help keep the drive toward those goals from turning ugly. Is goal tending legal in this "game"?

The players shinnied back to the game. Hamudi was just getting started. When the goals opened up at the three-minute mark, he'd be unstoppable.

"Hey, the people who stayed are sticking around," said DiFazio. "About time you let the team cut loose."

"Yeah, they'll stick around," smiled Wegener, leaning back to enjoy the closing minutes of her first victory as a coach. "This is just the beginning."

golf

To some people, the sport of golf is an activity which interrupts a good walk. But to many others (some estimates run as high as ten million!) it is a demanding game which places the emphasis upon skill rather than on strength. It is an individual rather than a team sport, and success in it derives partly from psychological factors—self-control and discipline being all-important.

The game of golf developed around A.D. 1000. It was invented in Scotland by the Romans during their occupation of the British Isles. It was a simple game then, consisting of hitting a leather, feather-filled "ball" around with a shaped stick. Golf has obviously come a long way since then, what with the golf business a multimillion-dollar industry in this country alone.

Golf became very popular in this country in the late 1800s, and the United States Golf Association (U.S.G.A.) was formed in 1894 to advance and regulate the game. Golf was among the first sports to attract women participants, and since the turn of the century women have played it in great numbers.

In addition, golf is an expensive and time-consuming sport. It is also an "in" game among the upper-middle and upper classes around the world. It is organized around the country-club life in the United States. For this and other reasons, golf seems to have excluded minority groups and the poor. This situation is changing for the better, and golf, like tennis, is one of the fastest-growing sports among all segments of the population.

To Hell
with the
Odds

robert l. fish

This chilling story deals not only with matters that
are peculiar to golf but also with major themes that apply
to all sports. Of these themes, three seem to be particularly important. First, each sport is a culture unto itself.
Within that culture, there are norms and values that
regulate the conduct and motivate the behavior of the
players. These are separate from the formal rules and
regulations of the game itself. For example, in this story
about golf, Marty Russell gives us a rather sad insight
into the "class system" of golf as a game. Players are
first class, second class, and so on, within the golf culture. Star golf players have privileges and are accorded a
high degree of respect—and envy—by other players.

The second major theme exemplified about sports in
this story concerns the prototype of the "has-been." Marty
Russell is depicted as a has-been in golf. Although his
anguish and anxiety about his status lead him to make a
peculiar arrangement with the Devil which in real life
would not be a problem faced by a has-been, the picture
presented is a sad commentary on the immediacy and the
precariousness of being a star player in any sport. During
a three- to five-year period, one may be a star in a

particular sport and receive all the honors and wealth associated with it. However, after this relatively short period of time, it is likely that younger players will outperform the "stars" and make former stars "obsolete." One of the most tragic aspects of modern professional sports is the likelihood that a young man who trains all of his life to reach stardom in a particular sport may, after having accomplished that goal, be faced with the prospect of not being able to do anything else.

The third major theme which relates to all sports in this story is Marty Russell's viewpoint of golf as simply a source of income. Russell no longer looks at golf for its intrinsic satisfactions but looks at it as a business—as a source of livelihood—as he contemplates "that even fifteenth place is worth a new set of tires and enough to live on for a couple of months." Many modern professional golf—and other sports—players are criticized on the basis of their high salaries and dominant interest in sports as a business. But this criticism is usually countered by the argument that the prime, productive period for a top player in any sport is relatively short and justifies a high salary which helps a player form a base for an alternative profession. Marty Russell presents us with a sometimes funny but always sad picture of a thirty-eight-year-old golf player who is "all played out."

To Hell
with the
Odds

The Devil could not have selected a more likely prospect. . . .

Marty Russell sat slumped in the last booth of the dimly lit bar of the Nineteenth Tee Motel, a half mile down the road from the Rocky Hollow Country Club. The top professional golfers for the Open were being accommodated at the club; most of the second-flighters were having their expenses paid at the Waldorf in the city by generous members of the club. It was only the golf-bums and the has-beens who paid their own way and stayed at dumps like the Nineteenth Tee.

Marty stared into the murky depths of his drink and smiled bitterly. He remembered when the main suite at Rocky Hollow had automatically been reserved for Marty Russell. When he drove up in his Cadillac convertible, there had been eager hands to help with his bags; caddies had fought for the privilege of taking his clubs from the car trunk. The thought brought a sudden reminder: the Chevy needed tires. It was doubtful if the right rear one would last to Sandy Beach. He shoved the thought aside, letting his mind go back to the club. Today they fought for Carter's bag—what a laugh! Carter, the leading money winner in the country; Carter, the kid he taught to play. Marty sighed. Nowadays, he thought, if Carter even mentions me, it's just to get in a nasty crack about the old man! Well, I suppose maybe that's what it takes to get ahead today. . . .

The old man . . . thirty-eight years old and all played out. An ancient at thirty-eight, who couldn't help thinking of the cost every time he unwrapped a new golf ball; who left immediately after a day's play and showered back at the motel, because he knew he couldn't afford to stand his share of rounds at the bar, equating each one to so many gallons of gasoline, or so many quarts of oil. A has-been at thirty-eight, painfully aware that he was becoming an object of either pity or derision on the circuit. Sure there were a lot of top golfers older than he was; he just wasn't one of them. He was an old man at thirty-eight who couldn't play without his rest, and couldn't sleep without a couple of drinks under his belt. And drinks—even at a dump like the Nineteenth Tee—a buck each, too! And speaking of drinks, he thought, let's knock this one down and get another. To hell with it.

As he reached for his glass he was vaguely aware that a shadowy figure had slipped into the seat opposite him. The thought of company was suddenly irritating; he leaned back, his fist locked about his drink, peering across at the wavering figure belligerently.

"And who invited you?" he asked angrily.

"Why, you did," said the Devil calmly. "Back on Route 406, near Carlisle. You said, 'I'd give my soul to win that Open.'" The nebulous shape seemed to shrug.

"I've heard that sort of thing before, of course, but you actually meant it. You develop an ear for nuances in my business, you know."

"I haven't a clue as to what you're talking about, and I couldn't care less," Marty said, and felt his unwarranted irritation with the stranger fade. It wasn't this character's fault he was a golf bum. "But now that you're here, have a drink."

"I don't drink," said the Devil piously. "Well, you did mean it, didn't you? You were serious?"

"Serious about what?" Marty asked.

"About giving your soul to win the Open."

"What's the pitch?" Marty asked curiously, and then smiled bitterly. "If you're trying to set things up to make a fast buck on a fix, you're talking to the wrong guy. Man, are you talking to the wrong guy! You ought to be up at the clubhouse working on Carter, or Jamison, or one of those boys."

"I never gamble," said the Devil virtuously. "Just answer my question. How would you like to win the Open?"

Marty grinned. "How would you like to be John D. Rockefeller?"

"It was nothing special," said the Devil, and frowned. "I'm afraid I must ask you to be more serious about this. If you want to win the Open, I can arrange it."

Marty stared across the table. The figure there seemed to shimmer, to fade and return in smoky wisps. Boy, oh boy! he thought; I'd better go easy on these drinks. He put his hand to his forehead; it came away damp. "Who are you?" he asked.

"I'm the Devil."

"Man!" Marty said in relief and admiration. "You're drunker than I am! On the level, who are you?"

"I told you. I'm the Devil." The voice was beginning to sound impatient. "Well? Is it a deal?"

Marty shook his head wonderingly. Staying in crummy motels and patronizing crummy bars you certainly run into some prime weirdos. Marty figured he'd humor him. "And what's in it for you?"

"You."

"Me?" Marty laughed. This one was really out on cloud six! "And what would you do with an old broken-down ex–golf pro like me?"

The Devil shrugged. "We'd find a use. We always do. Well, do we have a deal?"

Marty grinned. "Just what would I have to do? Poison everybody else in the tournament?"

The Devil was not amused. "All you have to do is agree. I'll do the rest."

"And when would I have to pay off? I mean, when would my lily-white soul be collected?"

"We'd come to an arrangement that would be mutually satisfactory. Well? Do we do business?"

It was getting late and Marty was getting tired. He suddenly decided he'd wasted enough time on this nut. "OK, buddy," he said. "It's a deal. Just for you I'll go out and win the Open."

But he was talking to an empty seat. The smokiness opposite him was gone; the plastic-backed bench across from him was sharp in outline. This is the end, Marty thought. I've really reached the very end. I'll be seeing polka-dot snakes next. . . .

The young bartender turned to the old bartender.

"Better cut off the drinks on that character in the last booth. He's talkin' to hisself."

"Leave him alone," said the old bartender curtly. He continued to rub his rag across the polished mahogany. "You know who that is? That's Marty Russell. I remember him when he was away up on top. I was working over at the club in those days, and it was nothing for him to tip five bucks, just for a beer. He's a great guy."

"Well, he looks like an old bum now," said the young bartender.

"He's under forty," said the old bartender.

"He still looks like an old bum," said the young bartender.

The old bartender paused in his task of wiping the bar. He looked at the other in deep disgust. "You ain't going to stay a kid all your life, neither," he said, and then turned back to his work.

Marty Russell was scheduled to tee off in the second threesome, a position almost of disrespect, but a position he had become accustomed to in recent years. The gallery hadn't even begun to form yet; most of the other players hadn't even gotten up. One advantage, of course, Marty thought; teeing off after lunch I'd probably want a drink. This way I save dough.

He was teeing off with a professional from a small club upstate, and one of the low-handicap amateurs from Rocky Hollow. They all shook hands and smiled at each other as strangers do, while they waited for the players ahead to hit their second shots and get out of range. The amateur won the toss, nodded, teed up his ball, and waggled his club.

"Well," he said, fixing his feet, "I'm damn glad I'm not playing this afternoon with the big boys. I'd get so nervous I wouldn't be able to even hit the ball." He swung and sent his drive down the fairway in a better-than-fair hit.

The small-time pro cleared his throat and avoided looking at Marty. Damned stupid kid! he thought. Somebody should have taught him to keep his mouth shut, as well as how to swing a golf club! The small-time pro remembered Marty from the old days; he had seen Marty win the Open on this same course fifteen years before. He sent his ball sailing down the fairway and picked up his tee.

"Lay it out there, Marty," he said. It was evident from his tone that he meant it.

Marty nodded absently. The club felt strangely heavy in his hands as he swung his wrists in practice. His arms felt heavy, too. Too much sleeping-juice the night before, he thought; too much conversation with goof-balls. Well, what the hell! It's only one more round of golf, not the first and not the last. He addressed his ball and glanced down the fairway. What I would really like, he thought as always, is to lay it out there about three hundred yards, right down the middle. Right between the legs of that guy who is pitching for the green. He went into his backswing automatically and hit the ball.

"Jee-sus!" said the amateur in a tone of shocked disbelief.

"A beauty, Marty," said the small-time pro happily.

"Good God!" exclaimed the amateur. "It's going to hit that guy ahead—no; it went between his legs! It must be over three hundred yards out there!"

"Felt good," Marty said shortly, and bent down to pick up his tee. Well, he thought as they stepped off the tee and started down the spongy fairway, at least I started off with a decent drive, even if there wasn't anyone around to admire it. But it didn't really feel that good when I hit it. Maybe I'm even losing the feel, now.

The green lay seventy yards from his ball, a narrow, twisting pocket of velvet flanked on each side by gaping traps. The flag was on a small plateau to the left, well to the rear of the green with tricky rolls in all directions. Marty paused beside his caddy, studying the shot carefully. Drop it about two yards past the flag with plenty of backspin, he thought. No—the roll is bad for that. Drop it in front, maybe four, five yards, and run it up. Take a seven if you're thinking of that. . . . No, as a matter of fact, the best way to play it. . . . Ah, to hell with the whole business! he thought. Hit the damn ball and pray it falls in the cup. He took his wedge from the bag; his arms came down smoothly. The ball rose cleanly in the air, bounced once on the green, and rolled over to drop in the cup.

"Holy Kee-rist!" said the amateur. "An eagle!"

"Lovely, Marty!" said the small-time pro proudly.

"Yeah," Marty said in a puzzled tone. "A little lucky."

A memory was teasing his brain as he teed up the ball for the second hole. He shrugged it off. Keep your mind on the game, he said to himself sternly. Even fifteenth place in this tournament is worth a new set of tires and enough to live on for a couple of months, with care. And you're two under par even if there are seventy-one holes left to play. Or, as they used to say, two under par if you never see the back of your neck. He glanced down the fairway.

The second hole was a sharp dogleg to the right, a short but wicked par four with an open invitation to disaster. To the left, a low outcropping of rock formed a wall; to the right, heavy woods waited patiently for any error. Straight ahead, beyond the bend in the fairway, a small refreshment stand was in the process of being erected to serve the gallery during the Open; it separated the second fairway from a practice green where several of the contestants were attempting to improve their putting. Marty smiled to himself. Over the woods was too dangerous, even assuming he still had the strength to carry such a distance. The smart play was to take a low iron, play it straight down the middle to the bend, and then have a straight pitch to the green. His smile widened. Of course—if wishes were drives—the real way to play this hole would be to slap one out there about three-ten or three-twenty, hit the stand, and bounce it right onto the green and save all that extra effort. The fore-caddy at the bend windmilled his arms, indicating they were free to hit. Marty went into his backswing and connected with the ball solidly.

"Very good. Straight as an arrow." The amateur was not only being condescending; he was also being helpful. Then his tone became worried. "But—my God—it's too long! It's going right over the fairway. It's going to hit that stand. . . ." His voice became doleful. "I lost it. . . ."

There was a yell, faint on the breeze but still tinged with justified outrage, from the direction of the green. The fore-marker was pointing excitedly. Marty raised his arms in pantomime, trying to determine if he should hit a provisional ball. The fore-caddy managed to get across the message that it wasn't necessary, and Marty stepped off the tee.

When they came to the bend in the fairway, Marty could see his ball on the green, lying about ten feet from the pin. "Talk about the luck of the Irish!" someone was saying. "Hit the corner post of the stand and bounced on the green. I don't know who he is, but I wish I'd bought him in the Calcutta!"

Marty said nothing. A cold feeling was beginning to grip him. He started toward the green when a familiar voice made him pause.

"Hi, Pops." It was Carter, standing on the edge of the practice putting green, watching him sardonically. "You came close to hitting a couple of golfers. I thought you taught me never to do that."

Marty clenched his jaw and advanced on the green. When his turn came to putt, his hands began to tremble, and he stepped away from his ball, attempting to calm himself. Relax! he instructed himself fiercely. Don't blow up now! At the very worst it's going to be a birdie. He crouched back of the ball, lining it up, well aware that Carter had moved up and was watching. No! he thought, suddenly stubborn; this one goes in! The ball obediently trickled across the green, hesitated momentarily, and then dropped into the cup.

"Two eagles! In a row!" said the amateur, and then grinned broadly, almost as if he had had something to do with them personally. "Hey, hey! What do you know?"

Marty was still alone at the motel that night. His name had led the rest on the big board before the clubhouse, and many had been the congratulations and old memories revived after his first round, but in the end he found himself alone, back at the Nineteenth Tee, back in the last booth in the dimly lit bar. After all, anyone can have a hot round, and you have to remember that back in the dark ages the guy did used to play damned good golf. But you also had to remember that there were still fifty-four holes to go, and that he'd started off hot before —not this hot, but still hot—and still missed the cutoff. And you had to keep in mind that Carter is only two strokes back, and he always plays his best under pressure, and you couldn't forget that a man like Jamison has come from behind to win a lot more often than not. . . .

But still, it felt mighty good to see your name posted in the number-one spot on the big board, just like in the old days. Fifteenth place, my eye! he thought happily, forgetting for the moment the feeling of uneasiness that had gripped him throughout the day. Two under the field, and everything clicking! If I don't fall apart, I could place fourth—maybe even third, maybe second— and trade the Chevy in, finally. Not on anything fancy, but on a compact, maybe. They don't eat too much gas, and one thing is always true about a new car—new tires they got. And maybe I could also get some new clothes. I look like a tramp next to Carter and that gang.

He sipped his drink in quiet triumph, reliving the remarkable game he had played. I couldn't do anything wrong, he thought with satisfaction. Whatever I wanted.

A shadowy figure slipped into the booth opposite him.

"You see?" said the Devil, and spread the two wisps that served as its hands.

Memory struck Marty like a blow. He almost spilled his drink. "You were here last night, weren't you?" he asked, suddenly tense. "Right here—in this booth?"

"Relax," said the Devil. "Take it easy." He studied the man across from him in the manner of one used to facing this reaction. "It always comes as something of a shock, but you'll get used to it."

"Get used to it?" Marty asked fiercely. "Get used to what?"

The Devil chose to change the subject. "You're quite a gambler, you know? That bounce off that refreshment stand they're building—that really had me humping, believe me!" He looked reproachful. "Let's keep them within reason, shall we?"

"You were there?" Marty asked incredulously.

"Of course I was there," said the Devil disdainfully. "Naturally, I always watch my investments." He suddenly seemed to understand Marty's question. "Oh! No, I wasn't there in this form, of course. I was there in the form of a man. Otherwise people would get confused," he explained.

Marty stared across the table, trying to focus his eyes on the mist.

"Look," he said at last, picking his words with care, "last night maybe I was pretty tired. I'd driven over four hundred miles to get here, and I'd had a drink or two on an empty stomach on the way. Plus what I had after I got here." He hesitated a moment and then plunged.

"Maybe I said something out of turn, but if I did, I'm sorry. If I made any deal, forget it."

The Devil giggled.

"You're quite a kidder, aren't you?" he said. He made a vague movement that resembled nothing as much as a swirl of fog, but to Marty's confused eye it almost appeared as if the other were consulting a wristwatch. "Well, keep up the good work. Just wish 'em where you want 'em. I'll do the rest."

The swirl darkened and then faded. Marty was alone.

"Buddy-boy is talkin' to hisself again," said the young bartender.

"So let him talk," said the old bartender with glee. "Let him whistle Dixie if he wants." He did a fast buck-and-wing beneath the protective cover of the battery of beer faucets. "See what he done today? Six under par and two under the field! Man, oh man, oh man! Two under the youngsters!" He did a slight shuffle-off-to-Buffalo. "How I'd love to see him clobber those infants! How I'd love it! Two under the field!"

"Two under the field?"

"That's what I said! Two under!"

"Well, don't look at me like I was no moron or some-thin'," said the young bartender resentfully. "Two under the field don't mean nothin' to me. I don't know one end of a golf club from another. . . ."

The second day the groupings were the same, but Marty's threesome had been scheduled for later in the day, and now a small portion of the gallery accompanied them. Under these circumstances the amateur couldn't do anything right, and he chopped his way down the fairway morosely, grumbling to himself. The small-time pro, on the other hand, inspired by Marty's example and happy to see his favorite winning, was playing over his head and even beginning to get visions of placing in the top ten. Marty glumly hit his fantastic shots and dropped his incredible putts, paying no attention to the gasps of the awe-stricken gallery. By the end of nine, he was three more under par and had widened his lead over Carter by an additional stroke.

As he came to the tenth tee, Marty paused to think. Why did it necessarily have to be some supernatural agency that was controlling his magnificent shots? After all, he'd played some pretty top golf in his day without the help of anyone, and what made him suddenly believe in ghosts or devils? Just because he happened to be having a series of rounds that any professional golfer might put together when everything was working. He waggled his club, relief flooding him at the thought, and decided to prove he had been a fool.

He glanced down the fairway. To the left, and at least three hundred yards from the tee, a finger of the lake poked out toward the fairway. He nodded and commanded the ball. Hook into that tiny spit of water, he said silently, and then took both the stance and the grip for an extreme slice. He'd have trouble recovering from the lie that would result from the slice, but it was worth it to know. He swung; there was a gasp from the gallery. The ball fled from the clubhead, hooking just enough to carry it to the water. A cold hand seemed to grip Marty's stomach, twisting cruelly. Not only was the thing he had feared true, but he had lost two valuable strokes to Carter, who had been playing almost perfect golf! Marty blanked his mind to the significance of the experience, and bent down to tee up another ball. This time he stared straight down the fairway to a clear spot in the middle and swung. This time the ball was more obedient.

By the end of the eighteen holes for that day, he had managed to recover the two strokes lost so stupidly by his shot into the pond, but his lead over Carter had been cut to one stroke. He handed his putter to his caddy silently and ducked into his battered Chevy. For some reason he didn't feel like facing the sudden-friends at the big board, or hearing the congratulations of the other players in the locker room. He wanted to be alone.

As he sat in his accustomed place in the last booth of the darkened bar that night, he waited impatiently for his visitor. As his thick fingers twiddled nervously with the glass before him, he reviewed arguments, threats, anything to get out of the spot in which he found himself. Now look here, he said to his imaginary booth-companion: if I can hit them where I want, what's to prevent me from putting them all in the pond? I did it once today, didn't I? Under your conditions I can lose this thing just as easily as I can win it. After all, second money is still a young fortune to me. So why don't we make a deal . . . ?

The word stuck in his mind. They already had a deal; that was the trouble. He sighed and drank deeply, peering across the table, but the clear-cut back of the plastic seat was all that was facing him.

Come on! Get here! Let's clear this thing up! his mind whispered to his missing tormentor. Let's get it over with. If you won't let me out of this stupid arrangement, I'll throw the match. I swear I'll throw it! I promise I'll lose!

He sighed. He wouldn't and he knew it. Not after over ten years on the skids; not after beating from tournament to tournament in that damn falling-apart Chevy, praying for a fifteenth, or even a twentieth place sometimes, just to pay for coffee and cakes. He couldn't and he knew he couldn't. And especially not to lose to Carter. He reached for his glass again, his hand shaking. Damn! Damn! Damn! How did I ever get myself in a mess like this?

He was still waiting alone at 2 A.M. when they closed the bar.

"Buddy-boy ain't talkin' to hisself tonight," said the young bartender. "Musta had a bad day."

"Bad day?" said the old bartender jubilantly. "Bad day? Nine under par and still one up on Carter and you call that a bad day?" He looked at the young bartender witheringly. "A bad day is what your mother had when you was born!"

For the final day's round the tournament committee rearranged the match to put the top three contenders together as usual, scheduling them for a tee-off time that would allow them to hit the fifteenth tee in time for the TV cameras to meet their commercial obligations. Marty stood on the first tee with Carter and Jamison while the gallery sized them up with that unconscious self-aggrandizement of people within touching distance of the great.

"That Marty Russell sure looks like he was out on one hell of a toot last night," one spectator said to another.

"He should worry," said the second. "The way he's playing, he should worry! Maybe he plays better when he's bushed."

Jamison leaned over and set his tee firmly in the ground, placed his ball on top of it, and rotated it until the brand mark was up. He straightened up, and smiled over his shoulder.

"Let's see if I can get one of those Russell specials," he said, and laid one far down the fairway.

Marty came up next. "Show you how I used to play when I was young and healthy," he said, but his heart wasn't in it. He swung at the ball listlessly, placing it fifty yards ahead of Jamison's.

Carter teed up. "Not bad, Pops," he said. "I always did say that goofpills will beat skill any day. . . ." He put one a bite behind Marty's ball, and the three men filed off the tee with Marty in the rear, his face white, his jaw clenched almost painfully. No, sir! he thought. Not to Carter . . . !

It was more or less a repeat on the front nine. Marty played each shot as if disinterested, and by the time they had holed out on the ninth, he had added one shot to his lead over Carter and two to his lead over Jamison. It was as they were teeing off from the tenth that Jamison said something that caught Marty's attention. His head came up.

"What?"

"I said, we'll have to be careful of that gallery," Jamison said. "They're beginning to get out of the marshal's control, wandering all over the fairway."

Marty was teeing up at the time.

"Show us one of those Russell miracle shots," Carter

said sarcastically. "Bounce it off some character's head
right onto the green, like you did at the second hole the
first day." He shook his head. "Lucky for you I was
there, because otherwise I'd never have believed it."

Marty almost jerked on his backswing, but his ball
still sailed out as if fired from a gun. Lucky for me
Carter was there, eh? Was it possible? The way the guy
was playing golf, it certainly was possible! But, no—the
Devil could scarcely make the same deal with two
people. . . . Still, there were such things as agents, and
except for Carter, who else had been around the refreshment stand at the time? A couple of carpenters, working
on it, and some other people. . . . It could be anyone.
What a pity! If I could be sure it was Carter. . . .

As they stepped off the tee his mind was still busy.
Even if it wasn't Carter, it had to be someone in the
gallery, and Jamison's comment—no, it had actually
been Carter's comment—had given him a wonderful idea.
Bounce it off someone's head, eh? How about that? Old
wispy said he watched his investments, and do you have
any idea what a well-hit golf ball can do to a man's
head? Especially from up close? Well, well, what do you
know . . . ?

The problem, of course, would be where to pull it.
The eleventh was no good: a water hole that kept the
gallery well back from the fairway. And the twelfth just
didn't seem to suit. Marty reviewed the possibilities of
each hole as he played. His game remained as flawless
as ever, but his brain was racing, concentrating on his
problem. The sixteenth might do, but the best place
without a doubt would be the eighteenth. Of course if
you failed, there wouldn't be another chance, but—but

how could you fail? Or who was going to? The eighteenth it was! The gallery would all be crowded around the green, and old pal—whether he was Carter or not—would be sure to be there.

He smiled grimly as he perfected the plan, unaware that the odd look on his face was puzzling the gallery that marched along with him. That was how it would be: an unfortunate accident on the eighteenth green. After that, of course, he would be too upset to finish the round. It would cost him the tournament, but he wouldn't have lost, and that was the important thing. If his target was Carter, then Jamison would win—and he liked that idea. And if Carter was *not* his target, then let the smug little bastard pick up the dough—the money was no longer important. The fact remained that Carter would not have won; he would have been handed the prize in default. . . .

When they came to the eighteenth, Marty studied the lie carefully, biting his lip in concentration. It was a straightaway hole, four hundred and sixty yards to a saucerlike green nestling alongside the clubhouse. Behind the green was a tall television tower; to the left of the green, a deep trap. But it was the right side of the green that Marty studied; it was as if he had never seen it before, the way he looked at it now. That sharp spur of rocks that had given the club its name. . . . Lovely. Exactly as he remembered it. Perfect . . .

The gallery had rushed ahead and now stood jammed, encircling the final green. In the distance the crowd looked like a multicolored collar about the smooth green, ruffled a bit where it bent around the trap and the rock spur. Very pretty, Marty thought with a grim twist of his lips. Prettiest thing I've seen in the past four days. No eagle here, nor any par. This was a hole that wasn't going to be finished. A topped drive to begin with, about a hundred and twenty yards. That would give him an excuse to be short of the green on his second, but close enough to be in a good position to do real damage with a low iron. Wish them where you want them, eh? That's just what we'll do. . . .

He teed up his ball as his opponents watched, went into his accustomed backswing, and swung downward. The ball obediently dribbled one hundred and twenty yards before the tee. There was a sharp gasp from the gallery spread along the fairway; it was his first missed shot of the tournament.

"What's the trouble?" Carter asked as he teed up. "Getting nervous this close to the payoff?"

Marty clamped his jaws on the first words that came to his lips. Keep it cool! he said to himself almost viciously. Let him have his rope; let either one of them have their rope! He was shaking as he walked to his ball; he had to force himself to calmness, to keep his plan in mind. Now, let's see. . . . A three-wood would look logical, and would bring the ball to about fifteen yards from the green. But not in front of the trap; it would be too illogical to take a low iron there. And the left side was better, anyway; the greatest portion of the crowd was there. Assuming that Carter wasn't his man. . . . Of course the crowd would be disappointed, figuring he should reach from there, but they'd have to live with their disappointment. He took his three-wood from his caddy, made a great pretense of swinging as hard as he could, and laid the ball exactly fifteen yards from the green, a bit to the left.

He felt an unusual mixture of icy calmness and bubbling excitement as he came up to his ball, and then paused at the sudden scream from the crowd. Carter had dropped his approach! A wave of applause broke wildly from the gallery. For a second Marty felt again that cold feeling he knew so well, and then he smiled bitterly to himself. So I could drop mine to win, he thought. So what? If he's my target, let them pay off to his widow. If he isn't, let him win!

Both Carter and Jamison were on the green, watching him. He glanced with veiled eyes at the gallery; they presented a mosaic of one-face, a mass of colorful curiosity watching him. You're here, he thought. Either on the green or behind it. I'll find you!

He affected to study his shot in the hushed silence, and then at last leaned toward his caddy. "Three-iron," he said quietly, and slipped the club from the bag before the caddy could question the choice. "Just roll it up," he said, half to himself, as if in explanation. The caddy shrugged. You didn't argue with a guy with the lowest score ever recorded in an Open.

Marty glanced once in the direction of the green, where Carter seemed to be watching him with secret amusement. For one second Marty stared, and then bent to address his ball. Maybe you, maybe not. It makes no difference. In the silence that held the frozen gallery, he placed the clubhead back of the ball. His mind was ice and fire at the same time. Then suddenly it seemed to clear; his brain was a funnel of twisting light shapes, and a brilliant point of clarity peeped at him from the open end. Find him! he prayed. The one that got me into this horrible mess—find him and kill him! Kill him! *Kill him!*

He felt his arms being lifted as by an outside force, felt the clubhead come whirling through. As he felt the solid impact of the club against the ball, he smiled secretly; he had never hit a ball as well or as hard in his life. . . .

Too much sleeping-juice drunk in too many crummy motels over the years, they play hell with the reflexes. Marty didn't even hear the sharp gasp of the gallery, or the woman's high scream as the ball came back from the rock spur. When his head came up, the ball seemed to be waiting for him. For one split second it seemed to hover before his eyes; then it came on.

And, of course, he was in no condition to see that odd bounce, and see the ball trickle over, still spotted with red, and drop into the waiting cup. . . .

boxing

Two men trying to beat each other's brains out is probably as old as mankind itself. Boxing is perhaps one of the simplest, most basic of sports. It places a premium on speed, stamina, and guts. Historically it has been a sport (at least in the United States) to which the poor of society have been attracted. It offered—or appeared to offer—strong young men a way out of poverty and out of a potential life of crime.

Boxing was a popular sport in ancient Rome, where it was a featured event in the arena. The fighters used a form of glove called the *cestus*, which was equipped with spikes. The bouts were so brutal that the Romans finally refused to permit the matches, thereby gaining the distinction of being the first group to ban a "sport."

The sport then entered into a decline which lasted for many centuries. Disputes between men were settled in these later periods by duels, usually with swords. "Gentlemen" would never consider using their fists. However, boxing reappeared in England, largely for unknown reasons, during the eighteenth century. The Englishman John Figg was the first famous boxing champion, to be followed by a long line of immortals. The fighters of this era fought with bare knuckles until the sport was standardized by the Marquis of Queensberry in 1867. He advocated the wearing of gloves, a standard round of three minutes of fighting and one minute of rest, and the count of ten to constitute a knockout. Much later, the mandatory eight-count rule was instituted in the United States as a precautionary device.

Heavyweight champions like John L. Sullivan helped to popularize boxing, although the sport had trouble receiving the sanction of local and national authorities who were concerned about the brutality and the type of people attracted to it. For many years the police raided boxing matches, hence many of them had to be held in secret. Eventually, state boxing commissions were established to regulate and control the sport, although they failed to keep the undesirable element away. Boxing has been infiltrated to greater or lesser degrees by underworld figures and groups, but the situation is much better today than in the past, when numerous young men were deprived of their earnings by unscrupulous managers and promoters.

Boxing seems to have reached its peak in the United States during the period 1920 to 1940, with champions like Jack Dempsey and Joe Louis attracting large followings. The sport has always lent itself to ethnic and racial identification, and Irish, Italian, Jewish, and black fighters have had large followings within their own communities. During the 1950s, boxing was a very popular television attraction, but many have argued overexposure on television killed the sport. While there may be some truth to that assertion, it is more likely that increased opportunities for social mobility combined with opportunities for college scholarships for other sports have been equally responsible for its decline in the United States. It remains very popular in other areas of the world, however, and with the exception of the heavier weight divisions, the focus of boxing has shifted to Europe and to the Third World countries. Boxing in the United States still has its charismatic figures like Muhammad Ali, but it is highly doubtful that it will ever regain its former prominence in American sports.

Title Fight
william campbell gault

Sports are reflections of the society in which they take place. In the case of the United States, this has meant the spillover of racial, religious, and ethnic identities into the world of sports. Blacks were excluded from many sports until after World War II, and Jews found it difficult to participate in sports like golf and yachting because of the restrictive policies of country and yacht clubs.

After about 1920, boxing was not one of these restrictive sports. Fighters from all ethnic groups competed for titles in the various weight divisions. Boxing provided a way out of poverty for members of these groups. Indeed, the ethnic makeup of boxing at any given time provides an excellent guide to the economic makeup of a given period in American history.

Each group has had its favorites, and entire rooting sections could be found at the bouts. The folk heroes who emerged in boxing never exercised the potential for leadership that was (and is) clearly present within their communities. But what if they did? What kind of leadership could they offer, and what would be their goals? Would they be a force for good, or would they be a force for evil?

Title Fight

The sounds from above were dim in the dressing room. Over his head, between him and the thousands of fans, were the tons of concrete, robot-made concrete. Man conceived but robot made.

He looked down at his hands, his strong, short-fingered hands. Complete with fingerprints—but of protonol. Who'd know it, to look at them? In man's image, he was made. In God's image, man was made, if one believed in that, anymore. In man's image, he was made, but not with man's status.

His name was Alix 1340, which meant only that he was the thirteen hundred and fortieth of the Alix type. The short, broad Nordic type. In about twenty minutes, he was due in the ring. He was fighting for the middle-weight championship of the world.

Joe Nettleton had dreamed that one up. It had been born in the verbiage of his daily syndicated sports column, nurtured by the fans' clamor, and fanned into reality—by what? Animosity? These robots were coming up in the world, getting too big for their britches. Nick Nolan would show this Alix his place.

Nick was the champ, a man, made in His image. He

butted and thumbed and gouged and heeled. His favorite target was the groin. But *he* was a man. Oh, yes, he was a man. A champion among men.

Manny came in. His real title was Manuel 4307, but robots like to forget the numbers. He was Manny, Alix's manager and number-one second. A deft and sharp and able robot, Manny.

He said, "I thought it would be better if we were alone. No fans, especially. And I've had a bellyful of sportswriters."

"Even Joe Nettleton?" Alix asked. "Joe's on our side, isn't he?"

"It's hard to say. Do you ever wonder about him, Alix?"

Alix didn't answer, right away. He knew there were robots who "passed," went over to the status line and lived as humans. He didn't know how many there were, and he often wondered about them. In every robot brain, there was a remote-controlled circuit breaker. They could be stopped with the throwing of a switch at the personnel center. There was a well-guarded office and a man on duty at that center twenty-four hours of every day.

Now Alix said, "I never thought much about Joe, either way."

"What have you been thinking?" Manny asked

"I've been thinking," Alix said slowly, "that we fight man's wars and pulverate his garbage and dehydrate his sewerage, but we're not citizens. Why, Manny?"

"We're not human. We're not—orthodox." Manny was watching him closely as he spoke.

"Not human? They feed us Bach and Brahms and

Beethoven and Shakespeare and Voltaire in our incubation period, don't they? And all the others I've forced myself to forget. Does this—this *soul* come from somewhere outside the system?"

"I guess it does. They don't feed us much religion, but I guess it comes from God."

"And what's He like?"

"It would depend upon who you ask, I guess," Manny said. "Sort of a superman. From Him they get their charity and tolerance and justice and all the rest of their noble attributes." Manny's laugh was bitter. "How they love themselves."

"They're so sure about everything else," Alix said, "but not very sure of their God. Is that it?"

"That's about it. I heard one man say He watched when a sparrow falls. I guess we're less than the sparrows, Alix."

There was a silence, and then Manny put a hand on Alix's shoulder. "We've got about fifteen minutes, and I've got a million things to say. Maybe I should have said them earlier."

Alix turned at the gravity of Manny's voice. His lumagel eyes went over Manny's dark face, absorbing his rigid intensity. Whatever it was that was coming, it was more important than the fight.

Manny said quietly, "Win this one, and blood will run in the streets, Alix."

"Human blood?"

"White man's blood. We've got the Negro, and the Jap, and the Chinamen and all the rest of them who got their rights so recently. And what kind of rights have they got? Civil, not in the people's hearts. You think those races don't know it? We were talking of their God, Alix. Well, the robots have one, too. His name is Alix 1340."

"Manny, you've gone crazy."

"Have I? Joe Nettleton's one of us, Alix. This was his scheme, and the four men who run the switch at the personnel center; they're ours, too. Top robots. Their IQ's all crowding two hundred. We've got the brains, Alix, and the manpower. We've got the combined venom of a billion nonwhites. And now we've got you."

"A pug. What kind of god would I make? You're off the beam, Manny."

"Am I? Did I ever give you anything but the straight dope? They adore you, Alix. You've been a model to them. You could be their king, if you say the word."

"You've been setting this up, you and Joe Nettleton? This fight tonight's the crisis? You've been building toward tonight?"

"But it takes a front man, a symbol. You're the only one who can be that. You're the only one they'd all back."

Alix looked again at his hands, the hands that had taken him to the first mixed fight in history, to a title fight. "Man Versus The Machine," most of the sports scribes had labeled it, though not Joe Nettleton. Machine? A machine that had assimilated Voltaire? A machine that had listened to Brahms?

What differentiates man from his machines? Supremacy? Supremacy would be established tonight. No, it wasn't physical supremacy. And there were robots far beyond man's mental powers.

The spark, then, the spark from their God? How did

they know they had it? In all the wrangling mysticism that had gone through so many directed misinterpretations, where could they find their God?

"Thinking it over?" Manny asked. "Why so quiet, Alix?"

Alix's grin was saturnine. "Believe it or not, I was thinking of God."

"*Their* God?"

Alix frowned. "I suppose. Their's and the sparrows'."

There were three spaced knocks at the door. Manny said, "Joe Nettleton. He wants to talk to you. We've got about eight minutes, Alix." He went to the door.

Joe Nettleton was tall, and pale, and brown-eyed. The eyes should be lumagel, and Alix studied them, but could note no difference from those of a man.

Joe said to Manny, "He knows?"

Manny nodded.

Joe turned back. "Well—Alix—?"

"I don't know. It's—it's—monstrous, it's—" He shrugged his shoulders and pounded one hand into the palm of the other.

"You're *it*, Alix. King, god, what you will. For six years, I've built you up—in *their* papers, in *their* minds. Clean, quiet, hardworking Alix. And humble. Oh, the humility I gave you has made me cry, at times."

Manny said in mild protest, "You didn't have to build that angle much. Alix is humble. Alix is—he's—he's—" And the articulate Manny had no words.

Joe Nettleton's pale face was cynical. He said, "The way you feel is the way they all feel—the black ones out there and the brown ones and the yellow ones."

"They've got their rights," Alix said.

"Have they? Take a look at the first twenty rows, ringside. You'll see what rights they have, word rights, paper rights. But not in the hearts of men. Oh, the grapes of wrath are out there, Alix, beyond the twentieth row. Haven't you any sense of history, of destiny?"

Alix didn't answer.

Manny said, "He's been thinking of God, he tells me."

Joe Nettleton's face was blank. "God? Their God?" He looked at Alix wonderingly. "This Superman they scare us with? You don't eat that malarkey, do you, Alix?"

Alix shrugged, saying nothing.

"They don't believe it themselves," Joe protested. "It's one of those symbols they set up, to make them superior. They ever tell you what He looks like? Oh, they give Him a prophet sure, and the prophet gives them words to live by. Don't kill, don't steal, don't lie, don't lust, don't envy— Words, Alix, words, words, words— Judge them by their actions."

Alix looked up. "I'm not—cut out to be a leader."

"Yes, you are. And I cut you out, in their minds, with words. The brown ones read me and the black ones and the yellow ones, and I built you up, in their minds—*and tonight they'll wait for a signal from you.*"

"A signal from me? Are you—what—?"

"A signal from you. To those in the crowd, to those watching on the video screens, the ones who are briefed and *know* about rioting, about how to steer a revolution. Think of the irony of it—man's prejudice building the army of resentment and man's genius building the machines that army can use to destroy man—white man. White man—first."

"First—?" Manny said. "You've dreams beyond tonight, Joe?"

Joe smiled disarmingly. "I use too many words. That one got away. We can't think beyond tonight, now." He turned to Alix. "It's not an involved signal, Alix. It's just one word. The word is 'kill.' From *you* it's more than a word, it's an order."

There was a knock at the door, and the sono-bray above the door said, "Time to go up. Time for the big one."

All three were silent, and then Joe put a hand on Alix's shoulder. "You can't give the signal from your back, Alix. You'd better be standing up, when this one is over with."

Alix looked at Joe, trying to read behind those brown eyes. Alix said, "I'll be standing up. There's never been a second I doubted that."

They went out, and there was a clamor, a ring of scribes in the corridor beyond the showers. One of them voiced it for all of them, "What the hell is this, Manny? Joe a cousin, or something? How about a statement?"

Manny looked at them bleakly. "We hope to win, but we're up against a superior being. It's in God's lap."

Cynical men, but they resented the blasphemy— coming from a robot.

Joe said, "And Alix is his prophet. Who's betting what?"

No answer. They stared at Joe, and some wrote down a few words. One of them looked at Alix.

"How about you, Alix? How do you feel?"

Alix the humble, the new-day Uncle Tom, the subservient. Alix lifted his chin and didn't smile. "Confident. I'll win."

"How?" another asked.

"Hitting him harder, and oftener. What's he got but a hook and an iron jaw?"

"Guts," one of them said. "You've got to hand him that, Alix."

"I concede nothing," Alix answered. "We'll see, tonight."

There were no further questions. They went down the long aisle that led to the bright ring, Manny and Alix and the other handler, who'd been waiting in the prelim boys' shower room.

Eighty thousand people in the Bowl, a clear, warm night, and millions watching on the video screens around the globe. Video hadn't hurt this one—this was history, a robot crossing the status line. They wanted to be a part of this.

The referee was black, Willie Newton. It would look like less favoritism if the referee was black, reasoned the white men in their left-handed reasoning.

Bugs around the arcs, and big, ebony Willie in his striped shirt, waiting in the ring, smiling, just *happening* to be in Alix's corner as he climbed through.

Willie bent, pretending to help part the ropes. Willie whispered, "You'll get all the breaks you need, Alix."

Alix came through and stood erect. "I don't want a single break, Willie, just a fair shake. *You* can understand it has to be like that."

"I can, Alix. I'm sorry. About the name—just Alix? Or I could blur the rest."

"Alix one-three-four-oh, not blurred. It's my name."

He turned from Willie then, acknowledging the thunder behind him, both hands high in salute. He could see the rows stretching out from ringside—the first twenty all white. Most of the thunder came from high in the stands.

And now the champ came down his aisle, his faded purple dressing robe across his bulky shoulders, his handlers a respectful few paces behind him.

Nick Nolan, the middleweight champion of the world. His ears were lumpy, his brows ridged with scar tissue. His round head centered on those bulky shoulders, apparently with no neck to connect them. A fringe of red hair and a brutal, thick-featured face.

Made in His image?

Some words ran through Alix's mind— "Is this the Thing Lord God made and gave— To have dominion over sea and land . . . ?"

This was a hell of a time to be recalling Markham.

Nick came over to his corner, the false geniality on his face as phony as the gesture of a champ coming to the challenger's corner. Nick said, "Best—between us, huh?"

"The better," Alix corrected him. "Keep them above the belt, Nick."

Nick grinned. "Don't I always? I came up the hard way, Alix."

Alix said nothing, staring . . . *when this dumb Terror shall rise to judge the world . . .*

A man with a hook and an urge to combat. The hard way? Maybe. He'd taken enough punches to give him a lifetime lease on Queer Street. But he'd handed out more than he'd received. A spoiler and a mixer. A weight-draper and infighter and an easy bleeder.

Blood will run in the streets, Alix. . . .

In the ring, Nick's blood would flow, and further stain the spotted canvas. In the streets, the blood of Nick's brothers would flow, in the streets around the world.

Title fight? Oh, yes.

The Irishman first, he'd come up through the ring to his grudging equality, and the Jew, then, and the Filipino and the Negro and the Cuban and all the others who wouldn't stay down. Who had their fists and their guts. Mickey Walker, Benny Leonard, Joe Louis—immortals all. Great men, great champs, great memories.

And he? Alix 1340? Different, a machine, no spark. He'd almost forgotten about no spark.

Nick's manager came over to inspect the bandages on Alix's hands, and then went back to his corner with Manny to inspect those on the battered hands of the champ.

Alix's hands were clean-lined, no breaks, no lumps. Alix was a scientific hitter, and his protonol was better than the natural product.

He watches the sparrows, Manny had said. *A signal,* Joe had said. I wish somebody would give me a signal, Alix thought. It's too big for me.

The introductions, the numbers not blurred. The instructions, and Willie saying, "Clean tonight, Nick. I know you well, Nick. But this one is touchy, remember."

"Ah, save it," Nick told him. Champ, big man, Nick Nolan.

The buzzer and Manny's brief pat on the shoulder. Rising, and flexing on the ropes, looking down into that sea of faces, white faces. The ones who held dominion over sea and land.

Bugs in the arcs, a hush on the crowd, and the bell.

Alix turned and here came Nick, shuffling across, wasting no time, bringing the fight to the upstart.

Nick had a right hand, too, but it was clumsy. The hook was better trained. Alix circled to his left, away from Nick's left, and put his jab easily to Nick's nose.

There are sportswriters, Alix knew, who talked of a *right* hook, but a man would need to be a contortionist to throw it. Unless he was *completely* unorthodox. Or a southpaw.

Nick was neither. Nick had a right hand like a mallet, but it came from below or above, and was telegraphed by the pulling up of his right foot. Nick saved that for the time his opponent couldn't see or react.

Nick came in with the hook, trying to slide under Alix's extended left hand, trying to time the pattern of his feet to Alix's circling, looking for the hole.

Alix peppered him with the left, and then saw the low left hand of Nick. Alix stopped circling—and tossed a singing right.

It traveled over Nick's left and found the button. Nick took two stumbling backward steps, and went down.

Resin dust swirled and the scream of the stands was like a single anguished cry.

Alix went to a neutral corner, shrugging his shoulder muscles loose, trying to still the sudden pounding of his heart. Nick had been knocked down before, often.

He took a full count, under the rules, but was on one knee at three. The big black semaphore of Willie's right hand and then those hands wiping the gloves and Willie stepping clear.

Nick stormed in. He got through Alix's left, this time, and sent a looping right hand high. It missed, but it was meant to miss. Nick's elbow smashed Alix's mouth.

Rage, a red rage, and they stood in the corner, trading leather.

The hook came in low, and pain knifed into Alix's groin. In his aching blindness he could feel Nick's feet groping for his, trying to find his instep.

Champion, model.

Alix grabbed, and hung on. This one he had to win. This one could be lost, right now.

Nick said, "Break it up, phony man. I can't hit you when you're hanging on."

The big slap of Willie's hand. Willie, playing it straight. Alix broke at the touch.

Alix broke—and Nick threw the right hand, on the break.

Foul? Of course, but Alix went down, his senses numb, his mind turning black. He lay on his face, not moving, the blackness moving through his body.

What's this God like? It would depend upon who you ask. They ever tell you what He looks like? The blackness turned red, the red of blood, running in the streets. And there was suddenly a cross, and a dim figure, and he heard Willie's sonorous, "Five, six—"

He turned over at seven, was on one knee at eight, and up at nine. And Nick came bulling in, both hands ready.

The bell.

He got to his corner without Manny's help. The magic of Manny's hands dug at his neck, bringing clarity. The ice, the other handler probing at his flaccid legs.

"I saw a cross, Manny."

"Nobody's crossing us, Alix. Don't think, Alix. Here." He gave him the water bottle.

Alix rinsed his mouth, and spit it out. "He's rough, Manny. He knows all the tricks."

"Don't you?"

"I don't want to. I saw a cross when I was unconscious, Manny. A cross like you see on a church."

"Don't tell me about it. Get him, boy. Don't try to mix with him, but get him, with that left, with your speed, with your brain. Get him."

"I'll try. But he's not typical, Manny. They're not all like Nick."

"The hell they aren't. He's one of the better ones. Get him."

The buzzer, the bell, and Nick.

Nick with the iron jaw, Nick with the hook and the bulging shoulders, Nick the champion.

Alix put the left into Nick's face, but it wasn't a jab. It was a straight left, with shoulder in it. It twisted Nick's nose, and brought blood.

Nick was nettled, and he charged. He charged into a straight, sweet right hand that was delivered from a flat-footed stance. Nick wavered, and tried to grab.

Alix felt his strength pour back and the pattern of his feet was sure and planned. A left, a feint, a jolting right, moving around this hulk, this blundering knot of flesh and muscle, beating a tattoo on him, spreading the blood. *Get him.*

It looked like a slaughterhouse. Blood all over Nick's face, and blood matting the curled, sweaty hair on his chest. Starting to look dazed, starting to wonder, the champ. The untypical man? He must be, he had to be, to have dominion over sea and land.

Why didn't he go down? Couldn't he see the pattern of it, the pattern Alix was tracing for him with his blood-soaked gloves? Why didn't he go down? Why didn't he quit?

He hadn't quit by the end of the fifth round. Out there, those eighty thousand were silent. This was no fight, this was now murder. Why didn't he quit?

Alix asked Manny, on the stool, before the sixth, "Why doesn't he quit? He can't win. Manny, I hate to hit him."

"Don't be a sucker. Don't be a damned fool." Manny's voice was hoarse. "As long as there's a spark of life in those bastards, they won't quit. He's dangerous yet, Alix."

A spark, a spark— Life? Cognizance? No, life, a spark of life.

In the sixth, Nick almost went to his knees, in the middle of the ring. But he got control, and stumbled toward Alix.

Alix came in fast and carelessly—and the earth erupted.

He's dangerous, yet, Alix. There was no blackness this

time, just the blood red. There was no cross. But a voice? "In the sky, in the sky—" Silence.

Get up, Alix. For the black and brown and red and yellow who are watching you, around the world, get up. You're their hope, you're their WORD. Up, to one knee, and up just under the wire.

Nick didn't charge, this time. Wary and careful, he was, after the pasting he'd been taking. Let Alix make the mistakes, like the one he just had. Nick only needed one more.

Manny said, "Can you hit him, now? Still mourning for him, are you?"

Alix said, "I'm a machine, Manny. He can't hurt me. I can hurt him, but he can't hurt me."

"That's my boy," Manny said. "I'm glad you know what side of the fence you're on, finally."

"I know my place," Alix said. "I know my job."

"That you do. Get him."

He got him. They don't quit, these men. Not while they're conscious. Not while they're alive. Alix hit him everywhere there was room to hit, with both hands, knocking him down four times in the seventh round.

Each time, Nick got up. And in the eighth, he came out to meet Alix, walking into his doom, not flinching, not hiding, putting his crown on the line.

Supremacy? Nick had it, bastard though he was. But for how long? How long could he stay that dumb and still live?

Nick came out, his low hands a farce of a defense.

How long could he hold the animosity down with his arrogance and his brutality and his shoddiness? How much time did he have? Alix knew.

Nick came out for the eighth, and Alix hit him with a solid right hand. He didn't set it up, or feint Nick into the spot, or hesitate. There wasn't any need to.

He put all his weight and most of his bitterness into the button shot that made him middleweight champion of the world.

Silence, a shocked silence at the history before them, and then, from the far seats, from the cheap seats, acclamation. The video cameras covered the ring, the crowd; the lights went on all over the huge bowl.

Manny hugged him, Joe Nettleton hugged him, and others.

In the far seats, no one moved. In the near seats, no one moved. Joe said, "The word, Alix."

They were bringing the banked microphones over, the microphones that would carry the word all over the world. The cameras trained on him. The word.

He looked at Joe, and Manny. He brought the mikes to mouth level, and moved back a bit. He said, "I won, tonight. I've no message for you. But someone has. It's in the sky."

Craning necks, a murmur, the cameras leaving Alix as the operators swung the huge machines toward the red letters in the sky.

Beside him, Manny gasped. Joe Nettleton stared, unbelieving, his mouth slack.

Red letters? Something like red, but luminous and miles high, and definite. The cameras were trained directly on it, now:

FIND YOUR GOD

Manny said, "Alix—how— Are you, did you? Alix, what in hell are you?"

"There's more to it they don't know," Alix said. "It's 'Find your God or your machines will kill you.' I don't think there's any need to tell them the rest if they obey the first."

Manny said hoarsely, "But this message came through you? You're a—"

"A prophet? Me, a machine, Alix 1340?"

Joe said, "You're not sending out the other word?"

"Not yet. It's not time."

"How do *you* know," Manny cut in. "How do you know if it's time or not? And if their God wanted to send a message, why should he use a machine? Why should he use you?"

"Because," Alix said, "no man would listen. And if they don't listen, now, Manny, our time *will* come. . . ."

Steel
richard matheson

There is no sadder scene in all of sports than that of the washed-up fighter who continues to fight. Overage, overweight, abused and confused by managers who don't care about him, the fighter fights on, because that is the only way he knows of making a living. The fighter as slave was graphically portrayed in films like *The Harder They Fall* and *Requiem for a Heavyweight*.

Much has been written about the seamy side of boxing —the gangster element, the violence, the pain, and the deaths. There have been periodic calls for the banning of boxing in "civilized" countries. The question of the banning of boxing is a complex one with no easy answers. Fighters compete because boxing is a big business. Banning it would only drive it underground. However, it needs close governmental regulation in order to ensure both the safety and the honor of the sport.

In this story, Richard Matheson envisions a society which does not permit fights between men but allows bouts between androids, artificial men. Watching competition between nonhumans is not new—witness, for example, dog racing. But as science and technology create changes in all areas of life, we can expect technology to alter the form of our sports. As in the story, someday sports trainers may have to be trained in mechanics as well as in first aid, able to change transistors as easily as they wrap ankles in tape. The team physician of the future may require a degree in electronics rather than a degree in medicine. The transition will not be easy. Here is an example of that classic science fiction theme: the struggle between man and machine.

Steel

The two men came out of the station rolling a covered object. They rolled it along the platform until they reached the middle of the train, then grunted as they lifted it up the steps, the sweat running down their bodies. One of its wheels fell off and bounced down the metal steps and a man coming up behind them picked it up and handed it to the man who was wearing a rumpled brown suit.

"Thanks," said the man in the brown suit and he put the wheel in his side coat pocket.

Inside the car, the men pushed the covered object down the aisle. With one of its wheels off, it was lopsided and the man in the brown suit—his name was Kelly—had to keep his shoulder braced against it to keep it from toppling over. He breathed heavily and licked away tiny balls of sweat that kept forming over his upper lip.

When they reached the middle of the car, the man in the wrinkled blue suit pushed forward one of the seat backs so there were four seats, two facing two. Then the two men pushed the covered object between the seats and Kelly reached through a slit in the covering and felt around until he found the right button.

The covered object sat down heavily on a seat by the window.

"Oh, God, listen to'm squeak," said Kelly.

The other man, Pole, shrugged and sat down with a sigh.

"What d'ya expect?" he asked.

Kelly was pulling off his suit coat. He dropped it down on the opposite seat and sat down beside the covered object.

"Well, we'll get 'im some o' that stuff soon's we're paid off," he said worriedly.

"If we can find some," said Pole, who was almost as thin as one. He sat slumped back against the hot seat watching Kelly mop at his sweaty cheeks.

"Why shouldn't we?" asked Kelly, pushing the damp handkerchief down under his shirt collar.

"Because they don't make it no more," Pole said with the false patience of a man who has had to say the same thing too many times.

"Well, that's crazy," said Kelly. He pulled off his hat and patted at the bald spot in the center of his rust-colored hair. "There's still plenty B-twos in the business."

"Not many," said Pole, bracing one foot upon the covered object.

"*Don't*," said Kelly.

Pole let his foot drop heavily and a curse fell slowly from his lips. Kelly ran the handkerchief around the lining of his hat. He started to put the hat on again, then changed his mind and dropped it on top of his coat.

"God, but it's hot," he said.

"It'll get hotter," said Pole.

Across the aisle a man put his suitcase up on the rack, took off his suit coat, and sat down, puffing. Kelly looked at him, then turned back.

"Ya think it'll be hotter in Maynard, huh?" he asked.

Pole nodded. Kelly swallowed dryly.

"Wish we could have another o' them beers," he said.

Pole stared out the window at the heat waves rising from the concrete platform.

"I had three beers," said Kelly, "and I'm just as thirsty as I was when I started."

"Yeah," said Pole.

"Might as well've not had a beer since Philly," said Kelly.

Pole said, "Yeah."

Kelly sat there staring at Pole a moment. Pole had dark hair and white skin and his hands were the hands of a man who should be bigger than Pole was. But the hands were as clever as they were big. Pole's one o' the best, Kelly thought, one o' the best.

"Ya think he'll be all right?" he asked.

Pole grunted and smiled for an instant without being amused.

"If he don't get hit," he said.

"No, no, I mean it," said Kelly.

Pole's dark, lifeless eyes left the station and shifted over to Kelly.

"So do I," he said.

"Come on," Kelly said.

"Steel," said Pole, "ya know just as well as me. He's shot t'hell."

"That ain't true," said Kelly, shifting uncomfortably. "All he needs is a little work. A little overhaul 'n' he'll be good as new."

"Yeah, a little three-four-grand overhaul," Pole said, "with parts they don't make no more." He looked out the window again.

"Oh . . . it ain't as bad as that," said Kelly. "Hell, the way you talk you'd think he was ready for scrap."

"Ain't he?" Pole asked.

"No," said Kelly angrily, "he *ain't.*"

Pole shrugged and his long white fingers rose and fell in his lap.

"Just 'cause he's a little old," said Kelly.

"Old." Pole grunted. "*Ancient.*"

"Oh . . ." Kelly took a deep breath of the hot air in the car and blew it out through his broad nose. He looked at the covered object like a father who was angry with his son's faults but angrier with those who mentioned the faults of his son.

"Plenty o' fight left in him," he said.

Pole watched the people walking on the platform. He watched a porter pushing a wagon full of piled suitcases.

"Well . . . is he okay?" Kelly asked finally as if he hated to ask.

Pole looked over at him.

"I dunno, Steel," he said. "He needs work. Ya know that. The trigger spring in his left arm's been rewired so many damn times it's almost shot. He's got no protection on that side. The left side of his face's all beat in, the eye lens is cracked. The leg cables is worn, they're pulled slack, the tension's gone to hell. Even his gyro's off."

Pole looked out at the platform again with a disgusted hiss.

"Not to mention the oil paste he ain't got in 'im," he said.

"We'll get 'im some," Kelly said.

"Yeah, *after* the fight, *after* the fight!" Pole snapped. "What about *before* the fight? He'll be creakin' around that ring like a goddam—*steam shovel*. It'll be a miracle if he does two rounds. They'll prob'ly ride us outta town on a rail."

Kelly swallowed. "I don't think it's that bad," he said.

"The *hell* it ain't," said Pole. "It's worse. Wait'll that crowd gets a load of 'Battling Maxo' from Philadelphia. They'll blow a nut. We'll be lucky if we get our five hundred bucks."

"Well, the contract's signed," said Kelly firmly. "They can't back out now. I got a copy right in the old pocket." He leaned over and patted at his coat.

"That contract's for Battling Maxo," said Pole. "Not for this—steam shovel here."

"Maxo's gonna do all right," said Kelly as if he was trying hard to believe it. "He's not as bad off as you say."

"Against a B-*seven*?" Pole asked.

"It's just a *starter* B-*seven*," said Kelly. "It ain't got the kinks out yet."

Pole turned away.

"Battling Maxo," he said. "One-round Maxo. The battling steam shovel."

"Aw, shut the hell up!" Kelly snapped suddenly, getting redder.

"You're always knockin' 'im down. Well, he's been doin' OK for twelve years now and he'll keep on doin'

OK. So he needs some oil paste. And he needs a little work. *So what?* With five hundred bucks we can get him all the paste he needs. And a new trigger spring for his arm and—and new leg cables! And everything. Chris-*sake.*"

He fell back against the seat, chest shuddering with breath, and rubbed at his cheeks with his wet handkerchief. He looked aside at Maxo. Abruptly, he reached over a hand and patted Maxo's covered knee clumsily and the steel clanked hollowly under his touch.

"You're doin' all right," said Kelly to his fighter.

The train was moving across a sun-baked prairie. All the windows were open but the wind that blew in was like blasts from an oven.

Kelly sat reading his paper, his shirt sticking wetly to his broad chest. Pole had taken his coat off too and was staring morosely out the window at the grass-tufted prairie that went as far as he could see. Maxo sat under his covering, his heavy steel frame rocking a little with the motion of the train.

Kelly put down his paper.

"Not even a word," he said.

"What d'ya expect?" Pole asked. "They don't cover Maynard."

"Maxo ain't just some clunk from Maynard," said Kelly. "He was big time. Ya'd think they'd"—he shrugged —"remember him."

"Why? For a coupla prelims in the Garden three years ago?" Pole asked.

"It wasn't no three years, buddy," said Kelly definitely.

"It was in 1977," said Pole, "and now it's 1980. That's three years where I come from."

"It was late '77," said Kelly. "Right before Christmas. Don't ya remember? Just before—Marge and me . . ."

Kelly didn't finish. He stared down at the paper as if Marge's picture were on it—the way she looked the day she left him.

"What's the difference?" Pole asked. "They don't remember *them*, for Chrissake. With a coupla thousand o' the damn things floatin' around? How could they remember 'em? About the only ones who get space are the champeens and the new models."

Pole looked at Maxo. "I hear Mawling's puttin' out a B-nine this year," he said.

Kelly refocused his eyes. "Yeah?" he said uninterestedly.

"Hyper-triggers in both arms—*and* legs. All steeled aluminum. Triple gyro. Triple-twisted wiring. God, they'll be beautiful."

Kelly put down the paper.

"Think they'd remember him," he muttered. "It wasn't so long ago."

His face relaxed in a smile of recollection.

"Boy, will I ever forget that night," he said. "No one gives us a tumble. It was all Dimsy the Rock, Dimsy the Rock. *Three* t'one for Dimsy the Rock. Dimsy the Rock—fourth-rankin' light heavy. On his way t'the top."

He chuckled deep in his chest. "And did we ever put him away," he said. "*Oooh.*" He grunted with savage pleasure. "I can see that left cross now. *Bang!* Right in the chops. And old Dimsy the Rock hittin' the canvas like a—like a *rock*, yeah, *just* like a rock!"

He laughed happily. "Boy, what a night, what a night," he said. "Will I ever forget that night?"

Pole looked at Kelly with a somber face. Then he turned away and stared at the dusty sun-baked plain again.

"I wonder," he muttered.

Kelly saw the man across the aisle looking again at the covered Maxo. He caught the man's eye and smiled, then gestured with his head toward Maxo.

"That's my fighter," he said loudly.

The man smiled politely, cupping a hand behind one ear.

"My fighter," said Kelly. "Battling Maxo. Ever hear of 'im?"

The man stared at Kelly a moment before shaking his head.

Kelly smiled. "Yeah, he was almost light-heavyweight champ once," he told the man. The man nodded politely.

On an impulse, Kelly got up and stepped across the aisle. He reversed the seat back in front of the man and sat down facing him.

"Pretty damn hot," he said.

The man smiled. "Yes. Yes it is," he said.

"No new trains out here yet, huh?"

"No," said the man. "Not yet."

"Got all the new ones back in Philly," said Kelly. "That's where"—he gestured with his head—"my friend 'n' I come from. And Maxo."

Kelly stuck out his hand.

"The name's Kelly," he said. "Tim Kelly."

The man looked surprised. His grip was loose.

When he drew back his hand he rubbed it unobtrusively on his pants leg.

"I used t'be called 'Steel' Kelly," said Kelly. "Used t'be in the business m'self. Before the war, o' course. I was a light heavy."

"Oh?"

"Yeah. That's right. Called me 'Steel' 'cause I never got knocked down once. Not *once*. I was even number nine in the ranks once. Yeah."

"I see." The man waited patiently.

"My—fighter," said Kelly, gesturing toward Maxo with his head again. "He's a light heavy too. We're fightin' in Maynard t'night. You goin' that far?"

"Uh-no," said the man. "No, I'm—getting off at Hayes."

"Oh." Kelly nodded. "Too bad. Gonna be a good scrap." He let out a heavy breath. "Yeah, he was—fourth in the ranks once. He'll be *back* too. He—uh—knocked down Dimsy the Rock in late '77. Maybe ya read about that."

"I don't believe. . . ."

"Oh. Uh-huh." Kelly nodded. "Well . . . it was in all the East Coast papers. You know. New York, Boston, Philly. Yeah it—got a hell of a spread. Biggest upset o' the year."

He scratched at his bald spot.

"He's a B-two, y'know, but—that means he's the second model Mawling put out," he explained, seeing the look on the man's face. "That was back in—let's see—'67, I think it was. Yeah, '67."

He made a smacking sound with his lips. "Yeah, that was a good model," he said. "The best. Maxo's still goin' strong." He shrugged depreciatingly. "I don't go for these new ones," he said. "You know. The ones made o' steeled aluminum with all the doo-dads."

The man stared at Kelly blankly.

"Too . . . flashy—flimsy. Nothin' . . ." Kelly bunched his big fist in front of his chest and made a face. "Nothin' *solid*," he said. "No. Mawling don't make 'em like Maxo no more."

"I see," said the man.

Kelly smiled.

"Yeah," he said. "Used t'be in the game m'self. When there was enough men, o' course. Before the bans." He shook his head, then smiled quickly. "Well," he said, "we'll take this B-seven. Don't even know what his name is," he said, laughing.

His face sobered for an instant and he swallowed.

"We'll take 'im," he said.

Later on, when the man had gotten off the train, Kelly went back to his seat. He put his feet up on the opposite seat and, laying back his head, he covered his face with the newspaper.

"Get a little shut-eye," he said.

Pole grunted.

Kelly sat slouched back, staring at the newspaper next to his eyes. He felt Maxo bumping against his side a little. He listened to the squeaking of Maxo's joints. "Be all right," he muttered to himself.

"What?" Pole asked.

Kelly swallowed. "I didn't say anything," he said.

When they got off the train at six o'clock that evening they pushed Maxo around the station and onto the sidewalk. Across the street from them a man sitting in his taxi called them.

"We got no taxi money," said Pole.

"We can't just push 'im through the streets," Kelly said. "Besides, we don't even know where Kruger Stadium is."

"What are we supposed to eat with then?"

"We'll be loaded after the fight," said Kelly. "I'll buy you a steak three inches thick."

Sighing, Pole helped Kelly push the heavy Maxo across the street that was still so hot they could feel it through their shoes. Kelly started sweating right away and licking at his upper lip.

"God, how d'they live out here?" he asked.

When they were putting Maxo inside the cab the base wheel came out again and Pole, with a snarl, kicked it away.

"What're ya *doin'*?" Kelly asked.

"Oh . . . sh—" Pole got into the taxi and slumped back against the warm leather of the seat while Kelly hurried over the soft tar pavement and picked up the wheel.

"Chris*sake*," Kelly muttered as he got in the cab. "What's the—?"

"Where to, chief?" the driver asked.

"Kruger Stadium," Kelly said.

"You're there." The cab driver pushed in the rotor button and the car glided away from the curb.

"What the hell's wrong with you?" Kelly asked Pole in a low voice. "We wait more'n half a damn year t'get us a bout and you been nothin' but bellyaches from the start."

"Some bout," said Pole. "Maynard, Kansas—the prize-fightin' center o' the nation."

"It's a start, ain't it?" Kelly said. "It'll keep us in coffee 'n' cakes a while, won't it? It'll put Maxo back in shape. And if we take it, it could lead to—"

Pole glanced over disgustedly.

"I don't *get* you," Kelly said quietly. "He's our fighter. What're ya writin' 'im off for? Don't ya want 'im t'win?"

"I'm a class-A mechanic, Steel," Pole said in his falsely patient voice. "I'm not a daydreamin' kid. We got a piece o' dead iron here, not a B-seven. It's simple mechanics, Steel, that's all. Maxo'll be lucky if he comes out o' that ring with his head still on."

Kelly turned away angrily.

"It's a *starter* B-seven," he muttered. "Full o' kinks. *Full* of 'em."

"Sure, sure," said Pole.

They sat silently a while looking out the window, Maxo between them, the broad steel shoulders bumping against theirs. Kelly stared at the building, his hands clenching and unclenching in his lap as if he was getting ready to go fifteen rounds.

"Have you seen this Maynard Flash?" Pole asked the driver.

"The Flash? You bet. Man, there's a fighter on his way. Won seven straight. He'll be up there soon, ya can bet ya life. Matter o' fact he's fightin' t'night too. With some B-two heap from back East, I hear."

The driver snickered. "Flash'll slaughter 'im," he said.

Kelly stared at the back of the driver's head, the skin tight across his cheekbones.

"Yeah?" he said flatly.

"Man, he'll—"

The driver broke off suddenly and looked back. "Hey, you ain't—" he started, then turned front again. "Hey, I didn't know, mister," he said. "I was only ribbin'."

"Skip it," Pole said. "You're right."

Kelly's head snapped around and he glared at the sallow-faced Pole.

"*Shut up*," he said in a low voice.

He fell back against the seat and stared out the window, his face hard.

"I'm gonna get 'im some oil paste," he said after they'd ridden a block.

"Swell," said Pole. "We'll eat the tools."

"Go to hell," said Kelly.

The cab pulled up in front of the brick-fronted stadium and they lifted Maxo out onto the sidewalk. While Pole tilted him, Kelly squatted down and slid the base wheel back into its slot. Then Kelly paid the driver the exact fare and they started pushing Maxo toward the alley.

"Look," said Kelly, nodding toward the poster board in front of the stadium. The third fight listed was

MAYNARD FLASH

(B-7, L.H.)

VS.

BATTLING MAXO

(B-2, L.H.)

"Big deal," said Pole.

Kelly's smile disappeared. He started to say something, then pressed his lips together. He shook his head irritably and big drops of his sweat fell to the sidewalk.

Maxo creaked as they pushed him down the alley and carried him up the steps to the door. The base wheel fell out again and bounced down the cement steps. Neither one of them said anything.

It was hotter inside. The air didn't move.

"Get the wheel," Kelly said and started down the narrow hallway, leaving Pole with Maxo. Pole leaned Maxo against the wall and turned for the door.

Kelly came to a half-glassed office door and knocked.

"Yeah," said a voice inside. Kelly went in, taking off his hat.

The fat bald man looked up from his desk. His skull glistened with sweat.

"I'm Battling Maxo's owner," said Kelly, smiling. He extended his big hand but the man ignored it.

"Was wonderin' if you'd make it," said the man whose name was Mr. Waddow. "Your fighter in decent shape?"

"The best," said Kelly cheerfully. "The best. My mechanic—he's class-A—just took 'im apart and put 'im together again before we left Philly."

The man looked unconvinced.

"He's in good shape," said Kelly.

"You're lucky t'get a bout with a B-two," said Mr. Waddow. "We ain't used nothin' less than B-fours for more than two years now. The fighter we was after got stuck in a car wreck though and got ruined."

Kelly nodded. "Well, ya got nothin' t'worry about," he said. "My fighter's in top shape. He's the one knocked down Dimsy the Rock in Madison Square year or so ago."

"I want a good fight," said the fat man.

"You'll get a good fight," Kelly said, feeling a tight

pain in his stomach muscles. "Maxo's in good shape. You'll see. He's in top shape."

"I just want a good fight."

Kelly stared at the fat man a moment. Then he said, "You got a ready room we can use? The mechanic 'n' me'd like t'get something t'eat."

"Third door down the hall on the right side," said Mr. Waddow. "Your bout's at eight thirty."

Kelly nodded. "OK."

"Be there," said Mr. Waddow, turning back to his work.

"Uh . . . what about—?" Kelly started.

"You get ya money after ya deliver a fight," Mr. Waddow cut him off.

Kelly's smile faltered.

"OK," he said. "See ya then."

When Mr. Waddow didn't answer, he turned for the door.

"Don't slam the door," Mr. Waddow said. Kelly didn't.

"Come on," he said to Pole when he was in the hall again. They pushed Maxo down to the ready room and put him inside it.

"What about checkin' 'im over?" Kelly said.

"What about my *gut?*" snapped Pole. "I ain't eaten in six hours."

Kelly blew out a heavy breath. "All right, let's go then," he said.

They put Maxo in a corner of the room.

"We should be able t'lock him in," Kelly said.

"Why? Ya think somebody's gonna *steal* 'im?"

"He's valuable," said Kelly.

"Sure, he's a priceless antique," said Pole.

Kelly closed the door three times before the latch caught. He turned away from it, shaking his head worriedly. As they started down the hall he looked at his wrist and saw for the fiftieth time the white band where his pawned watch had been.

"What time is it?" he asked.

"Six twenty-five," said Pole.

"We'll have t'make it fast," Kelly said. "I want ya t'check 'im over good before the fight."

"What for?" asked Pole.

"Did ya *hear* me?" Kelly said angrily.

"Sure, sure," Pole said.

"He's gonna take that son-of-a-bitch B-seven," Kelly said, barely opening his lips.

"Sure he is," said Pole. "With his teeth."

"Some town," Kelly said disgustedly as they came back in the side door of the stadium.

"I told ya they wouldn't have any oil paste here," Pole said. "Why should they? B-twos are dead. Maxo's probably the only one in a thousand miles."

Kelly walked quickly down the hall, opened the door of the ready room and went in. He crossed over to Maxo and pulled off the covering.

"Get to it," he said. "There ain't much time."

Blowing out a slow, tired breath, Pole took off his wrinkled blue coat and tossed it over the bench standing against the wall. He dragged a small table over to where Maxo was, then rolled up his sleeves. Kelly took off his hat and coat and watched while Pole worked loose the nut that held the tool cavity door shut. He stood with his big hands on his hips while Pole drew out the tools one by one and laid them down on the table.

"Rust," Pole muttered. He rubbed a finger around the inside of the cavity and held it up, copper-colored rust flaking off the tip.

"Come on," Kelly said irritably. He sat down on the bench and watched as Pole pried off the sectional plates on Maxo's chest. His eyes ran up over Maxo's leonine head. If I didn't see them coils, he thought once more, I'd swear he was real. Only the mechanics in a B-fighter could tell it wasn't real men in there. Sometimes people were actually fooled and sent in letters complaining that real men were being used. Even from ringside the flesh tones looked human. Mawling had a special patent on that.

Kelly's face relaxed as he smiled fondly at Maxo.

"Good boy," he murmured. Pole didn't hear. Kelly watched the sure-handed mechanic probe with his electric pick, examining connections and potency centers.

"Is he all right?" he asked, without thinking.

"Sure, he's great," Pole said. He plucked out a tiny steel-caged tube. "If this doesn't blow out," he said.

"Why should it?"

"It's sub-par," Pole said jadedly. "I told ya that after the last fight *eight months* ago."

Kelly swallowed. "We'll get 'im a new one after this bout," he said.

"Seventy-five bucks," muttered Pole as if he were watching the money fly away on green wings.

"It'll hold," Kelly said, more to himself than to Pole. Pole shrugged. He put back the tube and pressed in the row of buttons on the main autonomic board. Maxo stirred.

"Take it easy on the left arm," said Kelly. "Save it."

"If it don't work here, it won't work out there," said Pole.

He jabbed at a button and Maxo's left arm began moving with little, circling motions. Pole pushed over the safety-block switch that would keep Maxo from counterpunching and stepped back. He threw a right at Maxo's chin and the robot's arm jumped up with a hitching motion to cover his face. Maxo's left eye flickered like a ruby catching the sun.

"If that eye cell goes . . ." Pole said.

"It *won't*," said Kelly tensely. He watched Pole throw another punch at the left side of Maxo's head. He saw the tiny ripple of the flexo-covered cheek, then the arm jerked up again. It squeaked.

"That's enough," he said. "It works. Try the rest of 'im."

"He's gonna get more than two punches throwed at his head," Pole said.

"*His arm's all right*," Kelly said. "Try something else, I said."

Pole reached inside Maxo and activated the leg-cable centers. Maxo began shifting around. He lifted his left leg and shook off the base wheel automatically. Then he was standing lightly on black-shoed feet, feeling at the floor like a cured cripple testing for stance.

Pole reached forward and jabbed in the FULL button, then jumped back as Maxo's eye beams centered on him and the robot moved forward, broad shoulders rocking slowly, arms up defensively.

"Damn," Pole muttered, "they'll hear 'im squeakin' in the back row."

Kelly grimaced, teeth set. He watched Pole throw another right and Maxo's arm lurch up raggedly. His throat moved with a convulsive swallow and he seemed to have trouble breathing the close air in the little room.

Pole shifted around the floor quickly, side to side. Maxo followed lumberingly, changing direction with visibly jerking motions.

"Oh, he's *beautiful*," Pole said, stopping. "Just beautiful." Maxo came up, arms still raised, and Pole jabbed in under them, pushing the OFF button. Maxo stopped.

"Look, we'll have t'put 'im on *de*fense, Steel," Pole said. "That's all there is to it. He'll get chopped t'pieces if we have 'im movin' in."

Kelly cleared his throat. "No," he said.

"Oh for—will ya use ya *head?*" snapped Pole. "He's a B-two, f'Chrissake. He's gonna get slaughtered anyway. Let's save the pieces."

"They want 'im on the *of*fense," said Kelly. "It's in the contract."

Pole turned away with a hiss.

"What's the use?" he muttered.

"Test 'im some more."

"What for? He's as good as he'll ever be."

"Will ya do what I say!" Kelly shouted, all the tension exploding out of him.

Pole turned back and jabbed in a button. Maxo's left arm shot out. There was a snapping noise inside it and it fell against Maxo's side with a dead clank.

Kelly started up, his face stricken. "My God! what did ya *do!*" he cried. He ran over to where Pole was pushing the button again. Maxo's arm didn't move.

"I *told* ya not t'fool with that arm!" Kelly yelled. "What the hell's the *matter* with ya!" His voice cracked in the middle of the sentence.

Pole didn't answer. He picked up his pry and began working off the left shoulder plate.

"So help me God, if you broke that arm . . ." Kelly warned in a low, snaking voice.

"If *I* broke it!" Pole snapped. "Listen, you dumb mick! This heap has been runnin' on borrowed time for three years now! Don't talk t'me about breakages!"

Kelly clenched his teeth, his eyes small and deadly.

"Open it up," he said.

"Son-of-a—" Pole muttered as he got the plate off. "You find another goddam mechanic that coulda kep' this steam shovel together any better these last years. You just *find* one."

Kelly didn't answer. He stood rigidly, watching while Pole put down the curved plate and looked inside.

When Pole touched it, the trigger spring broke in half and part of it jumped across the room.

Pole started to say something, then stopped. He looked at the ashen-faced Kelly without moving.

Kelly's eyes moved to Pole.

"Fix it," he said hoarsely.

Pole swallowed. "Steel, I—"

"*Fix* it!"

"I can't! That spring's been fixin' t'break for—"

"You broke it! Now *fix* it!" Kelly clamped rigid fingers on Pole's arm. Pole jerked back.

"Let go of me!" he said.

"What's the matter with you!" Kelly cried. "Are you crazy? He's got t'be fixed. He's *got* t'be!"

"Steel, he needs a new spring."

"Well, *get* it!"

"They don't *have* 'em here, Steel," Pole said. "I *told* ya. And if they *did* have 'em, we ain't got the sixteen fifty t'get one."

"Oh— Oh, God," said Kelly. His hand fell away and he stumbled to the other side of the room. He sank down on the bench and stared without blinking at the tall, motionless Maxo.

He sat there a long time, just staring, while Pole stood watching him, the pry still in his hand. He saw Kelly's broad chest rise and fall with spasmodic movements. Kelly's face was a blank.

"If he don't watch 'em," muttered Kelly finally.

"What?"

Kelly looked up, his mouth set in a straight, hard line. "If he don't watch, it'll work," he said.

"What're ya talkin' about?"

Kelly stood up and started unbuttoning his shirt.

"What're ya—"

Pole stopped dead, his mouth falling open. "Are you *crazy?*" he asked.

Kelly kept unbuttoning his shirt. He pulled it off and tossed it on the bench.

"Steel, you're out o' your mind!" Pole said. "You can't do that!"

Kelly didn't say anything.

"But you'll— Steel, you're *crazy!*"

"We deliver a fight or we don't get paid," Kelly said.

"But—you'll get *killed!*"

Kelly pulled off his undershirt. His chest was beefy, there was red hair swirling around it. "Have to shave this off," he said.

"Steel, *come on*," Pole said. "You—"

His eyes widened as Kelly sat down on the bench and started unlacing his shoes.

"They'll never let ya," Pole said. "You can't make 'em think you're a—" He stopped and took a jerky step forward. "Steel, fuh Chrissake!"

Kelly looked up at Pole with dead eyes.

"You'll help me," he said.

"But they—"

"Nobody knows what Maxo looks like," Kelly said. "And only Waddow saw me. If he don't watch the bouts we'll be all right."

"But—"

"They won't know," Kelly said. "The B's bleed and bruise too."

"Steel, come on," Pole said shakily. He took a deep breath and calmed himself. He sat down hurriedly beside the broad-shouldered Irishman.

"Look," he said. "I got a sister back East—in Maryland. If I wire 'er, she'll send us the dough t'get back."

Kelly got up and unbuckled his belt.

"Steel, I know a guy in Philly with a B-five wants t'sell cheap," Pole said desperately. "We could scurry up the cash and— Steel, fuh Chrissake, you'll get *killed!* It's a B-seven! Don't ya understand? A B-*seven!* You'll be mangled!"

Kelly was working the dark trunks over Maxo's hips.

"I won't let ya do it, Steel," Pole said, "I'll go to—"

He broke off with a sucked-in gasp as Kelly whirled and moved over quickly to haul him to his feet. Kelly's grip was like the jaws of a trap and there was nothing left of him in his eyes.

"You'll help me," Kelly said in a low, trembling voice. "You'll help me or I'll beat ya brains out on the wall."

"You'll get killed," Pole murmured.

"Then I will," said Kelly.

Mr. Waddow came out of his office as Pole was walking the covered Kelly toward the ring.

"Come on, come on," Mr. Waddow said. "They're waitin' on ya."

Pole nodded jerkily and guided Kelly down the hall.

"Where's the owner?" Mr. Waddow called after them.

Pole swallowed quickly. "In the audience," he said.

Mr. Waddow grunted and, as they walked on, Pole heard the door to the office close. Breath emptied from him.

"I should've told 'im," he muttered.

"I'd o' killed ya," Kelly said, his voice muffled under the covering.

Crowd sounds leaked back into the hall now as they turned a corner. Under the canvas covering, Kelly felt a drop of sweat trickle down his temple.

"Listen," he said, "you'll have t'towel me off between rounds."

"Between what rounds?" Pole asked tensely. "You won't even last one."

"Shut up."

"You think you're just up against some tough fighter?" Pole asked. "You're up against a machine! Don't ya—"

"I said shut up."

"Oh . . . you dumb—" Pole swallowed. "If I towel ya off, they'll know," he said.

"They ain't seen a B-two in years," Kelly broke in. "If anyone asks, tell 'em it's an oil leak."

"Sure," said Pole disgustedly. He bit his lips. "Steel, ya'll never get away with it."

The last part of his sentence was drowned out as, suddenly, they were among the crowd, walking down the sloping aisle toward the ring. Kelly held his knees locked and walked a little stiffly. He drew in a long, deep breath and let it out slowly.

The heat burdened in around him like a hanging weight. It was like walking along the sloping floor of an ocean of heat and sound. He heard voices drifting past him as he moved.

"Ya'll take 'im home in a box!"

"Well, if it ain't *Rattlin'* Maxo!"

And the inevitable, "*Scrap iron!*"

Kelly swallowed dryly, feeling a tight, drawing sensation in his loins. Thirsty, he thought. The momentary vision of the bar across from the Kansas City train station crossed his mind. The dim-lit booth, the cool fan breeze on the back of his neck, the icy, sweat-beaded bottle chilling his palm. He swallowed again. He hadn't allowed himself one drink in the last hour. The less he drank the less he'd sweat, he knew.

"Watch it."

He felt Pole's hand slide in through the opening in the back of the covering, felt the mechanic's hand grab his arm and check him.

"Ring steps," Pole said out of a corner of his mouth.

Kelly edged his right foot forward until the shoe tip touched the riser of the bottom step. Then he lifted his foot to the step and started up.

At the top, Pole's fingers tightened around his arm again.

"Ropes," Pole said, guardedly.

It was hard getting through the ropes with the covering on. Kelly almost fell and hoots and catcalls came at him like spears out of the din. Kelly felt the canvas give slightly under his feet and then Pole pushed the stool against the back of his legs and he sat down a little too jerkily.

"Hey, get that derrick out o' here!" shouted a man in the second row. Laughter and hoots.

Then Pole drew off the covering and put it down on the ring apron.

Kelly sat there staring at the Maynard Flash.

The B-seven was motionless, its gloved hands hanging across its legs. There was imitation blonde hair, crew cut, growing out of its skull pores. Its face was that of an impassive Adonis. The simulation of muscle curve on its body and limbs was almost perfect. For a moment Kelly almost thought that years had been peeled away and he was in the business again, facing a young contender. He swallowed carefully. Pole crouched beside him, pretending to fiddle with an arm plate.

"Steel, *don't*," he muttered again.

Kelly didn't answer. He kept staring at the Maynard Flash, thinking of the array of instant-reaction centers inside that smooth arch of chest. The drawing sensation reached his stomach. It was like a cold hand pulling in at strands of muscle and ligament.

A red-faced man in a white suit climbed into the ring and reached up for the microphone which was swinging down to him.

"Ladies and gentlemen," he announced, "the opening bout of the evening. A ten-round light-heavyweight bout. From Philadelphia, the B-two, *Battling Maxo.*"

The crowd booed and hissed. They threw up paper airplanes and shouted *"Scrap iron!"*

"His opponent, our own B-seven, the *Maynard Flash!"*

Cheers and wild clapping. The Flash's mechanic touched a button under the left armpit and the B-seven jumped up and held his arms over his head in the victory gesture. The crowd laughed happily.

"God," Pole muttered, "I never saw that. Must be a new gimmick."

Kelly blinked to relieve his eyes.

"Three more bouts to follow," said the red-faced man and then the microphone drew up and he left the ring. There was no referee. B-fighters never clinched—their machinery rejected it—and there was no knockdown count. A felled B-fighter stayed down. The new B-nine, it was claimed by the Mawling publicity staff, would be able to get up, which would make for livelier and longer bouts.

Pole pretended to check over Kelly.

"Steel, it's your last chance," he begged.

"Get out," said Kelly without moving his lips.

Pole looked at Kelly's immobile eyes a moment, then sucked in a ragged breath and straightened up.

"Stay *away* from him," he warned as he started through the ropes.

Across the ring, the Flash was standing in its corner,

hitting its gloves together as if it were a real young fighter anxious to get the fight started. Kelly stood up and Pole drew the stool away. Kelly stood watching the B-seven, seeing how its eye centers were zeroing in on him. There was a cold sinking in his stomach.

The bell rang.

The B-seven moved out smoothly from its corner with a mechanical glide, its arms raised in the traditional way, gloved hands wavering in tiny circles in front of it. It moved quickly toward Kelly, who edged out of his corner automatically, his mind feeling, abruptly, frozen. He felt his own hands rise as if someone else had lifted them and his legs were like dead wood under him. He kept his gaze on the bright, unmoving eyes of the Maynard Flash.

They came together. The B-seven's left flicked out and Kelly blocked it, feeling the rock-hard fist of the Flash even through his glove. The fist moved out again. Kelly drew back his head and felt a warm breeze across his mouth. His own left shot out and banged against the Flash's nose. It was like hitting a doorknob. Pain flared in Kelly's arm and his jaw muscles went hard as he struggled to keep his face blank.

The B-seven feinted with a left and Kelly knocked it aside. He couldn't stop the right that blurred in after it and grazed his left temple. He jerked his head away and the B-seven threw a left that hit him over the ear. Kelly lurched back, throwing out a left that the B-seven brushed aside. Kelly caught his footing and hit the Flash's jaw solidly with a right uppercut. He felt a jolt of pain run up his arm. The Flash's head didn't budge. He shot out a left that hit Kelly on the right shoulder.

Kelly backpedaled instinctively. Then he heard someone yell, "Get 'im a bicycle!" and he remembered what
Mr. Waddow had said. He moved in again.

A left caught him under the heart and he felt the
impact shudder through his frame. Pain stabbed at his
heart. He threw a spasmodic left which banged against
the B-seven's nose again. There was only pain. Kelly
stepped back and staggered as a hard right caught him
high on the chest. He started to move back. The B-seven
hit him on the chest again. Kelly lost his balance and
stepped back quickly to catch equilibrium. The crowd
booed. The B-seven moved in without making a single
mechanical sound.

Kelly regained his balance and stopped. He threw a
hard right that missed. The momentum of his blow
threw him off center and the Flash's left drove hard
against his upper right arm. The arm went numb. Even
as Kelly was sucking in a teeth-clenched gasp the
B-seven shot in a hard right under his guard that
slammed into Kelly's spongy stomach. Kelly felt the
breath go out of him. His right slapped ineffectively
across the Flash's right cheek. The Flash's eyes glinted.

As the B-seven moved in again, Kelly sidestepped and,
for a moment, the radial eye centers lost him. Kelly moved
out of range dizzily, pulling air in through his nostrils.

"Get that heap out o' there!" a man yelled

Breath shook in Kelly's throat. He swallowed quickly
and started forward just as the Flash picked him up
again. He stepped in close, hoping to outtime electrical
impulse, and threw a hard right at the Flash's body.

The B-seven's left shot up and Kelly's blow was
deflected by the iron wrist. Kelly's left was thrown off

too and then the Flash's left shot in and drove the breath out of Kelly again. Kelly's left barely hit the Flash's rock-hard chest. He staggered back, the B-seven following. He kept jabbing but the B-seven kept deflecting the blows and counterjabbing with almost the same piston-like motion. Kelly's head kept snapping back. He fell back more and saw the right coming straight at him. He couldn't stop it.

The blow drove in like a steel battering ram. Spears of pain shot behind Kelly's eyes and through his head. A black cloud seemed to flood across the ring. His muffled cry was drowned out by the screaming crowd as he toppled back, his nose and mouth trickling bright blood that looked as good as the dye they used in the B-fighters.

The rope checked his fall, pressing in rough and hard against his back. He swayed there, right arm hanging limp, left arm raised defensively. He blinked his eyes instinctively, trying to focus them. I'm a robot, he thought, a robot.

The Flash stepped in and drove a violent right into Kelly's chest, a left to his stomach. Kelly doubled over, gagging. A right slammed off his skull like a hammer blow, driving him back against the ropes again. The crowd screamed.

Kelly saw the blurred outline of the Maynard Flash. He felt another blow smash into his chest like a club. With a sob he threw a wild left that the B-seven brushed off. Another sharp blow landed on Kelly's shoulder. He lifted his right and managed to deflect the worst of a left thrown at his jaw. Another right concaved his stomach. He doubled over. A hammering right drove him back on the ropes. He felt hot, salty blood in his mouth and the roar of the crowd seemed to swallow him. Stay up!—he screamed at himself. Stay up, goddam you! The ring wavered before him like dark water.

With a desperate surge of energy, he threw a right as hard as he could at the tall, beautiful figure in front of him. Something cracked in his wrist and hand and a wave of searing pain shot up his arm. His throat-locked cry went unheard. His arm fell, his left went down, and the crowd shrieked and howled for the Flash to finish it.

There were only inches between them now. The B-seven rained in blows that didn't miss. Kelly lurched and staggered under the impact of them. His head snapped from side to side. Blood ran across his face in scarlet ribbons. His arm hung like a dead branch at his side. He kept getting slammed back against the ropes, bouncing forward and getting slammed back again. He couldn't see anymore. He could only hear the screaming of the crowd and the endless swishing and thudding of the B-seven's gloves. Stay up, he thought. I have to stay up. He drew in his head and hunched his shoulders to protect himself.

He was like that seven seconds before the bell when a clubbing right on the side of his head sent him crashing to the canvas.

He lay there gasping for breath. Suddenly, he started to get up, then, equally as suddenly, realized that he couldn't. He fell forward again and lay on his stomach on the warm canvas, his head throbbing with pain. He could hear the booing and hissing of the dissatisfied crowd.

When Pole finally managed to get him up and slip the

cover over his head the crowd was jeering so loudly that Kelly couldn't hear Pole's voice. He felt the mechanic's big hand inside the covering, guiding him, but he fell down climbing through the ropes and almost fell again on the steps. His legs were like rubber tubes. Stay up. His brain still murmured the words.

In the ready room he collapsed. Pole tried to get him up on the bench but he couldn't. Finally, he bunched up his blue coat under Kelly's head and, kneeling, he started patting with his handkerchief at the trickles of blood.

"You dumb bastard," he kept muttering in a thin, shaking voice. "You dumb bastard."

Kelly lifted his left hand and brushed away Pole's hand.

"Go—get the—money," he gasped hoarsely.

"What?"

"The money!" gasped Kelly through his teeth.

"But—"

"*Now!*" Kelly's voice was barely intelligible.

Pole straightened up and stood looking down at Kelly a moment. Then he turned and went out.

Kelly lay there drawing in breath and exhaling it with wheezing sounds. He couldn't move his right hand and he knew it was broken. He felt the blood trickling from his nose and mouth. His body throbbed with pain.

After a few moments he struggled up on his left elbow and turned his head, pain crackling along his neck muscles. When he saw that Maxo was all right he put his head down again. A smile twisted up one corner of his lips.

When Pole came back, Kelly lifted his head painfully. Pole came over and knelt down. He started patting at the blood again.

"Ya get it?" Kelly asked in a crusty whisper.

Pole blew out a slow breath.

"*Well?*"

Pole swallowed. "Half of it," he said.

Kelly stared up at him blankly, his mouth fallen open. His eyes didn't believe it.

"He said he wouldn't pay five C's for a one rounder."

"What d'ya mean?" Kelly's voice cracked. He tried to get up and put down his right hand. With a strangled cry he fell back, his face white. His head thrashed on the coat pillow, his eyes shut tightly.

"He can't—he can't do that," he gasped.

Pole licked his dry lips.

"Steel, there—ain't a thing we can do. He's got a bunch o' toughs in the office with 'im. I can't. . . ." He lowered his head. "And if—you was t'go there he'd know what ya done. And—he might even take back the two and a half."

Kelly lay on his back staring up at the naked bulb without blinking. His chest labored and shuddered with breath.

"No," he murmured. "No."

He lay there for a long time without talking. Pole got some water and cleaned off his face and gave him a drink. He opened up his small suitcase and patched up Kelly's face. He put Kelly's right arm in a sling.

Fifteen minutes later Kelly spoke.

"We'll go back by bus," he said.

"What?" Pole asked.

"We'll go by bus," Kelly said slowly. "That'll only cost fifty-six bucks." He swallowed and shifted on his back. "That'll leave almost two C's. We can get 'im a—a new trigger spring and a—eye lens and—" He blinked his eyes and held them shut a moment as the room started fading again.

"And oil paste," he said then. "Loads of it. He'll be— good as new again."

Kelly looked up at Pole. "Then we'll be all set up," he said. "Maxo'll be in good shape again. And we can get us some decent bouts." He swallowed and breathed laboriously. "That's all he needs is a little work. New spring, a new eye lens. That'll shape 'im up. We'll show those bastards what a B-two can do. Old Maxo'll show 'em. *Right?*"

Pole looked down at the big Irishman and sighed.

"Sure, Steel," he said.

chess

There are some who argue that chess is a *game* and not a *sport*. This distinction may have some validity for certain card and board games, but it does not hold true in the case of chess. In championship chess, physical conditioning and stamina are of the utmost importance. Chess champions train many months before important matches because the tension and strain of chess are so great that physical fitness can make the difference between victory and defeat, especially in tournament play, which can last for weeks.

The popularity of chess in the United States has increased dramatically since the recent world championship matches between Bobby Fischer and Boris Spassky. Fischer acted like the young Cassius Clay (later Muhammad Ali), speaking arrogantly, making wild predictions (most of which came true!), and acting temperamentally. Because his opponent was a Russian, the match had an aura of international politics attached to it. Millions of Americans who did not know anything about chess were rooting for Fischer in order to witness the dethroning of the Soviet world champion.

Chess is a very old sport. Some experts place its origin in India as early as A.D. 500. The Arabs introduced chess into Europe at the height of their conquests, where it quickly became a popular sport among royalty. Later, its popularity spread to other sectors of the population, and it was played in coffee houses and inns.

Chess is a very demanding sport which puts participants under great mental and physical pressure. It demands constant study, since the variations in the game are endless. In fact, there have been few great chess players who did not devote most of their lives to chess. Although it is played for pleasure by millions around the world, it also requires continuous study for those who wish to excell.

The Immortal Game

poul anderson

The military strategy characteristic of chess has been noted by many observers. However, it poses no risks for its participants apart from bruised egos.

In this story, Poul Anderson describes a military engagement based on a classic chess match played between Adolf Anderssen and Lionel Kieseritzky in London in 1851. The game is considered one of the most brilliant ever played and has become known as "The Immortal Game." The game is reproduced below:

Anderssen	(White)	Kieseritzky	(Black)
1. P-K4	(e2-e4)	P-K4	(e7-e5)
2. P-KB4	(f2-f4)	PxP	(e5:f4)
3. B-B4	(♗ f1-c4)	P-QKt4	(b7-b5)
4. BxP	(♗ c4:b5)	Q-R5ch	(♛ d8-h4+)
5. K-B1	(♔ e1-f1)	Kt-KB3	(♞ g8-f6)
6. Kt-KB3	(♞ g1-f3)	Q-R3	(♛ h4-h6)
7. P-Q3	(d2-d3)	Kt-R4	(♞ f6-h5)
8. Kt-R4	(♞ f3-h4)	P-QB3	(c7-c6)
9. Kt-B5	(♞ h4-f5)	Q-Kt4	(♛ h6-g5)
10. P-KKt4	(g2-g4)	Kt-B3	(♞ h5-f6)
11. R-Kt1	(♜ h1-g1)	PxB	(c6:b5)
12. P-KR4	(h2-h4)	Q-Kt3	(♛ g5-g6)

Anderssen	(White)		Kieseritzky	(Black)
13. P-R5	(h4-h5)		Q-Kt4	(♛ g6-g5)
14. Q-B3	(♛ d1-f3)		Kt-Kt1	(♞ f6-g8)
15. BxP	(♝ c1:f4)		Q-B3	(♛ g5-f6)
16. Kt-B3	(♞ b1-c3)		B-B4	(♝ f8-c5)
17. Kt-Q5	(♞ c3-d5)		QxP	(♛ f6:b2)
18. B-Q6	(♝ f4-d6)		QxRch	(♛ b2:a1+)
19. K-K2	(♚ f1-e2)		BxR	(♝ c5:g1)
20. P-K5	(e4-e5)		Kt-QR3	(♞ b8-a6)
21. KtxPch	(♞ f:g7+)		K-Q1	(♚ e8-d8)
22. Q-B6ch	(♛ f3-f6+)		KtxQ	(♞ g8:f6)
23. B-K7 mate	(♝ d6-e7++)			

If you own a chess set, play along as you read this
story. In science fiction, the stakes for the pieces can be
higher than those for the players!

The
Immortal
Game

The first trumpet sounded far and clear and brazen cold, and Rogard the Bishop stirred to wakefulness with it. Lifting his eyes, he looked through the suddenly rustling, murmuring line of soldiers, out across the broad plain of Cinnabar and the frontier, and over to the realm of LEUKAS.

Away there, across the somehow unreal red-and-black distances of the steppe, he saw sunlight flash on armor and caught the remote wild flutter of lifted banners. *So it is war*, he thought. *So we must fight again.*

Again? He pulled his mind from the frightening dimness of that word. Had they ever fought before?

On his left, Sir Ocher laughed aloud and clanged down the vizard on his gay young face. It gave him a strange, inhuman look, he was suddenly a featureless thing of shining metal and nodding plumes, and the steel echoed in his voice: "Ha, a fight! Praise God, Bishop, for I had begun to fear I would rust here forever."

Slowly, Rogard's mind brought forth wonder. "Were you sitting and thinking—before now?" he asked.

"Why—" Sudden puzzlement in the reckless tones: "I

think I was. . . . Was I?" Fear turning into defiance: "Who cares? I've got some LEUKANS to kill!" Ocher reared in his horse till the great metallic wings thundered.

On Rogard's right, Flambard the King stood, tall in crown and robes. He lifted an arm to shade his eyes against the blazing sunlight. "They are sending DIOMES, the royal guardsman, first," he murmured. "A good man." The coolness of his tone was not matched by the other hand, its nervous plucking at his beard.

Rogard turned back, facing over the lines of Cinnabar to the frontier. DIOMES, the LEUKAN King's own soldier, was running. The long spear flashed in his hand, his shield and helmet threw back the relentless light in a furious dazzle, and Rogard thought he could hear the clashing of iron. Then that noise was drowned in the trumpets and drums and yells from the ranks of Cinnabar, and he had only his eyes.

DIOMES leaped two squares before coming to a halt on the frontier. He stopped then, stamping and thrusting against the Barrier which suddenly held him, and cried challenge. A muttering rose among the cuirassed soldiers of Cinnabar, and spears lifted before the flowing banners.

King Flambard's voice was shrill as he leaned forward and touched his own guardsman with his scepter. "Go, Carlon! Go to stop him!"

"Aye, sire." Carlon's stocky form bowed, and then he wheeled about and ran, holding his spear aloft, until he reached the frontier. Now he and DIOMES stood face to face, snarling at each other across the Barrier, and for a sick moment Rogard wondered what those two had done,

once in an evil and forgotten year, that there should be
such hate between them.

"Let me go, sire!" Ocher's voice rang eerily from the
slit-eyed mask of his helmet. The winged horse stamped
on the hard red ground, and the long lance swept a
flashing arc. "Let me go next."

"No, no, Sir Ocher." It was a woman's voice. "Not
yet. There'll be enough for you and me to do, later in
this day."

Looking beyond Flambard, the Bishop saw his Queen,
Evyan the Fair, and there was something within him
which stumbled and broke into fire. Very tall and
lovely was the gray-eyed Queen of Cinnabar, where she
stood in armor and looked out at the growing battle. Her
sun-browned young face was coifed in steel, but one
rebellious lock blew forth in the wind, and she brushed
at it with a gauntleted hand while the other drew her
sword snaking from its sheath. "Now may God
strengthen our arms," she said, and her voice was low
and sweet. Rogard drew his cope tighter about him and
turned his mitered head away with a sigh. But there was
a bitter envy in him for Columbard, the Queen's Bishop
of Cinnabar.

Drums thumped from the LEUKAN ranks, and another
soldier ran forth. Rogard sucked his breath hissingly in,
for this man came till he stood on DIOMES' right. And
the newcomer's face was sharp and pale with fear. There
was no Barrier between him and Carlon.

"To his death," muttered Flambard between his teeth.
"They sent that fellow to his death."

Carlon snarled and advanced on the LEUKAN. He had
little choice—if he waited, he would be slain, and his

King had not commanded him to wait. He leaped, his spear gleamed, and the LEUKAN soldier toppled and lay emptily sprawled in the black square.

"First blood!" cried Evyan, lifting her sword and hurling sunbeams from it. "First blood for us!"

Aye, so, thought Rogard bleakly, *but King* MIKILLATI *had a reason for sacrificing that man. Maybe we should have let Carlon die. Carlon the bold, Carlon the strong, Carlon the lover of laughter. Maybe we should have let him die.*

And now the Barrier was down for Bishop ASATOR of LEUKAS, and he came gliding down the red squares, high and cold in his glistening white robes, until he stood on the frontier. Rogard thought he could see ASATOR's eyes as they swept over Cinnabar. The LEUKAN Bishop was poised to rusn in with his great mace should Flambard, for safety, seek to change with Earl Ferric as the Law permitted.

Law?

There was no time to wonder what the Law was, or why it must be obeyed, or what had gone before this moment of battle. Queen Evyan had turned and shouted to the soldier Raddic, guardsman of her own Knight Sir Cupran: "Go! Halt him!" And Raddic cast her his own look of love, and ran, ponderous in his mail, up to the frontier. There he and ASATOR stood, no Barrier between them if either used a flanking move.

Good! Oh, good, my Queen! thought Rogard wildly. For even if ASATOR did not withdraw, but slew Raddic, he would be in Raddic's square, and his threat would be against a wall of spears. *He will retreat, he will retreat—*

Iron roared as ASATOR's mace crashed through helm and skull and felled Raddic the guardsman.

Evyan screamed, once only. "And I sent him! I sent him!" Then she began to run.

"Lady!" Rogard hurled himself against the Barrier. He could not move, he was chained here in his square, locked and barred by a Law he did not understand, while his lady ran toward death. "O Evyan, Evyan!"

Straight as a flying javelin ran the Queen of Cinnabar. Turning, straining after her, Rogard saw her leap the frontier and come to a halt by the Barrier which marked the left-hand bound of the kingdoms, beyond which lay only dimness to the frightful edge of the world. There she wheeled to face the dismayed ranks of LEUKAS, and her cry drifted back like the shriek of a stooping hawk: "MIKILLATI! Defend yourself!"

The thunder-crack of cheering from Cinnabar drowned all answer, but Rogard saw, at the very limits of his sight, how hastily King MIKILLATI stepped from the line of her attack, into the stronghold of Bishop ASATOR. Now, thought Rogard fiercely, now the white-robed ruler could never seek shelter from one of his Earls. Evyan had stolen his greatest shield.

"Hola, my Queen!" With a sob of laughter, Ocher struck spurs into his horse. Wings threshed, blowing Rogard's cope about him, as the Knight hurtled over the head of his own guardsman and came to rest two squares in front of the Bishop. Rogard fought down his own anger; he had wanted to be the one to follow Evyan. But Ocher was a better choice.

Oh, much better! Rogard gasped as his glittering eyes

took in the broad battlefield. In the next leap, Ocher could cut down DIOMES, and then between them he and Evyan could trap MIKILLATI!

Briefly, that puzzlement nagged at the Bishop. Why should men die to catch someone else's King? What was there in the Law that said Kings should strive for mastery of the world and—

"Guard yourself, Queen!" Sir MERKON, King's Knight of LEUKAS, sprang in a move like Ocher's. Rogard's breath rattled in his throat with bitterness, and he thought there must be tears in Evyan's bright eyes. Slowly, then, the Queen withdrew two squares along the edge, until she stood in front of Earl Ferric's guardsman. It was still a good place to attack from, but not what the other had been.

BOAN, guardsman of the LEUKAN Queen DOLORA, moved one square forward, so that he protected great DIOMES from Ocher. Ocher snarled and sprang in front of Evyan, so that he stood between her and the frontier: clearing the way for her, and throwing his own protection over Carlon.

MERKON jumped likewise, landing to face Ocher with the frontier between them. Rogard clenched his mace and vision blurred for him; the LEUKANS were closing in on Evyan.

"Ulfar!" cried the King's Bishop. "Ulfar, can you help her?"

The stout old yeoman who was guardsman of the Queen's Bishop nodded wordlessly and ran one square forward. His spear menaced Bishop ASATOR, who growled at him—no Barrier between those two now!

MERKON of LEUKAS made another soaring leap, landing three squares in front of Rogard. "Guard yourself!" the voice belled from his faceless helmet. "Guard yourself, O Queen!"

No time now to let Ulfar slay ASATOR. Evyan's great eyes looked wildly about her; then, with swift decision, she stepped between MERKON and Ocher. Oh, a lovely move! Out of the fury in his breast, Rogard laughed.

The guardsman of the LEUKAN King's Knight clanked two squares ahead, lifting his spear against Ocher. It must have taken boldness thus to stand before Evyan herself; but the Queen of Cinnabar saw that if she cut him down, the Queen of LEUKAS could slay her. "Get free, Ocher!" she cried. "Get away!" Ocher cursed and leaped from danger, landing in front of Rogard's guardsman.

The King's Bishop bit his lip and tried to halt the trembling in his limbs. How the sun blazed! Its light was a cataract of dry white fire over the barren red-and-black squares. It hung immobile, enormous in the vague sky, and men gasped in their armor. The noise of bugles and iron, hoofs and wings and stamping feet, was loud under the small wind that blew across the world. There had never been anything but this meaningless war, there would never be aught else, and when Rogard tried to think beyond the moment when the fight had begun, or the moment when it would end, there was only an abyss of darkness.

Earl RAFAEON of LEUKAS took one ponderous step toward his King, a towering figure of iron readying for combat. Evyan whooped. "Ulfar!" she yelled. "Ulfar, your chance!"

Columbard's guardsman laughed aloud. Raising his

spear, he stepped over into the square held by ASATOR. The white-robed Bishop lifted his mace, futile and feeble, and then he rolled in the dust at Ulfar's feet. The men of Cinnabar howled and clanged sword on shield.

Rogard held aloof from triumph. ASATOR, he thought grimly, had been expendable anyway. King MIKILLATI had something else in mind.

It was like a blow when he saw Earl RAFAEON's guardsman run forward two squares and shout to Evyan to guard herself. Raging, the Queen of Cinnabar withdrew a square to her rearward. Rogard saw quickly how unprotected King Flambard was now, the soldiers scattered over the field and the hosts of LEUKAS marshaling. But Queen DOLORA, he thought with a wild, clutching hope, Queen DOLORA, her tall, cold beauty was just as open to a strong attack.

The soldier who had driven Evyan back took a leap across the frontier. "Guard yourself, O Queen!" he cried again. He was a small, hard-bitten, unkempt warrior in dusty helm and corselet. Evyan cursed, a bouncing, soldierly oath, and moved one square forward to put a Barrier between her and him. He grinned impudently in his beard.

It is ill for us, it is a bootless and evil day. Rogard tried once more to get out of his square and go to Evyan's aid, but his will would not carry him. The Barrier held, invisible and uncrossable, and the Law held, the cruel and senseless Law which said a man must stand by and watch his lady be slain, and he railed at the bitterness of it and lapsed into a gray waiting.

Trumpets lifted brazen throats, drums boomed, and Queen DOLORA of LEUKAS stalked forth into battle. She came high and white and icily fair, her face chiseled and immobile in its haughtiness under the crowned helmet, and stood two squares in front of her husband, looming over Carlon. Behind her, her own Bishop SORKAS poised in his stronghold, hefting his mace in armored hands. Carlon of Cinnabar spat at DOLORA's feet, and she looked at him from cool blue eyes and then looked away. The hot dry wind did not ruffle her long pale hair; she was like a statue, standing there and waiting.

"Ocher," said Evyan softly, "out of my way."

"I like not retreat, my lady," he answered in a thin tone.

"Nor I," said Evyan. "But I must have an escape route open. We will fight again."

Slowly, Ocher withdrew, back to his own home. Evyan chuckled once, and a wry grin twisted her young face.

Rogard was looking at her so tautly that he did not see what was happening until a great shout of iron slammed his head around. Then he saw Bishop SORKAS, standing in Carlon's square with a bloodied mace in his hands, and Carlon lay dead at his feet.

Carlon, your hands are empty, life has slipped from them and there is an unending darkness risen in you who loved the world. Goodnight, my Carlon, goodnight.

"Madame—" Bishop SORKAS spoke quietly, bowing a little, and there was a smile on his crafty face. "I regret, madame, that—ah—"

"Yes. I must leave you." Evyan shook her head, as if she had been struck, and moved a square backward and sideways. Then, turning, she threw the glance of an

eagle down the black squares to LEUKAS' Earl ARACLES.
He looked away nervously, as if he would crouch behind
the three soldiers who warded him. Evyan drew a deep
breath sobbing into her lungs.

Sir THEUTAS, DOLORA's Knight, sprang from his stronghold, to place himself between Evyan and the Earl.
Rogard wondered dully if he meant to kill Ulfar the
soldier; he could do it now. Ulfar looked at the Knight
who sat crouched, and hefted his spear and waited for
his own weird.

"Rogard!"

The Bishop leaped, and for a moment there was fire-
streaked darkness before his eyes.

"Rogard, to me! To me, and help sweep them from
the world!"

Evyan's voice.

She stood in her scarred and dinted armor, holding her
sword aloft, and on that smitten field she was laughing
with a newborn hope. Rogard could not shout his reply.
There were no words. But he raised his mace and ran.

The black squares slid beneath his feet, footfalls
pounding, jarring his teeth, muscles stretching with a
resurgent glory and all the world singing. At the frontier,
he stopped, knowing it was Evyan's will though he could
not have said how he knew. Then he faced about, and
with clearing eyes looked back over that field of iron
and ruin. Save for one soldier and a knight, Cinnabar
was now cleared of LEUKAN forces, Evyan was safe, a
counterblow was readying like the first whistle of hurricane. Before him were the proud banners of LEUKAS—
now to throw them into the dust! Now to ride with
Evyan into the home of MIKILLATI!

"Go to it, sir," rumbled Ulfar, standing on the Bishop's right and looking boldly at the white Knight who could slay him. "Give 'em hell from us."

Wings beat in the sky, and THEUTAS soared down to land on Rogard's left. In the hot light, the blued metal of his armor was like running water. His horse snorted, curveting and flapping its wings; he sat it easily, the lance swaying in his grasp, the blank helmet turned to Flambard. One more such leap, reckoned Rogard wildly, and he would be able to assail the King of Cinnabar. Or—no—a single spring from here and he would spit Evyan on his lance.

And there is a Barrier between us!

"Watch yourself, Queen!" The arrogant LEUKAN voice boomed hollow out of the steel mask.

"Indeed I will, Sir Knight!" There was only laughter in Evyan's tone. Lightly, then, she sped up the row of black squares. She brushed by Rogard, smiling at him as she ran, and he tried to smile back but his face was stiffened. Evyan, Evyan, she was plunging alone into her enemy's homeland!

Iron belled and clamored. The white guardsman in her path toppled and sank at her feet. One fist lifted strengthlessly, and a dying shrillness was in the dust: "Curse you, curse you, MIKILLATI, curse you for a stupid fool, leaving me here to be slain—no, no, no—"

Evyan bestrode the body and laughed again in the very face of Earl ARACLES. He cowered back, licking his lips—he could not move against her, but she could annihilate him in one more step. Beside Rogard, Ulfar whooped, and the trumpets of Cinnabar howled in the rear.

Now the great attack was launched! Rogard cast a
fleeting glance at Bishop SORKAS. The lean, white-coped
form was gliding forth, mace swinging loose in one
hand, and there was a little sleepy smile on the pale face.
No dismay—? SORKAS halted, facing Rogard, and smiled a
little wider, skinning his teeth without humor. "You can
kill me if you wish," he said softly. "But do you?"

For a moment Rogard wavered. To smash that head—!

"Rogard! Rogard, to me!"

Evyan's cry jerked the King's Bishop around. He saw
now what her plan was, and it dazzled him so that he
forgot all else. LEUKAS *is ours!*

Swiftly he ran. DIOMES and BOAN howled at him as he
went between them, brushing impotent spears against
the Barriers. He passed Queen DOLORA, and her lovely
face was as if cast in steel, and her eyes followed him as
he charged over the plain of LEUKAS. Then there was no
time for thinking, Earl RAFAEON loomed before him, and
he jumped the last boundary into the enemy's heartland.

The Earl lifted a meaningless ax. The Law read death
for him, and Rogard brushed aside the feeble stroke.
The blow of his mace shocked in his own body, slamming his jaws together. RAFAEON crumpled, falling
slowly, his armor loud as he struck the ground. Briefly,
his fingers clawed at the iron-hard black earth, and then
he lay still.

*They have slain Raddic and Carlon—we have three
guardsmen, a Bishop, and an Earl— Now we need only
be butchers! Evyan, Evyan, warrior Queen, this is your
victory!*

DIOMES of LEUKAS roared and jumped across the frontier. Futile, futile, he was doomed to darkness. Evyan's

lithe form moved up against ARACLES, her sword flamed and the Earl crashed at her feet. Her voice was another leaping brand: "Defend yourself, King!"

Turning, Rogard grew aware that MIKILLATI himself had been right beside him. There was a Barrier between the two men—but MIKILLATI had to retreat from Evyan, and he took one step forward and sideways. Peering into his face, Rogard felt a sudden coldness. There was no defeat there, it was craft and knowledge and an unbending steel will—*what was* LEUKAS *planning?*

Evyan tossed her head, and the wind fluttered the lock of hair like a rebel banner. "We have them, Rogard!" she cried.

Far and faint, through the noise and confusion of battle, Cinnabar's bugles sounded the command of her King. Peering into the haze, Rogard saw that Flambard was taking precautions. Sir THEUTAS was still a menace, where he stood beside SORKAS. Sir Cupran of Cinnabar flew heavily over to land in front of the Queen's Earl's guardsman, covering the route THEUTAS must follow to endanger Flambard.

Wise, but—Rogard looked again at MIKILLATI's chill white face, and it was as if a breath of cold blew through him. Suddenly he wondered why they fought. For victory, yes, for mastery over the world—but when the battle had been won, what then?

He couldn't think past that moment. His mind recoiled in horror he could not name. In that instant he knew icily that this was not the first war in the world, there had been others before, and there would be others again. *Victory is death.*

But Evyan, glorious Evyan, she could not die. She
would reign over all the world and—

Steel blazed in Cinnabar. MERKON of LEUKAS came
surging forth, one tigerish leap which brought him
down on Ocher's guardsman. The soldier screamed,
once, as he fell under the trampling, tearing hoofs, but it
was lost in the shout of the LEUKAN Knight: "Defend
yourself, Flambard! Defend yourself!"

Rogard gasped. It was like a blow in the belly. He had
stood triumphant over the world, and now all in one
swoop it was brought toppling about him. THEUTAS
shook his lance, SORKAS his mace, DIOMES raised a bull's
bellow—somehow, incredibly somehow, the warriors of
LEUKAS had entered Cinnabar and were thundering at
the King's own citadel.

"No, no—" Looking down the long, empty row of
squares, Rogard saw that Evyan was weeping. He
wanted to run to her, hold her close and shield her
against the falling world, but the Barriers were around
him. He could not stir from his square, he could only
watch.

Flambard cursed lividly and retreated into his Queen's
home. His men gave a shout and clashed their arms—
there was still a chance!

No, not while the Law bound men, thought Rogard,
not while the Barriers held. Victory was ashen, and
victory and defeat alike were darkness.

Beyond her thinly smiling husband, Queen DOLORA
swept forward. Evyan cried out as the tall white woman
halted before Rogard's terrified guardsman, turned to
face Flambard where he crouched, and called to him:
"Defend yourself, King!"

"No—no—you fool!" Rogard reached out, trying to break the Barrier, clawing at MIKILLATI. "Can't you see, none of us can win, it's death for us all if the war ends. Call her back!"

MIKILLATI ignored him. He seemed to be waiting.

And Ocher of Cinnabar raised a huge shout of laughter. It belled over the plain, dancing, joyous mirth, and men lifted weary heads and turned to the young Knight where he sat in his own stronghold, for there was youth and triumph and glory in his laughing. Swiftly, then, a blur of steel, he sprang, and his winged horse rushed out of the sky on DOLORA herself. She turned to meet him, lifting her sword, and he knocked it from her hand and stabbed with his own lance. Slowly, too haughty to scream, the white Queen sank under his horse's hoofs.

And MIKILLATI smiled.

"I see," nodded the visitor. "Individual computers, each controlling its own robot piece by a tight beam, and all the computers on a given side linked to form a sort of group-mind constrained to obey the rules of chess and make the best possible moves. Very nice. And it's a pretty cute notion of yours, making the robots look like medieval armies." His glance studied the tiny figures where they moved on the oversized board under one glaring floodlight.

"Oh, that's pure frippery," said the scientist. "This is really a serious research project in multiple computer-linkages. By letting them play game after game, I'm getting some valuable data."

"It's a lovely setup," said the visitor admiringly. "Do you realize that in this particular contest the two sides are reproducing one of the great classic games?"

"Why, no. Is that a fact?"

"Yes. It was a match between Anderssen and Kieseritzky, back in—I forget the year, but it was quite some time ago. Chess books often refer to it as The Immortal Game. . . . So your computers must share many of the properties of a human brain."

"Well, they're complex things, all right," admitted the scientist. "Not all their characteristics are known yet. Sometimes my chessmen surprise even me."

"Hm." The visitor stooped over the board. "Notice how they're jumping around inside their squares, waving their arms, batting at each other with their weapons?" He paused, then murmured slowly: "I wonder—I wonder if your computers may not have consciousness. If they might not have—minds."

"Don't get fantastic," snorted the scientist.

"But how do you know?" persisted the visitor. "Look, your feedback arrangement is closely analogous to a human nervous system. How do you know that your individual computers, even if they are constrained by the group linkage, don't have individual personalities? How do you know that their electronic senses don't interpret the game as, oh, as an interplay of free will and necessity; how do you know they don't receive the data of the moves as their own equivalent of blood, sweat, and tears?" He shuddered a little.

"Nonsense," grunted the scientist. "They're only robots. Now—Hey! Look there! Look at that move!"

Bishop SORKAS took one step ahead, into the black square adjoining Flambard's. He bowed and smiled. "The war has ended," he said.

Slowly, very slowly, Flambard looked about him. SORKAS, MERKON, THEUTAS, they were crouched to leap on him wherever he turned; his own men raged helpless against the Barriers; there was no place for him to go.

He bowed his head. "I surrender," he whispered.

Rogard looked across the red and black to Evyan. Their eyes met, and they stretched out their arms to each other.

"Checkmate," said the scientist. "That game's over."

He crossed the room to the switchboard and turned off the computers.

fishing

Fishing is—or seems to be—the most popular of all modern sports. Unlike most professional sports, which have turned into big business, fishing has long been a means of livelihood—from the subsistence level to huge industries. It is impossible to discover the precise point at which early man fished for fun instead of food, since fishermen usually eat their catch even when fishing for relaxation. However, there is a category of fishing, known as big-game fishing, whose goal is the defeat of a large fish and its retention as a trophy.

Fishing is also very relaxing (except for the fish), and millions of Americans use it as an excuse to escape from the pressures of urban living. After all, it provides a chance to "get away" and escape from the drudgery of work, a chance for solitude and the quiet life. In some areas, many fishermen arrive at the same trout stream on the same weekend so that the competition of life is transferred to the sport itself.

However, the future of fishing is not assured. We can fish in the oceans, rivers, and lakes of the world only as long as these bodies of water can support life. If we are not careful, the peril of pollution will put an end to one of the oldest of mankind's pleasures.

The Doors of
His Face, the Lamps of
His Mouth

roger zelazny

The mystery of fishing is one of the major attractions of millions of people to this form of sport. Man cannot peer through the waters in order to be certain of what is there, and this sense of the unknown and of uncertainty provides modern man with one of the few genuine challenges open to him today. This sense of mystery is also related to the disposition of most fishermen to graduate from "small" to "large" fishing. There seems to be a graduation which most fishermen experience from the thrill of small freshwater fishing to the increased excitement of fishing for larger fish which swim the oceans: From small to big to biggest seems to be part of the natural maturation of the average fisherman.

However, modern fishing is not only a matter of challenge associated with size. Among fishermen as a group, preferences are developed—and sophisticated codes and norms of fishing are formed—to deal with specialization. For example, snook are considered to be the "fisherman's fish" of saltwater fishing. This is a ranking given by fishermen based upon the taste as well as the spirit and fighting ability of the snook.

In addition, most mature fishermen will attribute to

fish the characteristics and personality traits of human beings. Aggressive, vicious, lazy, beautiful, patient, sneaky, and treacherous—these are adjectives commonly associated with different kinds of fish. Perhaps this relates to man's having evolved from essentially water-living creatures millions and millions of years ago. Or perhaps it simply relates to man's persistent inclination to attribute human traits to anything with whom or with which he is in conflict or competition.

The life of a fishing baitman on Venus—the central theme of this story—underscores all of these points. The gigantic three-hundred-foot-long *Ichthysaurus elasmognathus* which is the object of the fishing expedition is represented with humanlike characteristics which forebode evil. The relationships between the fish and fishermen, between the element of play and the element of tragedy, and between the element of rationality and the element of chance are all graphically portrayed in the context of this expedition. Stories about the fish–fisherman relationship and the myths and symbols associated with it have tremendous appeal to a broad range of Americans. For example, Hemingway's *The Old Man and the Sea* finds its more contemporary counterpart in the best-selling novel by Peter Benchley, *Jaws*, a story about a huge shark and the implications of its presence for a small Long Island town.

The Doors of
His Face, the Lamps of
His Mouth

I'm a baitman. No one is born a baitman, except in a
French novel where everyone is. (In fact, I think that's
the title, *We Are All Bait*. Pfft!) How I got that way is
barely worth the telling and has nothing to do with
neo-exes, but the days of the beast deserve a few words,
so here they are.

The Lowlands of Venus lie between the thumb and
forefinger of the continent known as Hand. When you
break into Cloud Alley it swings its silverblack bowling
ball toward you without a warning. You jump then,
inside that firetailed tenpin they ride you down in, but
the straps keep you from making a fool of yourself. You
generally chuckle afterward, but you always jump first.

Next, you study Hand to lay its illusion and the two
middle fingers become dozen-ringed archipelagoes as the
outers resolve into greengray peninsulas; the thumb is
too short, and curls like the embryo tail of Cape Horn.

You suck pure oxygen, sigh possibly, and begin the
long topple to the Lowlands.

There, you are caught like an infield fly at the Lifeline
landing area—so named because of its nearness to the

great delta in the Eastern Bay—located between the first
peninsula and "thumb." For a minute it seems as if
you're going to miss Lifeline and wind up as canned sea-
food, but afterward—shaking off the metaphors—you
descend to scorched concrete and present your middle-
sized telephone directory of authorizations to the short,
fat man in the gray cap. The papers show that you are
not subject to mysterious inner rottings and etcetera. He
then smiles you a short, fat, gray smile and motions you
toward the bus which hauls you to the Reception Area.
At the R.A. you spend three days proving that, indeed,
you are not subject to mysterious inner rottings and
etcetera.

Boredom, however, is another rot. When your three
days are up, you generally hit Lifeline hard, and it
returns the compliment as a matter of reflex. The effects
of alcohol in variant atmospheres is a subject on which
the connoisseurs have written numerous volumes, so I
will confine my remarks to noting that a good binge is
worthy of at least a week's time and often warrants a
lifetime study.

I had been a student of exceptional promise (strictly
undergraduate) for going on two years when the *Bright
Water* fell through our marble ceiling and poured its
people like targets into the city.

Pause. The *Worlds Almanac* re Lifeline: ". . . Port
city on the eastern coast of Hand. Employees of the
Agency for Nonterrestrial Research comprise approxi-
mately 85% of its 100,000 population (2010 Census).
Its other residents are primarily personnel maintained
by several industrial corporations engaged in basic
research. Independent marine biologists, wealthy fishing

enthusiasts, and waterfront entrepreneurs make up the remainder of its inhabitants."

I turned to Mike Perrin, a fellow entrepreneur, and commented on the lousy state of basic research.

"Not if the mumbled truth be known."

He paused behind his glass before continuing the slow swallowing process calculated to obtain my interest and a few oaths, before he continued.

"Carl," he finally observed, poker playing, "they're shaping Tensquare."

I could have hit him. I might have refilled his glass with sulfuric acid and looked on with glee as his lips blackened and cracked. Instead, I grunted a noncommittal: "Who's fool enough to shell out fifty grand a day? ANR?"

He shook his head.

"Jean Luharich," he said, "the girl with the violet contacts and fifty or sixty perfect teeth. I understand her eyes are really brown."

"Isn't she selling enough facecream these days?"

He shrugged.

"Publicity makes the wheels go round. Luharich Enterprises jumped sixteen points when she picked up the Sun Trophy. You ever play golf on Mercury?"

I had, but I overlooked it and continued to press.

"So she's coming here with a blank check and a fishhook?"

"*Bright Water*, today," he nodded. "Should be down by now. Lots of cameras. She wants an Ikky, bad."

"Hmm," I hmmed. "How bad?"

"Sixty-day contract, Tensquare. Indefinite extension clause. Million and a half deposit," he recited.

"You seem to know a lot about it."

"I'm Personnel Recruitment. Luharich Enterprises approached me last month. It helps to drink in the right places.

"Or own them," he smirked, after a moment.

I looked away, sipping my bitter brew. After a while I swallowed several things and asked Mike what he expected to be asked, leaving myself open for his monthly temperance lecture.

"They told me to try getting you," he mentioned. "When's the last time you sailed?"

"Month and a half ago. The *Corning*."

"Small stuff," he snorted. "When have you been under, yourself?"

"It's been awhile."

"It's been over a year, hasn't it? That time you got cut by the screw, under the *Dolphin*?"

I turned to him.

"I was in the river last week, up at Angleford where the currents are strong. I can still get around."

"Sober," he added.

"I'd stay that way," I said, "on a job like this."

A doubting nod.

"Straight union rates. Triple time for extraordinary circumstances," he narrated. "Be at Hangar Sixteen with your gear, Friday morning, five hundred hours. We push off Saturday, daybreak."

"You're sailing?"

"I'm sailing."

"How come?"

"Money."

"Ikky guano."

"The bar isn't doing so well and baby needs new minks."

"I repeat—"

". . . And I want to get away from baby, renew my contact with basics—fresh air, exercise, make cash. . . ."

"All right, sorry I asked."

I poured him a drink, concentrating on H_2SO_4, but it didn't transmute. Finally I got him soused and went out into the night to walk and think things over.

Around a dozen serious attempts to land *Ichthysaurus elasmognathus*, generally known as "Ikky," had been made over the past five years. When Ikky was first sighted, whaling techniques were employed. These proved either fruitless or disastrous, and a new procedure was inaugurated. Tensquare was constructed by a wealthy sportsman named Michael Jandt, who blew his entire roll on the project.

After a year on the Eastern Ocean, he returned to file bankruptcy. Carlton Davits, a playboy fishing enthusiast, then purchased the huge raft and laid a wake for Ikky's spawning grounds. On the nineteenth day out he had a strike and lost one hundred and fifty bills' worth of untested gear, along with one *Ichthysaurus elasmognathus*. Twelve days later, using tripled lines, he hooked, narcotized, and began to hoist the huge beast. It awakened then, destroyed a control tower, killed six men, and worked general hell over five square blocks of Tensquare. Carlton was left with partial hemiplegia and a bankruptcy suit of his own. He faded into waterfront atmosphere and Tensquare changed hands four more times, with less spectacular but equally expensive results.

Finally, the big raft, built only for one purpose, was

purchased at auction by ANR for "marine research." Lloyd's still won't insure it, and the only marine research it has ever seen is an occasional rental at fifty bills a day—to people anxious to tell Leviathan fish stories. I've been baitman on three of the voyages, and I've been close enough to count Ikky's fangs on two occasions. I want one of them to show my grandchildren, for personal reasons.

I faced the direction of the landing area and resolved a resolve.

"You want me for local coloring, gal. It'll look nice on the feature page and all that. But clear this— If anyone gets you an Ikky, it'll be me. I promise."

I stood in the empty Square. The foggy towers of Lifeline shared their mists.

Shoreline a couple eras ago, the western slope above Lifeline stretches as far as forty miles inland in some places. Its angle of rising is not a great one, but it achieves an elevation of several thousand feet before it meets the mountain range which separates us from the Highlands. About four miles inland and five hundred feet higher than Lifeline are set most of the surface airstrips and privately owned hangars. Hangar Sixteen houses Cal's Contract Cab, hop service, shore to ship. I do not like Cal, but he wasn't around when I climbed from the bus and waved to a mechanic.

Two of the hoppers tugged at the concrete, impatient beneath flywing halos. The one on which Steve was working belched deep within its barrel carburetor and shuddered spasmodically.

"Bellyache?" I inquired.

"Yeah, gas pains and heartburn."

He twisted setscrews until it settled into an even keening, and turned to me.

"You're for out?"

I nodded.

"Tensquare. Cosmetics. Monsters. Stuff like that."

He blinked into the beacons and wiped his freckles. The temperature was about twenty, but the big overhead spots served a double purpose.

"Luharich," he muttered. "Then you *are* the one. There's some people want to see you."

"What about?"

"Cameras. Microphones. Stuff like that."

"I'd better stow my gear. Which one am I riding?"

He poked the screwdriver at the other hopper.

"That one. You're on videotape now, by the way. They wanted to get you arriving."

He turned to the hangar, turned back.

"Say 'cheese.' They'll shoot the close close-ups later."

I said something other than "cheese." They must have been using telelens and been able to read my lips, because that part of the tape was never shown.

I threw my junk in the back, climbed into a passenger seat, and lit a cigarette. Five minutes later, Cal himself emerged from the office Quonset, looking cold. He came over and pounded on the side of the hopper. He jerked a thumb back at the hangar.

"They want you in there!" he called through cupped hands. "Interview!"

"The show's over!" I yelled back. "Either that, or they can get themselves another baitman!"

His rustbrown eyes became nailheads under blond brows and his glare a spike before he jerked about and

stalked off. I wondered how much they had paid him to
be able to squat in his hangar and suck juice from his
generator.

Enough, I guess, knowing Cal. I never liked the guy,
anyway.

Venus at night is a field of sable waters. On the coasts,
you can never tell where the sea ends and the sky begins.
Dawn is like dumping milk into an inkwell. First, there
are erratic curdles of white, then streamers. Shade the
bottle for a gray colloid, then watch it whiten a little
more. All of a sudden you've got day. Then start heating
the mixture.

I had to shed my jacket as we flashed out over the
bay. To our rear, the skyline could have been under
water for the way it waved and rippled in the heatfall. A
hopper can accommodate four people (five, if you want
to bend Regs and underestimate weight), or three pas-
sengers with the sort of gear a baitman uses. I was the
only fare, though, and the pilot was like his machine.
He hummed and made no unnecessary noises. Lifeline
turned a somersault and evaporated in the rear mirror at
about the same time Tensquare broke the fore-horizon.
The pilot stopped humming and shook his head.

I leaned forward. Feelings played flopdoodle in my
guts. I knew every bloody inch of the big raft, but the
feelings you once took for granted change when their
source is out of reach. Truthfully, I'd had my doubts I'd
ever board the hulk again. But now, now I could almost
believe in predestination. There it was!

A tensquare football field of a ship. A-powered. Flat as

a pancake, except for the plastic blisters in the middle and the "Rooks" fore and aft, port and starboard.

The Rook towers were named for their corner positions—and any two can work together to hoist, co-powering the graffles between them. The graffles—half gaff, half grapple—can raise enormous weights to near water level; their designer had only one thing in mind, though, which accounts for the gaff half. At water level, the Slider has to implement elevation for six to eight feet before the graffles are in a position to push upward, rather than pulling.

The Slider, essentially, is a mobile room—a big box capable of moving in any of Tensquare's crisscross groovings and "anchoring" on the strike side by means of a powerful electromagnetic bond. Its winches could hoist a battleship the necessary distance, and the whole craft would tilt, rather than the Slider come loose, if you want any idea of the strength of that bond.

The Slider houses a section-operated control indicator which is the most sophisticated "reel" ever designed. Drawing broadcast power from the generator beside the center blister, it is connected by shortwave with the sonar room, where the movements of the quarry are recorded and repeated to the angler seated before the section control.

The fisherman might play his "lines" for hours, days even, without seeing any more than metal and an outline on the screen. Only when the beast is graffled and the extensor shelf, located twelve feet below waterline, slides out for support and begins to aid the winches, only then does the fisherman see his catch rising before him like a fallen seraph. Then, as Davits learned, one looks into the Abyss itself and is required to act. He didn't, and a hundred meters of unimaginable tonnage, undernarcotized and hurting, broke the cables of the winch, snapped a graffle, and took a half-minute walk across Tensquare.

We circled till the mechanical flag took notice and waved us on down. We touched beside the personnel hatch and I jettisoned my gear and jumped to the deck.

"Luck," called the pilot as the door was sliding shut. Then he danced into the air and the flag clicked blank.

I shouldered my stuff and went below.

Signing in with Malvern, the de facto captain, I learned that most of the others wouldn't arrive for a good eight hours. They had wanted me alone at Cal's so they could pattern the pub footage along twentieth-century cinema lines.

Open: landing strip, dark. One mechanic prodding a contrary hopper. Stark-o-vision shot of slow bus pulling in. Heavily dressed baitman descends, looks about, limps across field. Close-up: He grins. Move in for words: "Do you think this is the time? The time he *will* be landed?" Embarrassment, taciturnity, a shrug. Dub something.—"I see. And why do you think Miss Luharich has a better chance than any of the others? Is it because she's better equipped? [Grin.] Because more is known now about the creature's habits than when you were out before? Or is it because of her will to win, to be a champion? Is it any one of these things, or is it all of them?" Reply: "Yeah, all of them."—"Is that why you signed on with her? Because your instincts say, 'This one will be it'?" Answer: "She pays union rates. I couldn't rent that damned thing myself. And I want in." Erase. Dub something else. Fade-out as he moves toward hopper, etcetera.

"Cheese," I said, or something like that, and took a walk around Tensquare, by myself.

I mounted each Rook, checking out the controls and the underwater video eyes. Then I raised the main lift. Malvern had no objections to my testing things this way. In fact, he encouraged it. We had sailed together before and our positions had even been reversed upon a time. So I wasn't surprised when I stepped off the lift into the Hopkins Locker and found him waiting. For the next ten minutes we inspected the big room in silence, walking through its copper coil chambers soon to be Arctic.

Finally, he slapped a wall.

"Well, will we fill it?"

I shook my head.

"I'd like to, but I doubt it. I don't give two hoots and a damn who gets credit for the catch, so long as I have a part in it. But it won't happen. That gal's an egomaniac. She'll want to operate the Slider, and she can't."

"You ever meet her?"

"Yeah."

"How long ago?"

"Four, five years."

"She was a kid then. How do you know what she can do now?"

"I know. She'll have learned every switch and reading by this time. She'll be up on all the theory. But do you remember one time we were together in the starboard Rook, forward, when Ikky broke water like a porpoise?"

"How could I forget?"

"Well?"

He rubbed his emery chin.

"Maybe she can do it, Carl. She's raced torch ships and she's scubaed in bad waters back home." He glanced in the direction of invisible Hand. "And she's hunted in the Highlands. She might be wild enough to pull that horror into her lap without flinching.

". . . For Johns Hopkins to foot the bill and shell out seven figures for the corpus," he added. "That's money, even to a Luharich."

I ducked through a hatchway.

"Maybe you're right, but she was a rich witch when I knew her.

"And she wasn't blonde," I added, meanly.

He yawned.

"Let's find breakfast."

We did that.

When I was young I thought that being born a sea creature was the finest choice Nature could make for anyone. I grew up on the Pacific coast and spent my summers on the Gulf or the Mediterranean. I lived months of my life negotiating coral, photographing trench dwellers, and playing tag with dolphins. I fished everywhere there are fish, resenting the fact that they can go places I can't. When I grew older I wanted bigger fish, and there was nothing living that I knew of, excepting a Sequoia, that came any bigger than Ikky. That's part of it. . . .

I jammed a couple extra rolls into a paper bag and filled a thermos with coffee. Excusing myself, I left the galley and made my way to the Slider berth. It was just the way I remembered it. I threw a few switches and the shortwave hummed.

"That you, Carl?"

"That's right, Mike. Let me have some juice down here, you doublecrossing rat."

He thought it over, then I felt the hull vibrate as the generators cut in. I poured my third cup of coffee and found a cigarette.

"So why am I a doublecrossing rat this time?" came his voice again.

"You knew about the cameramen at Hangar Sixteen?"

"Yes."

"Then you're a doublecrossing rat. The last thing I want is publicity. 'He who fouled up so often before is ready to try it, nobly, once more.' I can read it now."

"You're wrong. The spotlight's only big enough for one, and she's prettier than you."

My next comment was cut off as I threw the elevator switch and the elevator switch and the elephant ears flapped above me. I rose, settling flush with the deck. Retracting the lateral rail, I cut forward into the groove. Amidships, I stopped at a juncture, dropped the lateral, and retracted the longitudinal rail.

I slid starboard, midway between the Rooks, halted, and threw on the coupler.

I hadn't spilled a drop of coffee.

"Show me pictures."

The screen glowed. I adjusted and got outlines of the bottom.

"Okay."

I threw a Status Blue switch and he matched it. The light went on.

The winch unlocked. I aimed out over the waters, extended the arm, and fired a cast.

"Clean one," he commented.

"Status Red. Call strike." I threw a switch.

"Status Red."

The baitman would be on his way with this, to make the barbs tempting.

It's not exactly a fishhook. The cables bear hollow tubes, the tubes convey enough dope for an army of hopheads, Ikky takes the bait, dandled before him by remote control, and the fisherman rams the barbs home.

My hands moved over the console, making the necessary adjustments. I checked the narco-tank reading. Empty. Good, they hadn't been filled yet. I thumbed the Inject button.

"In the gullet," Mike murmured.

I released the cables. I played the beast imagined. I let him run, swinging the winch to simulate his sweep.

I had the air conditioner on and my shirt off and it was still uncomfortably hot, which is how I knew that morning had gone over into noon. I was dimly aware of the arrivals and departures of the hoppers. Some of the crew sat in the "shade" of the doors I had left open, watching the operation. I didn't see Jean arrive or I would have ended the session and gotten below.

She broke my concentration by slamming the door hard enough to shake the bond.

"Mind telling me who authorized you to bring up the Slider?" she asked.

"No one," I replied. "I'll take it below now."

"Just move aside."

I did, and she took my seat. She was wearing brown

slacks and a baggy shirt and she had her hair pulled
back in a practical manner. Her cheeks were flushed, but
not necessarily from the heat. She attacked the panel
with a nearly amusing intensity that I found disquieting.

"Status Blue," she snapped, breaking a violet finger-
nail on the toggle.

I forced a yawn and buttoned my shirt slowly. She
threw a side glance my way, checked the registers, and
fired a cast.

I monitored the lead on the screen. She turned to me
for a second.

"Status Red," she said levelly.

I nodded my agreement.

She worked the winch sideways to show she knew
how. I didn't doubt she knew how and she didn't doubt
that I didn't doubt, but then—

"In case you're wondering," she said, "you're not going
to be anywhere near this thing. You were hired as a
baitman, remember? Not a Slider operator! A baitman!
Your duties consist of swimming out and setting the
table for our friend the monster. It's dangerous, but
you're getting well paid for it. Any questions?"

She squashed the Inject button and I rubbed my
throat.

"Nope," I smiled, "but I am qualified to run that
thingamajigger—and if you need me I'll be available, at
union rates."

"Mister Davits," she said, "I don't want a loser operat-
ing this panel."

"Miss Luharich, there has never been a winner at this
game."

She started reeling in the cable and broke the bond

at the same time, so that the whole Slider shook as the big yo-yo returned. We skidded a couple feet backward as it curled into place, and she retracted the arm. She raised the laterals and we shot back along the groove. Slowing, she transferred rails and we jolted to a clanging halt, then shot off at a right angle. The crew scrambled away from the hatch as we skidded onto the elevator.

"In the future, Mister Davits, do not enter the Slider without being ordered," she told me.

"Don't worry. I won't even step inside if I am ordered," I answered. "I signed on as a baitman. Remember? If you want me in here, you'll have to *ask* me."

"That'll be the day," she smiled.

I agreed, as the doors closed above us. We dropped the subject and headed in our different directions after the Slider came to a halt in its berth. She did say "good day," though, which I thought showed breeding as well as determination, in reply to my chuckle.

Later that night Mike and I stoked our pipes in Malvern's cabin. The winds were shuffling waves, and a steady spattering of rain and hail overhead turned the deck into a tin roof.

"Nasty," suggested Malvern.

I nodded. After two bourbons the room had become a familiar woodcut, with its mahogany furnishings (which I had transported from Earth long ago on a whim) and the dark walls, the seasoned face of Malvern, and the perpetually puzzled expression of Perrin set between the big pools of shadow that lay behind chairs and splashed in corners, all cast by the tiny table light and seen through a glass, brownly.

"Glad I'm in here."

"What's it like underneath on a night like this?"

I puffed, thinking of my light cutting through the insides of a black diamond, shaken slightly. The meteor-dart of a suddenly illuminated fish, the swaying of grotesque ferns, like nebulae—shadow, then green, then gone—swam in a moment through my mind. I guess it's like a spaceship would feel, if a spaceship could feel, crossing between worlds—and quiet, uncannily, preter-naturally quiet; and peaceful as sleep.

"Dark," I said, "and not real choppy below a few fathoms."

"Another eight hours and we shove off," commented Mike.

"Ten, twelve days, we should be there," noted Malvern.

"What do you think Ikky's doing?"

"Sleeping on the bottom with Mrs. Ikky, if he has any brains."

"He hasn't. I've seen ANR's skeletal extrapolation from the bones that have washed up—"

"Hasn't everyone?"

". . . Fully fleshed, he'd be over a hundred meters long. That right, Carl?"

I agreed.

". . . Not much of a brain box, though, for his bulk."

"Smart enough to stay out of our locker."

Chuckles, because nothing exists but this room, really. The world outside is an empty, sleet-drummed deck. We lean back and make clouds.

"Boss lady does not approve of unauthorized fly-fishing."

"Boss lady can walk north till her hat floats."

"What did she say in there?"

"She told me that my place, with fish manure, is on the bottom."

"You don't Slide?"

"I bait."

"We'll see."

"That's all I do. If she wants a Slideman she's going to have to ask nicely."

"You think she'll have to?"

"I think she'll have to."

"And if she does, can you do it?"

"A fair question," I puffed. "I don't know the answer, though."

I'd incorporate my soul and trade forty percent of the stock for the answer. I'd give a couple years off my life for the answer. But there doesn't seem to be a lineup of supernatural takers, because no one knows. Supposing when we get out there, luck being with us, we find ourselves an Ikky? Supposing we succeed in baiting him and get lines on him. What then? If we get him shipside will she hold on or crack up? What if she's made of sterner stuff than Davits, who used to hunt sharks with poison-darted air pistols? Supposing she lands him and Davits has to stand there like a video extra.

Worse yet, supposing she asks for Davits and he still stands there like a video extra or something else—say, some yellowbellied embodiment named Cringe?

It was when I got him up above the eight-foot horizon of steel and looked out at all that body, sloping on and on till it dropped out of sight like a green mountain range. . . . And that head. Small for the body, but still immense. Flat, craggy, with lidless roulettes that had spun black and red since before my forefathers decided to try the New Continent. And swaying.

Fresh narco-tanks had been connected. It needed another shot, fast. But I was paralyzed.

It had made a noise like God playing a Hammond organ. . . .

And looked at me!

I don't know if seeing is even the same process in eyes like those. I doubt it. Maybe I was just a gray blur behind a black rock, with the plexi-reflected sky hurting its pupils. But it fixed on me. Perhaps the snake doesn't really paralyze the rabbit, perhaps it's just that rabbits are cowards by constitution. But it began to struggle and I still couldn't move, fascinated.

Fascinated by all that power, by those eyes, they found me there fifteen minutes later, a little broken about the head and shoulders, the Inject still unpushed.

And I dream about those eyes. I want to face them once more, even if their finding takes forever. I've got to know if there's something inside me that sets me apart from a rabbit, from notched plates of reflexes and instincts that always fall apart in exactly the same way whenever the proper combination is spun.

Looking down, I noticed that my hand was shaking. Glancing up, I noticed that no one else was noticing.

I finished my drink and emptied my pipe. It was late and no songbirds were singing.

I sat whittling, my legs hanging over the aft edge, the chips spinning down into the furrow of our wake. Three days out. No action.

"You!"

"Me?"

"You."

Hair like the end of the rainbow, eyes like nothing in Nature, fine teeth.

"Hello."

"There's a safety rule against what you're doing, you know."

"I know. I've been worrying about it all morning."

A delicate curl climbed my knife, then drifted out behind us. It settled into the foam and was plowed under. I watched her reflection in my blade, taking a secret pleasure in its distortion.

"Are you baiting me?" she finally asked.

I heard her laugh then, and turned, knowing it had been intentional.

"What, me?"

"I could push you off from here, very easily."

"I'd make it back."

"Would you push me off, then—some dark night, perhaps?"

"They're all dark, Miss Luharich. No, I'd rather make you a gift of my carving."

She seated herself beside me then, and I couldn't help but notice the dimples in her knees. She wore white shorts and a halter and still had an offworld tan to her which was awfully appealing. I almost felt a twinge of guilt at having planned the whole scene, but my right hand still blocked her view of the wooden animal.

"Okay, I'll bite. What have you got for me?"

"Just a second. It's almost finished."

Solemnly, I passed her the wooden jackass I had been

carving. I felt a little sorry and slightly jackassish myself, but I had to follow through. I always do. The mouth was split into a braying grin. The ears were upright.

She didn't smile and she didn't frown. She just studied it.

"It's very good," she finally said, "like most things you do—and appropriate, perhaps."

"Give it to me." I extended a palm.

She handed it back and I tossed it out over the water. It missed the white water and bobbed for awhile like a pigmy seahorse.

"Why did you do that?"

"It was a poor joke. I'm sorry."

"Maybe you are right, though. Perhaps this time I've bitten off a little too much."

I snorted.

"Then why not do something safer, like another race?"

She shook her end of the rainbow.

"No. It has to be an Ikky."

"Why?"

"Why did you want one so badly that you threw away a fortune?"

"Man reasons," I said. "An unfrocked analyst who held black therapy sessions in his basement once told me, 'Mister Davits, you need to reinforce the image of your masculinity by catching one of every kind of fish in existence.' Fish are a very ancient masculinity symbol, you know. So I set out to do it. I have one more to go.— Why do you want to reinforce *your* masculinity?"

"I don't," she said. "I don't want to reinforce anything but Luharich Enterprises. My chief statistician once said, 'Miss Luharich, sell all the cold cream and face powder in the System and you'll be a happy girl. Rich, too.' And he was right. I am the proof. I can look the way I do and do anything, and I sell most of the lipstick and face powder in the System—but I have to be *able* to do anything."

"You do look cool and efficient," I observed.

"I don't feel cool," she said, rising. "Let's go for a swim."

"May I point out that we are making pretty good time?"

"If you want to indicate the obvious, you may. You said you could make it back to the ship, unassisted. Change your mind?"

"No."

"Then get us two scuba outfits and I'll race you under Tensquare.

"I'll win, too," she added.

I stood and looked down at her, because that usually makes me feel superior to women.

"Daughter of Lir, eyes of Picasso," I said, "you've got yourself a race. Meet me at the forward Rook, starboard, in ten minutes."

"Ten minutes," she agreed.

And ten minutes it was. From the center blister to the Rook took maybe two of them, with the load I was carrying. My sandals grew very hot and I was glad to shuck them for flippers when I reached the comparative cool of the corner.

We slid into harnesses and adjusted our gear. She had changed into a trim one-piece green job that made me shade my eyes and look away, then look back again.

I fastened a rope ladder and kicked it over the side. Then I pounded on the wall of the Rook.

"Yeah?"

"You talk to the port Rook, aft?" I called.

"They're all set up," came the answer. "There's ladders and draglines all over that end."

"You sure you want to do this?" asked the sunburned little gink who was her publicity man, Anderson yclept.

He sat beside the Rook in a deckchair, sipping lemonade through a straw.

"It might be dangerous," he observed, sunkenmouthed. (His teeth were beside him, in another glass.)

"That's right," she smiled. "It *will* be dangerous. Not overly, though."

"Then why don't you let me get some pictures? We'd have them back to Lifeline in an hour. They'd be in New York by tonight. Good copy."

"No," she said, and turned away from both of us.

She raised her hands to her eyes.

"Here, keep these for me."

She passed him a box full of her unseeing, and when she turned back to me they were the same brown that I remembered.

"Ready?"

"No," I said, tautly. "Listen carefully, Jean. If you're going to play this game there are a few rules. First," I counted, "we're going to be directly beneath the hull, so we have to start low and keep moving. If we bump the bottom, we could rupture an air tank. ...."

She began to protest that any moron knew that and I cut her down.

"Second," I went on, "there won't be much light, so we'll stay close together and we will *both* carry torches."

Her wet eyes flashed.

"I dragged you out of Govino without—"

Then she stopped and turned away. She picked up a lamp.

"Okay. Torches. Sorry."

". . . And watch out for the drive-screws," I finished. "There'll be strong currents for at least fifty meters behind them."

She wiped her eyes again and adjusted the mask.

"All right, let's go."

We went.

She led the way, at my insistence. The surface layer was pleasantly warm. At two fathoms the water was bracing; at five it was nice and cold. At eight we let go the swinging stairway and struck out. Tensquare sped forward and we raced in the opposite direction, tattooing the hull yellow at ten-second intervals.

The hull stayed where it belonged, but we raced on like two darkside satellites. Periodically, I tickled her frog feet with my light and traced her antennae of bubbles. About a five-meter lead was fine; I'd beat her in the home stretch, but I couldn't let her drop behind yet.

Beneath us, black. Immense. Deep. The Mindanao of Venus, where eternity might eventually pass the dead to a rest in cities of unnamed fishes. I twisted my head away and touched the hull with a feeler of light; it told me we were about a quarter of the way along.

I increased my beat to match her stepped-up stroke, and narrowed the distance which she had suddenly opened by a couple meters. She sped up again and I did, too. I spotted her with my beam.

She turned and it caught on her mask. I never knew whether she'd been smiling. Probably. She raised two fingers in a V-for-Victory and then cut ahead at full speed.

I should have known. I should have felt it coming. It was just a race to her, something else to win. Damn the torpedoes!

So I leaned into it, hard. I don't shake in the water. Or, if I do it doesn't matter and I don't notice it. I began to close the gap again.

She looked back, sped on, looked back. Each time she looked I was nearer, until I'd narrowed it down to the original five meters.

Then she hit the jatoes.

That's what I had been fearing. We were about halfway under and she shouldn't have done it. The powerful jets of compressed air could easily rocket her upward into the hull, or tear something loose if she allowed her body to twist. Their main use is in tearing free from marine plants or fighting bad currents. I had wanted them along as a safety measure, because of the big suck-and-pull windmills behind.

She shot ahead like a meteorite, and I could feel a sudden tingle of perspiration leaping to meet and mix with the churning waters.

I swept ahead, not wanting to use my own guns, and she tripled, quadrupled the margin.

The jets died and she was still on course. Okay, I was an old fuddyduddy. She *could* have messed up and headed toward the top.

I plowed the sea and began to gather back my yardage, a foot at a time. I wouldn't be able to catch her or beat her now, but I'd be on the ropes before she hit deck.

Then the spinning magnets began their insistence and she wavered. It was an awfully powerful drag, even at this distance. The call of the meat grinder.

I'd been scratched up by one once, under the *Dolphin*, a fishing boat of the middle-class. I *had* been drinking, but it was also a rough day, and the thing had been turned on prematurely. Fortunately, it was turned off in time, also, and a tendon-stapler made everything good as new, except in the log, where it only mentioned that I'd been drinking. Nothing about it being off-hours when I had a right to do as I damn well pleased.

She had slowed to half her speed, but she was still moving crosswise, toward the port, aft corner. I began to feel the pull myself and had to slow down. She'd made it past the main one, but she seemed too far back. It's hard to gauge distances under water, but each red beat of time told me I was right. She was out of danger from the main one, but the smaller port screw, located about eighty meters in, was no longer a threat but a certainty.

Each air bubble carried a curse to daylight as I moved to flank her from the left.

She had turned and was pulling away from it now. Twenty meters separated us. She was standing still. Fifteen.

Slowly, she began a backward drifting. I hit my jatoes, aiming two meters behind her and about twenty back of the blades.

Straightline! Thankgod! Catching, softbelly, leadpipe

on shoulder SWIMLIKEHELL! maskcracked, not broke though AND UP!

We caught a line and I remember brandy.

Into the cradle endlessly rocking I spit, pacing. Insomnia tonight and left shoulder sore again, so let it rain on me—they can cure rheumatism. Stupid as hell. What I said. In blankets and shivering. She: "Carl, I can't say it." Me: "Then call it square for that night in Govino, Miss Luharich. Huh?" She: nothing. Me: "Any more of that brandy?" She: "Give me another, too." Me: sounds of sipping. It had only lasted three months. No alimony. Many $ on both sides. Not sure whether they were happy or not. Wine-dark Aegean. Good fishing. Maybe he should have spent more time on shore. Or perhaps she shouldn't have. Good swimmer, though. Dragged him all the way to Vido to wring out his lungs. Young. Both. Strong. Both. Rich and spoiled as hell. Ditto. Corfu should have brought them closer. Didn't. I think that mental cruelty was a trout. He wanted to go to Canada. She: "Go to hell if you want!" He: "Will you go along?" She: "No." But she did, anyhow. Many hells. Expensive. He lost a monster or two. She inherited a couple. Lot of lightning tonight. Stupid as hell. Civility's the coffin of a conned soul. By whom?—Sounds like a bloody neo-ex . . . But I hate you, Anderson, with your glass full of teeth and her new eyes. . . . Can't keep this pipe lit, keep sucking tobacco. Spit again!

Seven days out and the scope showed Ikky.

Bells jangled, feet pounded, and some optimist set the

thermostat in the Hopkins. Malvern wanted me to sit it out, but I slipped into my harness and waited for whatever came. The bruise looked worse than it felt. I had exercised every day and the shoulder hadn't stiffened on me.

A thousand meters ahead and thirty fathoms deep, it tunneled our path. Nothing showed on the surface.

"Will we chase him?" asked an excited crewman.

"Not unless she feels like using money for fuel," I shrugged.

Soon the scope was clear, and it stayed that way. We remained on alert and held our course.

I hadn't said over a dozen words to my boss since the last time we went drowning together, so I decided to raise the score.

"Good afternoon," I approached. "What's new?"

"He's going north-northeast. We'll have to let this one go. A few more days and we can afford some chasing. Not yet."

Sleek head . . .

I nodded. "No telling where this one's headed."

"How's your shoulder?"

"All right. How about you?"

Daughter of Lir . . .

"Fine. By the way, you're down for a nice bonus."

Eyes of perdition!

"Don't mention it," I told her back.

Later that afternoon, and appropriately, a storm shattered. (I prefer "shattered" to "broke." It gives a more accurate idea of the behavior of tropical storms on Venus and saves lots of words.) Remember that inkwell I mentioned earlier? Now take it between thumb and forefinger and hit its side with a hammer. Watch yourself! Don't get splashed or cut—

Dry, then drenched. The sky one million bright fractures as the hammer falls. And sounds of breaking.

"Everyone below!" suggested loudspeakers to the already scurrying crew.

Where was I? Who do you think was doing the loudspeaking?

Everything loose went overboard when the water got to walking, but by then no people were loose. The Slider was the first thing below decks. Then the big lifts lowered their shacks.

I had hit it for the nearest Rook with a yell the moment I recognized the pre-brightening of the holocaust. From there I cut in the speakers and spent half a minute coaching the track team.

Minor injuries had occurred, Mike told me over the radio, but nothing serious. I, however, was marooned for the duration. The Rooks do not lead anywhere; they're set too far out over the hull to provide entry downward, what with the extensor shelves below.

So I undressed myself of the tanks which I had worn for the past several hours, crossed my flippers on the table, and leaned back to watch the hurricane. The top was black as the bottom and we were in between, and somewhat illuminated because of all that flat, shiny space. The waters above didn't rain down—they just sort of got together and dropped.

The Rooks were secure enough—they'd weathered any number of these onslaughts—it's just that their positions gave them a greater arc of rise and descent when Tensquare makes like the rocker of a very nervous grandma.

I had used the belts from my rig to strap myself into the bolted-down chair, and I removed several years in purgatory from the soul of whoever left a pack of cigarettes in the table drawer.

I watched the water make teepees and mountains and hands and trees until I started seeing faces and people. So I called Mike.

"What are you doing down there?"

"Wondering what you're doing up there," he replied. "What's it like?"

"You're from the midwest, aren't you?"

"Yeah."

"Get bad storms out there?"

"Sometimes."

"Try to think of the worst one you were ever in. Got a slide rule handy?"

"Right here."

"Then put a one under it, imagine a zero or two following after, and multiply the thing out."

"I can't imagine the zeroes."

"Then retain the multiplicand—that's all you can do."

"So what are you doing up there?"

"I've strapped myself in the chair. I'm watching things roll around the floor right now."

I looked up and out again. I saw one darker shadow in the forest.

"Are you praying or swearing?"

"Damned if I know. But if this were the Slider—if only this were the Slider!"

"*He's out there?*"

I nodded, forgetting that he couldn't see me.

Big, as I remembered him. He'd only broken surface

for a few moments, to look around. *There is no power on Earth that can be compared with him who was made to fear no one.* I dropped my cigarette. It was the same as before. Paralysis and an unborn scream.

"You all right, Carl?"

He had looked at me again. Or seemed to. Perhaps that mindless brute had been waiting half a millennium to ruin the life of a member of the most highly developed species in business . . .

"You okay?"

. . . Or perhaps it had been ruined already, long before their encounter, and theirs was just a meeting of beasts, the stronger bumping the weaker aside, body to psyche. . . .

"Carl, dammit! Say something!"

He broke again, this time nearer. Did you ever see the trunk of a tornado? It seems like something alive, moving around in all that dark. Nothing has a right to be so big, so strong, and moving. It's a sickening sensation.

"Please answer me."

He was gone and did not come back that day. I finally made a couple wisecracks at Mike, but I held my next cigarette in my right hand.

The next seventy or eighty thousand waves broke by with a monotonous similarity. The five days that held them were also without distinction. The morning of the thirteenth day out, though, our luck began to rise. The bells broke our coffee-drenched lethargy into small pieces, and we dashed from the galley without hearing what might have been Mike's finest punchline.

"Aft!" cried someone. "Five hundred meters!"

I stripped to my trunks and started buckling. My stuff is always within grabbing distance.

I flipflopped across the deck, girding myself with a deflated squiggler.

"Five hundred meters, twenty fathoms!" boomed the speakers.

The big traps banged upward and the Slider grew to its full height, m'lady at the console. It rattled past me and took root ahead. Its one arm rose and lengthened.

I breasted the Slider as the speakers called, "Four-eighty, twenty!"

"Status Red!"

A belch like an emerging champagne cork and the line arced high over the waters.

"Four-eighty, twenty!" it repeated, all Malvern and static. "Baitman, attend!"

I adjusted my mask and hand-over-handed it down the side. Then warm, then cool, then away.

Green, vast, down. Fast. This is the place where I am equal to a squiggler. If something big decides a baitman looks tastier than what he's carrying, then irony colors his title as well as the water about it.

I caught sight of the drifting cables and followed them down. Green to dark green to black. It had been a long cast, too long. I'd never had to follow one this far down before. I didn't want to switch on my torch.

But I had to.

Bad! I still had a long way to go. I clenched my teeth and stuffed my imagination into a straitjacket.

Finally the line came to an end.

I wrapped one arm about it and unfastened the squiggler. I attached it, working as fast as I could, and plugged in the little insulated connections which are the reason it can't be fired with the line. Ikky could break them, but by then it wouldn't matter.

My mechanical eel hooked up, I pulled its section plugs and watched it grow. I had been dragged deeper during this operation, which took about a minute and a half. I was near—too near—to where I never wanted to be.

Loath as I had been to turn on my light, I was suddenly afraid to turn it off. Panic gripped me and I seized the cable with both hands. The squiggler began to glow, pinkly. It started to twist. It was twice as big as I am and doubtless twice as attractive to pink squiggler-eaters. I told myself this until I believed it, then I switched off my light and started up.

If I bumped into something enormous and steel-hided, my heart had orders to stop beating immediately and release me—to dart fitfully forever along Acheron, and gibbering.

Ungibbering, I made it to green water and fled back to the nest.

As soon as they hauled me aboard I made my mask a necklace, shaded my eyes, and monitored for surface turbulence. My first question, of course, was: "Where is he?"

"Nowhere," said a crewman, "we lost him right after you went over. Can't pick him up on the scope now. Musta dived."

"Too bad."

The squiggler stayed down, enjoying its bath. My job ended for the time being, I headed back to warm my coffee with rum.

From behind me, a whisper: "Could you laugh like that afterward?"

Perceptive Answer: "Depends on what he's laughing at."

Still chuckling, I made my way into the center blister with two cupfuls.

"Still hell and gone?"

Mike nodded. His big hands were shaking, and mine were steady as a surgeon's when I set down the cups.

He jumped as I shrugged off the tanks and looked for a bench.

"Don't drip on that panel! You want to kill yourself and blow expensive fuses?"

I toweled down, then settled down to watching the unfilled eye on the wall. I yawned happily; my shoulder seemed good as new.

The little box that people talk through wanted to say something, so Mike lifted the switch and told it to go ahead.

"Is Carl there, Mister Perrin?"

"Yes, ma'am."

"Then let me talk to him."

Mike motioned and I moved.

"Talk," I said.

"Are you all right?"

"Yes, thanks. Shouldn't I be?"

"That was a long swim. I—I guess I overshot my cast."

"I'm happy," I said. "More triple-time for me. I really clean up on that hazardous duty clause."

"I'll be more careful next time," she apologized. "I guess I was too eager. Sorry—" Something happened to

the sentence, so she ended it there, leaving me with
half a bagful of replies I'd been saving.

I lifted the cigarette from behind Mike's ear and got a
light from the one in the ashtray.

"Carl, she was being nice," he said, after turning to
study the panels.

"I know," I told him. "I wasn't."

"I mean, she's an awfully pretty kid, pleasant. Head-
strong and all that. But what's she done to you?"

"Lately?" I asked.

He looked at me, then dropped his eyes to his cup.

"I know it's none of my bus—" he began.

"Cream and sugar?"

Ikky didn't return that day, or that night. We picked up
some Dixieland out of Lifeline and let the muskrat
ramble while Jean had her supper sent to the Slider.
Later she had a bunk assembled inside. I piped in "Deep
Water Blues" when it came over the air and waited for
her to call up and cuss us out. She didn't, though, so I
decided she was sleeping.

Then I got Mike interested in a game of chess that
went on until daylight. It limited conversation to several
"chocks," one "checkmate," and a "damn!" Since he's a
poor loser it also effectively sabotaged subsequent talk,
which was fine with me. I had a steak and fried potatoes
for breakfast and went to bed.

Ten hours later someone shook me awake and I
propped myself on one elbow, refusing to open my eyes.

"Whassamadder?"

"I'm sorry to get you up," said one of the younger

crewmen, "but Miss Luharich wants you to disconnect the squiggler so we can move on."

I knuckled open one eye, still deciding whether I should be amused.

"Have it hauled to the side. Anyone can disconnect it."

"It's at the side now, sir. But she said it's in your contract and we'd better do things right."

"That's very considerate of her. I'm sure my Local appreciates her remembering."

"Uh, she also said to tell you to change your trunks and comb your hair, and shave, too. Mister Anderson's going to film it."

"Okay. Run along, tell her I'm on my way—and ask if she has some toenail polish I can borrow."

I'll save on details. It took three minutes in all, and I played it properly, even pardoning myself when I slipped and bumped into Anderson's white tropicals with the wet squiggler. He smiled, brushed it off; she smiled, even though Luharich Complectacolor couldn't completely mask the dark circles under her eyes; and I smiled, waving to all our fans out there in videoland.— Remember, Mrs. Universe, you, too, can look like a monster-catcher. Just use Luharich facecream.

I went below and made myself a tuna sandwich, with mayonnaise.

Two days like icebergs—bleak, blank, half-melting, all frigid, mainly out of sight, and definitely a threat to peace of mind—drifted by and were good to put behind. I experienced some old guilt feelings and had a few disturbing dreams. Then I called Lifeline and checked my bank balance.

"Going shopping?" asked Mike, who had put the call through for me.

"Going home," I answered.

"Huh?"

"I'm out of the baiting business after this one, Mike. The Devil with Ikky! The Devil with Venus and Luharich Enterprises! And the Devil with you!"

Up eyebrows.

"What brought that on?"

"I waited over a year for this job. Now that I'm here, I've decided the whole thing stinks."

"You knew what it was when you signed on. No matter what else you're doing, you're selling facecream when you work for facecream sellers."

"Oh, that's not what's biting me. I admit the commercial angle irritates me, but Tensquare has always been a publicity spot, ever since the first time it sailed."

"What, then?"

"Five or six things, all added up. The main one being that I don't care anymore. Once it meant more to me than anything else to hook that critter, and now it doesn't. I went broke on what started out as a lark and I wanted blood for what it cost me. Now I realize that maybe I had it coming. I'm beginning to feel sorry for Ikky."

"And you don't want him now?"

"I'll take him if he comes peacefully, but I don't feel like sticking out my neck to make him crawl into the Hopkins."

"I'm inclined to think it's one of the four or five other things you said you added."

"Such as?"

He scrutinized the ceiling.

I growled.

"Okay, but I won't say it, not just to make you happy you guessed right."

He, smirking: "That look she wears isn't just for Ikky."

"No good, no good," I shook my head. "We're both fission chambers by nature. You can't have jets on both ends of the rocket and expect to go anywhere—what's in the middle just gets smashed."

"That's how it *was*. None of my business, of course—"

"Say that again and you'll say it without teeth."

"Any day, big man," he looked up, "any place . . ."

"So go ahead. Get it said!"

"She doesn't care about that bloody reptile, she came here to drag you back where you belong. You're not the baitman this trip."

"Five years is too long."

"There must be something under that cruddy hide of yours that people like," he muttered, "or I wouldn't be talking like this. Maybe you remind us humans of some really ugly dog we felt sorry for when we were kids. Anyhow, someone wants to take you home and raise you —also, something about beggars not getting menus."

"Buddy," I chuckled, "do you know what I'm going to do when I hit Lifeline?"

"I can guess."

"You're wrong. I'm torching it to Mars, and then I'll cruise back home, first class. Venus bankruptcy provisions do not apply to Martian trust funds, and I've still got a wad tucked away where moth and corruption enter not. I'm going to pick up a big old mansion on the Gulf, and if you're ever looking for a job you can stop around and open bottles for me."

"You are a yellowbellied fink," he commented.

"OK," I admitted, "but it's her I'm thinking of, too."

"I've heard the stories about you both," he said. "So you're a heel and a goofoff and she's a bitch. That's called compatibility these days. I dare you, baitman, try keeping something you catch."

I turned.

"If you ever want that job, look me up."

I closed the door quietly behind me and left him sitting there waiting for it to slam.

The day of the beast dawned like any other. Two days after my gutless flight from empty waters I went down to rebait. Nothing on the scope. I was just making things ready for the routine attempt.

I hollered a "good morning" from outside the Slider and received an answer from inside before I pushed off. I had reappraised Mike's words, sans sound, sans fury, and while I did not approve of their sentiment or significance, I had opted for civility anyhow.

So down, under, and away. I followed a decent cast about two hundred ninety meters out. The snaking cables burned black to my left and I paced their undulations from the yellow-green down into the darkness. Soundless lay the wet night, and I bent my way through it like a cockeyed comet, bright tail before.

I caught the line, slick and smooth, and began baiting. An icy world swept by me then, ankles to head. It was a draft, as if someone had opened a big door beneath me. I wasn't drifting downward that fast either.

Which meant that something might be moving up, something big enough to displace a lot of water. I still didn't think it was Ikky. A freak current of some sort, but not Ikky. Ha!

I had finished attaching the leads and pulled the first plug when a big, rugged, black island grew beneath me. . . .

I flicked the beam downward. His mouth was opened. I was rabbit.

Waves of the death-fear passed downward. My stomach imploded. I grew dizzy.

Only one thing, and one thing only. Left to do. I managed it, finally. I pulled the rest of the plugs.

I could count the scaly articulations ridging his eyes by then.

The squiggler grew, pinked into phosphorence . . . squiggled!

Then my lamp. I had to kill it, leaving just the bait before him.

One glance back as I jammed the jatoes to life.

He was so near that the squiggler reflected on his teeth, in his eyes. Four meters, and I kissed his lambent jowls with two jets of backwash as I soared. Then I didn't know whether he was following or had halted. I began to black out as I waited to be eaten.

The jatoes died and I kicked weakly.

Too fast, I felt a cramp coming on. One flick of the beam, cried rabbit. One second, to know . . .

Or end things up, I answered. No, rabbit, we don't dart before hunters. Stay dark.

Green water, finally, to yellow-green, then top.

Doubling, I beat off toward Tensquare. The waves from the explosion behind pushed me on ahead. The world closed in, and a screamed, "He's alive!" in the distance.

A giant shadow and a shock wave. The line was alive, too.

—Good-bye Perrin, Violet Eyes, Ikky. I go to the Happy Fishing Grounds. Maybe I did something wrong. . . .

Somewhere Hand was clenched. What's bait?

A few million years. I remember starting out as a one-celled organism and painfully becoming an amphibian, then an air-breather. From somewhere high in the tree-tops I heard a voice.

"He's coming around."

I evolved back into homo sapience, then a step further into a hangover.

"Don't try to get up yet."

"Have we got him?" I slurred.

"Still fighting, but he's hooked. We thought he took you for an appetizer."

"So did I."

"Breathe some of this and shut up."

A funnel over my face. Good. Lift your cups and drink. . . .

"He was awfully deep. Below scope range. We didn't catch him till he started up. Too late, then."

I began to yawn.

"We'll get you inside now."

I managed to uncase my ankle knife.

"Try it and you'll be minus a thumb."

"You need rest."

"Then bring me a couple more blankets. I'm staying."

I fell back and closed my eyes.

Someone was shaking me. Gloom and cold. Spotlights bled yellow on the deck. I was in a jury-rigged bunk, bulked against the center blister. Swaddled in wool, I still shivered.

"It's been eleven hours. You're not going to see anything now."

I tasted blood.

"Drink this."

Water. I had a remark but I couldn't mouth it.

"Don't ask how I feel," I croaked. "I know that comes next, but don't ask me. OK?"

"OK. Want to go below now?"

"No. Just get me my jacket."

"Right here."

"What's he doing?"

"Nothing. He's deep, he's doped but he's staying down."

"How long since last time he showed?"

"Two hours, about."

"Jean?"

"She won't let anyone in the Slider. Listen, Mike says come on in. He's right behind you in the blister."

I sat up and turned. Mike was watching. He gestured; I gestured back.

I swung my feet over the edge and took a couple deep breaths. Pains in my stomach. I got to my feet and made it into the blister.

"Howza gut?" queried Mike.

I checked the scope. No Ikky. Too deep.

"You buying?"

"Yeah, coffee."

"Not coffee."

"You're ill. Also, coffee is all that's allowed in here."

"Coffee is a brownish liquid that burns your stomach. You have some in the bottom drawer."

"No cups. You'll have to use a glass."

"Tough."

He poured.

"You do that well. Been practicing for that job?"

"What job?"

"The one I offered you—"

A blot on the scope!

"Rising, ma'am! Rising!" he yelled into the box.

"Thanks, Mike. I've got it in here," she crackled.

"Jean!"

"Shut up! She's busy!"

"Was that Carl?"

"Yeah," I called. "Talk later," and I cut it.

Why did I do that?

"Why did you do that?"

I didn't know.

"I don't know."

Damned echoes! I got up and walked outside.

Nothing. Nothing.

Something?

Tensquare actually rocked! He must have turned when he saw the hull and started downward again. White water to my left, and boiling. An endless spaghetti of cable roared hotly into the belly of the deep.

I stood awhile, then turned and went back inside.

Two hours sick. Four, and better.

"The dope's getting to him."

"Yeah."

"What about Miss Luharich?"

"What about her?"

"She must be half dead."

"Probably."

"What are you going to do about it?"

"She signed the contract for this. She knew what might happen. It did."

"I think you could land him."

"So do I."

"So does she."

"Then let her ask me."

Ikky was drifting lethargically, at thirty fathoms.

I took another walk and happened to pass behind the Slider. She wasn't looking my way.

"Carl, come in here!"

Eyes of Picasso, that's what, and a conspiracy to make me Slide . . .

"Is that an order?"

"Yes— No! Please."

I dashed inside and monitored. He was rising.

"Push or pull?"

I slammed the "wind" and he came like a kitten.

"Make up your own mind now."

He balked at ten fathoms.

"Play him?"

"No!"

She wound him upward—five fathoms, four . . .

She hit the extensors at two, and they caught him. Then the graffles.

Cries without and a heat lightning of flashbulbs.

The crew saw Ikky.

He began to struggle. She kept the cables tight, raised the graffles. . . .

Up.

Another two feet and the graffles began pushing.

Screams and fast footfalls.

Giant beanstalk in the wind, his neck, waving. The green hills of his shoulders grew.

"He's big, Carl!" she cried.

And he grew, and grew, and grew uneasy. . . .

"*Now!*"

He looked down.

He looked down, as the god of our most ancient ancestors might have looked down. Fear, shame, and mocking laughter rang in my head. Her head, too?

"Now!"

She looked up at the nascent earthquake.

"I can't!"

It was going to be so damnably simple this time, now the rabbit had died. I reached out.

I stopped.

"Push it yourself."

"I can't. You do it. Land him, Carl!"

"No. If I do, you'll wonder for the rest of your life whether you could have. You'll throw away your soul finding out. I know you will, because we're alike, and I did it that way. Find out now!"

She stared.

I gripped her shoulders.

"Could be that's me out there," I offered. "I am a green

sea serpent, a hateful, monstrous beast, and out to destroy
you. I am answerable to no one. Push the Inject."

Her hand moved to the button, jerked back.

"Now!"

She pushed it.

I lowered her still form to the floor and finished
things up with Ikky.

It was a good seven hours before I awakened to the
steady, sea-chewing grind of Tensquare's blades.

"You're sick," commented Mike.

"How's Jean?"

"The same."

"Where's the beast?"

"Here."

"Good." I rolled over. ". . . Didn't get away this time."

So that's the way it was. No one is born a baitman, I
don't think, but the rings of Saturn sing epithalamium
the sea-beast's dower.

hunting

Hunting, like fishing, grew out of early man's struggle to survive. Man had to eat in order to live, and hunting was one of the means to obtain food.

Hunting has decimated much of the big game that used to be abundant all throughout North America. Many hunters will state that it is the hunt and not the kill that provides the fun and excitement associated with the sport. Nevertheless, relatively few hunters fail to kill their quarry if they are able to. In the hunt itself, the animals have the advantage in knowing the terrain and have senses superior to those of the human hunter. All the hunter has going for him are an accurate high-powered rifle, telescopic sights, airplanes, snowmobiles, powerful lights which hypnotize the animal, and other items like decoys and birdcalls! It hardly seems fair. The relative equality of the old days when men had to rough it has ended for those who do not want to be inconvenienced.

For the more daring, hunting with bow and arrow is an exciting sport as is hunting with a camera, which provides permanent memories for the hunter—and the right to live for the animals. Like fishing, hunting is tremendously popular today, but it remains to be seen whether the advantages of technology will permit this sport to continue in the twenty-first century.

Poor
Little
Warrior!

brian w. aldiss

One of the paradoxes of hunting is that the act of killing
can be talked about in terms of beauty, dignity, and
honor. To some people, modern hunting is nothing less
than virtual murder; to others, it is the "king of sports."
Unlike other sports, points are not at stake; the object
of the "game" is the life of an animal. In this story,
hunting is alluded to as being beautiful, although the
author of the story does this with a cynical tone. The
beauty perceived by the hunter of the original hunt
winds up, at the end of the story, in a deadly scene of
retribution.

Moreover, it should be noted that hunting is very
much like tourism. The hunter enters the territory and
the domain of the animal, trying to learn as much as
possible about the behavior of the hunted, just as the
tourist tries to learn as much as he can about the behavior of the residents of the host country. This tourist
dimension of hunting is exaggerated but credible in this
story, since the hunter is sent back in time in order to
hunt a brontosaurus. The "host country" holds surprising
events for the hunter-tourist in this story.

Finally, this story points out the fundamental question

of whether hunting is truly a sport. In most sports, competition is the core of activity, and this takes place between two or more players who are presumed to be fairly equal in terms of prior training and abilities. Can this be said of hunting? What are the relative strengths and weaknesses of modern hunters and the hunted? Does equality prevail?

Poor
Little
Warrior!

Claude Ford knew exactly how it was to hunt a bronto-saurus. You crawled heedlessly through the mud among the willows, through the little primitive flowers with petals as green and brown as a football field, through the beauty-lotion mud. You peered out at the creature sprawl-ing among the reeds, its body as graceful as a sock full of sand. There it lay, letting the gravity cuddle it nappy-damp to the marsh, running its big rabbit-hole nostrils a foot above the grass in a sweeping semicircle, in a snoring search for more sausagy reeds. It was beautiful: here horror had reached its limits, come full circle and finally disappeared up its own sphincter. Its eyes gleamed with the liveliness of a week-dead corpse's big toe, and its compost breath and the fur in its crude aural cavities were particularly to be recommended to anyone who might otherwise have felt inclined to speak lovingly of the work of Mother Nature.

But as you, little mammal with opposed digit and .65 self-loading, semiautomatic, dual-barreled, digitally com-puted, telescopically sighted, rustless, high-powered rifle gripped in your otherwise defenseless paws, slide along under the bygone willows, what primarily attracts you is the thunder lizard's hide. It gives off a smell as deeply resonant as the bass note of a piano. It makes the elephant's epidermis look like a sheet of crinkled lavatory paper. It is gray as the Viking seas, daft-deep as cathedral foundations. What contact possible to bone could allay the fever of that flesh? Over it scamper—you can see them from here!—the little brown lice that live in those gray walls and canyons, gay as ghosts, cruel as crabs. If one of them jumped on you, it would very likely break your back. And when one of those parasites stops to cock its leg against one of the bronto's vertebrae, you can see it carries in its turn its own crop of easy-livers, each as big as a lobster, for you're near now, oh, so near that you can hear the monster's primitive heart-organ knocking, as the ventricle keeps miraculous time with the auricle.

Time for listening to the oracle is past: you're beyond the stage for omens, you're now headed in for the kill, yours or his; superstition has had its little day for today, from now on only this windy nerve of yours, this shaky conglomeration of muscle entangled untraceably beneath the sweat-shiny carapace of skin, this bloody little urge to slay the dragon, is going to answer all your orisons.

You could shoot now. Just wait till that tiny steam-shovel head pauses once again to gulp down a quarry load of bulrushes, and with one inexpressibly vulgar bang you can show the whole indifferent Jurassic world that it's standing looking down the business end of evolution's sex-shooter. You know why you pause, even as you pretend not to know why you pause; that old worm conscience, long as a baseball pitch, long-lived as a

tortoise, is at work; through every sense it slides, more
monstrous than the serpent. Through the passions: saying here is a sitting duck, O Englishman! Through the
intelligence: whispering that boredom, the kite hawk
who never feeds, will settle again when the task is done.
Through the nerves: sneering that when the adrenalin
currents cease to flow the vomiting begins. Through the
maestro behind the retina: plausibly forcing the beauty
of the view upon you.

Spare us that poor old slipper-slopper of a word,
beauty; holy mom, is this a travelogue, nor are we out of
it? *"Perched now on this titanic creature's back, we see a
round dozen—and, folks, let me stress that round—of
gaudily plumaged birds, exhibiting between them all
the color you might expect to find on lovely, fabled
Copacabana Beach. They're so round because they feed
from the droppings that fall from the rich man's table.
Watch this lovely shot now! See the bronto's tail lift. . . .
Oh, lovely, yep, a couple of hayricksful at least emerging
from his nether end. That sure was a beauty, folks,
delivered straight from consumer to consumer. The birds
are fighting over it now. Hey, you, there's enough to go
round, and anyhow, you're round enough already. . . .
And nothing to do now but hop back up onto the old
rump steak and wait for the next round. And now as the
sun sinks in the Jurassic West, we say 'Fare well on that
diet'. . . ."*

No, you're procrastinating, and that's a lifework. Shoot
the beast and put it out of your agony. Taking your
courage in your hands, you raise it to shoulder level and
squint down its sights. There is a terrible report; you
are half stunned. Shakily, you look about you. The

monster still munches, relieved to have broken enough wind to unbecalm the Ancient Mariner.

Angered (or is it some subtler emotion?), you now burst from the bushes and confront it, and this exposed condition is typical of the straits into which your consideration for yourself and others continually pitches you. Consideration? Or again something subtler? Why should you be confused just because you come from a confused civilization? But that's a point to deal with later, if there is a later, as these two hog-wallow eyes pupiling you all over from spitting distance tend to dispute. Let it not be by jaws alone, O monster, but also by huge hooves and, if convenient to yourself, by mountainous rollings upon me! Let death be a saga, sagacious, Beowulfate.

Quarter of a mile distant is the sound of a dozen hippos springing boisterously in gymslips from the ancestral mud, and next second a walloping great tail as long as Sunday and as thick as Saturday night comes slicing over your head. You duck as duck you must, but the beast missed you anyway because it so happens that its coordination is no better than yours would be if you had to wave the Woolworth Building at a tarsier. This done, it seems to feel it has done its duty by itself. It forgets you. You just wish you could forget yourself as easily; that was, after all, the reason you had to come the long way here. *Get Away from It All*, said the time travel brochure, which meant for you getting away from Claude Ford, a husbandman as futile as his name with a terrible wife called Maude. Maude and Claude Ford. Who could not adjust to themselves, to each other, or to he world they were born in. It was the best reason in the as-it-is-at-present-constituted world for coming back here to shoot giant saurians—if you were fool enough to think that one hundred and fifty million years either way made an ounce of difference to the muddle of thoughts in a man's cerebral vortex.

You try and stop your silly, slobbering thoughts, but they have never really stopped since the coca-collaborating days of your growing up; God, if adolescence did not exist it would be unnecessary to invent it! Slightly, it steadies you to look again on the enormous bulk of this tyrant vegetarian into whose presence you charged with such a mixed death-life wish, charged with all the emotion the human orga(ni)sm is capable of. This time the bogeyman is real, Claude, just as you wanted it to be, and this time you really have to face up to it before it turns and faces you again. And so again you lift Ole Equalizer, waiting till you can spot the vulnerable spot.

The bright birds sway, the lice scamper like dogs, the marsh groans, as bronto sways over and sends his little cranium snaking down under the bile-bright water in a forage for roughage. You watch this; you have never been so jittery before in all your jittered life, and you are counting on this catharsis wringing the last drop of acid fear out of your system forever. OK, you keep saying to yourself insanely over and over, your million-dollar twenty-second-century education going for nothing, OK, OK. And as you say it for the umpteenth time, the crazy head comes back out of the water like a renegade express and gazes in your direction.

Grazes in your direction. For as the champing jaw with its big blunt molars like concrete posts works up and down, you see the swamp water course out over rimless lips, lipless rims, splashing your feet and sousing the ground. Reed and root, stalk and stem, leaf and loam, all are intermittently visible in that masticating maw and, struggling, straggling, or tossed among them, minnows, tiny crustaceans, frogs—all destined in that awful, jaw-full movement to turn into bowel movement. And as the glump-glump-glumping takes place, above it the slime-resistant eyes again survey you.

These beasts live up to two hundred years, says the time travel brochure, and this beast has obviously tried to live up to that, for its gaze is centuries old, full of decades upon decades of wallowing in its heavyweight thoughtlessness until it has grown wise on twitterpatedness. For you it is like looking into a disturbing misty pool; it gives you a psychic shock, you fire off both barrels at your own reflection. Bang-bang, the dumdums, big as pawpaws, go.

With no indecision, those century-old lights, dim and sacred, go out. These cloisters are closed till Judgment Day. Your reflection is torn and bloodied from them forever. Over their ravaged panes nictitating membranes slide slowly upward, like dirty sheets covering a cadaver. The jaw continues to munch slowly, as slowly the head sinks down. Slowly, a squeeze of cold reptile blood toothpastes down the wrinkled flank of one cheek. Everything is slow, a creepy Secondary Era slowness like the drip of water, and you know that if you had been in charge of creation you would have found some medium less heartbreaking than Time to stage it all in.

Never mind! Quaff down your beakers, lords, Claude Ford has slain a harmless creature. Long live Claude the Clawed!

You watch breathless as the head touches the ground, the long laugh of neck touches the ground, the jaws close for good. You watch and wait for something else to happen, but nothing ever does. Nothing ever would. You could stand here watching for a hundred and fifty million years, Lord Claude, and nothing would ever happen here again. Gradually your bronto's mighty carcass, picked loving clean by predators, would sink into the slime, carried by its own weight deeper; then the waters would rise, and old Conqueror Sea come in with the leisurely air of a cardsharp dealing the boys a bad hand. Silt and sediment would filter down over the mighty grave, a slow rain with centuries to rain in. Old bronto's bed might be raised up and then down again perhaps half a dozen times, gently enough not to disturb him, although by now the sedimentary rocks would be forming thick around him. Finally, when he was wrapped in a tomb finer than any Indian rajah ever boasted, the powers of the Earth would raise him high on their shoulders until, sleeping still, bronto would lie in a brow of the Rockies high above the waters of the Pacific. But little any of that would count with you, Claude the Sword; once the midget maggot of life is dead in the creature's skull, the rest is no concern of yours.

You have no emotion now. You are just faintly put out. You expected dramatic thrashing of the ground, or bellowing; on the other hand, you are glad the thing did not appear to suffer. You are like all cruel men, sentimental; you are like all sentimental men, squeamish. You tuck the gun under your arm and walk round the dinosaur to view your victory.

You prowl past the ungainly hooves, round the septic white of the cliff of belly, beyond the glistening and how-thought-provoking cavern of the cloaca, finally posing beneath the switchback sweep of tail-to-rump. Now your disappointment is as crisp and obvious as a visiting card: the giant is not half as big as you thought it was. It is not one half as large, for example, as the image of you and Maude is in your mind. Poor little warrior, science will never invent anything to assist the titanic death you want in the contraterrene caverns of your fee-fi-fo fumblingly fearful id!

Nothing is left to you now but to slink back to your timemobile with a belly full of anticlimax. See, the bright dung-consuming birds have already cottoned onto the true state of affairs; one by one, they gather up their hunched wings and fly disconsolately off across the swamp to other hosts. They know when a good thing turns bad, and do not wait for the vultures to drive them off; all hope abandon, ye who entrail here. You also turn away.

You turn, but you pause. Nothing is left but to go back, no, but A.D. 2181 is not just the home date; it is Maude. It is Claude. It is the whole awful, hopeless, endless business of trying to adjust to an overcomplex environment, of trying to turn yourself into a cog. Your escape from it into *the Grand Simplicities of the Jurassic*, to quote the brochure again, was only a partial escape, now over.

So you pause, and as you pause, something lands socko on your back, pitching you face forward into tasty mud. You struggle and scream as lobster claws tear at your neck and throat. You try to pick up the rifle but cannot, so in agony you roll over, and next second the crab-thing is greedying it on your chest. You wrench at its shell, but it giggles and pecks your fingers off. You forgot when you killed the bronto that its parasites would leave it, and that to a little shrimp like you they would be a deal more dangerous than their host.

You do your best, kicking for at least three minutes. By the end of that time there is a whole pack of the creatures on you. Already they are picking your carcass loving clean. You're going to like it up there on top of the Rockies; you won't feel a thing.